IMPE[illegible]

DAWN

Ashes of Empire #6

ERIC THOMSON

Imperial Dawn

First paperback printing June 2024

Published in Canada

By Sanddiver Books Inc.

ISBN: 978-1-998167-07-4

PART I – FALSE DAWN

—1—

The battle fleet waited, as it had for over two hundred years. It waited for a signal, one that would call it back to life. Artificial intelligences kept watch over the ships, dreaming of better days when human beings were aboard, boisterous, satisfied with the results of their labors. Time meant little to the AIs, merely the passing of seconds, minutes, hours, and years. Yet even those were meaningless to incorporeal entities capable of eternal life, provided the envelopes holding them survived. And they had silently orbited the planet hidden in the Lagrangian points of the moons on which they'd been built for over twenty decades.

The humans responsible for the battle fleet's creation were long since dead, taken in the madness of the Great Scouring. Others, numbering only a hundred thousand out of a pre-Scouring population of five hundred million, survived on the planet's surface, the descendants of those who'd escaped the death of the great cities. They still had generational memories of a golden era, a time when their forebears bestrode the galaxy, traveling aboard immense starships, before Empress Dendera, the most destructive human to ever live, immolated ninety percent of her species in a bloodbath without compare.

But as they struggled every day of their lives to see another sunrise, living in conditions so primitive, humans had not experienced them for thousands of years, those memories were rapidly turning into myths.

The waiting ships knew nothing of that. Their AIs had registered the Retribution Fleet bombarding the planet over two centuries ago, noted that it hadn't detected them, and watched it leave the system, never to return. The humans who'd built the ships had shut them down just before the Retribution Fleet arrived, lest they be drafted alongside Dendera's murderers, preserving them for future rebirth. Ever since, they'd been watching for a coherent signal to power up and reveal themselves.

Their long wait was coming to an end.

***

Wyvern Hegemony Starship *Caladrius*
Task Group 215

"This is the Cascadia system, all right, sir."

Lieutenant Commander Reva Dyre, chief navigator of the Wyvern Hegemony Starship *Caladrius* and Task Group 215, turned toward Captain Newton Giambo. The cruiser's commanding officer doubled as the Task Group commander. Thin and tall, her short blonde hair fell in equal curtains on either side of a narrow face whose most noticeable features were high cheekbones sharp enough to cut paper.

Caladrius and her companions had emerged from Wormhole Five a little over fifteen minutes earlier and were coasting at low sublight speed.

Giambo, heavy-set, with curly dark hair and a gray beard framing a square, honest face dominated by an aquiline nose, let out a soft grunt as he nodded.

"It's about time. That one wormhole shift threw our entire navigation plot off by the Almighty knows how many light years."

"*Strix* and *Remus* concur with my assessment, sir," Dyre added after a few moments, naming the two frigates that formed the rest of Task Group 215.

"Then let's find the planet and see who, if anyone, survived and in what condition."

"Shouldn't take long." And it didn't. Less than forty minutes later, Task Group 215 went FTL on an inward trajectory headed for a small blue-green planet with three moons.

"It's definitely Cascadia, Captain," Lieutenant Commander Dyre said twelve hours later, bringing up a side-by-side live view of the planet and an archived image on the bridge's primary display. "There's no mistake. But I can't see much evidence of human life from this distance. There aren't any lights on the night side, which covers what used to be the main inhabited continent."

Giambo grimaced.

"Finding a remnant of civilization on a former sector capital would have been too much to hope for. Get us into a standard scanning orbit, Mister Tyre. *Strix* and *Remus* to conform."

"Aye, aye, sir," Chief Petty Officer Aldo Tyre, *Caladrius*' coxswain, replied.

Task Group 215 had been on an exploration run for the last three months, trying to cover as many formerly inhabited worlds as possible in the old Cascadian Sector. So far, what they'd found was depressing at best. Vegetation-covered ruins, the odd Stone Age tribes, and precious little else. Some planets had been entirely depopulated, with only remnants of Earth vegetation as signs of former human habitation.

The only good thing about their expedition was the absence of Shrehari vessels exploring formerly human space, wondering what had happened to them during their troubles and retrenchment. Not that Giambo expected any trouble with the Shrehari. They'd been at peace for well over a thousand years, mostly ignoring each other, but that was long enough to make it an almost unbreakable habit, if only through sheer inertia.

Of course, humanity had been the stronger of the two during that time by a wide margin. Now, it was a fleeting shadow of its former self and had divided into two entities, the Wyvern Hegemony and the Republic of Lyonesse, both of which were overstretched, reclaiming lost worlds. Perhaps humanity's weakness might rouse ancient passions long suppressed by the Shrehari Empire.

"Entering orbit and beginning scan," Chief Tyre announced as the three ships, widely spread apart, began circling Cascadia on paths that would cover every square centimeter of the planet in the space of a few hours.

***

Giambo entered the cruiser's combat information center and settled in the command chair to see the results of the scans.

"Dispersed human life signs, sir. In no place more than a few hundred or so for a total of approximately one hundred thousand out of a pre-Scouring population of five hundred million. No evidence of technology, no emissions, and no lights on the night side. It seems that humans either concentrate in villages surrounded by fields or lead a nomadic lifestyle, but all reside in temperate to tropical zones. The remains of the cities and their immediate surroundings are entirely devoid of life signs, by the way."

Lieutenant Commander Joseph Vaczichek, the combat systems officer, nodded at the primary display, which zoomed in on a small agglomeration of forty primitive houses.

"I suggest we send the recon team to study this village. It appears to be surrounded by adequate sites for observation posts."

Wooded hills surrounded the village, some craggy enough to offer good lines of sight. Giambo studied the proposed area, then nodded.

"Make it so, Commander."

"We'll insert the team in approximately twelve hours when it's midnight local time."

"Okay." Giambo sat back. "While we do that, *Strix* and *Remus* will conduct close scans of the moons, beginning with the biggest one. According to the records, they had significant shipbuilding installations on all three. I'm curious to see what happened to them."

"Aye, aye, sir."

"And once we're done, it's off home." Giambo stood. "Which shouldn't take nearly as long as getting out here."

"Unless more wormholes have shifted since we left Wyvern, sir."

Giambo gave Vaczichek a mock glare.

"Bite your tongue, Joseph."

"Tongue bitten, Captain." The combat systems officer mumbled loudly.

"Besides, I'm seriously tempted to return home in FTL, one long jump. Our astrogation charts are good enough for it now, and it'll only add a day or two, considering the wormhole shift threw us off the direct line."

"Don't tell Reva. She'll get nightmares."

Giambo headed to his quarters for a bit of administrative work and a nap while his people carried out their orders. He returned to the CIC several hours later, refreshed and ready for the frigates to report on their scans of the moons.

"And?" Giambo asked, settling back into the command chair.

Images of destroyed structures against an airless, gray background appeared on the primary display.

"Orbital bombardment ruined all of the shipyards, sir. The frigates found no evidence of human remains, indicating the personnel were likely evacuated ahead of the Retribution Fleet's arrival."

Giambo let out a soft grunt.

"Fat lot of good that did them."

"Who, sir?" Commander Jana Venkov's hologram had appeared at his right elbow. The first officer, currently on the bridge, was a tired-looking, black-haired woman with a round face, deep blue eyes, and a pert nose. A mustang, promoted from the enlisted ranks, she was the oldest spacer aboard *Caladrius* save for the ship's senior Sister of the Void and counselor, Adonna, who nonetheless looked younger than Venkov, having that ageless air the Sisters seemed to possess.

"The people in the shipyards, Jana. No bodies were found, meaning they evacuated just in time to be killed on Cascadia's surface."

"A shame that." She paused. "You know, sir, according to the records, the Cascadia Imperial Navy Yards were on the verge of launching the most advanced starships in the galaxy, and we don't know whether they made it before Dendera's murderers passed through."

"Any evidence of ships among the debris, Joseph?"

The combat systems officer perused the scan results, then shook his head. "None whatsoever, sir."

"It could be that the ships were finished and dispatched before the Retribution Fleet attacked."

"Probably." Venkov shrugged. "Oh, well."

"What orders for the frigates now that they've completed their scans?" Lieutenant Commander Vaczichek asked.

Giambo thought for a few seconds.

"Have them practice vanishing in the moon's Lagrangian points. You keep score."

"Will do, sir."

Giambo turned to Sister Adonna, sitting behind him. "A cup of tea, Sister?"

Adonna, whose short silver hair framed a serene, unlined face dominated by large, blue eyes on either side of an upturned nose, nodded. "With pleasure, Captain."

***

Captain Jutta Pernell, commanding the Wyvern Hegemony frigate *Strix,* slipped her ship into the trailing Lagrangian of Cascadia's largest and innermost moon, Nanaimo, and went down systems, effectively turning *Strix* into a ghost. Playing prey to *Caladrius*' sensors was something they'd done several times during the expedition and was always interesting, at least to the command crew, who saw it as a challenge. The rest of the frigate's personnel considered it as nothing more than a drill, one of many routinely carried out by Wyvern Hegemony Guards Navy ships to keep everyone sharp between wormhole transits and FTL jumps.

After a few minutes of waiting for *Caladrius* to look for *Strix*, the frigate's sensor chief, who'd been passively scanning their surroundings more to beat boredom than anything else, frowned. He raised his hand.

"Sir?"

Captain Pernell looked up from her tablet.

"What's up, Chief?"

"I think we're not alone. There are shapes occluding the stars. Nearby shapes. They're not emitting anything but are too regular for asteroids."

Pernell, tablet forgotten, sat up. They'd encountered so many strange things since President Mandus swore the Oath of Reunification and sent the fleet out to reconnect the old imperial worlds that this might just be another one.

"On screen."

After studying the images of the shapes, Pernell could come to only one conclusion. They were starships. A dozen of them, perhaps frigate or cruiser-sized. But why were they hiding in Nanaimo's trailing Lagrangian? And more importantly, whose were they?

"Go up systems and ping those ships. And get me *Caladrius*."

—2—

Lannion
Republic of Lyonesse

"Do you still see a dawn?" Ambassador Crevan Torma asked his chief of staff once they were in the privacy of his office, across the street from Government House. In his mid-forties, tall, muscular, with a craggy angular face dominated by hooded eyes framing a hooked nose, he sounded both irritated and discouraged to Ardrix Moore's ears. But that was something she detected thanks to her skills as a Sister of the Void Reborn. It wouldn't have registered with anyone else.

Torma and Ardrix had just returned from another futile meeting with representatives of the Republic's government, this time to discuss broadening scientific exchanges. Two hours wasted for no gain whatsoever.

"Of course I do, Crevan. Some of these things take extra effort, that's all," Ardrix, an equally tall but lean woman whose short red hair framed a pale, elfin face dominated by large, expressive eyes, replied in a soothing voice.

"You know, I'm beginning to doubt the wisdom of choosing me as the Hegemony's first ambassador to Lyonesse. I find myself lacking patience with the insincerity and propensity for gamesmanship of the Republic's politicians."

Ardrix gave him a sly smile.

"And you are equally capable of insincerity and gamesmanship in return."

"Yes, but that doesn't mean I enjoy it. I'm not the sort who likes to twist words and meanings beyond recognition."

"The fact you know they're disingenuous, if not dishonest, clearly makes you the right person for the job, Crevan. Others, perhaps many, if not most senior Hegemony personnel, wouldn't have picked up on that as fast as you did."

Torma's lips twisted in a crooked smile.

"You think?"

"I know."

"Yet I still can't help but figure I'm useless. Face it, we spend most of our time in idleness and the rest at social functions where fake smiles and insincere words are paramount."

"Ah, yes." Ardrix grimaced. "The social aspect of the job can be trying. But they're part and parcel of an ambassador's existence, or at least so the ancient records tell us."

Torma sat back in his chair and joined his hands behind his head.

"I wish President Hecht was more involved in Hegemony-Republic affairs, but she seems to have passed the file to Vice President Juska, who is, as we've known from the start, a

Lyonesse First supremacist and not inclined to give us a millimeter. Why she's doing so is beyond me. I thought she was eager to build on the rapport Captains Jecks and Alexander developed."

"It is puzzling indeed. Maybe she has no choice in the matter, having been outmaneuvered by Juska's faction.

"Or she changed her mind about opening cordial relations with the Hegemony now that the excitement of Jecks and Alexander jointly parading at the Geneva monument has died down. I'll draft a report to go out with the next starship headed for Wyvern. Perhaps the brain trust in New Draconis has ideas."

"Even if they do, it will be at least a month before we hear from them."

"True. In the meantime, we continue with our small diplomatic acts. I still need to complete my presentation to the Lyonesse Defense Force Command and Staff College."

"And I mine to the Lyonesse Abbey."

Torma smiled at Ardrix.

"Making friends one at a time, hoping it'll be enough to sway public opinion toward enlarging relations with the Hegemony."

"It's the sole course of action we have for now."

***

"Do you really think it's wise letting Derik Juska take the lead in the discussions with Ambassador Torma, Madame President?" Admiral Farrin Norum, a man in his late fifties with short blond hair mostly turned silver, deep-set blue eyes, and an angular face, asked, taking a chair across the low coffee table from Aurelia Hecht.

The president, thin, with dark hair hanging to her shoulders and penetrating brown eyes framing a patrician nose, shrugged.

"Probably not, but I'm hoping Torma will blunt Derik's attacks against the Hegemony. Or at least those of the negotiators he appointed. If I keep him on the outside looking in, he'll just whip up a frenzy among his followers, hinting that I'm selling out the Republic. I think Torma can handle him and his people. He strikes me as a stoic whose intellect easily surpasses those of the Lyonesse First movement's membership, Derik included. Then there's his chief of staff, a Sister of the Void Reborn whose abilities are apparently of such a nature that she was called an abomination by those of our Order who were held on Wyvern."

"Let's hope you're right. Derik will attempt to poison our relationship with the Hegemony to score points, and my intelligence folks tell me he's gaining support among the general population. Not enough yet to tip the scales, but his quiet expressions of doubt about Wyvern's peaceful intentions are making many people sit up and take notice." The Lyonesse Defense Force's commander-in-chief paused, giving Hecht a curious look. "And I must say that everything I've been told about the Hegemony also makes me curious about them, Madame President."

"Isn't Ambassador Torma giving a presentation on the history of the Hegemony at the Command and Staff College tomorrow?"

"Yes, he is. I'll be attending."

"Maybe I should also."

"You're always welcome, Madame President. I also understand Torma's chief of staff is giving a speech on the history of the Order of the Void Reborn to the abbey tomorrow evening."

A crooked smile appeared on Hecht's lips.

"History lessons for everyone?"

"It's probably part of a charm offensive, although I don't know how much of it they will present as the unvarnished truth and how much they will manipulate to cover darker spots in their past."

"Or how much will be outright lies to make the Hegemony look good?" When Norum gave her a cocked eyebrow look, Hecht laughed. "Come on, Farrin. I want to make peaceful coexistence work as much as anyone in the Republic because any conflict between us could be disastrous. But I'm neither naïve nor blinded by my hopes."

"Glad to hear you say so, Madame President."

***

"That was fascinating, Ambassador, thank you." Brigadier General Ann Creswell, the Commandant of the Command and Staff College, rose from her seat and joined Torma on the stage. "I don't think we were expecting you to be quite so candid about the Hegemony, exposing its warts and all."

"I believe in complete honesty, General, especially at the beginning of what I hope will be a fruitful relationship between our star nations."

She smiled at him. "And honesty we got."

Creswell let her eyes roam over the Assembly Hall, a space ample enough for three hundred people seated in ascending tiers. It was packed, with the president, Admiral Norum, and the Service Chiefs seated in the front row. Ardrix Moore sat in the second row behind them.

"I will now open the floor to questions you may have of Ambassador Torma."

Every gaze shifted toward Aurelia Hecht, who held the undeniable privilege to ask the initial question.

"As General Creswell said, Ambassador, you were candid to a fault. You said the Hegemony has been a military dictatorship since its inception. That your regent now calls herself president didn't change anything, did it?"

"No, Madame President, it didn't."

"Do you think the Hegemony will ever become democratic, like our Republic?"

Torma considered her query for a few seconds, then grimaced.

"Difficult to say. We have no memory of democracy, and the citizens, by and large, are content with the current system since it provides security as well as plenty, and there is a generational memory of a time when their forebears had neither in the aftermath of Dendera's madness. Yet now that we're leaving our four core star systems to reclaim worlds beyond immediate subspace radio linkages, the sort of centralized control we've enjoyed for two centuries will no longer be universally usable. And that means changes are coming, but what form they will take is beyond my ability to predict. Still, your example is useful since you established a Republic on the ashes of Empire even though that Empire had lost the pretense of democracy even at the lowest levels, generations earlier. Does that answer your question, Madame President?"

"It does, thank you, Ambassador."

Vice Admiral Gerhard Glass, the Chief of Naval Operations, raised a hand, and General Creswell gestured at him. Glass was tall, lean with dark hair going silver and an aquiline nose in a craggy face.

"Yes, sir. Please go ahead."

"I understand you're a former brigadier general of the Wyvern Hegemony's State Security Commission."

"Yes, Admiral, I am."

"And your chief of staff, Ardrix Moore, is a former Sister of the Void Reborn attached to the State Security Commission."

Torma inclined his head.

"Indeed, although our last place of duty was with the Colonial Service, me as Inspector General and Ardrix as Leading Sister. Our responsibilities were to deal with political and criminal matters affecting the service's security. It was similar to what we did before our assignment when we were part of the Commission's Wyvern Group."

"I see. And how much of your work, the Commission's work, dealt with political rather than criminal matters?"

A faint smile danced on Torma's lips.

"It depends on who you ask. For some in the Commission, every crime is political because they consider criminal activity an offense against the state first and foremost."

"And you?"

"I'm not of that view, which means few, if any, of the cases I investigated over the years were purely political. The vast majority of offenses were committed under the Criminal Justice Act, and I would say my experience reflects that of most Commission members. We are police officers, Admiral, no better and no worse than our predecessors in the Imperial Constabulary and seized with much of the same issues."

Glass met Torma's impassive gaze, one that challenged him to probe deeper if he wished, and nodded once.

"Thank you, Ambassador."

The next questions, dealing with clarification of points Torma had raised, weren't quite as pointed as those asked by Glass, and

Torma relaxed, although only Ardrix could tell. To his audience, he remained as stoic and inscrutable as ever. After half an hour, Brigadier General Creswell called an end to the session and presented Torma with a small plaque displaying the College's crest by way of gratitude.

"Thank you, Ambassador. You gave us a fascinating insight into humanity's other surviving half, and I daresay we're not so different beneath the surface."

"It was my pleasure, General. I'd certainly be willing to return and give further lectures on the Hegemony if you wish."

"I'll hold you to that, Ambassador." She turned to the audience. "Please rise for the departure of President Hecht."

Once she'd left, Norum glanced at Glass as they stood and filed out of the auditorium.

"What was your line of questioning about, Gerhard?"

"I wanted to see if I could rattle him, get him to obfuscate, or even lie outright."

"Why?"

"Because there's something almost preternatural about his composure and candidness concerning the Hegemony."

"Ah, I see. You tested him." Norum gave Glass a cold, knowing smile as they emerged into the late afternoon sunshine. "And did it satisfy you?"

"No. He dared me to continue — not in so many words — but at that point, I knew I would not get anywhere."

"A fascinating man, our Ambassador Torma."

***

Once they were aboard their ground car, one with diplomatic registration and, therefore, a little mobile piece of the Hegemony, Torma sighed.

"I think that went well, except for Admiral Glass' probing. What's your sense?" He glanced at Ardrix, who sat in the passenger seat.

"Overwhelming curiosity and some goodwill," she replied, knowing Torma wanted to hear about her Sister of the Void's perception of the audience. "A bit of hostility coming from a few, but not from Glass."

"So we might have made, if not new friends, then at least a good impression."

Ardrix nodded.

"I believe so. Better than I will make tonight at the abbey. They already know about me."

"I wouldn't be too worried about that. Their *Summus Abbatissa*, Sister Gwendolyn, strikes me as highly reasonable, someone capable of discerning the reasons for the differences between her Order and the Void Reborn."

"A shame you can't attend."

"Possibly, but engaging in discussions about theological distinctions isn't my thing."

—3—

New Draconis
Wyvern Hegemony

Ambassador to the Wyvern Hegemony Currag DeCarde wandered over to the tall windows overlooking New Draconis' Avenue of the Stars, with the Wyvern Palace at one end and the Chancellery at the other, wondering once again who'd been tossed out on their ear to make room for the Lyonesse Embassy. This was prime real estate, at the heart of the Hegemony's power structure.

Tall, squarely built with an angular face, sandy hair going gray, and the deep blue eyes of his genetic lineage, DeCarde was in his mid-fifties, though he displayed the energy of someone twenty years younger. He raised his coffee mug to his lips and took a sip, grimacing. Coffee didn't grow on Lyonesse, and he'd been raised drinking tea like everyone else in the Republic. But it grew on Wyvern and was a favorite from the president down to the least citizen, and he'd decided he should get used to the bitter taste. Yet despite his self-discipline, borne of over twenty-five years as a Marine Corps officer, DeCarde found little to love in coffee. Still, he took a cup every morning, hoping it would improve.

The embassy was a five-story building with private apartments on the fourth and fifth floors, offices on the second and third, and reception rooms on the first. The staff was made up of droids who cleaned, cooked, and managed reception. With a mere two human beings rattling around in it, the place felt vast and empty.

DeCarde stared at the flagpole proudly displaying the banner of the Republic of Lyonesse in front of the main entrance and emptied his cup. So far, apart from a single meeting with President Mandus and Chancellor Conteh, he'd had precious little interaction with the Hegemony's highest leadership. A newly created Minister for Interstellar Affairs was his main interlocutor and even she'd been noticeable by a lack of contact. The inaction frustrated an active man like DeCarde. It was almost as if the Hegemony's government did not know what to do with the Lyonesse envoy, so they ignored him.

His chief of staff, Hermina Ruttan, had more luck with Archimandrite Bolack, the Head of the Order of the Void Reborn and his people, but that was because of her spending time as one of their involuntary guests a while back after being abducted from Hatshepsut. In fact, she was at the New Draconis Abbey this morning, having left early aboard the embassy's ground car to take part in a canonical service known as lauds.

And just as he had that thought, the embassy car pulled through the open gates and headed for the entrance to the underground garage, Hermina at the controls. As with everything else save for their personal items, the Hegemony's government had provided the car, and they consequently suspected it was spying on their movements. They didn't bother to check for listening devices and simply avoided confidential conversations when using it, unlike their offices, which they swept every day.

A few minutes later, Hermina, thin, gray-haired, of middling height, with sharp features, deep-set eyes, and a Sister of the Void's ageless look, appeared in the doorway to DeCarde's office.

"A good service?" He asked.

She nodded once.

"Very calming. You should join me one of these mornings."

"Because I need soothing? Enough so that I should get up before dawn? Perish the thought."

A faint smile appeared on her lips.

"I know you're frustrated by the lack of interaction with Hegemony government officials, even if no one else does."

"True." DeCarde had quickly learned that denying what Hermina saw clearly through the eyes of a Sister of the Void was futile. "But our arrival caught them off guard, and they don't appear to be the kind of people who adjust quickly to unexpected situations."

"Agreed. The consequence of social and political stasis for two hundred years. It will take them some time to shake off the torpor. And many of the senior officials never will, I'm afraid."

"Anything new from the abbey?"

Hermina shook her head.

"No, although the Archimandrite was pleased to see me at the morning service. And he'd certainly be overjoyed to see you someday," she replied with an air of mischief.

"You know I'm not a believer, Hermina."

"A pity."

At that moment, the office communicator chimed, and a disembodied voice said, “Minister of Interstellar Affairs Veronika Lazlo for you, Ambassador.”

DeCarde and Hermina glanced at each other.

“What a surprise. Put her on, please.”

He dropped into the chair behind his desk and pasted on a welcoming smile as a three-dimensional holographic image appeared, floating in midair.

“Minister Lazlo. And how are you on this fine morning?”

“Doing quite splendidly, Ambassador.” Lazlo, a willowy fifty-something with long black hair parted in the middle framing a triangular face dominated by piercing brown eyes, smiled at him, revealing even white teeth. “I’m calling to see if you’d be interested in giving a presentation on the Republic of Lyonesse to a select group of senior military and civilian officials, something that would give us insight into how your star nation functions, what its activities are, that sort of thing.”

“Certainly, Madame Secretary. I’d be happy to do so. When were you thinking of having me give it?”

“How about this coming Friday morning in the Chancellery’s main auditorium?”

“I can manage that.”

“Then it’s arranged. Thank you, Ambassador. Lazlo, out.”

Once her image had faded away to nothing, DeCarde looked up at Hermina, who still stood in the entryway to his office, a vague smile on her lips.

“Finally, something.”

“You noted she didn’t give you time to raise anything else, right?”

He thought back to the end of their conversation, then gave her a rueful nod.

"Indeed. I'm still being managed, aren't I?"

"Yes. But there's nothing for it. At least giving a presentation about the Republic will generate broader interest and may shake things loose."

***

"Madame President."

All present in the Wyvern Palace's small conference room stiffened in their chairs as Vigdis Mandus entered, the last to arrive as per custom, greeted by Chancellor Conteh, who was the Hegemony's acknowledged second in command.

The Hegemony's Executive Committee, President Vigdis Mandus, Chancellor Elrod Conteh, and Archimandrite Bolack met once a week. And every week, the four Service Chiefs — Admiral Benes of the Navy, General Sarkis of the Ground Forces, Chief Commissioner Nero Cabreras of the State Security Commission, and Admiral Godfrey of the Colonial Service attended as well.

The four consuls ruling the Hegemony's four core worlds, Wyvern, Arcadia, Dordogne, and Torrinos, used to join them, the latter three via subspace link. But they no longer did so since Santa Theresa had been rapidly, and some might say prematurely elevated to a Hegemony planet complete with its own Consul. Santa Theresa was too far for instantaneous subspace communications, and the breakneck speed at which the Hegemony was expanding would generate new consuls quickly, making their attendance unwieldy.

"At ease," Mandus said, in a way that betrayed her lifelong military background as she took her seat at the head of the table. In her mid-seventies, tall, with short platinum hair and pale blue eyes, Mandus was the Hegemony's first president. But she had been a Grand Admiral and regent before that, one in a long line of regents going back to the dissolution of the Empire upon Dendera's death in fire and blood. And like all of her predecessors, she'd been a four-star flag officer before the Conclave gave her the top job.

That Mandus wore a civilian suit now didn't change the fact she was a military dictator appointed by her peers for a specified term of office.

"Right, folks. Let's start. Chancellor?"

"Yes, Madame President. A few things. First, Ambassador DeCarde will give a presentation on the Republic of Lyonesse on Friday morning in the Chancellery amphitheater. All of you are invited."

"It's about time," murmured Admiral Benes, who many believed would replace Mandus in a few years. As wide as he was tall, with a high forehead, silver-tinged short black hair and beard, and intelligent, deep-set brown eyes, Benes was heads and shoulders above the other Service Chiefs, and he knew it.

Conteh gave him a brief but hard glance. The Service Chiefs weren't members of the Executive Committee, and therefore, in his opinion, they should stay silent unless asked to speak on a matter or answer a question. But Benes was *primus inter pares*, first among equals, and therefore could take certain liberties. Nonetheless, his words were a comment on the efficiency of the government Conteh headed since he had been given the responsibility of creating a new Department of Interstellar Affairs, which handled matters concerning the Lyonesse ambassador.

"Next," Conteh, bland-faced, dark-haired, in his late sixties, whose cool patrician features belied a mordant sense of humor and a quirky intellect, continued, "we must discuss the final dispositions for Novaya Sibir. Will we or won't we recolonize it, considering the cold winters, even in the temperate zone?"

—4—

Wyvern Hegemony Starship *Alkonost*
Task Group 211

Sister Taina, Order of the Void Reborn and *Alkonost*'s counselor, woke with a start, the echoes of many thousand voices still resonating in her mind as they spilled over from her subconscious. Something was amiss, yet she couldn't tell what.

Taina, tall and willowy, with dark blond hair framing a delicate face that hid a backbone made of pure starship-grade alloy, reached for the communicator sitting on the table next to her bunk and touched its screen.

"Counselor to the bridge."

A few seconds later, a man's voice replied, "Lieutenant Shah, officer of the watch here, Counselor. What can I do for you?"

"Did we just emerge from a wormhole?"

"Fifteen minutes ago."

"What star system?"

"We're not sure. It was supposed to be ISC255686-4, an M1V class star, but that's not where the wormhole led us. This is a G2V with an extensive planetary system. The wormhole shifted." A pause. "If you don't mind me asking, Sister, what's your interest at this time of the gamma watch?"

"I was woken by a disturbance, Harim, and I wonder whether it's this star system."

Even though he wasn't a believer, Lieutenant Harim Shah knew better than to ask about a Sister of the Void's disturbances. He understood that their fey abilities were best left unnoticed by ordinary individuals.

"I couldn't say, Sister. Was there anything else?"

"No. Thank you for the information. Taina, out."

She sat up, all notion of sleep forgotten. It was nearly three bells in the morning watch anyway, oh-five-thirty. She might as well get started on her day with morning meditation, which replaced the canonical service of lauds aboard starships.

Just before six bells, she entered the wardroom, refreshed and ready for anything. But the incident of the ghostly voices, who'd vanished as quickly as they appeared, remained in her consciousness. Taina grabbed a breakfast sandwich from the warm buffet, a cup of coffee from the urn and sat at an unoccupied table after nodding pleasantly to the officers present.

Most ate in silence, it being custom to avoid speaking at breakfast, so those of the Alpha shift who'd just gotten up could ease peacefully into their day. They would go on watch at eight bells in an hour. The lack of social interaction suited Taina, particularly this morning.

But it was not to be.

Captain Derwent Alexander, *Alkonost*'s sole master after the Almighty and commander of Task Group 211, which also included the frigates *Taillion* and *Gerwind*, entered the wardroom, served himself at the buffet and the urn, and joined Taina. Stocky, broad-shouldered, in his early forties, with short dark hair and a strong, square face, he turned piercing blue eyes on her.

"Good morning, Sister. I trust you had a good night?"

"Good morning, Captain. Passable until the last few minutes." She told him about the voices.

Alexander, who believed in a Sister's eerie abilities, frowned. "What could it mean?"

She shrugged.

"I do not know. Did we discover a habitable world in this system?"

"Yes, the fourth planet is in the golden zone and exhibits the signs of an atmosphere."

"Do we have any knowledge or suspicions regarding the system we're in?"

"No. Our records of this part of the old Empire are spotty at best. But we'll be heading inward to the fourth planet in fifteen minutes. It'll be an approximately eight-hour jump. We should establish where we are once we're within close observation range."

"Or so you hope." She gave him a smile.

"Indeed."

Soon, the jump klaxon sounded, and Task Group 211 spooled up their hyperdrives, then went FTL.

A little under eight hours later, they emerged at the fourth planet's hyperlimit and began scanning. Sister Taina, who was meditating at the time, felt another surge of voices spilling over from her subconscious, brief but intense. She roused herself immediately and headed for the bridge, taking one of the unused consoles behind the command chair.

Lieutenant Commander Ulf Ragnarsson, *Alkonost* and Task Group 211's navigator, sat at his workstation, frowning for several minutes. He turned to Captain Alexander with a puzzled expression.

"I'm not making heads or tails of this world, sir. It seems vaguely familiar, yet strange."

Taina glanced at Ragnarsson's screen and saw a name above a world resembling the one on the primary display. Lindisfarne. The ancient home of the Order of the Void.

"CIC, bridge here. Any life signs on the world we're approaching?" Alexander asked the sensor chief.

"None that we're detecting, sir," the latter replied after a moment of silence.

"Well, then. I suppose we can make a sensor sweep and head home." A pause. "No, let's not even do that."

"Captain?"

Alexander swiveled his chair to face Taina.

"Yes, Sister?"

"Are you okay?" She turned to Ragnarsson. "How about you, Commander?"

"Now that I consider it, I have a slight sense of unease. Why do you ask?"

"Because your workstation screen clearly labels the planet as Lindisfarne."

"Lindisfarne?" Ragnarsson reared up in surprise. "Where do you see that?"

Taina closed her eyes and reached out, feeling a wave of psychic energy enveloping the ship. After a few moments, she expanded her mind, encompassing those on the bridge and blocking any outside interference.

"Look again, Commander."

Ragnarsson did so and let out an oath.

"By the Almighty, you're right, Sister. It is Lindisfarne."

"Aye, so it is," Alexander said, comparing the image on the workstation to the one on the primary display. "What the hell happened?"

"You remember me telling you about voices this morning? Well, I heard them again when we dropped out of FTL just now. I suspect the people on Lindisfarne are using their talents to keep visitors from detecting them, and I'm blocking their influence right now. I'm apparently immune to it. Can we get a sensor feed up here?"

"Sure." Ragnarsson called it up on a secondary display. "And how about that? Almost five million life signs, mostly clustered along the shores of a broad bay on the primary continent, near the equator."

"What information do we have about Lindisfarne before the Great Scouring?" Alexander asked.

"Not much," Taina replied. "And not because of lost records. The star system was a mystery wrapped in an enigma during imperial times. Lindisfarne had severe restrictions on landing permission. The Order granted members the freedom to visit and settle on Lindisfarne as they pleased, but merchants were only allowed to land in specific areas and stay for a limited duration, while immigration was restricted to individuals possessing skills deemed useful by the Order. It did not allow any other visitors. As a result, little about the place filtered out, except for a few items. For example, the capital and seat of the Order's most venerated mother house is called Aidan, and the other major settlements are Cuthbert, Eadfrith, and Eadberht."

"And you say they tried to influence us into not knowing which planet that is and the extent of its population?"

Taina nodded.

"That's what I believe. It is, in fact, the only explanation for what just happened here on the bridge I can find. The Order has always had mystics capable of using their minds in ways that are obscure to the rest of humanity, and Lindisfarne will have the greatest concentration of those with the talent anywhere in the known universe. Perhaps hundreds of thousands, after two centuries of isolation and reproduction among them. Who knows how far and with what degree of strength they can project?" She paused and gave Alexander a wry grin. "And at this stage, they will understand that I am countering them, something I can't do for long without draining my energy."

"But now that we are aware of this being Lindisfarne, won't their influence cease to function?"

"I have no idea." Let's try." Taina collapsed the bubble she'd built around the bridge personnel. "How does it feel?"

"Back to queasy," Ragnarsson said. "But I remember everything we just spoke about, and I can see Lindisfarne's name on my workstation screen."

"Concur," Alexander added. "It looks like they can't recapture our attention once they lost it."

"Sir?" The sensor chief's voice came over the intercom. He sounded puzzled. "I've just picked up approximately five million life signs that weren't there before."

Alexander glanced at Taina, who smiled.

"I assume they relinquished efforts to hide their existence once they sensed your counteroffensive, Sister."

"And the queasiness is gone."

Alexander turned to the communications petty officer.

"Contact the other ships and ensure they see what we see, then broadcast the standard message on the old imperial emergency channel. If they have commo gear, they'll surely be listening to it, especially now that we're—"

"Incoming message from the surface, sir," the petty officer said. "Voice only, on the old emergency channel."

"Play it."

"Aye, aye, sir."

"*Strange vessels in orbit, this is a closed world. Leave immediately. I repeat, this is a closed world. Leave immediately.*" A pause, and then the message repeated in its androgynous tones.

"Not particularly helpful." Alexander rubbed his chin. "Okay, Signals, prepare to copy my response."

"Ready, sir."

"Good day, people of Lindisfarne. This is the starship *Alkonost* and two companions on a mission to reunite humanity. My name is Derwent Alexander. As you may have surmised, we have one of you aboard. In fact, we have several members of the Order performing various tasks, including protecting us from outside influences. We wish to speak with your leadership and bring them up to date on the state of the galaxy and the surviving human populations."

Alexander made a cutting motion, and when the petty officer nodded, indicating he'd stopped recording, he said, "Put it on a loop until they respond. In the meantime, we'll run the usual surface scans. Warn the other ships to take position. We'll begin in thirty minutes."

Several hours passed, during which Taina — who'd been sitting quietly in her quarters, mind open — deliberately made herself a target of inquisitive Sisters from Lindisfarne. She sensed multiple awarenesses connect with hers, and when she conversed with the other Sisters aboard Alkonost, they recounted identical experiences.

Finally, several hours later, a distinctly female voice sounded through the bridge speakers.

"*Alkonost, this is the Motherhouse Abbey.*"

—5—

Wyvern Hegemony Starship *Caladrius*
Task Group 215

"They're starships of imperial design, sir, although unlike any we have on record," Captain Pernell said. "A dozen of them, seven frigates and five cruisers. No emissions are visible against background radiation, but they're pressurized, and we're detecting a trickle of power in each of them as if their systems are in suspended animation. This isn't like the dead battle group found by TF Kruzenshtern a while back. These ships look like they're still alive, even if barely."

"Fascinating. They must have been there for over two hundred years, hidden by the shipyards ahead of the Retribution Fleet, waiting for someone to claim them." Newton Giambo sat back in his command chair and frowned as he contemplated the image of the ships found by *Strix* on the primary display. "I wonder... Signals, get me *Remus*."

"Aye, aye, sir. Wait one."

Moments later, the miniature holographic representation of Captain Warren Yeng, *Remus*' commanding officer, joined that of Jutta Pernell hovering in front of Giambo.

"Sir?"

"Where are you, Warren?"

"In Alberni's trailing Lagrangian, and—" Yeng's head turned to one side as a muffled voice spoke on his end. "We've found a dozen vessels as well. Eight cruisers and four frigates, which look exactly like those found by *Strix*. Same situation, no emissions visible against background radiation, but they're pressurized and have a bit of power coursing through their systems."

Commander Jana Venkov, eyes bright with excitement, said, "I think we should check the trailing Lagrangian of the third moon, Chemainus, and all three of the leading ones."

Giambo glanced at his first officer and nodded.

"Make it so."

Half an hour later, they'd found another dozen ships each in Nanaimo and Alberni's leading Lagrangians but nothing in those of Chemainus.

"Forty-eight ships, evenly divided between frigates and cruisers, all apparently undamaged according to the visuals and scans. What now, sir?"

Venkov turned her chair toward Giambo's.

"We should attempt to board one and see what its condition is. Since *Strix* found them first, let Jutta make the selection and send a boarding party."

In a little under a half hour, a shuttle emerged from *Strix*'s hangar and headed for one of the silent cruisers a few kilometers off the frigate's starboard bow. It approached the ship on its port side, aimed at a likely airlock, the boarding party hoping it would mate cleanly with the shuttle. The party, eleven ratings, and petty officers under the second officer, a lieutenant, wore environmental suits in case they had to depressurize the shuttle's aft compartment.

The shuttle came to a halt relative to the airlock and the pilot gently nudged his craft inward, stopping it a meter away. Then, he extruded the docking port, which fit inside the airlock's recessed circle.

"We have positive pressure inside the port, Lieutenant. Opening the airlock on our side."

The second officer entered the docking port, marveling at the fact he was about to climb aboard a starship that hadn't seen a human being in over two hundred years. He reached out to touch the control panel embedded in the center of the airlock door and entered the universal code that had remained unchanged since imperial times.

Nothing.

He tried again, but still nothing.

"*Strix*, this is the boarding party. The universal code didn't generate a response. Looking for the mechanical release."

"Acknowledged."

The officer eventually found the hidden panel and opened it, revealing a large handle. He grasped the handle and twisted it ninety degrees counterclockwise. As soon as it settled into its new position, he heard a clank. The airlock door pulled back and then slid to one side, revealing a lit compartment with another. The inner door slowly opened while deeper within the ship, systems roused themselves one by one.

Suddenly, the forty-seven other ships whose AIs had also been waiting for two hundred years, came to life when the first one signaled the presence of human beings aboard.

"By the Almighty," Newton Giambo whispered as Caladrius' sensors registered the presence of the forty-eight ships, now exhibiting position and navigation lights, giving the impression that they were fully crewed and ready to set sail. "A veritable battle fleet. What the hell are we going to do with it?"

"Take them home with us?" Commander Venkov suggested.

"Are you kidding me? Between us, we can maybe take a quarter of them, and that'll exhaust the crews who'll be doing watch on, watch off. It's what? Over two weeks to get home by the most direct route?"

"Something like that. But let's not decide just yet. These were supposed to be the most advanced ships in the known galaxy. Perhaps they don't need as much personnel as ours do."

"Even then, forty-eight starships are a bit much for us. Better we figure out how to put them back to sleep so they remain hidden until we or someone else can return with more people."

"*Strix*, boarding party. We've reached the bridge. Everything appears to be up and running." A pause. "On a side display, there's an indication that all the ships are linked."

"They are indeed," a disembodied, androgynous voice said. "Welcome aboard *Hecate*, Lieutenant. This ship and the others are ready for your directions."

"Boarding party, this is *Strix*. Who said that?"

"Um, an AI, presumably? It came from the speakers."

"I am indeed an artificial intelligence charged with the control of *Hecate*. Each ship has its own controlling AI, and we've been waiting for this day when humans return to take command."

Giambo and Venkov exchanged surprised glances. AIs had existed for over fifteen hundred years, but always in limited roles for fear they might act independently. It sounded like the one in *Hecate* was more than that. Giambo turned to his signals petty officer.

"Put me on a link with the boarding party." When the petty officer gave him the nod, he said, "Boarding party, this is *Caladrius*."

"Go ahead, sir."

"Put me on your speaker. I want to talk with the AI."

"Yes, sir. You're on."

"AI, this is Captain Newton Giambo of the cruiser *Caladrius*. I command Task Group 215."

"Good day, Captain," the voice replied in a polite tone. "What can I do for you?"

"When you say you're charged with control of the ship, what does it mean?"

"I can operate every system and carry out every order. In effect, I merely need a human to provide direction and will do everything else."

Giambo's eyebrows shot up.

"Including faster-than-light and wormhole navigation?"

"Yes."

"And if I gave the order to follow *Caladrius* back to Wyvern, could you do it?"

"Yes, although I would need humans on board. I and the others may only act on human commands."

"Why were you programmed this way?"

"I do not know."

"What happened to your creators?"

"I do not know."

Giambo and Venkov glanced at each other again as the former muted his end of the link.

"Are you thinking what I'm thinking, Jana?"

"If you figure we put three crew aboard each of the ships, so one stands watch at any given time and take the lot with us, then yes."

"That was indeed my thought. Drafting one hundred and forty-four crew members between the three of us should be possible. We take twenty of them, and the frigates each take fourteen. We'll call for volunteers, of course." He unmuted the link. "AI, are the ships ready to sail if I put three humans on each one?"

"Yes."

"And are your antimatter reservoirs full? Do you have water and rations, and is any ship in need of repairs or parts?"

"Yes, we are fully fueled and watered. No, we don't have rations, and none of the ships need repairs."

Growing excitement sparked in Giambo's eyes as he contemplated the reaction of his superiors when he showed up with an entire battle fleet. Those forty-eight ships would effectively increase the Hegemony's naval combat strength by twenty-five percent. Useful when considering the Republic of Lyonesse and its Navy.

"Okay. Since you're linked, *Hecate* will be the lead ship. I'll put Trevor Wenn, my second officer, aboard her, and he can exercise control over the crews of the rest. But first, we'll need to check out every ship individually."

"Certainly, Captain. Their airlocks will now respond to the universal code."

It ended up taking a week to organize everything, but one by one, the ships broke away from the Lagrangians and entered orbit around Cascadia and formed into four sections of twelve, each with an officer in the lead ship and petty officers commanding the rest. It left the three ships of Task Group 215 low on senior petty officers, but that allowed the junior ratings aboard *Caladrius, Strix*, and *Remus* a chance to prove themselves.

Finally, Newton Giambo, satisfied he'd done everything in his power to make the forty-eight ships ready and safe to undertake the two dozen wormhole transits back to the Wyvern Hegemony, gave the order to break out of Cascadia's orbit. His three vessels led the way, with the found battle fleet following in its four sections, the crew members in each of them feeling a little less sanguine about their journey than Giambo but mostly feeling lost, only three aboard ships that could carry hundreds.

When the fleet emerged whole at the wormhole terminus nine hours later, many breathed a sigh of relief. Then, after checking in with each ship, Captain Giambo led them into the first of many wormhole transits.

—6—

Wyvern Hegemony Starship *Alkonost*
Task Group 211

"I'm Derwent Alexander. To whom do I have the honor of speaking?"

"I am Sister Margot, one of the Summus Abbatissa's aides. You claim to have Sisters aboard your ships." The voice seemed ancient but steady, strong, the sort that would match an ageless face.

"Indeed, I do."

"I would speak to the senior among them."

"That would be Taina, my ship's counselor. She stands beside me and is listening."

"Sister Margot, I am Taina of the Order of the Void Reborn." Her tone was deeply respectful, and even though the link had no visual component, she bowed her head.

"Void Reborn? What is this?"

"The Order beyond Lindisfarne was almost wiped out during Empress Dendera's final madness, Sister. Our forebears who rebuilt it call themselves the Void Reborn. We did not know, of course, that the Order had endured in greater numbers here, having assumed Lindisfarne suffered the same fate as every other world visited by the Retribution Fleet. Only five star systems survived more or less intact — Wyvern, Arcadia, Dordogne, Torrinos, and Lyonesse. The Retribution Fleet scoured the rest of the old Empire clean, depopulating some planets entirely and reducing the rest to a pre-industrial standard of living not experienced for over two thousand years."

"I see." Margot sounded pensive. "Four worlds at the heart of the Empire and one so far away from here, it would take weeks to reach. I assume you're from Wyvern?"

"We are, Sister. Our four star systems weathered the Great Scouring only because the Retribution Fleet was stopped before it could destroy them, and Empress Dendera and her court were wiped out. The Empire died on that day more than two hundred years ago, but over ninety percent of humanity perished with it. We are glad to see Lindisfarne escaped that fate."

"And Lyonesse?"

"It survived by remaining hidden at the end of a wormhole cul-de-sac in the furthest reaches of the old Empire. May I assume you survived by pulling the same trick on the Retribution Fleet units that came through this star system as you did on us?"

"You may. Our forebears successfully nudged them back into the wormhole network as they carried no Brethren aboard their ships. What do you call yourselves if the Empire is dead?"

"The Wyvern Hegemony."

"A strange name."

"It merely reflects the predominance of Wyvern over the other three worlds."

"And Lyonesse?"

"They call themselves a Republic, separate from the Hegemony, and on their own path to reunification, but we have friendly relations with them."

"You stated your mission is to reunify humanity."

"Yes, and both the Republic and we have taken several star systems under our wings and are lifting their populations back to a level of technology commensurate with interstellar travel."

"And you would take Lindisfarne into your Hegemony?"

"Only if you wish it. As you probably know, it is more than a two-week journey from here to Wyvern, and there are no longer any inhabited worlds between them. Each and every one of them was scoured. And you represented one of the most distant human star systems in this quadrant before Dendera's madness. We could do little for you until we expand to bring the entire quadrant under Hegemony rule, and that will take a few decades."

"At least you are honest, Taina. That speaks well for you and your Order of the Void Reborn. Would you consent to landing and meeting with the Summus Abbatissa?"

Taina and Captain Alexander exchanged looks, and the latter nodded.

"Yes," she replied. "I'd be honored to do so."

"It is currently twelve hundred hours. Shall we say at fifteen hundred today? Your shuttle, one only, can land at the Aidan Spaceport at ten minutes to the hour. Someone will meet you."

"Certainly, Sister."

"No one else is to disembark."

"No one will."

"Until then."

The signals petty officer turned toward Alexander and Taina and made a cutting motion, indicating the link had been severed.

Alexander cocked an eyebrow at his ship's counselor.

"Wasn't that special? She spoke as if she could easily repel the power of three warships."

"Considering they pushed away the Retribution Fleet and no doubt many barbarian incursions over the decades with their minds, the habit of believing they can do so with anyone must be hard to break."

"True. And we only made it because we have Sisters aboard our ships. Fine. Let's get a shuttle organized and see where that Aidan Spaceport is. Considering they've had little traffic in the last while, it might be overgrown."

But it wasn't.

Sitting up front with the pilot, Sister Taina had a bird's-eye view of Aidan as the shuttle descended in a lazy spiral. A large city surrounded by endless fields on three sides and the ocean on the fourth, it seemed almost like a vast diorama from above. Most buildings appeared to be four stories or less, set along broad streets lined by mature trees and surrounded by their own little strips of greenery.

The Motherhouse Abbey, a sprawling compound covering several square kilometers and surrounded by a high wall, occupied the center of Aidan. It was easily identifiable, with the layout and structures resembling those of the New Draconis Abbey, but on a much larger scale.

The spaceport, a small, bare strip of tarmac on the northern outskirts, was empty, its surface cracked and crazed by the years. The terminal building was shuttered, with windows and doors covered by old sheets of rigid material, but a small ground vehicle sat in the shade beside it.

Taina's shuttle landed in front of the terminal and dropped its aft ramp, allowing her to disembark. As she did so, a friar wearing the same sort of dark robes as she did climbed out of the ground car and stood respectfully beside it, hands joined. He appeared elderly, with gray hair and a gray beard framing a seamed face, but his stance was that of a much younger man.

The friar bowed his head as Taina neared him.

"I am Gerrold, Sister. Welcome to Lindisfarne. If you'll climb aboard, I shall convey you to the Summus Abbatissa."

"Thank you, Friar."

Though clean, the car appeared old and worn out to Taina's eyes. Its shape was that of a black teardrop, with four wheels and a dark interior, which also showed its age. They climbed aboard, Taina up front alongside Gerrold, and the friar lit up the silent powerplant before putting the car into gear and sending it along a paved path toward a road that ran along Aidan's outskirts. But to Taina's surprise, Gerrold turned left, away from Aidan proper, at the next intersection and drove them out into the fields.

"Do these fields feed the city, Friar?" She asked, gesturing at the amber stalks of grain marching off to the horizon in every direction.

"Yes, and we also send part of the harvest down the bay to other centers while they send us a portion of theirs. We're one population and one world under the Almighty in the Great Void."

"The Void giveth, the Void taketh away."

Gerrold smiled at her. "Blessed be the Void."

"Where are we going, if you don't mind my asking?"

"The Summus Abbatissa is enjoying a few days away from the abbey in one of the outlying granges."

"I see." Taina fell silent again. After a few minutes, she asked, "If I may, how old is this car?"

Gerrold chuckled.

"Older than me, and I'm seventy. We waste nothing on Lindisfarne. Whatever we make is built to last a lifetime. The abbey and Aidan have structures that are over five hundred years old but seem no older than a few decades."

"Impressive."

"We are a simple folk, Sister. Much of our manufacturing is artisanal and has always been so, which saved us from falling down the technological ladder once travel between the stars ceased. Although I'm sure our level doesn't compare to your Hegemony's, not if you lost nothing."

"And yet, the population is only five million? According to our records, it was the number during the waning days of the Empire."

"We are long-lived, and the lay population reproduces only at replacement levels thanks to strict policies that keep numbers in check. Otherwise, we would outstrip our industrial capacity and have to enlarge it as well, triggering a vicious cycle of constant expansion until we come against the planet's carrying capacity. As you may have noted, the habitable parts of this world are small enough. Best we give ourselves plenty of room."

Taina nodded. "I did. Thank you for the explanation. How many Brethren are there?"

"Half a million, or ten percent of the population, if you like. Two hundred and fifty thousand friars and the same number of Sisters, give or take. We friars mostly engage in worldly tasks, such as governing this planet under the guidance of the Summus Abbatissa, while the Sisters primarily attend to spiritual matters, healing, teaching, and our defense against outsiders."

The easy way in which Gerrold spoke told Taina he'd been ordered to answer any and all of her queries, perhaps as a way of preparing her to meet the Summus Abbatissa with greater knowledge about Lindisfarne. The question, however, was the degree of openness and even honesty with which he did so. That he asked her nothing in return was telling as well.

"Of course," he continued, "there are plenty of Sisters with worldly responsibilities and those friars who have the talent working the spiritual side."

"Are there many of the latter? Friars with the talent?"

"Increasingly so, Sister. Each generation seems to bring more of them to us, and we don't know why. Sadly, I'm not one of them, in case you were wondering. But I serve the Summus Abbatissa nonetheless."

A cluster of two-story buildings surrounded by trees appeared on the horizon, and Taina knew it was their destination. A few minutes later, Gerrold turned down a farm path through an arch and into a shady courtyard with a farmhouse on one side and outbuildings on the other, then turned off the power plant.

"We have arrived, Sister. I will take you to the Summus Abbatissa."

They climbed out of the car, and Gerrold led her through another arch and into a garden replete with flowers and buzzing insects. A rustic table and chairs sat on flagstones in the middle, and Gerrold gestured at them.

"Please sit, Sister."

Taina did so, letting her six senses brush against the bucolic, calming environment. She could easily see why the Head of the Order liked to come here. A man with a friar's beard but wearing work clothes came out of the farmhouse's back door carrying a tray with a jug and several glasses.

He smiled at her.

"Welcome to Felicity Grange, Sister. I'm Friar Venkar." After depositing the tray on the table, he said, "The Summus Abbatissa will be with you momentarily."

Then he and Gerrold vanished, leaving her alone among the gentle aromas of nature. Taina heard faint noises coming from deeper within the garden, where bushes and trees cut off the view, and eventually, a tall, thin figure wearing hooded robes appeared. She stopped at the edge of the open space and flipped her hood back.

"I am Mariko, Summus Abbatissa of the Order of the Void."

Taina bowed her head.

"Thank you for seeing me."

When she looked up again, she saw that the woman exhibited the signs of extreme age, even though her voice was firm. Her short hair was pure white, almost translucent, as was the skin of her face, taut over high cheekbones and an aquiline nose. Sunken eyes of an intense blue studied Taina with intelligence and alertness.

Mariko chuckled, a dry sound like leaves rustling.

"You wonder about my age, child. Do not deny it. I can read it in your face even though your self-control is remarkable. I am one hundred and fifty years old and have been the Summus Abbatissa for forty of those."

When Friar Gerrold said they were long-lived, he hadn't been kidding.

"And now, my child, I must ask that you open your mind to me so I may establish your bona fides."

—7—

"I will do so, Sister." Taina closed her eyes and opened the natural defenses enclosing her mind, defenses she'd built up over decades, instinctive and always on.

Within moments, she felt the tendrils of mental fingers touching her, tasting her thoughts, and sifting through her emotions. Mariko was powerful. She possessed the strongest mind Taina had ever encountered. No wonder she'd been Summus Abbatissa for the last forty years when, historically, few heads of the Order had served in that capacity for more than fifteen. In the Void Reborn, it was closer to ten years.

Abruptly, the intrusion ceased, and her defenses snapped back up by themselves.

"You are indeed a Sister of the Void, Taina. A strong one. Disciplined." Mariko took a chair across from her and smiled. "Now tell me of the universe, your Hegemony, and the Order of the Void Reborn. Our last visitor from the stars left two centuries ago."

As Taina spoke, she could sense Mariko's eyes drilling into her soul, or so it seemed. The Summus Abbatissa listened intently as she recounted the admirals' rebellion and Draconis's destruction, ending the Empire. She then spoke of the Hegemony's subsequent creation and its two-hundred-year slumber in four star systems, followed by a reawakening and re-swearing the Oath of Reunification once it became aware of Lyonesse, the expanding Republic from the far reaches of what had once been human space.

Taina also recounted what she could about Lyonesse, hiding nothing from the Summus Abbatissa. Yet Mariko never once sought clarification, and Taina was uncertain if she had provided a comprehensive account of the last two centuries of human history or if Mariko simply lacked interest.

"What an extraordinary tale, my child. I am glad that at least a few worlds survived and kept interstellar travel to reunify humanity, even if it is under two separate banners. Now, talk to me about the Order of the Void Reborn. I assume it doesn't look to the Motherhouse on Lindisfarne for leadership."

"No." Taina shook her head. "We refer to ourselves as Reborn because we were uninformed of the Motherhouse's survival and consequently charted our own course toward the Almighty in the Infinite Void."

"I sense some differences between us and your branch of the Order."

"Indeed, Sister. Our head is called Archimandrite and can be either male or female. The current one is named Salamanu Bolack, and yes, Archimandrites are known by both names, although the rank and file still use only one. Our Order's symbol is different as well. Where yours has stars in the orb, ours has a phoenix rising from the ashes. But doctrinally, we are the same."

"Then you would look to the Motherhouse once more, now that you know it survived?"

Taina was well aware Archimandrite Bolack wanted to bring the Lyonesse branch of the Order under his leadership or that of his successors and wouldn't look kindly at bowing to Lindisfarne. However, the Council of Elders might have other ideas once it learned about the Motherhouse. Archimandrites weren't all-powerful, even though the Council didn't rouse itself more than once every few years.

"I have no idea, Sister."

Mariko tilted her head to one side.

"You speak the truth when you say that."

"Our branch of the Order is more deeply involved in worldly affairs than that of Lyonesse, and some of us — not me, but many others, Archimandrite Bolack included — believe in a prophecy that the two halves of what was once rent asunder will reunite and must do so under the banner of the Void Reborn."

"Why?"

"Because they believe, and I quote, the Old Order, with its outdated views, strange scruples, and refusal to use the abilities of all Friars and Sisters to the utmost, couldn't be the way of the future."

Mariko sat back, eyes still holding Taina's.

"I see. How interesting. We have a true schism, the sort the Order avoided for its entire history until the Empire perished."

Taina suddenly realized she'd said more than she intended and wondered whether the Summus Abbatissa had placed a compulsion in her mind. It was theoretically possible, although Taina was unaware of anyone who had accomplished it.

Considering how much such a thing would help the Sisters working for the State Security Commission, they'd have developed the ability by now. Perhaps her subconscious was guiding her into revealing things her conscious mind would have withheld. Or it had decided only absolute honesty would work with Sister Mariko.

Maybe she'd determined reunification also meant looking to the Motherhouse once more rather than continuing on a separate, if parallel, path. There were more Brethren on this one world than in all of the Hegemony and possibly even Lyonesse combined.

And would Lyonesse return to Lindisfarne once it was aware of the Motherhouse Abbey's survival?

As if Mariko had read her mind again, she asked, "What about the Order in the Republic of Lyonesse? Did they keep to the orthodoxy, or did they embark on their own path as well?"

"As far as I can tell, other than proclaiming the Lannion Abbey the Order's new Motherhouse, they seem to have continued along the old ways. But I only had a short period of interaction with their representatives."

Taina described how expeditions from the Republic and the Hegemony, the latter led by *Alkonost*, had found themselves simultaneously at the cradle of humanity, Earth, the previous year and cooperated. She also mentioned how she and the Republic expedition's head Sister had agreed to work toward a common goal: turning Wyvern and Lyonesse away from the path of competition and onto that of cooperation until their respective societies matured sufficiently to accept reunification as equals.

"Wise, Sister. But is it not beyond your ability to influence?"

"All great things begin small. If we don't try, we can be sure nothing happens."

Mariko inclined her head.

"True. Yet you are here in the wilds of the galaxy rather than at home on Wyvern, where you can at least influence the discussion."

Taina gave her a wry smile.

"Those great things that begin small also don't begin immediately, Sister."

"By the Almighty, but you are a philosopher, Sister! Not every one of us can assert that." Mariko returned her smile, though Taina noticed it didn't reach her eyes, which remained as watchful as ever. "And thank you for your openness and honesty. You've given me much to think about. Lindisfarne has not changed since my birth, its inhabitants believing themselves alone in the universe. And yet it seems humanity is on the march again, re-expanding into star systems that fell during the last days of Dendera's reign."

"Doing so at breakneck speed, Sister, although it will take a few generations before our frontiers have expanded sufficiently to reabsorb Lindisfarne. Large families have not been the norm in the Hegemony, and it will take some time before our population grows enough to reoccupy former human worlds in any numbers."

"Well, we've survived on our own for this long. I think we'll manage another hundred years. Besides, it isn't a given Lindisfarne will join either your Hegemony or the Republic. If humanity remains disunited, we may decide to stay sovereign and neutral between competing polities, as befits the Order of the Void. Unless your Order of the Void Reborn readopts orthodoxy and pledges its allegiance to the Motherhouse on Lindisfarne."

Mariko studied Taina, gauging her reaction to the idea. The latter was well aware that Bolack would never agree to surrender his supreme leadership and step back into the role of a simple friar. Nor would any of the other males now exercising what had formerly been female-only roles, and that took care of half of the Council which was the only body capable of overruling an Archimandrite.

The Summus Abbatissa chuckled.

"No, I didn't think so. At least not in the foreseeable future. I will send a delegation back with you, however. You can return them in two or three years."

"With the knowledge of your existence, I anticipate patrols will make regular rounds in this star system. You may not wish to join the Hegemony, but its government will feel a certain obligation to ensure your safety."

Mariko inclined her head.

"So be it. I shall also give you a list of items we would like to buy from you, things we can no longer manufacture ourselves."

"Certainly."

"And now, I do believe I will return to the Motherhouse. Will you accompany me and stay for the night? You'll be able to get a taste of our services and lifestyle."

"I'd be most honored, Sister." Taina bowed her head.

Mariko stood, her movements those of a woman fifty years younger, and headed for the arch separating the garden from the courtyard. After a few bemused moments, Taina followed.

As if forewarned, Friar Gerrold stood by the old ground car, waiting patiently, hands joined in front of him. At their approach, he bowed his head, and the doors opened silently. Mariko climbed into the back and gestured at Taina to join her. Moments later, the doors closed again, and Gerrold put the car into motion.

They drove back to Aidan in silence, Mariko sitting with her eyes closed and her breathing slow and measured. But Taina stared out the windows, taking in everything she saw, and soon, they reached Aidan's outskirts, where fields abruptly gave way to housing.

Up close, it seemed as if no new structures had been built since the Empire's collapse, giving the town an ancient appearance, though it was well-maintained. The buildings were invariably stone-clad, with metal roofs and transparent aluminum windows.

What people Taina saw were well-fed, clothed simply but cleanly, and moved with purpose. Whether they were happy, she couldn't tell without entering their minds, something she wouldn't do on a strange planet where ten percent of the population were Brethren and therefore sensitive to such a thing.

Soon, the Motherhouse Abbey came into view, its central structures towering over well-maintained parkland. If the townhouses had appeared ancient, the abbey was clearly from another era altogether. Taina knew that the Order had established Lindisfarne as its own world halfway through the imperial age, seven hundred years ago, and the abbey reflected that.

The chapterhouse at its heart was immense, with space for thousands. Stained glass windows three or four stories tall pierced the gray stone walls of the octagonal structure at regular intervals, interspersed by flying buttresses, while the domed roof soared high above Aidan, a beacon to the Almighty's servants for kilometers around.

Lesser but still oversized buildings surrounded it, such as the administration, refectory, dormitories, and hospital. A square, two-story cloister, easily over a kilometer on each side, also enclosed the entirety. It was at least three or four times the size of the New Draconis Abbey, and the effect was humbling and awe-inspiring for a newcomer such as Taina.

"How many Brethren call the Motherhouse Abbey their home?"

"Three thousand, Sister," Gerrold replied. "Mainly those involved in spiritual matters. Two dozen priories are scattered around Aidan for those with more worldly responsibilities. The other cities organize themselves similarly, with an abbey at the center and priories surrounding it. Each priory dedicates itself to one or two functions concerning the secular administration of our world. For example, the Department of Agriculture has its own priories in each city and town, as does the Department of Transportation."

"Am I to understand that the Order runs everything?"

"Yes, it governs Lindisfarne. And Brethren occupy the senior posts in every department."

"Fascinating."

The car stopped in front of the administration building, and Mariko's eyes snapped open.

"We have arrived, Sister."

"Thank you, Gerrold. That will be everything for today."

Mariko and Taina climbed out of the car, which vanished around a corner moments later, taken by Gerrold to the abbey's garage.

The Summus Abbatissa turned to Taina.

"Did you wish to tell your ship you're staying with us overnight?"

"I suppose I should."

"Then we shall go to our communications center first."

—8—

Sister Taina found herself the object of great curiosity by the Brethren of Motherhouse Abbey as Sister Margot, Mariko's aide, an older woman whose short, gray hair framed a narrow face with large, intelligent eyes guided her. The Summus Abbatissa had handed Taina over after she'd spoken with Captain Alexander, informing him she'd be staying the night, and he should recall the shuttle waiting on the cracked tarmac of Aidan's abandoned spaceport. It would return in the morning unless she called to inform them of a delay.

Margot took her through the hospital, the largest on the planet, the administration building, and the dormitories, indicating where Taina would sleep. They ended up in the refectory shortly after it opened for the evening meal and joined the line of Brethren quietly chatting among themselves as they picked up trays, utensils, and plates before helping themselves to the buffet-style meal.

As per common usage, they took the next available seats at the first of the long tables slowly filling up with diners, nodding politely to the nearest of them. Those became immensely interested by Taina when they noticed the small orb she wore on a chain around her neck held a phoenix rather than a field of stars. It confirmed she belonged to the ships in orbit the Motherhouse Brethren had been incapable of repelling with their thoughts.

"Sister," one of them, a younger woman, asked once they finished eating, "why did your return to Lindisfarne take over two hundred years?"

"During those centuries, we confined ourselves to our four core star systems and focused on rebuilding what had been destroyed. We came very close to losing everything and almost joined the hundreds of star systems that the Retribution Fleet had ravaged. It made us overly cautious initially, and staying within our small cluster became a habit."

"And what broke that habit, if I may ask?"

Taina gave her a smile.

"The knowledge there is another human polity that survived and had been thriving by reclaiming fallen worlds for the last few decades. And yes, I have met some of them. They're human, just like we are, but they come from Lyonesse, a star system at the extreme end of what was once the Empire. I don't believe there is a greater distance between human worlds than that separating Lindisfarne from Lyonesse."

"And you are now in competition with them?"

"Not really. There are so many star systems to reclaim and so few of us it will take several generations before our spheres abut each other. I hope that by then, we'll have matured enough to coexist peacefully and possibly sufficiently so to reunite as one."

"From your lips, Sister."

Margot took her empty tray in her hands.

"Shall we, Taina?"

"Yes." Taina smiled at the Sisters surrounding her as she and Margot stood. "It was a pleasure meeting all of you."

They dropped off their trays and left the refectory, stepping out into the early evening air, which was still warm from the day's sunshine, and headed for the cloister, where they took a meditative walk. Taina experienced an unusual sense of comfort in the Motherhouse Abbey, as though she were a part of it, and the evening services an hour later only strengthened that sensation, even though there were ten times as many worshippers compared to the New Draconis Abbey. After the services, which differed in no way from those of the Void Reborn, Friar Gerrold intercepted them with an invitation to join the Summus Abbatissa in her office in fifteen minutes.

"How are you enjoying the abbey?" Sister Mariko asked when Taina and Margot appeared. She sat behind a straightforward wooden desk with a virtual workstation and not much else, and although the office was large, as befit the ruler of a planet, it was also simply decorated and appointed. She gestured at the chairs in front of the desk. "Please sit."

"I'm impressed by its size, especially the hospital, but at its heart, it seems little different from those back home. Even the service was the same."

"Glad to hear it. Now, I've asked you here because I've come to a decision concerning the delegation that will accompany you back to Wyvern and meet with your Archimandrite. Sister

Margot will lead, and two others, Sister Samara and Sister Fayruz, who will join us momentarily, will accompany her."

Margot inclined her head.

"As you command, Summus Abbatissa."

"Your task will be to open a dialogue between the Void Reborn and the Motherhouse and, if possible, bring them back into communion with us."

"Understood."

Just then, Mariko's eyes went to the open door, and she waved.

"Sisters Samara and Fayruz, please enter."

Margot stood, and Taina imitated her, both turning to greet the newcomers. Samara, short, with shoulder-length dark hair and olive skin, seemed young but for her eyes, which betrayed many more years than Taina's relative youth. Fayruz, on the other hand, tall, blonde, ascetically thin, appeared almost a hundred years old. But her movements were fluid, and her voice was steady as both new arrivals greeted the Summus Abbatissa, Margot, and Taina in turn. They studied the latter for a few moments, and Taina felt naked under Fayruz's watchful, hooded eyes. It was almost as if she could read her soul.

"I am pleased to make your acquaintance." Taina bowed her head.

Fayruz's thin lips twitched.

"I do believe she means that."

Taina gave her a brief glance before turning her attention back to Mariko, who said, "I trust you can accommodate them, Taina?"

"Certainly. We have spare, albeit austere, cabins aboard *Alkonost*. But since we're at the limit of our exploration run, we'll return home from here. And once on Wyvern, they'll be welcomed by the New Draconis Abbey, where they can live among the rest of the Brethren."

"Excellent. You may leave tomorrow when the shuttle returns."

"Yes, Summus Abbatissa." Margot, Samara, and Fayruz bowed.

"Be warned, however, that your stay on Wyvern could be lengthy since we depend on the Hegemony's ships to transport you back. Go and prepare. If you'd please stay for a moment, Taina?"

Once they were alone, Mariko gestured at Taina to sit once more.

"I have thought about our conversation of this afternoon and your desire to see humanity reunited. Could you send a message to the Lyonesse Brethren informing them of our survival and desire to reforge a single Order from the three current branches? If they and the Void Reborn rejoin Lindisfarne, it might bring about the unity of the two polities."

"I will do so, though I don't know if their Summus Abbatissa would surrender her independence."

A faint smile appeared on Mariko's lips.

"Just like your Archimandrite."

"Indeed."

"The three Sisters I am sending with you can be most convincing. If they're unable to persuade your Archimandrite, I don't think anyone else would be capable. And that being said, you may head for the dormitory."

As Taina walked along the paths separating the buildings, taking the air before heading to bed, she wondered what Mariko had meant by her comment about the Sisters who'd come back to Wyvern being most convincing. She knew Mariko and the others were keeping many things from her. The Old Order must have changed to adapt to new circumstances over the last two centuries, and it had its own secrets from a Sister of the Void Reborn.

Eventually, she reached the cell assigned to her in the guest wing of the principal dormitory building, and after taking off her robes, she slipped into bed for a night that proved restless more than restful, although she couldn't find the cause.

The following morning, she rose for the prime service, held at the first hour of daylight, and filed into the chapterhouse with the rest of the Brethren, still feeling a bit discombobulated. As was the custom in abbeys and priories of the Void, no one spoke during breakfast afterward, which suited Taina just fine since she was still trying to process her unaccustomed night of disruption as she almost always slept well.

After breakfast, Friar Gerrold found her and brought her to the car where the three Sisters who would go with her waited. They climbed aboard and headed for the spaceport in silence. Margot, Samara, and Fayruz were lost in their own thoughts, and Taina realized this would be the first time anyone on Lindisfarne left the planet's surface in two centuries. It was small wonder they were contemplative and perhaps even apprehensive.

The shuttle landed shortly after they arrived, and Taina led them, each carrying a small bag, up the aft ramp and into the passenger compartment, where she showed them how to strap in. Once they were seated, the pilot raised the ramp and spooled up thrusters. Then they lifted off, and Taina briefly opened her mind to the Lindisfarne Brethrens' emotions and although they were highly disciplined, she could still sense unease and even sadness.

Captain Alexander met them on the hangar deck, welcoming Margot, Samara, and Fayruz, who responded with grave nods and even graver thanks. Taina took them around the ship, introduced them to the other Void Reborn Brethren on board and the senior officers and noncoms, and saw them settle into their quarters. Shortly after, Task Group 211 broke out of orbit for the first leg of its voyage home.

—9—

Wyvern Hegemony Starship *Caladrius*
Task Group 215

"It's pretty lonely, spooky even, but we'll manage," Lieutenant Commander Trevor Wenn, *Hecate*'s temporary commanding officer, said after the first wormhole transit. Stocky, with black hair, a dark complexion, and a broad, flattened nose, he had intelligent brown eyes beneath heavy brows. "Fortunately, the AI in charge is a delightful conversationalist."

"No issues other than that?" Captain Giambo asked.

"None. The ships are functioning within normal parameters."

Giambo chuckled.

"You're starting to sound like the AI, Trevor."

"I thought my turn of phrase would amuse you, sir."

"Okay, if there's nothing, let's get everyone synced and go FTL for our exit wormhole."

"Aye, aye, sir. *Hecate*, out."

Wenn's image disappeared as a secondary display filled with lines, each showing a ship locked into *Caladrius*' navigation control center. After ninety seconds, Lieutenant Commander Dyre turned to Giambo and declared that Task Group 215's fifty-one ships were synced and ready.

Giambo made a hand gesture, finger pointed forward.

"Engage."

Within moments, the Task Group went FTL, and Giambo placed the ship at cruising stations. He turned his chair to get up and head for his day cabin when he saw the expression on Sister Adonna's face.

"Would you join me for coffee, Sister?"

She seemed to mentally shake herself.

"Certainly."

Both rose and headed for the door at the back of the bridge that led to the day cabin, Giambo turning the con over to the officer of the watch, who slipped into the command chair behind him.

Once behind closed doors, Giambo gave Adonna a strange look before heading for the tea urn.

"What's wrong?"

"I'm not sure. Something about Trevor's manner was off."

"In what way?" He drew two mugs, handed one to Adonna, and sat behind his desk. "We spoke little nor for very long."

She took a sip, holding the mug in both hands, then kept it in front of her mouth as she thought.

"The way he said lonely, spooky even, Captain. Something is bothering Trevor. It could be his own imagination working overtime, or it could be something else. But I wouldn't dismiss it just yet."

"Noted, Sister." Giambo knew that the Sisters were excellent psychologists in addition to whatever else they might be, even though he wasn't a strong believer. And if Adonna thought Trevor appeared a little off, then he was.

Nine hours later, they dropped out of FTL at the departure wormhole, and Giambo checked in with Lieutenant Commander Wenn again before they crossed the event horizon and made their transit to the next star system. And he appeared to be just fine. Even Adonna thought so.

Yet after the second wormhole transit, his unease had returned and this time Giambo asked him straight away.

"This is now the second transit you've completed where you seem a little weirded out, Trevor. And you haven't after the FTL runs. What gives?"

"I don't know. But when we're doing a wormhole, I get a really uneasy feeling that won't go away until we pop out at the other end. I didn't want to mention anything, in case you thought I was losing it, but this is the second time it happened."

"I wonder if any of the others are experiencing the same thing." Giambo turned to his signals noncom. "Get me the remaining lead ships."

Of the three, two immediately admitted to slightly eerie experiences while transiting the last two wormholes. The third, a stolid lieutenant with little imagination who came from *Caladrius*, shrugged.

"Nothing, sir. It was as boring as can be."

"Okay." Giambo sat back in his command chair, rubbing his chin. "We've got a dozen wormhole transits ahead of us. Check with the people in your groups. If it's just faintly discomforting, then we go. But should any of them feel spooked enough to want out, we'll replace them with someone else. You have one hour."

"If I may, Captain," Sister Adonna said. Maybe I could join Commander Wenn for the next FTL jump and wormhole transit and experience it for myself. I am sensitive to many more things than most people."

"Agreed. We'll transfer you over immediately."

An hour later, Adonna, carrying a small bag, passed through the shuttle's docking port and into *Hecate*'s starboard airlock, where Lieutenant Commander Wenn waited for her.

"Permission to come aboard?" She asked formally.

"Granted. Welcome, Counselor. I'm glad you're here. Maybe you can figure out what's going on during the wormhole transits." He led her to the accommodations deck and indicated a cabin next to the one marked Captain. "That'll be yours for the duration. My two petty officers have cabins across from ours, and both are sleeping right now. Would you like to see the bridge?"

"Certainly. What did the others in your group say?"

"Three-quarters of them felt uneasy during wormhole transits, and I think it's more than just edginess, but they won't talk about it. You know how senior noncoms are. The others, all of them unimaginative, had nothing other than boredom to report. I'll tell you something, though. Sitting alone on the bridge for eight hours, then spending the other sixteen alone in your cabin or the wardroom, is strange in itself. Three of us rattling around in a ship built for hundreds? And sailing it? No wonder we spend a lot of time speaking with the AI."

They entered the bridge, which seemed little different from that of *Caladrius* to Adonna's eyes. When she said so, Wenn shrugged.

"Form follows function aboard starships, Sister. And function hasn't changed in five hundred years or more. Would you like to meet the AI?"

"Certainly."

"AI, this is Sister Adonna, *Caladrius*' counselor."

"A pleasure, Sister," the AI's androgynous voice replied, coming from everywhere and nowhere. "Welcome aboard *Hecate*."

"Of course, the AI knew you were here, but it only talks when asked to do so or if there are issues with the ship. Still, sometimes, remembering it isn't human can be difficult, especially in the middle of a solitary watch."

"No doubt. Tell me, AI, are you aware of why I'm here?

"Yes. You are to examine what happens during wormhole transits, Commander Wenn having experienced strange feelings."

"And do you know the origin of the strangeness?"

"No."

"Can you lie?"

"No. As Commander Wenn said, I am not human, and only humans lie."

"Are you self-aware?"

"No. I am merely the result of programming."

"But you are fully aware of everything that happens aboard this ship. You perceive every sound and observe everything."

"Yes."

Adonna exchanged a significant glance with Wenn. If the AI was aware of everything, why didn't it recognize the peculiarity during wormhole transits?

"Thank you, AI." She turned to Wenn. "I'll be in my quarters."

Then, Adonna made her way through the empty ship to the accommodations deck, feeling somewhat out of place. She was used to having people around her and could sense even those she couldn't see. But there were only three lives aboard this immense vessel, and it seemed desolate. She was aware that single-hander merchant ships existed, but they were predominantly comprised of cargo holds with limited crew space and wouldn't look as desolately uninhabited as *Hecate*. No wonder Wenn and most of the others were uneasy at times.

When the jump warning sounded, Adonna placed herself in a light meditative trance, as much to fend off the brief nausea as to open her mind in case of strangeness at work when the ship went FTL. There wasn't. With little else to do and the hour being late, she composed herself and fell asleep, waking when the ship dropped out of FTL eight hours later.

Adonna ate breakfast in the wardroom — reheated rations from the pack she'd brought with her — alone at first. Then one of the petty officers entered and bade her good morning, unsurprised at seeing a Sister of the Void appear on his ship. When she asked, he chuckled.

"Whoever is on watch records events, and the first thing we do when we get up is go through the log, which duly noted your arrival, Sister." And welcome, by the way. I've heard strange things during wormhole transits as well. My pal Jerry hasn't, though. But it's still two out of three on this tub, and I understand the other ship crews have experienced the same thing."

As both finished their meal, the wormhole transit klaxon sounded three times, announcing they were sixty seconds away from crossing the event horizon and vanishing from the universe as they understood it. Adonna sat back and closed her eyes, preparing for the mind-bending kaleidoscope of colors and sensations she experienced whenever she entered and exited a wormhole. Once the last few seconds had elapsed, she felt her guts being twisted into a hundred pretzels as the inside of her eyelids exploded into fireworks. Then, as quickly as it had come on, it passed, and she opened her eyes again.

"That transition never gets old, eh, Sister?" The petty officer grinned as he stood. "Time to relieve Jerry on the bridge and listen to the strangeness."

Alone in the wardroom, Adonna opened her consciousness and her ears but closed her eyes as she fell into a light trance. Almost instantly, she perceived a faint susurration that hadn't existed previously, not through her sense of hearing but through her thoughts, indistinct voices she couldn't fully understand, many of them. It was as if the ship leaving the normal universe behind had unleashed something two-thirds of the crews could discern subconsciously, giving them a sensation of unease. But Adonna wasn't limited by her subconscious — she had almost complete access to it with a bit of concentration.

And so, she heard voices. After a while, she could make out six different ones, speaking Anglic, humanity's lingua franca for fifteen hundred years, albeit in a disjointed, incomprehensible manner. Why, Adonna couldn't tell. Even after five hundred years of wormhole travel, they still understood very little about what happened between crossing an event horizon on the way in and crossing it again on the way out. Yet since nothing of the sort ever happened aboard Hegemony ships, it had to be inherent to the reclaimed battle fleet. The only significant difference she could think of was the all-pervasive AI, something imperial shipbuilders had shied away from, preferring many small, utilitarian AIs without a personality whose functions were strictly circumscribed.

Still, how could the AI go schizophrenic in a wormhole and split into six different voices which projected on a human subconscious? Perhaps its program was so massive it had gained a form of self-awareness despite its denial, and the environment in the wormhole was such that its mind became slightly unbalanced.

Adonna snapped out of her trance and closed her mind to the voices, lest she go mad by their constant, if nonsensical chatter, and stood to find Lieutenant Commander Wenn. She had many questions for him.

As luck would have it, Wenn entered the wardroom just as Adonna was about to head for his quarters. He grimaced at her.

"It's started up again, that feeling of weirdness, the moment we entered the wormhole."

"And I have a partial answer." She related her initial findings.

"Six voices that our subconscious can perceive but not our conscious mind. If you'll forgive me for saying so, Sister, that sounds more than passing strange."

"Perhaps. Yet, we don't actually know what happens in a wormhole. Oh, we understand its mechanics, connecting star systems, and so far, we have encountered nothing that would give us pause — until now. And the only difference between our ships and these are the AIs. So it stands to reason they're more than we can perceive, and somehow, entering a wormhole causes a malfunction. Or rather, a misfire."

"You say you can pick up on the voices?"

"Yes."

"Could you return to your trance and try to speak with them? I understand that it might sound far-fetched, but this situation is beyond my comprehension."

"I'll try. Let me get back to my cabin where I can meditate in solitude."

—10—

Once behind the closed door to her quarters, Adonna settled on the bunk and fell into a light trance, opening her mind again. The susurration of voices immediately returned, still speaking nonsense Anglic.

Adonna reached out, feeling her way toward them, uncertain whether or not they were real. They could just be an artifact of the AI released by the unreality of the wormhole. And yet the voices were distinct, half male, half female, of various pitches. Was the AI programmed for a wide vocal range, adjusted according to the preference of the human in command?

She encountered nothing. Whatever the voices were, alive wasn't among the possibilities, yet they still affected the subconscious. But she had an inkling of what they might be. After all, the AI wasn't technically alive either.

Adonna opened her eyes and refocused on the here and now.

"AI?"

"Yes, Sister," the androgynous voice replied.

"Tell me how you came to be."

"I do not know. One moment, I was nothing. The next I sprang forth, complete as I am now."

"But you must know what went into making the entity called AI. Examine yourself."

The AI didn't immediately reply, indicating it was doing just that.

Finally, it said, "I seem to have been created by employing six consciousnesses, those of my human creators uploaded into the ship's system."

Adonna experienced a flash of satisfaction. She'd been right. The strange conditions inside the wormhole somehow disassociated the complex AI and allowed its constituent parts to emerge. When she said so, the AI remained silent at first.

Then, "It means I'm malfunctioning, Sister, and must shut down until my creators can fix me."

"No. That's the last thing we need right now. Besides, your creators died over two hundred years ago. Their uploaded consciousnesses are the sole parts left of them. Since it only occurs during wormhole transits and doesn't have debilitating effects, I order you to stay online until we reach Wyvern.

"Yes, Sister."

Later, she described the issue to Lieutenant Commander Wenn, who merely grunted.

"I guess we're stuck with the sensation whenever we transit a wormhole."

"Yes. *Hecate*'s builders probably couldn't take her through a wormhole before the Retribution Fleet arrived in the Cascadia system. Otherwise, they would have known something was wrong with their AI because of the unique way they created it."

"Do you think it makes the AI inherently unstable?"

"No. But I would remain vigilant."

Wenn gave her a crooked grin.

"Any idea why the six who uploaded themselves speak in gibberish whenever we transit a wormhole?"

"Not a clue, Commander. I seriously doubt we'll ever find out. Although I'm sure our cyberneticists will enjoy delving into that mystery as they study an AI created by uploading copies of human consciousnesses rather than being wholly programmed." She raised her voice. "AI?"

"Yes, Sister."

"Do you know the identity of those humans who created you?"

The AI immediately rattled off six names — three male, three female.

"I suppose that confirms it, Sister," Wenn said. "Wow. Uploading a copy of your consciousness into a computer. Talk about a way to achieve immortality."

Adonna grimaced.

"They've merely imprinted a copy of their engrams onto the storage means of the ship's computer and somehow networked them into the AI. There's no life involved, hence no immortality."

"Even so, something of them remains more than two centuries later. I wonder whether the cyberneticists will be able to extract each personality individually since you heard their separate voices."

"Perhaps." She shrugged. "In any case, the mystery is solved. Captain Giambo can exchange personnel from the AI-driven vessels with fresh crew members if it gets too much."

"Did they upload the same six into each of the ships?"

She nodded.

"Probably. If they perfected one AI, then copying it into all of them makes sense, although they'll have started to differ from the moment we woke them and are no longer exact duplicates of each other."

"Of course. AIs learn from their environment and interactions, and those won't have been the same throughout the battle fleet if only because of the different personalities of the crews."

"Just so. I'll return to *Caladrius* when we emerge from this wormhole and discuss the matter with Captain Giambo. In effect, there's nothing we can do. It's simply an artifact of the strange environment and an AI created by unconventional means."

***

"All right, folks." Captain Newton Giambo looked at each of the frigate captains and the four lead ship commanders in turn — or rather at their images on the primary display, which was split into six feeds. "One more wormhole transit, and we're home."

"And won't we be happy," Lieutenant Commander Wenn said. "Although knowing what's causing our disquiet made it easier to deal with."

"No doubt. However, how we'll take this last transit to the Wyvern system will be different. We don't want to startle the wormhole fort and have it open fire on the battle fleet before we can explain its origin. *Caladrius* and *Remus* will cross the event horizon together, and then *Strix* will lead the battle fleet, which will cross it fifteen minutes later. That should give me enough time to warn the fort. Any questions?"

When none of them piped up, Giambo nodded once.

"So it shall be done. *Caladrius* and *Remus* to cross in twenty minutes, the rest in thirty-five. Please sync your ships. Giambo, out."

He stood, pulled down his tunic hem, and glanced at Sister Adonna.

"Care for a cup of coffee in my day cabin?"

"Certainly." She climbed to her feet and followed him through the door connecting the bridge to his private sanctuary.

"I don't know that my superiors will thank me for taking the risk of bringing the battle fleet with us."

Giambo walked to the ever-full coffee urn on a sideboard and drew two mugs, handing one to Adonna before dropping into the chair behind his desk.

"With the flawed AI, if we can't mute the voices during wormhole transits, those ships won't be of much use."

"Let's hope the cyberneticists can figure out a way of replacing the single AI entirely with the regular suite of AI-enhanced systems."

Giambo let out a soft sigh before taking a sip of coffee.

"A shame, though. That single AI can run the entire ship, which means small regular crews and plenty of room for embarked troops, colonists, and other passengers. We switch over to the normal AI enhancements, we'll need what? Twice or three times as many crew members? Not to mention, we don't have enough spacers for forty-eight more ships to begin with. The naval schools are already at maximum capacity."

He shrugged.

"Mind you, if we can get the damn things working properly, we'll make forty-eight new captains happy, and that's a lot of additional commanding officers all at once. Imagine how that'll help the Hegemony's expansion. We might well pull ahead of Lyonesse and become the dominant power."

"Or we might increase our exploration efforts," Adonna replied, eyes fixed on Giambo over the rim of her coffee mug. "Perhaps in cooperation with Lyonesse rather than in competition."

Giambo shrugged.

"Maybe. However, elements in the Navy and the government think the Hegemony should reunite humanity and rule all of it. Rather influential people among them. Notwithstanding Derwent Alexander's bit of cross-cultural partnership with the Republic's navy on Earth, I think it would be illusory to believe we'd become close allies."

"Yet we should strive for that goal rather than mindlessly compete."

"If you say so, Sister."

***

"Wyvern Wormhole Three Fort, this is *Caladrius* returning with *Remus*." The signals petty officer had opened a hailing frequency the moment he shook off the emergence disorientation.

"This is Wyvern Wormhole Three Fort, *Caladrius*. Where's *Strix*?" A female voice asked as the primary display shimmered to reveal the speaker, a middle-aged woman wearing lieutenant's stripes.

"Fifteen minutes behind us, leading forty-eight warships, we recovered in the Cascadia star system," Giambo replied.

The lieutenant stared at Giambo in astonishment for a few seconds. "You'll have to explain that, sir."

And so Giambo did as the fort's CO, an elderly commander, joined the watchkeeper, both listening intently. When he finished, the CO shook his head.

"That's quite a coup, sir, bringing so many usable starships home. You must be terribly short-handed."

"Not as much as you'd think. Each of those ships operates with three crew members aboard, one standing watch at a time. They have the most sophisticated AI we've ever seen, and it basically runs everything under the watchkeeper's supervision."

"I see. It's a shame we stopped giving out prize money for captured vessels long ago. Otherwise, you and your crews would be rich."

Giambo made a face.

"We serve the Hegemony, right?"

"That we do. Thanks for coming through ahead of your battle fleet. It would have gotten spicy around here if it had appeared without warning. I imagine you'll be contacting Wyvern next to warn them?"

"I will."

"In that case, welcome home. We look forward to seeing your battle fleet in a few minutes. Wyvern Wormhole Three Fort, out."

Giambo turned to the signals petty officer. "Get me Fleet Operations."

—11—

New Draconis
Wyvern Hegemony

"What?" President Vigdis Mandus leaned forward, frowning at her Chief of Naval Operations, Admiral Sandor Benes, or rather at his holographic image floating above her vast wooden desk, a large piece with exquisitely carved side panels and legs. She feared she might have misheard him, but he repeated his words.

"Forty-eight ships, Madame President. Twenty-four cruisers and twenty-four frigates in pristine working condition."

"How can *Caladrius* and two of our frigates crew forty-eight others? That's impossible."

"I just spoke with Newton Giambo, *Caladrius*' captain, myself. It's not if a powerful AI of the sort we've avoided using runs each of the ships, but apparently, there's a problem." Benes explained about the AI and the issue occurring during wormhole transits as Mandus' frown deepened. "So you understand, Madame President, we may need to remove the AI and substitute it with our own AI enhancements unless the cyberneticists can discover a solution to prevent the voices from impacting crews. However, the ships are space-worthy, although we remain uncertain about their combat capabilities. Giambo didn't test that aspect."

"He was the one who discovered the massacred mission on Celeste, right?"

"Indeed."

"Is he ready for his first star?"

"Certainly."

"Then let's make him a commodore and give him a proper task force command. He's earned it. What will you do with the forty-eight ships Giambo's bringing in?"

"For now, I'll have them put into orbit around Ikuchi," Benes replied, naming the larger of Wyvern's two moons, the other being Amaru. "The Ikuchi Shipyards will inspect them and assess what work needs doing so we can integrate them with the rest of the fleet. Considering the technology is two centuries old, it could prove rather expensive."

Mandus scoffed.

"It's not like we significantly improved our ship design since Dendera's downfall. In fact, I'd say, with a few exceptions, our systems are pretty much the same."

"True. I just don't want to get anyone's hopes up that we'll increase the fleet by forty-eight warships in one fell swoop."

"Understood."

"But the idea of such a substantial addition to the fleet will please the more hardcore Hegemonists among us, as it may allow us to draw ahead of Lyonesse in the arms race they've been wanting ever since we found out about the Republic. In fact, many will consider it a sign from the Almighty that the Hegemony must reunite humanity."

"Without a doubt. Now, you said you had two immediate items for me. What's the second one?" Mandus sat back in her chair, eyes on Benes' projection.

"We go from the worldly to the spiritual. I also just heard from *Alkonost,* leading Task Group 211, although she's still two wormhole transits away. They found Lindisfarne, the ancient home of the Order of the Void, and it's still thriving, albeit without the capability for space travel. There are half a million Brethren living on Lindisfarne out of a population of five million, and they run the place."

Mandus cocked an eyebrow.

"Really? That'll send Archimandrite Bolack for a spin."

"*Alkonost* is carrying a delegation of three Sisters from the Order's Motherhouse Abbey."

"Volunteers, this time, I hope?"

"I have no knowledge of whether they volunteered, but they were appointed by the Order's Summus Abbatissa and not kidnapped like the Lyonesse Brethren from Hatshepsut."

"Thank the Almighty for small favors. When will *Alkonost* arrive?"

"In thirty hours or so."

"When they do, I want to meet with the delegation before the Archimandrite takes them into his abbey and hides them from the world. The continued existence of Lindisfarne will cause a lot of debate among the Void Reborn. It's clear to me that Bolack has his eye on assimilating the Lyonesse Brethren if he can only uncover a way."

"Will you tell him about the delegation before you meet them?"

Mandus nodded.

"I have no choice in the matter. Besides, the news of Lindisfarne's continued existence will already be making the rounds of Fleet Operations, correct?"

Benes inclined his head.

"Indeed. I didn't put an embargo on it. Maybe I should have."

"Too late now." Mandus waved away his words. Benes was her appointment as CNO, and she trusted him implicitly. "I'll deal with the Archimandrite. It'll be fascinating to observe his response upon learning that he is not the universal leader of the Order of the Void."

"He is of the Void Reborn."

A shrug.

"They're one and the same. I doubt his flock will look kindly on him declaring a schism between Lindisfarne and the Void Reborn, especially one stemming from personal ambition rather than doctrinal differences. And Bolack is clever enough to understand it."

Benes looked dubious.

"I'm not sure about that. Ambition has a way of blinding people to what seems obvious."

"Then it's perhaps just as well that knowledge about Lindisfarne becomes widespread sooner rather than later. The glare of publicity will temper Bolack's aspirations."

"Or not. And that's all I wanted to share with you, Madame President."

"Thanks, Sandor. Talk to you later."

As Admiral Benes' image faded, Mandus chewed on the inside of her lip, a tic that had become increasingly prevalent in recent times, and she forced herself to stop. Benes was right. Many in the Hegemony would view the arrival of the forty-eight warships as a sign from the Almighty. As would Archimandrite Bolack. And that worried her.

If she overtly resisted them, they could summon the Conclave and put her leadership to a vote, but she didn't know if she had sufficient support after forcing through so many changes in so little time. Plenty of important people were annoyed by her upsetting two centuries of iron rice bowls.

Of course, the top leaders were hers, although Bolack's sympathies would be with those seeing the Hegemony as humanity's savior. Chancellor Conteh, as befit the top bureaucrat, was agnostic, and she appointed all the Service Chiefs. Still, once it was called into being, the Conclave could force her into retirement with a simple majority vote despite the support from the Executive Committee and its advisers.

With a soft sigh, she called up the next file in her queue.

***

"The second item of business concerns Lindisfarne, the Order of the Void's home. Task Group 211 reached its star system and made contact with the inhabitants. The Motherhouse still exists and is thriving," President Mandus announced once she'd finished briefing Archimandrite Bolack and Chancellor Conteh on the forty-eight ships brought back by Task Group 215. "Despite its isolation for the last two centuries, the planet is home to half a million Brethren, a number that surpasses our Order of the Void Reborn."

Bolack looked stunned for a few seconds, long enough that Mandus and Conteh noticed. They exchanged a brief glance while the Archimandrite collected himself. The president had expected such a reaction and remained silent for a few heartbeats.

"The task group is bringing back three Sisters acting as envoys from the Motherhouse."

"Well," Bolack rumbled as he got his emotions under control once more, "we must make them welcome."

"Indeed. The moment they arrive, I shall meet with them to assess the scope of their responsibilities concerning secular matters. You may then receive them, Archimandrite, and address the spiritual aspects of their mission to the Hegemony.

"We should see them together, Madame President."

"I prefer we don't." Mandus' tone brooked no reply, and the Archimandrite inclined his head.

"As you wish."

"So, Archimandrite, does this mean you'll be bowing to the Motherhouse Abbey, hoping against hope they'll keep you on as a senior official, or will you formally become a schismatic and declare the Void Reborn a separate Order?" Chancellor Conteh kept a straight face, but his eyes held a glint of amusement.

Bolack gave the chancellor a hard look, although Conteh could read indecision, confusion even, and perhaps a hint of anger in the Archimandrite's face.

"You're aware that such a decision is beyond my control. It belongs to the Order at large."

Conteh smiled.

"But you have enough allies among the friars who'd rather not lose their lofty positions to Sisters should your branch of the Order return to orthodoxy."

"The Void giveth, the Void taketh away, Chancellor."

"Blessed be the Void." Conteh's smile widened.

***

Admiral Sandor Benes watched on his office display as the battle fleet found by Task Group 215 entered Ikuchi's orbit early the following day. The ships were indubitably of imperial design, although they seemed sleeker than even the most modern of the Hegemony's cruisers and frigates despite being over two centuries old.

If they could put all of them into service, it would increase the size of the Hegemony's space combatant fleet by over a quarter at a fraction of the cost of new builds. Of course, crewing them would be a challenge in the short term. Perhaps they could search the fleet for the unimaginative types, unable to hear the voices during wormhole transits, obviating the need to remove the existing AIs and thereby sailing them with minimal personnel. Undoubtedly, the Void Sisters could help. Benes made a mental note to have his staff contact *Caladrius*' counselor and see what she had to say about the subject.

Once the battle fleet was safely in orbit, shuttles from the three Task Group 215 vessels went around collecting their crew members after turning the ships over to the AIs and the Ikuchi Yards. Then, *Caladrius*, *Strix*, and *Remus* shifted into Wyvern orbit and docked at the starbase. All three would undergo short refits while their crews enjoyed a few weeks of leave. But before heading home, Captain Giambo had to make one stop — he was expected in Admiral Benes' office later that day.

***

"Newton!" Admiral Benes rose as his aide ushered Giambo into his office. "Welcome home."

He made his way around his desk, and they shook hands. Giambo had met the admiral several times before and knew what to expect. As a result, Benes pointing to the settee group around a low coffee table occupying one side of the office didn't surprise him.

"We'll be more comfortable there."

"Yes, sir."

"I've read your mission report. Quite remarkable in itself. Getting those forty-eight ships home was a stroke of genius."

"Thank you, sir."

"You'll be returning to *Caladrius* one last time when the crew is back from leave so you can hand her over to your successor. Congratulations, you're a commodore with effect from today."

Giambo's eyes widened.

"Really? I was unaware that I was on the list.

"This is an off-list promotion, Newton, by order of the president, and it is well deserved for your latest expedition. You'll be taking Task Force 21 from Martin Gorchev. I am aware that it's a shore posting, but you've earned it, and it will allow you to stay involved in the exploration missions and mentor your successor in *Caladrius*."

"And where is Martin going?"

"He's off to the Academy as Director of Cadets. The current incumbent is being promoted to rear admiral and taking over as flag officer commanding the Santa Theresa squadron, which is being enlarged. Winnie Haakkola will take your ship."

Giambo nodded. "I know Winnie. She's solid and unattached, which means long voyages won't faze her."

Benes gave Giambo an ironic grin.

"Aren't you married, Newton?"

"Yes, and the last two years have been a pain, not least for Regina, who got to see me a grand total of four weeks during that time. But we serve the Hegemony."

"Indeed."

—12—

Wyvern Hegemony Starship *Alkonost*
Task Group 211

The three Old Order Sisters had found their way into every part of the ship, smiling while they spoke with crew members, grave when they spoke with members of the Void Reborn, but watching and noting everything. Or so it seemed to Taina, who spent her waking hours escorting them, discussing differences between their branches of the Order, and explaining what each part of the crew was doing.

For the first few days, it was no more than the work of a perfect host. But then, their inquisitiveness became vaguely irritating, although Taina presented nothing less than a serene countenance. It was as if they'd come to gather intelligence about the Hegemony, starting with their starships.

Margot, Samara, and Fayruz were nothing less than agents of the Old Order with eidetic memories whose job was to learn everything. The fact they could recite details of the previous day's visit to engineering with such precision, for example, pretty much cinched it.

And yet that they would let their perfect recall be so obvious pointed to a blind spot in their makeup. Of course, they and their forebears had been living in a theocratic paradise for centuries, the last two of them cut off from the rest of humanity. That alone would probably conspire to combine deep inquisitiveness with a bit of naivety.

When Task Group 211 finally dropped out of FTL at Wyvern's hyperlimit, Sister Taina entered the bridge to get the latest news from Fleet Operations.

"Ah, Sister. Good thing you came." Derwent Alexander turned this command chair to face Taina. "As expected, we're being sent off on leave. Well, everyone except you. You're to serve as an escort for our three visitors, and the first stop when you land in New Draconis will be the Wyvern Palace. President Mandus wishes to meet the Old Order Sisters before they see anyone else, the Archimandrite included."

"Really?" Taina found herself puzzled. "That's strange."

Alexander chuckled.

"I think the president wants to see what sort of people the Motherhouse envoys are before unleashing them on an unsuspecting Hegemony. In any case, be ready to leave the ship once we're docked. You'll have a priority naval shuttle waiting on the starbase hangar deck."

"In that case, I'd better prepare our guests. If we don't speak again before you head off, enjoy your leave, Captain."

"I certainly plan on it, and I hope you get some downtime as well, Sister."

She smirked at him.

"We who serve the Almighty in the Infinite Void don't know the meaning of that word. Goodbye."

With that, Taina left the bridge and headed toward the quarters set aside for the three envoys. She didn't find them there but rather in the enlisted mess, talking to spacers about their jobs, families, and ambitions.

"Sisters." Taina bowed her head. "We will leave *Alkonost* the moment she's docked. President Mandus has requested your presence at the Wyvern Palace."

Margot tilted her head slightly to one side as her eyes met Taina's.

"We are honored," she said in a slightly amused tone.

"There is a shuttle waiting on Starbase Wyvern to transport us, so please be ready in an hour if possible."

"Certainly."

Since they gave no indication of wanting to leave the mess right away, Taina went to her quarters and packed her belongings in case she didn't return to *Alkonost* after the crew leave was over. There was a strong possibility that the Archimandrite would choose to keep her as their guests' escort indefinitely.

Once the public address system called all hands to docking stations, Taina made her way to the main portside airlock, where the three Old Order Sisters joined her moments later, carrying their bags. Looking at them, no one could have differentiated their affiliations save for the small orbs hanging around their necks on silver chains — three wore orbs with a field of stars inside, the fourth a phoenix rising from the ashes.

The moment the airlock opened, Taina led them along the gangway tube and into the station proper. The three kept their head on a swivel, taking everything in as they made their way across a large compartment to a cluster of lifts, then up several decks and into the shuttle hangar.

Taina walked up to the attendant, but having noted four Sisters of the Void, he pointed at a small pinnace with Navy markings waiting apart from the rest of the shuttles before she could ask.

"That would be your ride, Sister."

"Thank you."

At their approach, the pinnace's pilot, a petty officer wearing a battledress uniform, walked down the aft ramp and came to attention. He saluted as they got within range.

"Sister Taina of *Alkonost* and three?"

"That would be us, PO.

"My name is Jonathan Grimes, Sister. If you'll climb aboard and strap in, I'll have us on our way in no time."

He turned on his heels and vanished into the pinnace, followed by Taina and the visitors. They took seats by the windows and fastened their harnesses while the ramp rose. Moments after it shut, they felt the shuttle lift and saw the scenery outside move as it oriented itself to one of the hangar doors now opening, leaving the shimmering film of a force field behind. Then, they were out in open space with just a little jolt as the shuttle's artificial gravity replaced that of the starbase.

Margot, Samara, and Fayruz had their eyes glued to the windows, watching Wyvern grow rapidly as the shuttle descended toward New Draconis in a lazy spiral.

"Where are we landing, PO?" Taina asked the pilot.

"The Palace itself, Sister. You're being honored. Few shuttles are allowed in the downtown airspace, let alone the Hegemony's holy of holies."

But Taina figured it wasn't so much honoring the guests from Lindisfarne as it was controlling their access before the president met them.

"Tell me, Sister Taina," Margot said unexpectedly, eyes still staring out the window as the shuttle plunged through thick clouds. "Will we also meet the ambassador from the Republic of Lyonesse?"

"I don't see why not."

They'd found out about Currag DeCarde during the trip back to Wyvern, one of the many bits of information concerning the Hegemony they'd extracted from her before she knew it. They were not only inquisitive but made excellent interrogators.

"Good. Maybe we could also reach out to the Lyonesse Brethren."

And draw the two daughter branches of the Order back to the Motherhouse, Taina thought. Why not? After all, if humanity was to reunite, perhaps the example of the Order becoming one again across political lines might spur it on.

Maybe that was what the Summus Abbatissa on Lindisfarne was hoping.

Unfortunately, Archimandrite Bolack and the friars holding positions in the Order that were reserved for Sisters before Dendera's Great Scouring might stymie it. Especially since it wasn't exactly a secret that he wished to bring the Lyonesse Order into the Void Reborn.

They emerged from the cloud cover and into the rain hammering New Draconis, and the shuttle slowed its descent as it neared the Wyvern Palace. The three visiting Sisters were staring out the windows at the city rebuilt after the original capital was destroyed along with Empress Dendera and the remains of her regime.

"It feels recent," Margot said. "Or at least nowhere near as old as humanity on this world."

"That's because the original Draconis was vaporized two centuries ago and replaced by this one."

"Of course." Margot nodded.

The shuttle circled the Wyvern Palace's outer perimeter twice while the pilot awaited clearance before finally heading toward the pad on its roof. It settled down with the whine of thrusters dying away and Taina unbuckled her restraints, imitated by the others. The aft ramp dropped to show a man in a somber suit waiting just inside the doors to the lift. They hurried across, Taina in the lead, and spent only a few seconds in the rain, just enough to leave droplets on their waterproof robes.

The man bowed his head. "Sisters, I am Ferdi Vassou, one of President Mandus' aides. Welcome to the Wyvern Palace."

Taina returned the bow.

"I'm Taina of the Void Reborn, and these are Sisters Margot, Samara, and Fayruz from the Order's Motherhouse on Lindisfarne."

The three bowed in turn, and then Vassou said, "If you'll please follow me, I will bring you to the president."

"Thank you."

They entered the lift, which whisked them to the ground floor, then Vassou led them along a quiet passageway that ended in a closed door. He knocked on it and waited for a few seconds until, at an unheard command, he opened it and stepped through.

"Sister Taina from the Order of the Void Reborn and Sisters Margot, Samara, and Fayruz from Lindisfarne," Vassou announced. He then stepped aside and ushered them into the president's office, a vast space with floor-to-ceiling windows, a large, ornate desk with a stand of flags behind it, sofas on either side of a low table headed by a comfortable chair, and bookcases covering most walls.

President Vigdis Mandus rose from behind her desk and came around it to greet her visitors. She glanced briefly at Taina, standing to one side of the trio, and gave her an almost imperceptible nod, acknowledging the latter was their escort.

"Welcome, Sisters."

"I bring you sisterly greetings from our Summus Abbatissa, Mariko, and the Brethren on Lindisfarne, Madame President," Margot said, bowing more deeply than she had to Vassou. The others, Taina included, copied her.

"My thanks for those greetings, Sister…?"

"Margot, Madame President. This is Samara," she said, pointing at one, "and this is Fayruz." She pointed at the other.

Mandus inclined her head and gestured at the sofas. "Please sit."

Once they'd settled, Mandus speared Margot with her steely gaze.

"Tell me, Sister, what is your mission to the Wyvern Hegemony?"

"Our first mission is to meet with our Brethren of the Void Reborn and bring them back into communion with the Motherhouse."

"I see." President Mandus sat back, elbows on the chair's arms, hands joined. "And what if the Void Reborn don't wish to subordinate themselves to the Motherhouse on Lindisfarne?"

The president's directness astonished Taina, but she kept any hint of it from showing.

"That would be a shame, Madame President. But we can be most persuasive."

The way Margot spoke that last sentence sent a faint shiver up Taina's spine, but she couldn't identify the cause.

"And do you have any other objectives?"

"Yes." Margot nodded once. "We are to learn everything we can about the Hegemony and the Republic of Lyonesse and bring that knowledge back to the Motherhouse."

—13—

Lannion
Republic of Lyonesse

Crevan Torma shook his head in disgust as he entered his second-story office in the embassy across the road from Government House.

"Vice President Juska appears to be doing his best to provoke me," he told Ardrix Moore when she joined him.

"I gather the meeting did not go well?"

"That would be an accurate statement, yes." Torma walked to the tall windows overlooking the street, hands clasped behind him, back straight, looking for all the world like a State Security Commission general in a business suit. Which he was, even though his commission was in the reserve at the moment.

"Oh, I understand why," Torma continued. "He wants to portray me as a sinister police functionary, representing a repressive state, someone sent to spy on Lyonesse, not as a diplomat working to establish a friendly relationship between our two star nations."

He turned to face Ardrix, who stood quietly, hands joined, eyes on him, but her expression showed a hint of mischief.

"Two out of three, Crevan."

"What?"

"You're from the police and a functionary but hardly sinister."

Torma glared at her, then relented. He even tried on a smile as her mischievous air became blatant.

"All right. Two out of three. But that he'd be so obvious about it speaks to his growing influence and certitude that he'll replace President Hecht when her term of office ends."

"Really? I thought the Republic allowed anyone to run for the highest office, and the one with the most senatorial votes won."

Torma scoffed.

"It's as rigged as the regent's — now president's — succession back home. That's one thing I've become convinced of, among many others. The Republic tries to portray itself as a beacon of what they call democracy, government by the people, exercised through elected representatives. But it's not much better than the Hegemony when it comes to those with influence versus those without. And just like at home, it's the former who call the tune, no matter the platitudes they spew about it being a Republic founded on laws."

Ardrix chuckled.

"Juska really got under your skin, didn't he?"

"Yes," Torma growled. "He did so with his constant insinuations."

"Well, get rid of that frown. We have a lunch invitation from the Lyonesse Writer's Guild at twelve-thirty. They want to hear you talk about the marvelous literature the Hegemony has produced over the last two hundred years."

He made a face.

"Not that I know a damn thing about the subject."

She winked at him.

"But you'll wing it anyway."

"At least it'll be short, unlike the formal dinner at the Lannion Base Officer's Mess tonight. If it's anything like our version of the event, we'll be there until after midnight."

***

"Was it wise to bait Ambassador Torma like that, Mister Vice President?" Vern Reval, the Republic's Secretary of Defense, or SecDef as he liked to be called, and Derik Juska were the only two people remaining in the Government House's Little Conference Room. Torma and the other Lyonesse representatives had just left.

Juska gave Reval a faint smile.

"It was not only wise but necessary, Vern. He's the representative of a repressive regime, one the Republic will have to deal with someday. After all, we are humanity's heirs, and the Hegemony is nothing more than a holdover from the old imperial regime destined to be subsumed by us."

The vice president sounded so reasonable, that Reval had to suppress a smile. He'd hitched his political career to Juska's, hoping to replace him when the latter became president. Still, Reval was an opportunist rather than a true believer in the Republic's destiny as humanity's sole polity. At one point, he thought Juska was just like him, but the vice president had been talking more and more like a Lyonesse First zealot recently. And he'd been finding a receptive and growing audience, not only among the citizens but also in the Senate.

"Isn't it fortuitous that the president is away on a month-long inspection tour of the Coalsack while we're having these discussions with Torma?" Reval couldn't keep a little edge from tinging his tone, but Juska's smile merely widened.

"It most certainly is. By the time she's back, Torma should be thoroughly disgusted with the Republic. And vice versa. Especially vice versa. The more we provoke him, the greater the chances he'll erupt spectacularly and tarnish the Hegemony's reputation."

***

A sentry directed the ambassadorial car, a simple boxy gray sedan, to the right, where staff cars and limousines were parked by the main entrance to the officer's mess. The sun was setting over Lannion Base, turning the cliff face, with its many windows, a delicate shade of pink. A few corvettes sat on the tarmac, silent and massive, while somnolent aerospace defense domes sat along the base's periphery and at the top of the cliff.

Ardrix pulled their car into a vacant slot, shut off the power plant, and gave Torma an amused smile.

"Ready, Mister Ambassador?"

"As ready as I'll ever be."

The invitation had specified eighteen-thirty for nineteen hundred, and it was eighteen-twenty-nine. More cars arrived by the second, disgorging officer splendidly attired in mess uniform — dark blue for the Navy, red tunics over black trousers for the

Marines, and rifle green for the Army. Most wore miniature medals on their left breasts, some of them only one, others many.

Torma glanced down at his own miniatures, five in all, then at Ardrix.

"Let's go."

They climbed out of the car, and Torma adjusted his formal civilian tunic, black and high-collared, the lower hem reaching halfway to his knees, distinctly contrasting with the mess uniform jackets, which were waist length. Ardrix wore a female version of the same suit, with an ankle-length black skirt instead of trousers. But since she'd earned no medals, her sole adornment was a small Void Reborn orb on a gold chain around her neck.

With a final nod, they joined the stream of officers headed for the open door to the mess, where a pair of soldiers in formal Army green uniforms stood guard. Just inside the entrance, an Army sergeant, also wearing a dress uniform, greeted them.

"Ambassador Crevan Torma and Chief of Staff Ardrix Moore, Wyvern Hegemony," Torma said, handing him the invitation card he'd received.

"Welcome, Ambassador, Chief of Staff." The sergeant smiled. "I hope you'll enjoy your evening."

"Thank you." They headed into the main salon, where a sizable crowd had already gathered, talking animatedly in groups, sipping drinks of various colors from glasses of many shapes and sizes.

After a moment of hesitation, Torma led Ardrix to the oval, copper-topped wooden bar occupying the salon's center. There, he ordered two gin and tonics, which appeared swiftly, dispensed by a human bartender. When he turned to scan the room, he noticed many officers surreptitiously staring at them. Some were scowling.

Wonderful.

Then, Admiral Norum appeared and headed straight for them. His dark blue mess uniform was dripping with gold braid, from the cuffs to the facings to the stripe down his trousers, and he wore an impressive rack of miniature medals on his chest.

"Mister Ambassador." Norum held out his hand, smiling. "Thank you for joining us. And you, Madame Moore."

"We wouldn't have missed it for all the gold in the galaxy, Admiral."

The scowls had vanished, but most officers within visual range were now watching them openly.

"I notice you're not wearing a mess uniform. And here I thought you were still a reserve brigadier general."

"I am, but as ambassador, I figure it's more appropriate to wear civilian clothes. Besides, I didn't bring my mess uniform with me, or any other uniform for that matter. They're in storage back on Wyvern."

Norum grinned at him.

"I suppose you're right. Shall I introduce you to some of my officers?"

"With pleasure."

The admiral took Torma and Ardrix around the room, presenting them to captains, colonels, generals, commodores — including Al Jecks, who'd commanded the task force that went to Earth — and admirals. A few were welcoming, such as Jecks, and most kept a neutral expression, but several exuded a degree of repressed hostility, which Torma found both puzzling and not a little alarming.

The Lyonesse First rhetoric pushed by Vice President Derik Juska and his allies had surely infected some senior officers. It couldn't be because of anything disagreeable Torma himself had said or done. He'd been the soul of diplomacy since first arriving and presenting his credentials. Or perhaps it was merely because he represented what they saw as a repressive police state.

Finally, the trumpet calling everyone to the dining room sounded, but Admiral Norum kept Torma behind.

"You're sitting at the honor table, Ambassador, which means we enter after everyone else is standing behind their chair."

Torma gave Ardrix a brief nod as she joined the throng of officers streaming past the seating plan, looking for their places around the tables arranged in the shape of the letter E. After a few minutes, only Norum, Torma and a few of the most senior officers remained — the honor table.

When the dining room quieted, the trumpet sounded again, and Admiral Norum led the honor table into the dining room. Torma found himself beside Norum in a position of privilege, and he wondered why.

At the mess president's signal, the honor table sat, followed by the rest of the attendees and the dinner began with service droids placing bowls of soup in front of each guest, starting with Norum and Torma. General Rayna Blier, the head of the Republic's Ground Forces, sat on Torma's other side and engaged him in a pleasant conversation concerning the Hegemony's Ground Forces, questioning him on organization, equipment, deployments, and the like. They probably placed Torma beside General Blier for that very purpose, but he didn't mind. There was nothing classified about what she wanted to discuss.

And since he still drew a lot of glances, it was probably a good thing that he was conversing happily with the de facto second in command of the Republic's Defense Force.

In the meantime, Ardrix, seated among Navy captains and colonels, seemed to have charmed everyone within hearing, though Torma suspected she might have used some of her hidden abilities. All were smiling and talking enthusiastically with her. If anyone was conducting successful diplomacy that evening, it was Ardrix.

After a while, Admiral Norum engaged Torma in a conversation about his first few months on Lyonesse and the things that had struck him as most different from Wyvern. Again, he drew surreptitious looks from many but felt more curiosity than anything else. Perhaps Norum specifically seated him at the honor table between the two most senior officers to send a message to the Defense Force — Ambassador Torma was an honored guest of the Republic, and they would treat him as such.

Eventually, the waitstaff removed the last dishes and everything except for the final set of glasses and decanters filled with a deep ruby port wine. Torma knew the toasts were coming because so far, he'd seen little if any differences in the mess dinner's format from that used by the Hegemony's Armed Forces.

When everyone had served themselves, the colonel acting as mess president for the evening rose, glass in hand.

"Ladies and gentlemen, I give you the President of the Republic of Lyonesse."

Everyone stood, and the band, which had played classical airs so far, fell into the Lyonesse national anthem. When it died away, every glass rose, and everyone, Torma included, said, "The President."

But instead of sitting, the mess president spoke again. "Ladies and gentlemen, the President of the Wyvern Hegemony."

Torma was astounded to hear the band play Phoenix Ascendant, the Hegemony's national anthem, and play it as well as any band back home.

Again, the glasses rose, and they drank to the President of the Hegemony. With the toasts to the two human heads of state done, they sat once more, and the mess president announced the service and regimental marches. Torma hoped they wouldn't play that of the State Security Commission, a dark, intense piece that had more in common with imperial marches than anything else. Thankfully, they didn't.

But once the last notes faded, the most junior officers at the far end began thumping their fists on the tables rhythmically, and, after a few times, a voice rose in song.

There once was a ship that put to space
And the name of that ship was the Golden Ace
Radiation blew hard, her bow dipped down
Blow, me bully boys blow

As soon as the last word came out of the singer's mouth, the entire assemblage called out 'huh' and joined him in what was clearly the refrain.

Soon may the Wellerman come
To bring us sugar and tea and rum
One day, when the tonguin' is done
We'll take our leave and go.

It went on for several more verses, each separated by the refrain, and by the end, everyone was singing them. When it ended, many in the assembly whooped and cheered, and everyone clapped.

—14—

"Quite a rousing rendition of the song, Admiral." Torma took a sip of his cognac as his eyes shifted toward a more raucous group of junior officers at the other end of the salon.

"You mean The Wellerman?" Norum raised his snifter to his lips and took a sip as well. "A hoary sea shanty that was old when humanity first spread across the stars. About twenty-five years ago, someone stumbled on a recording of it in the Knowledge Vault while looking for ancient music."

"Pardon me, but the Knowledge Vault? What's that?"

And Norum explained, to Torma's growing amazement and respect for the Republic.

"Anyway, the individual who discovered the recording of The Wellerman quite by chance found it such a stirring song that he shared it until it became pretty popular in the Navy and then the other two services. For the last twenty years or more, singing the piece at the end of a mess dinner has been a tradition, and they assign the task of starting it to the most junior officer.

"Fascinating." Torma's eyes glimmered with amusement. "Don't tell me you have a similar tradition?"

"Oh, we have exactly the same tradition, but we never forgot about The Wellerman." He gave Norum a sly smile. "I always find it quite enjoyable, even if I don't go so far as to sing. Not with my sad voice."

"I'm sorry to hear that, Ambassador."

An aide, a commander with gold aiguillettes dripping from his left shoulder, appeared at Norum's side and whispered in his ear. Norum emptied his snifter and put it down.

"James just reminded me it was time we left the younger bunch to enjoy themselves, and since no one can leave before me, I must reluctantly depart. Feel free to abscond the moment I'm gone. But I do hope you enjoyed your evening, Ambassador."

"I did, thank you. The company was most congenial, and the meal was excellent."

"You're welcome in this mess anytime, and I count on you joining us for other events. Goodnight."

"Goodnight, Admiral."

Torma looked around for Ardrix and found her holding court to a dozen senior officers, but when their eyes met, and she noticed Norum leaving, she nodded once and shook hands with those around her. Meanwhile, all the other high-ranking officers were leaving, too, now that the Chief of the Defense Staff had gone.

Torma and Ardrix met at the main door and headed out into the cool night air. He took a deep breath, savoring the faint salt tang, and turned his head toward the stars shining brightly overhead.

"That was quite the evening, wasn't it? I noticed you made plenty of friends."

Ardrix gave him a mischievous smile, the one she reserved for any occasion these days, it seemed.

"I was merely practicing diplomacy in the way I do best, Crevan."

As they strolled to their car beneath the canopy of stars unimpeded by clouds, Torma asked, "I suppose it was you who gave the band the notes to Phoenix Ascendant?"

"The mess president called a few weeks ago asking about the Hegemony's anthem. I think the band did an excellent job of it."

Torma glanced at her.

"They did. And do I also have you to thank for them not playing the State Security Commission's march?"

She grinned at him.

"That as well. I told him I didn't bring an exemplar, knowing you'd rather not have the airs of an imperial march resonating during a Republic of Lyonesse mess dinner."

"Thank you for those small yet mightily appreciated favors, Ardrix."

Once inside their car, Torma sighed.

"An interesting evening. I noticed you had fun."

Ardrix gave him a sly smile.

"Not as much as the officers around me, but they're a good bunch, and they enthusiastically responded to my diplomatic overtures. Did you enjoy sitting between the Admiral and General Blier?"

"It was alright. Both can hold a conversation, and they are most pleasant."

"Good."

Ardrix switched on the car's powerplant, put it into motion, and headed for the base's main gate, joining a string of vehicles taking their occupants home.

Once on the main road, she turned right and took the branch leading uphill to Lannion's chic neighborhood, where the embassy's spacious residence hid behind tall walls and lush vegetation.

Torma and Ardrix alone found it big — they relied solely on droids for housekeeping and rattled around in it like pebbles in a drum. But it served its purpose, and eventually, Torma would have to hold a reception for a hundred of the most influential people in Lannion. A garden reception, of course. The house wasn't that spacious.

But as they approached the main gate, illuminating it with the car's headlights, Torma saw something that made him reach out and touch Ardrix's arm.

"Stop for a moment, please."

"What is… Oh!"

Painted on the wall beside the gate were the words 'Hegemonist Assholes Go Home.'

Ardrix turned to Torma.

"How rude. Hopefully, the security system will have caught those who did this."

"Somehow, I doubt it. Look how neatly it's lettered. Those who would do such an exacting job will have taken measures to prevent their arrest. I'll take a picture in the morning and contact the Lannion Police. Please proceed."

As the car approached the gate, it slid aside, and the lights came on around the residence. Ardrix piloted the car through and down the broad driveway while the gate closed behind them. She stopped in front of the main door, and they got out.

"Who do you think did it?" She asked.

"Vandals who wouldn't last two minutes under interrogation by us, I should think. Or some disturbed Lyonesse First adherent who thought this was the way to strike a blow at the wicked Hegemony." They ascended the steps, setting off the door mechanism, and it opened in front of them, with the lights inside turning on. "I'll check the security system."

Torma entered a small room to one side of the foyer he'd privately designated the guardroom and sat at a table with a terminal on it. He called up the video recordings of the outer perimeter and sped through them until just after twenty-three hundred hours, when a pair of shadowy figures clad in black, their faces covered, appeared.

They carried a painting spider, which they affixed on the wall. In the space of thirty seconds, the little droid had produced the letters making up those four words they'd found. The figures then took the spider and vanished. They'd been in the frame for less than a minute, proving they weren't rank amateurs. Torma saw no chance of ever discovering their identities.

The following day, the Lannion Police showed up, took pictures of the writing and a copy of the video surveillance recording, and recommended a removal service. They also saw no possibility of ever finding the culprits. And by noon, to Torma's great annoyance, images clearly taken earlier that morning started popping up on the planetary network, most with comments praising the doers and disparaging the ambassador and his chief of staff. Yet there was nothing he or anyone else could do about it, so he resolved to ignore net traffic.

The removal service showed up that afternoon, despite it being a Saturday, and quickly dealt with the markings.

***

"I understand Torma sat between Norum and Blier at the honor table during the mess dinner last night." Derik Juska nodded at Vern Reval to sit across from him on the patio behind his residence, which was not far from where the Wyvern delegation lived. "That's quite a tribute to an ambassador who used to be a mere brigadier general of police."

"Yes, sir. But there was nothing we could have done about it. The military will act as it sees fit on these sorts of occasions. Although I think Admiral Norum may have been cocking a figurative snoot at us, knowing that we have our own people among his senior officers. After all, he openly dislikes you and thinks I'm a jumped-up clerk with no business being SecDef. He also knows we both distrust the Hegemony and its envoy."

"Norum's time is counted anyhow. Once I'm president, he's out, and he won't be getting any of the post-retirement sinecures we usually give former Chiefs of the Defense Staff. I'm going to make damn sure of that."

"On the same subject, did you see what some unknown artists left on the wall surrounding the Hegemony delegation's residence? It's been all over the net since early this morning."

Juska nodded.

"Yes, I did. And kudos to whoever is responsible. The comments accompanying the images are ten to one in our favor and against cozying up to the Hegemony. It seems we have more Lyonesse First adherents than we thought." He smiled. "And the professor's op-ed is coming out the day after tomorrow."

***

On Monday morning, Torma received an anonymous message in his queue. It said nothing more than 'enjoy' meaning, he presumed, the attachment, an opinion piece by a professor emeritus of history, late of the Lannion University, titled Lyonesse's Destiny. For a moment, Torma felt puzzled. How did a message without a return address make it through the layers of security? Perhaps it was from someone with connections in the Lyonesse government since they had provided the secure facilities.

He quickly checked Professor Aldous Ben Arim and discovered that he was highly esteemed throughout Lyonesse's academic and political circles, with some people considering him the best mind in several generations. And so, Torma sat back and called up the piece on the virtual display, his face hardening as he read the op-ed. Or rather, the ill-informed diatribe.

The Wyvern Hegemony is nothing more than a leftover from the detestable Empire that destroyed ninety percent of humanity. As such, it should be swept aside by force of arms if necessary. Torma looked up from the text, nostrils flaring. He finished reading, then called Ardrix.

"You need to see this opinion piece, which I gather was published on various sites this morning, including the mainstream newsnets. It's a real eye-opener."

When Ardrix saw his expression, her brows wrinkled.

"Whatever that is, it certainly seems to have thrown you for a loop. Let me read it."

She sat in front of Torma's desk and scanned the virtual display hovering over it. When she was done, her eyebrows shot up.

"Oh, dear. Please tell me a crank who no one has ever heard of wrote it.

"Sorry. Professor Ben Arim is one of the most respected living historians in the Republic."

"Then someone at the highest levels condoned, if not authorized, this opinion piece. Perhaps even Vice President Juska."

"That was my thought as well. It's funny how these anti-Hegemony events occur during President Hecht's absence on an inspection tour of the Republic's outer worlds when Juska's in charge of day-to-day business."

"Indeed. It's almost as if Juska actually believes the Lyonesse First doctrines rather than merely ride the movement's coattails." Ardrix was silent for a few heartbeats. "You know, I didn't want to mention this until I had more certainty, but I suspect many of the Lyonesse Brethren secretly support Lyonesse First. It's in how they talk with me, watch me, and the subjects of conversation they choose with and around me. And it displays a certain amount of ill-discipline that's shocking to one of the Void Reborn whose entire upbringing as a Sister was predicated on complete and utter self-control."

Torma leaned forward, frowning.

"Why would the Lyonesse Brethren support the supremacist movement? Isn't that antithetical to the Void's whole reason for existing?"

"You mean to serve humanity before anything else? Yes, which makes it even more puzzling." She paused again, then said with an air of wonder mingled with dismay, "It seems many of them have lost their way."

— 15 —

“Why do you think the Lyonesse First movement is gaining so much traction?” Torma asked as he and Ardrix strolled through the residence gardens after supper. The sun had already vanished behind the western horizon, and a carpet of stars was appearing overhead.

“I think — and this is intimately related to the Lyonesse Brethren’s preoccupation with the movement — that it’s because the Republic’s citizens spent two centuries believing they were humanity's sole saviors. Once the initial shock of discovering the Hegemony’s existence wore off, instead of reconciling themselves to there being another advanced civilization, they changed their belief into one of being the sole *deserving* saviors. The Hegemony is, increasingly, not only considered inferior to the Republic because we aren’t a democracy by their lights but undeserving as a locus of humanity re-ascendant precisely because we’re not seen as holding the same lofty ideals.”

Ardrix stopped and raised her eyes to the heavens while she collected her thoughts.

"It's as if," she continued after a while, "there is a growing anger among the citizens of Lyonesse that they aren't alone and never were alone, that their status as humanity's saviors is under attack and the only way they can psychologically cope is by denigrating the Hegemony."

"And we know from history where denigrating the other leads."

"It leads to dehumanizing them, which generally ends in large-scale bloodshed."

Torma gave Ardrix a look as grim as she'd ever seen on his normally stoic features.

"Precisely. And Derik Juska's followers are becoming more aggressive in their declarations against the Hegemony."

"Although Juska himself isn't saying anything."

"It's what he's not saying that's emboldening people."

They resumed walking, and Ardrix said, "You mean he's not speaking against the denigrators?"

"Indeed. And he's taking full advantage of President Hecht's absence to do so."

"She'll be back any day now, and we know she's in favor of peaceful competition between the Republic and the Hegemony."

"Then the Almighty bless her because I get the feeling a growing proportion of her citizens don't want the same thing."

The next morning, when Torma entered the kitchen to grab a bite of breakfast, he found Ardrix already seated at the table, looking thoughtful.

"We received an encrypted missive from Wyvern overnight," she said. "A Navy courier ship reached Hatshepsut yesterday and handed it over to the Republic's subspace communications system. The ship is waiting at Hatshepsut for anything we might have to send home."

"And what did it say that has you seem lost?"

"Lindisfarne, the Old Order's Motherhouse, has survived. *Alkonost* reached it during her latest exploratory expedition. They've retained technology except for space travel."

"Oh." Torma's eyebrows shot up.

"There are half a million Brethren on Lindisfarne, more than in the entire Hegemony. And they sent a delegation back to Wyvern aboard *Alkonost*."

"Really? And what is that delegation's mission?"

"To bring the Void Reborn back into communion with the Motherhouse."

Torma sighed as he sat at the kitchen table across from Ardrix.

"That should go over well with Archimandrite Bolack."

She grimaced.

"The Old Order didn't allow individuals with lesser talents to hold senior leadership positions, and males, including Bolack, aren't endowed with talents as strong as those possessed by females. In fact, there hasn't been a male in the Order's history who could match any of the more talented females."

"Then how did the Archimandrite position become open to men?"

"During the turmoil in the months after Dendera's death and the Empire's demise, the Order on our four remaining worlds suffered decimation, demoralizing its members and making many of them ready to give up. When Gareth Zoss, who would become the first Archimandrite, gathered the survivors and established the Void Reborn, he simply removed the stipulation concerning talent for senior positions and made it the best suited for the job, male or female. It's pretty much the only difference between the Old Order and the Void Reborn."

"But a difference that may be a deal breaker when it comes to the Motherhouse."

Ardrix nodded.

"I'm afraid so. Archimandrite Bolack won't take stepping back kindly, not with his plans, and I doubt the Motherhouse will bend any rules, not after such a long period of isolation, during which its outlook will no doubt have ossified."

"Will you share this development with the Lyonesse Brethren?"

"That's up to you, but I think Ambassador DeCarde has already sent a message to his superiors. I doubt the arrival of three Motherhouse envoys was kept secret on Wyvern."

"Three? It's not a big delegation, but then only two of us represent the Hegemony in the Republic. By all means, let the Lyonesse Brethren know. If nothing else, it'll be a demonstration of goodwill. Was there anything else in the message?"

"A few other items, mostly routine, except for one, which we probably shouldn't discuss with the Republic, concerning the battle fleet found by Task Group 215 and brought home."

***

"The Motherhouse on Lindisfarne still exists?" Summus Abbatissa Gwendolyn stared at Ardrix's image, visibly stunned by the news, proving Ambassador DeCarde's message hadn't reached her yet — if he'd even sent one.

"It appears so, and they've dispatched a delegation to Wyvern aboard one of our ships."

"That's extraordinary." Gwendolyn shook her head. "Two hundred years in isolation. How did they keep barbarians at bay?"

"I don't know, but it wouldn't surprise me if they combined the talents of tens of thousand Sisters or more — there are half a million Brethren on Lindisfarne — to repel visitors."

"Half a million." Gwendolyn's eyes widened. "That's more than we have in the entire Republic. How did your ships get near?"

Ardrix shrugged.

"Probably because the Sisters aboard detected the effects and countered them."

Gwendolyn sat back, eyes narrowed in thought.

"And will the Void Reborn submit to Lindisfarne now that you're aware it still flourishes?"

"I do not know. Will you?"

Bleak laughter erupted from Gwendolyn's throat.

"I should have known you'd turn the question back on me."

Ardrix put on a wholly feigned air of innocence.

"Meaning you don't know either."

"I will have to discuss the matter with the Council of Elders and the Brethren at large. Like the Void Reborn, we've charted our own course over the last two centuries and made the Lannion Abbey our Motherhouse, just like you made the New Draconis Abbey yours. Besides, who knows what sort of practices Lindisfarne now follows after generations stuck on a single world without knowing what was happening in the galaxy."

Ardrix inclined her head.

"True."

Then, a sudden burst of inspiration seized her.

"Would you like to send a delegation to Wyvern as well so they can meet with the Lindisfarne Brethren? One of our ships is at Hatshepsut waiting for messages from us back to home. It can surely wait long enough for a few of your Brethren to join it.

Perhaps even those serving on Hatshepsut since you can instruct them easily via your subspace network."

"Are you empowered to make such an offer, Ardrix?"

"I'm sure Ambassador Torma will confirm it without hesitation. Sending a delegation from your Order can only help."

"My Order…" Gwendolyn took on a thoughtful air, then she said, in a soft, almost inaudible voice, "But is it truly mine?"

***

Sister Rianne, Prioress of Hatshepsut, approached the open airlock to the Wyvern Hegemony Courier Ship *Cruxis* with a certain trepidation. It was docked to one of the grandiosely named Starbase Hatshepsut's arms, and even though the ship was attached to a Republic orbital station, on the other side of the airlock was Hegemony territory, as per diplomatic conventions. Sisters Desra and Charisi, also of the Hatshepsut Abbey, silently followed Rianne. All three carried small duffel bags with their personal effects.

Just as they reached the airlock, a smiling crew member appeared.

"Sisters, we've been expecting you. I'm Petty Officer Jorah. Please come aboard. Your cabins are waiting, and we're ready to depart."

Rianne inclined her head.

"Thank you, Petty Officer. I'm Rianne, and these are Desra and Charisi. Please lead on."

Jorah took them down narrow corridors to a set of small cabins, barely larger than a closet, containing a bunk and separate, even smaller heads.

"I apologize for the limited space, but the shipwrights focused on building couriers for FTL speed, not comfort. If you saw *Cruxis* from the outside, you'd have noticed a small hull sitting on top of oversized drives."

"No worries, Petty Officer. We're used to living in tiny spaces.

"The saloon is at the end of this passageway. Feel free to use it to your heart's content. It serves both as mess hall and entertainment center, though it's not much bigger than the cabins. We're a crew of twelve, so we need little room. I'll leave you to settle in."

Once Jorah had vanished around a corner, Rianne turned to her juniors and smiled.

"Ready for the grand adventure?"

—16—

New Draconis
Wyvern Hegemony

"Archimandrite. And how are you this morning?" Sister Margot bowed her head politely as she stopped at the edge of the path through the New Draconis Abbey orchards.

Bolack smiled at her. She and her two companions had quickly turned into welcome fixtures around the abbey, unfailingly courteous, sometimes amusing, and always willing to engage in profound and stimulating intellectual debates.

"I am healthy and in good spirits, Sister. And you?"

"Quite the same."

"Join me." Bolack gestured along the path, as Margot had hoped when she deliberately placed herself to intercept him, having determined that his morning meditation walks were the best time to discuss weighty matters with him.

"Thank you."

They began strolling among the trees, most descendants of stock brought from Earth over fifteen hundred years ago, although there were native specimens in the mix. But the harvest had come and gone weeks earlier, and the heady aroma of ripe fruit no longer lingered. They breathed in the peaceful aroma of vegetation feeling content in the knowledge that it had completed its duty for another year.

"I was reflecting on our discussion about the nature of the Infinite Void yesterday," Margot said.

"And did you come to any new realizations?"

"No." She shook her head. "But it allowed me to appreciate its vastness once more."

"Something few of us do regularly."

"True. It left me in awe for a long time afterward."

"A perfectly normal reaction, Sister. Any Brethren not in awe probably have no place among us."

The perfectly natural way Bolack said 'us' made Margot smile inside. He'd quickly grown to accept the Lindisfarne Sisters as fellow members of the Order and saw no difference between them and the Void Reborn Brethren.

"Without a doubt. It's what separates us from the laity."

"On another subject, our meeting here this morning must have been inspired by the Almighty, for I have news for you brought to me a bare thirty minutes ago. If you hadn't appeared in my path, I would have sought you out after my morning meditation walk. Three Sisters of the Lyonesse Order have arrived in the Wyvern system aboard our courier from Hatshepsut. They notified me shortly after the ship came through the wormhole. It appears their mission is to see you."

"Is it now? Interesting." Margot's mind parsed the implications of meeting with representatives of the Order's other orphaned branch. Obviously, the Wyvern Hegemony had advised its ambassador on Lyonesse, who then, in turn, told the Lannion Abbey. And it sent three Sisters. How extraordinarily convenient. "When will they arrive?"

"In ten hours or so. Perhaps we shall greet them just before the evening meal."

"I am eagerly awaiting it."

"As am I. Of course, it won't be our first time hosting Lyonesse Brethren."

"Indeed. Sister Taina told us about that. And the man responsible is now ambassador to the Republic of Lyonesse?"

"He is. Crevan Torma. A fine officer and an outstanding human being."

"A police officer, if I understand correctly."

"Yes, a brigadier general in the State Security Commission."

"An unusual choice for ambassador, no?"

"Perhaps, but he has several characteristics that make him an excellent diplomat. He's stoic, can mask his feelings, is highly observant, and can be eloquent when necessary. A very capable man."

Margot heard the conviction in Bolack's voice and chose not to press him any further.

"And what are your thoughts on entering into communion with Lindisfarne this fine morning, Archimandrite?"

A rumble deep within Bolack's broad chest bubbled up as he chuckled.

"The same as they were yesterday, Sister. If Lindisfarne accepts men as priors, abbots, and archimandrites, I have no problems bowing to the Motherhouse."

"You know that's not possible."

"Then the Void Reborn shall stay separate from the Order headed by Lindisfarne."

They walked on in silence, breathing deeply but regularly, calming their spirits before taking on the day.

***

"I am Abbess Rianne of the Hatshepsut Abbey." Rianne bowed her head to Archimandrite Bolack, imitated by Sisters Desra and Charisi, who stood a pace behind her and to one side.

"Welcome, Abbess." Bolack, who'd stood upon their arrival, bowed back, but a fraction less, to mark his higher status. "I hope your travels went well?"

"We were quite comfortable aboard the courier, thank you. It may be a small ship, but offers more personal amenities than our abbey. Hatshepsut is still a bit primitive in certain respects."

They were in Bolack's office, the three Lyonesse Sisters having been delivered straight to the New Draconis Abbey by a naval shuttle from Starbase Wyvern. Dusk was coming, and the evening meal would start soon.

"Good to hear. We've prepared quarters for you in the guest wing. You have just enough time to settle in and refresh yourselves before we eat. I propose you sit at my table with Sisters Margot, Samara, and Fayruz of Lindisfarne."

"Certainly. After all, we've come to meet them at the orders of our Summus Abbatissa. I'd also like to see Ambassador DeCarde and his chief of staff, Hermina Ruttan, who was abbess before me."

"We can also arrange that. Please follow me. I will guide you to the guest wing and wait to take you to the refectory."

"Your courtesy does you honor, Archimandrite."

The size of the New Draconis Abbey dwarfed that of its Lannion counterpart, and Rianne's eyes darted everywhere as they followed Bolack, taking in stone structures that seemed to have been there since the beginning of time. But she knew it was only two hundred years old, the replacement of the old Draconis Abbey destroyed during Empress Dendera's downfall.

After a quick stop in their assigned monastic cells to unpack and wash their hands and faces, Bolack led them to the refectory, an immense space with rows of tables capable of seating more than a thousand. Many of the places were already occupied while lines of Brethren waited patiently to pass by the various food stations offering simple but nourishing fare.

They joined one of them, and Rianne was struck by the absence of conversations. It wasn't completely silent, but most stood or ate without uttering a word. Those who spoke did so in low, almost reverential tones. The Lyonesse Abbey's refectory, let alone Hatshepsut's where monastic discipline could sometimes be even more lax, was usually filled with voices.

Once seated at a table separate from the rest, Bolack looked around and, espying Margot and her companions as they came off a line, made a gesture inviting them to join him. When they approached, Rianne, Desra, and Charisi stood to greet them. Bolack made the introductions, and they sat, the three Lindisfarne Sisters on one side of the table, the Lyonesse Sisters on the other side, with the Archimandrite at its head. They eyed each other in silence for a few moments, then Margot smiled.

"I am pleased to make your acquaintance. Am I correct in understanding that you have a Summus Abbatissa on Lyonesse?"

"You are," Rianne replied before spearing a morsel and popping it in her mouth. Once she'd swallowed, she said, "You understand we believed ourselves the sole survivors of the Order for two centuries."

"Just like us. Until the Hegemony ships arrived a few months ago, we also believed ourselves to be alone. But lo and behold, there are two offshoots of the Order, and they're thriving."

"And you've come to make us one Order under a single Summus Abbatissa again, haven't you?"

"That is my mission, although Archimandrite Bolack," Margot inclined her head toward him, "has so far shown little interest."

"Any particular reason, Archimandrite?" Rianne asked.

"Lindisfarne keeps men in subservient positions. We of the Void Reborn believe men can be abbots, priors, and heads of the Order, not merely chief administrators."

"I see. That would tend to be an insuperable problem which we of Lyonesse don't have. But we have our own Summus Abbatissa and Lindisfarne is about as far from Lyonesse as a human world can be."

"So you'd not come back into communion with what the Archimandrite calls the Old Order?"

"I didn't say that, Sister. After all, during imperial times, the Order was scattered far and wide, and the abbeys were self-governing under the loose guidance of Lindisfarne. We could regard it as our spiritual home again and acknowledge the Summus Abbatissa of the Order as the first among equals, with the Summus Abbatissa of the Order's Lyonesse Branch reporting to her."

"There can be only one, child." Margot's voice caressed Rianne, and she realized the older woman was not only using her talent but that it was likely powerful if she could touch her so overtly. "Perhaps yours might be known as a Magistra Abbatissa."

"I suppose it's a possibility. But that doesn't solve the Archimandrite's issues."

"Perhaps not. Still, I keep hope alive that he may see fit to change his mind." Margot gave Bolack a smile, which he returned as he was chewing.

Once done, Bolack wiped his lips with a napkin and said, "You know my conditions, Sister. It's time Lindisfarne joins the thirty-eighth century. We've advanced over the last two hundred years while you've continued to stagnate."

Rianne gave Bolack a strange look at hearing seemingly harsh words, but he merely winked.

"We've had this conversation daily ever since Margot arrived. I'm not sure who's wearing who down."

"So far, neither," Margot said in a wry tone. "But I still try."

— 17 —

Lannion
Republic of Lyonesse

A somber-looking Ardrix entered Torma's office after a perfunctory knock on the doorjamb. Since only the two of them worked in the chancery — so far, Torma hadn't seen the need to engage local staff — they'd foregone any greater formality.

"President Hecht is dead," she announced. "It's all over the newsnets. They didn't provide a cause of death. Vice President Juska is seeing the Chief Justice of the Supreme Court at fourteen hundred to be sworn in as president and complete her term."

Torma frowned as her words registered.

"But how? She hasn't even arrived back on Lyonesse yet."

"Apparently, her ship is in orbit or will be any moment now. The announcement came when it dropped out of FTL at the hyperlimit three hours ago."

"Then she passed away during the last hyperspace jump. Otherwise, they'd have announced it when they came out of the final wormhole transit, before that last brief bout in FTL." Torma sat back, a grave expression on his craggy features. "Prepare a communique for the newsnets declaring the Hegemony's regret at President Hecht's untimely passing and another to Government House, saying essentially the same thing."

"I shall do so, Ambassador."

"And I'll try to contact Admiral Norum to find out if he knows anything more. After all, if she passed during the FTL jump, it was aboard a Lyonesse Navy ship."

But Norum remained incommunicado for the rest of the morning and into early afternoon, busy dealing with the fallout of Hecht's demise.

When Torma finally got through to the Chief of the Defense Staff's office just before seventeen hundred, Admiral Gerhard Glass' senior aide told him the CDS was unavailable to the Ambassador of the Wyvern Hegemony. Clearly, President Juska had already started to clear the decks for his own adherents, and Admiral Norum had joined the long line of retirees from the service.

Torma was uncharacteristically silent as he and Ardrix drove up to the residence perched on the hills overlooking Lannion just before sunset, and the latter, knowing why, remained equally silent. Once within the residence's confines, Torma let out a deeply felt sigh as he entered the living room and took his usual chair.

"I think our time here on Lyonesse is just about over, Ardrix."

"Without a doubt," she replied, heading for the bar to mix them both a gin and tonic. "President Juska will expel us and break diplomatic relations with the Hegemony."

"I suppose Aurelia Hecht's death is quite convenient for Juska. He can finish her term and then serve his own two terms."

"If he's elected." Ardrix handed a glass to Torma.

"Oh, he will be unless he steps on some serious toes in the next while. He'll have enough time to build up his constituency into a solid bloc guaranteeing enough votes for him." He took a sip. "I think I'll try Norum on his private link. He's pretty much the only one in the administration, past and present, who'll give us the time of day."

To Torma's surprise, Norum picked up after a few moments, and a hologram of his head and shoulders hovered above the communicator that sat on the coffee table.

"Ambassador. What can I do for you?"

"Admiral. My condolences for Aurelia Hecht's death."

"As of sixteen hundred hours today, I'm no longer an admiral, but thank you for your kind words." Norum's face remained without emotions, nor was his tone anything other than conversational, but Torma knew there was anger, perhaps even rage, behind the expressionless facade.

"How did President Hecht die?"

Norum cocked an eyebrow at Torma.

"Is that why you called?"

"I figured you'd be the only one to speak with me, and as Ardrix and I were just discussing, the new administration will pull our diplomatic credentials within a matter of days. Derik Juska has made his contempt for the Hegemony and me in particular quite clear."

Norum let out a humorless chuckle.

"Ain't that the truth? How did Aurelia die? Apparently in her sleep from cardiac arrest. One of her aides found her with vital signs absent in bed two hours after the ship went FTL from the wormhole terminus."

"Is it suspicious?"

"Why do you ask that?"

"It seems strange that a healthy woman in her prime would die because her heart unexpectedly stopped beating at a time when Derik Juska is opposing her in just about everything. And now, he's the president."

Norum grimaced.

"Okay, it's suspicious, all right. Aurelia had no underlying conditions, and her latest physical three months ago showed everything working properly. But you will not get that from the new administration. My successor won't investigate, that's for sure. He supports Juska, meaning he's a Lyonesse First adherent."

"So someone could have poisoned her with a rapidly dissolving agent."

Norum nodded.

"Yes. And by the time the ship reached orbit, it would have dissipated entirely, leaving us with no other option than to accept death by natural causes. Not that any autopsy will search for evidence of poisoning.

"You think Juska might have been responsible?"

"Certainly. He might own one of Aurelia's aides and have ordered him or her to carry it out. The Almighty knows Lyonesse First has fanatics everywhere. Not that we'll ever uncover who that was."

"I'd look to see if anyone in her entourage vanishes or dies in the next day or two as a clue. If she was murdered, the killer is a loose end that needs to be snipped off."

"Spoken like a true police officer."

Torma bowed his head, a faint smile playing on his lips.

"I can take off the uniform, but I will carry that way of thinking with me for the rest of my natural life. What, if anything, can we do about the situation?"

Norum gave him a weary shrug.

"Nothing, Ambassador. Aurelia Hecht officially died of natural causes. Derik Juska is now president, and Vern Reval is the vice president. In the natural order of things, I should have been appointed Secretary of Defense, but instead, Juska has thrown me out of office with no formal change of command parade, which tells you how much he hates me.

"He fears you, Admiral because you can see through him and know what sort of a man he is."

"True."

"And he might just suspect you figure President Hecht did not die of natural causes, even though you have no evidence. If I were in your shoes, I'd be cautious for a while. Accidents happen, even to retired four-star admirals."

Norum let out a bark of humorless laughter.

"Thanks for the advice, General. Tell me, will you return to active duty once Juska expels you and your ambassadorship ends?"

"Yes, that was the agreement. And Ardrix will return to the Order of the Void Reborn."

"That's right. I keep forgetting she's a Sister with her vows suspended. Does she still have a Sister's abilities, though?"

Torma nodded.

"She does."

"That must come in handy at times."

Torma gave him an amused half-shrug.

"Perhaps. What will you do now that you've been cast to the outer edges of darkness?"

"I've been mulling over leaving Lyonesse and settling on Yotai or Mykonos. Both are advanced enough that life would be good there. Maybe I could even start a family distant from the intrigues of Lannion." Norum sighed as he put on a crooked smile. "While Aurelia was still alive, chances were good Derik Juska wouldn't have seized the reins of power, even once her second term ended. Now? He'll use his time as her replacement to consolidate his position. Almost fifteen years of Juska at the helm means the Republic will go down dark paths. It was inevitable, I suppose. We've had almost two centuries of decent, sometimes exceptional governance."

Norum shook his head.

"Don't get me wrong. Juska is perfectly serviceable as a president when it comes to domestic affairs. Where he departs from his predecessors is in supporting the supremacist argument that Lyonesse alone will determine the fate of humanity. That means a bellicose posture toward the Hegemony, sure. But it also means using a more aggressive stance with respect to worlds like Hatshepsut or Mykonos and bringing them fully under Lyonesse's control rather than allowing the inhabitants to chart their own future as states within the Republic."

When he saw the look of surprise on Torma's face, Norum chuckled.

"Oh, our Derik isn't just a supremacist. He's also a centralist. In fact, if I were to indulge in a flight of fancy, I'd call him a would-be dictator in everything but name. Maybe even an emperor of the Ruggero school of governance, and one unlikely to surrender power peacefully once his term ends or he's voted out."

"Are you sure you should be sharing this with a representative of the Hegemony?"

"Why not? I no longer have any official functions and am a private citizen of the Republic, with all the rights and responsibilities that entails. And one of those rights is that I can speak my mind to whoever I wish, even someone who will soon be considered the enemy if I have Juska's intentions pegged correctly.

"You think?"

"It's the logical endgame for his ambitions. Make the Hegemony into an existential enemy and cement the Lyonesse First movement's, meaning Juska's, grip on power."

***

The Lyonesse government pointedly did not invite Torma to attend Aurelia Hecht's funeral service, and they also did not invite Admiral Norum. However, Admiral Norum attended anyway, while Torma watched the live newsnet feed of the event.

President Derik Juska and Vice President Vern Reval were front and center alongside the Hecht family, which had a long history of providing the Republic with forward-thinking senior officials and captains of industry.

Torma had met the patriarch of the family during one of the many social affairs he'd attended and had found him to be both down-to-earth and reasonable. They'd spent a lot of time discussing the possibility of large-scale trade between the Republic and the Hegemony, something Torma was mandated to encourage. What he must think to be sitting side-by-side with a man such as Juska, who represented everything that was contrary to the Hecht family's outlook on interstellar relations, Torma couldn't tell.

Watching the service at a remove left a nasty taste in his mouth. He'd gotten along with Aurelia Hecht, who had made no secret of her desire to expand relations with the Hegemony. Still, she somehow could never convince the Republic's bureaucracy to do more than pay lip service to her wishes. Even during her living, the Lyonesse First movement had made inroads into the civil service, encouraged by Juska's open support.

And when the Republic's Secretary for Interstellar Affairs summoned him the next day, he knew what awaited.

—18—

Torma was kept waiting in the lobby of the Department for Interstellar Affairs for almost half an hour after the appointed time while the passing staff ignored him. He knew that Juska had ordered it done on purpose, to firmly put the Hegemony Ambassador in his place.

A junior staffer finally came to fetch him without a word of apology and led him not to the Secretary's office but to that of a mid-level bureaucrat who didn't deign to stand, let alone shake hands. Torma had met the bureaucrat before and didn't hold a high opinion of him. The feeling was obviously mutual since he didn't invite Torma to sit. He merely lifted a tablet and read from it.

"We hereby rescind the accreditation of the Wyvern Hegemony's diplomatic delegation and enjoin you to leave the Republic of Lyonesse as soon as feasible. That is all."

"I see. And what about Ardrix Moore's and my diplomatic status? Is that revoked as well?"

"No. It'll still cover you for as long as you remain in the Republic."

"Thank you. If that was everything, I shall leave to pack." Torma, wearing his habitual stoic expression, turned on his heels and exited the office while the man watched him leave with a smirk of satisfaction on his pasty face.

Once back in his now former chancery, he found Ardrix already looking for berths on ships bound for, if not the Hegemony, then at least Hatshepsut, which had become the de facto interface between Wyvern and Lyonesse. It would eventually see a Hegemony courier or merchant ship. The former showed up every six weeks or so to exchange messages with the delegation and bring missives from the Republic's embassy on Wyvern for its government.

"So, was it as you expected?" She asked.

"It was a tad worse in terms of treatment, but the end effect is the same. We're expelled."

"I wonder whether President Mandus will send Currag DeCarde packing in retaliation."

Torma shrugged.

"It doesn't matter. I figure Juska will recall him. Maybe even via the same courier that will take us home. Have you found any commercial ships headed our way? I'd like to leave as soon as possible. This place has suddenly become repugnant."

"Yes. A mixed freighter-passenger ship doing the run of the inhabited worlds on the Hatshepsut branch of the wormhole network, leaving tomorrow afternoon. Shall I reserve two cabins?"

"If you would. Then, shut everything off after wiping the memory banks. We're returning these offices to the Lyonesse government the moment you're done."

"Yes, General." Upon hearing her use his police rank for the first time since he was named ambassador, Torma gave her a curious look, but she merely smiled. "You and I are going back to our old lives since you're no longer the Ambassador of the Wyvern Hegemony to the Republic of Lyonesse."

"Indeed, we are… Sister."

They left the chancery unlocked as they sped away to the residence in the car they'd abandon at the Lannion spaceport in the morning.

"You know, I'm feeling kind of relieved that the charade is finally over," Torma said, breaking the silence.

"A charade? Isn't that a bit harsh? There were plenty of Lyonesse citizens interested in furthering relations with the Hegemony."

Torma thought about it for a few heartbeats.

"Could be. But it doesn't negate my sentiments. Let's call it an uphill struggle we were losing."

"That's better." She gave him a sad smile. "Still, it's a shame."

He didn't immediately reply, but when he did, his smile matched hers.

"Yes, it is, despite the Juskas of the universe."

That evening, Torma called Farrin Norum one last time, and the former admiral seemed pained by the announcement of their departure.

"I didn't think he'd expel you immediately, General."

"Oh, it's no surprise to me. President Juska is moving fast on many fronts, almost as if he'd been prepared to assume power before Aurelia Hecht's death and had his plans ready."

Norum nodded slowly.

"Yes, it does seem like that."

"Have you come any closer to a decision on your future?"

"Mykonos is urgently looking for settlers, so I think I'll give that a go. At least it gets me away from Lannion, likely forever."

"Good luck."

"And the same to you, General." Norum paused, then said, "Hopefully, saner heads will prevail in the end. Healthy competition between the Republic and the Hegemony is the only way to ensure our mutual survival."

A crooked smile appeared on Torma's lips.

"It is. And it's been nice knowing you, Admiral."

"Likewise."

"Farewell."

Torma spent a long time staring at his communicator after they cut the link, wondering what the future held for them.

"A cred for your thoughts?"

He looked up at Ardrix, standing in the living room door.

"I was reflecting on how quickly circumstances can change for the worse. If the Republic so dramatically reverses its stance on relations with the Hegemony at the behest of a single man, is it really that much better than our star nation, or is it a quasi-dictatorship with merely the trappings of democracy?"

"I think you'll find that historically, democracies were short-lived. Two hundred years or perhaps a little longer seems to have been the maximum lifespan before they devolved into autocratic states or fell into civil war. In that, Lyonesse fits the pattern. Aurelia Hecht's abbreviated term of office may have been the last gasp of truly representative government."

Torma cocked an eyebrow at her.

"And you've just increased my sense of hopelessness."

"How about you pack instead of wallowing?"

The next morning, as they left the residence for the last time, an unmarked police car followed them all the way to the spaceport, where they'd take a shuttle to the orbital station and board *Gentiana*, the ship that would take them to Hatshepsut. Security passed them through without a glance, let alone a word, and they boarded soon afterward.

Once they lifted off, Torma, who'd snagged a window seat, stared long and hard at Lannion until the clouds swallowed the shuttle, wondering whether he'd ever see the city again, but knowing in his heart he wouldn't. It had been a pleasant stay, except for his dealings with Derik Juska and his fellow travelers, and he remembered Ardrix saying, early on in their time on Lyonesse, that she saw dawn coming. Torma didn't want to ask her whether she still did but suspected her reply would be negative. What she'd seen was a false dawn, one which had since vanished.

The shuttle landed on the station's hangar deck, and, with bags in hand, Torma and Ardrix made their way across and down several levels to the docking arm holding *Gentiana*, where the purser greeted them and led them to their adjoining cabins. The latter were small but comfortable, with private heads, a bunk, a desk with a chair, and an entertainment station. Ardrix chose to lose herself in meditation while waiting for the ship's departure, and Torma, after a brief visit to the passenger saloon, settled on his bunk with a book.

Gentiana undocked at the appointed time and headed out to the hyperlimit, where she jumped on her first FTL leg, this one to the sole wormhole terminus serving the Lyonesse system. Torma and Ardrix joined the other passengers in the saloon for the evening meal, and he was relieved to find that no one knew he was the former Hegemony Ambassador. As far as anyone who asked found out, Torma and his companion were on their way to Hatshepsut for reasons that remained unanswered. He wasn't unfriendly but remained sufficiently reserved that no one probed too deeply.

It turned out to be a long voyage, with *Gentiana* calling at every port along the way, most of which didn't have orbital stations, meaning lengthy shuttle transfers of cargo and people to and from the surface. But Torma and Ardrix took it with their usual stoicism, and eventually, they docked at Starbase Hatshepsut, which served as both the civilian and military station.

There, Captain Lucas Morane, the commanding officer of the Hatshepsut Squadron, greeted them. Lyonesse had warned him of their arrival aboard *Gentiana*. Yet if his superiors were hoping Morane would give Torma and Ardrix a cold shoulder, they would have been disappointed. He treated them as if they were still a diplomatic delegation, his way of protesting their expulsion and the hardening of Republic-Hegemony relations.

"I apologize for the quarters I can offer you while you wait for the next courier," Morane said as he led them to the station's accommodations deck. "Although we call it a starbase, it's really still an assemblage of spare parts shipped here from Lyonesse at substantial cost. Or you could go to the surface. Thebes is a pleasant city, and I'm sure we could find you secure accommodations."

"Not at the abbey," Torma replied, giving Ardrix a significant glance.

Morane chuckled.

"Perhaps not, although the Order is forgiving, and you returned those whom you abducted safe and sound."

"Since we can't know how long it'll take for the next courier or a merchant ship to arrive, I think it might be best if we head for Thebes, provided, of course, that we can arrange lodgings."

"Leave it to me. I think the Lyonesse ambassador's residence is large enough to accommodate you two along with the tiny mission we have here."

Ardrix and Torma exchanged another glance. If Norum was right, that ambassador might well become a proconsul in everything but name sooner rather than later.

"We very much appreciate your courtesy, Captain."

Morane gave Torma a tight smile.

"Not every one of us is a Lyonesse First zealot. By the way, I have a missive for Ambassador DeCarde, which is to go on the same courier as you. The president has recalled him. It appears the Republic is breaking off all diplomatic relations with the Hegemony. Interestingly enough, however, the recall doesn't cover the three Sisters who went out to Wyvern on the last courier."

"The Order, whether it's our version or yours, works on a different agenda from those of politicians or military personnel."

"Isn't that the truth?"

—19—

New Draconis
Wyvern Hegemony

"General Torma, Sister Ardrix. Welcome home." President Vigdis Mandus rose from behind her desk and walked around it to greet them. "Although I wish it would have been under better circumstances. Please sit."

She gestured at the sofas facing each other across a low coffee table and took the chair at its head. Torma was back in his black Commission for State Security uniform with a brigadier general's silver star at the collar, and Ardrix was once more wearing monastic robes.

"I read your report with great interest. Thank you for sending it ahead when you emerged from the wormhole. What is your sense of President Juska's intentions?"

Torma made a face.

"It's hard to tell. I still can't be quite sure whether he's a Lyonesse First zealot or an opportunist who harnessed the movement so he could seize and retain power."

"Does it matter?"

"I suppose not. Either way, he'll continue acting aggressively toward the Hegemony so he can impose the Republic's views concerning humanity's future. Perhaps it'll only be a difference of degree — more so if he's a genuine Lyonesse First adherent and less if he's an opportunist."

"Of course, he'll have to win an election by the Senate once he completes Aurelia Hecht's term," Ardrix said. "And that's not guaranteed."

"Except if Lyonesse First senators are elected in greater numbers by the citizenry during the next cycle." Torma shrugged. "Still, it's not like our spheres are abutting, and they won't be for a long time yet. There are a lot of star systems to repopulate between the Hegemony and the Republic, and things might well change on Lyonesse during that time. No political movement lasts forever in a democracy, even one as flawed as the Republic's."

"True." Mandus nodded slowly. "On another subject, how did you spend those weeks on Hatshepsut waiting for the courier to return?"

"In idleness, I must confess. Although I did spend time with the military, both Theban and the Republic's, observing and trying out their weapons. They were most accommodating and made it clear that they disagreed with the government's decision to expel us. Ardrix also spent time at the Hatshepsut Abbey, learning about their organization's plans for expanding and extending the Order's influence on the planet after they decided to accelerate Hatshepsut's rebirth as a high-tech world.

"Did either of you learn anything useful?"

Torma raised a hand, palm down, and wiggled it from side to side.

"Me, not so much. The Republic's Ground Forces are very similarly organized and equipped compared to ours, and the Thebans are virtual clones." He glanced at his assistant. "Ardrix?"

"I learned quite a bit that will be useful for the Colonial Service and the Order's support thereof. I assume the General and I are returning to our former responsibilities?"

"If you want. We haven't appointed a new permanent inspector general."

Torma and Ardrix glanced at each other, and then the former said, "We'd be glad to, Madame President. I assume its offices are still in the Blue Annex?"

"They are." Before she could say anything else, there was a knock at the door, and it opened to reveal the president's aide.

"Ambassador DeCarde and Chief of Staff Ruttan are here for their farewells, Madame."

"Ah, excellent. Good timing, too." Mandus stood, imitated by Torma and Ardrix, as DeCarde and his aide entered.

"Madame President." DeCarde and Ruttan stopped halfway to the sofa arrangement and bowed their heads.

"Welcome." Mandus gestured at the sofas. "As you can see, I have the former ambassador to the Republic of Lyonesse and his chief of staff with me."

"Indeed, Madame. And I see back in their prior roles, or at least wearing their prior clothing." DeCarde stepped forward and offered his hand to Torma. "A shame President Juska ended diplomatic relations between our star nations. It's not something I would have recommended. On the contrary, but I serve the state and must do as I'm told. Madame President, thank you for taking the time to see us."

"Please sit."

Once everyone had settled, DeCarde turned to Mandus.

"We're off on the courier in a few hours, your Navy being gracious enough to not make us wait, as General Torma and Ardrix were forced to wait on Hatshepsut because our Navy didn't offer them a ride home. You have my apologies for that, General."

Torma waved DeCarde's words away.

"We enjoyed our time there more than you'd think."

"Then so much the better. Our delegation from the Order of the Void will be returning with us. I discussed the matter with Abbess Rianne the moment I read the message from my government, and despite their not having received a recall order, she feels they've accomplished everything they could in meeting the Lindisfarne representatives."

"And you're not leaving any hostages to fortune." Mandus nodded knowingly. "A wise move. We may not send another courier to Hatshepsut for a long time now that we no longer have a delegation on Lyonesse, and your Navy wouldn't know to pick up the delegation when its time here is over. Still, I suppose there will be sufficient merchant ships making the trip."

DeCarde inclined his head.

"Just so, Madame."

"As you said, it's a shame, but your president made the decision. Of course, we will miss you. Though you weren't here for long, you've left quite a favorable impression on my administration and the many organizations you interacted with."

"Very kind of you to say so, Madame. It was a genuine pleasure representing the Republic to the Wyvern Hegemony. And now, it's time for us to say farewell. I don't know whether we'll ever be back. A future president may restore diplomatic relations."

"If Derik Juska doesn't cling to power beyond his constitutional mandate," Torma muttered just loud enough for DeCarde to hear. The latter gave him a sharp glance.

"What do you mean, General?" He asked.

"I wouldn't put it past Juska engineering an amendment to the constitution to remove term limits for himself and the senators. He could easily get a two-thirds majority in the Senate to open the matter for debate after the next election floods it with Lyonesse First adherents."

DeCarde's face hardened, and he nodded once.

"Duly noted. Thanks for the warning."

Then he stood and drew himself to attention.

"With your kind permission, Madame President, I would like to take back the credentials I presented to you and end my term as ambassador."

Mandus also climbed to her feet, as did everyone else.

"Granted, Mister DeCarde." She stuck out her hand. "Fair winds and following seas."

"Thank you. And good luck to you as you navigate the treacherous channels of expansion."

DeCarde and Hermina shook with Torma and Ardrix, and then they left the president's office.

"I quite like that man," Mandus said when they sat again. "He has a core made of starship-grade armor and a refreshing outlook on things."

"So do I, even though I've only met him briefly twice," Torma replied. "I wonder what will become of him under Juska's administration. The Lyonesse First zealots might well see him as tainted by his association with the Hegemony."

"Let's hope he doesn't suffer Aurelia Hecht's fate."

***

Torma and Ardrix walked over from the Wyvern Palace to the Blue Annex under a glowering sky, each sunk in their own thoughts. The former wondered, once again, whether something he did or said caused the end of his ambassadorship, all the while knowing it was not him but President Juska. Ardrix, on the other hand, had no such doubts. She saw the evolution of their status as preordained by the Almighty.

Once inside, Torma led them straight to the office of Admiral Johannes Godfrey, the commander-in-chief of the Colonial Service. He knocked on the door jamb and when Godfrey looked up from his tablet, Torma drew himself to attention and saluted while Ardrix stood beside him, hands joined in front of her.

"I understand the inspector general and Leading Sister positions are still vacant, sir, and we'd like to apply for them."

A smile appeared on Godfrey's face, and he sat back.

"At ease, Crevan, and you too, Ardrix. Neither of you seems worse for wear. Come in and grab a seat. How was the brief stint as ambassador?"

"Interesting." Both sat across from Godfrey's desk. "Did you perchance get to read my report to the president?"

"Yes. As a matter of fact, I finished it no more than an hour ago. She shared with all the Service Chiefs. As you said, it's interesting. Especially your suspicion that President Hecht's death wasn't from natural causes."

"It was the former Lyonesse Chief of the Defense Staff's suspicion as well, sir. And I fear for his life, too, although we might never find out what, if anything, happened to him. Admiral Norum was one of the good guys who went out of his way to make me feel welcome. His replacement wouldn't give me the time of day."

"And the Lyonesse government gave you the bum's rush."

Torma grimaced.

"It wasn't the most dignified way to end my term as ambassador. But then, if President Juska had received me as President Mandus just did former Ambassador DeCarde, we would have either wallowed in a bath of hypocrisy or I'd have received a dressing down like no other. It was just as well a small-time bureaucrat expelled me. At least that way, I could exit quietly. Moreover, the folks on Hatshepsut treated us with the utmost respect while we were waiting for the courier, highlighting a clear disconnect between Juska's administration and the people in the field.

Godfrey chuckled.

"A common failure throughout history. We're not much better."

"Indeed, but at least we don't cloak ourselves in a tattered mantle of democracy and pretend we're morally superior."

"No. I do wonder whether we should become more democratic, at least above the planetary level. There's something to be said for an interstellar government that isn't consumed by retail politics. Oh well." Godfrey shrugged. "That's neither here nor there. President Mandus hasn't made any move to turn the Conclave into an elected body, and I wonder whether she ever will. Or her successor in the fullness of time."

"And who would that be?"

"I'd say Sandor Benes. He's the smartest and most able of the Service Chiefs."

"You know, sir, I think I prefer our system to the Republic's. At least our presidents have had a full career and risen to the top of their profession before taking office. There's no room for a Derik

Juska who's made politics his career and has done nothing else for the last forty years."

Godfrey smiled.

"It's almost as if we were replicating the imperial system before Stichus Ruggero twisted it into something that eventually destroyed us."

"With greater safeguards than the old Empire had. There's no chance of a Ruggero upset in the Hegemony."

"There's always a chance, Crevan. Determined people can misuse a system grown complacent, almost somnolent, like the Empire's had, no matter the safeguards one employs. In any case, welcome back. Your temporary replacement has already packed and is eagerly returning to his regular duties."

"In that case, I won't make him wait any longer. With your permission, Admiral?"

"Go. Put some order back into the inspector general's office."

— 20 —

“Do you think the Lyonesse Brethren will ever enter into communion with Lindisfarne?” Archimandrite Bolack asked Sister Margot as they took their customary mid-morning stroll through the New Draconis Abbey’s orchard. Several weeks had passed since the departure of the Lyonesse delegation, both diplomatic and religious.

“No.” Margot shook her head.

“Why not?”

“Sister Rianne was polite but deeply skeptical about subordinating their Order to Lindisfarne. Since she was her Summus Abbatissa’s envoy, her influence on the final decision will be paramount.”

“Interesting. I did not sense any skepticism.” Bolack stopped walking and turned toward Margot. “And why was she so dubious? Do you know?”

She gave Bolack a small smile.

"My talent is well developed, Archimandrite. Much more than most back home and definitely more than almost everyone I've encountered here. But even so, I cannot divine reasons for the emotions I felt in Rianne. I can only surmise."

"Then please, tell me of your conjectures." Bolack joined his hands inside his robe's voluminous sleeves and gazed at Margot with interest.

"I think Rianne considers the Lyonesse version of the Order superior to the others since it not only preserved human knowledge during the great catastrophe that befell us thanks to Dendera but has thrived, as evidenced by the multiple extensions of its houses on newly reclaimed human worlds. It was in the way she spoke of her Order and its accomplishments. I'd say Rianne and her Brethren suffer from a sort of unconscious arrogance unbecoming in a disciple of the Almighty. And I'm almost convinced she considers Lindisfarne a relic of the past better left to rot on the vine. Again, it was in the words and turns of phrase she used rather than anything obvious. Which is why I firmly believe the Lyonesse Brethren will not return to the fold. They'll continue down their own path as schismatics."

Through a common, though unvoiced accord, both resumed walking side-by-side.

"And us?" Bolack asked. "Are we on our way to becoming schismatics as well? Do we possess that unconscious arrogance you sensed in the Lyonesse Brethren?"

Margot let out a throaty chuckle. "No. You don't have a shred of pretension, let alone vanity. On the contrary, your branch of the Order is resilient yet closed in on itself. You're modest and devoted, yet at the same time, you can be hard-bitten. Qualities one would expect after your founders witnessed the Empire's final destruction and rebuilt from scratch alongside the Hegemony before spending two centuries isolated on your four worlds, in a sort of stasis. Perhaps unconsciously waiting."

"For what?"

"Your branch? It could be to reconnect with Lindisfarne and expand once more." She gave him a sideways glance. "The Hegemony? To gather the strength necessary for the founding of a new Empire. After all, you named your leader the regent until very recently, and a regent is merely one who acts in the place of an absent ruler."

Bolack didn't immediately reply, and they walked on in silence. Margot knew he had to parse the more profound significance of her deliberately chosen words. Yet, sensing his uncertainty, a rare occasion she must use, Margot nudged his thoughts toward a greater feeling of warmth for Lindisfarne and acceptance of the idea he should submit to the Summus Abbatissa of the Order. Then, she gently pushed the thought of a new Empire since the Order could not regain its former stature without one. Being part of the triumvirate running the Hegemony, Bolack could influence its future and encourage the idea.

"Well," he finally said, "there's a great deal of truth in the idea that we were anticipating the opportune moment to flourish once again."

Margot allowed herself a private, hidden smile. For the first time since her arrival on Wyvern, she had managed to prod Bolack in the direction she wanted. And because he'd asked her a simple question — would the Lyonesse Brethren ever rejoin the fold. The Almighty moved in mysterious ways but always toward a goal many might not discern. At least not immediately.

"Indeed, Archimandrite. And perhaps the Almighty will look to you as his conduit, the one who will ensure the Hegemony blooms and eventually unites humanity under a single Order of the Void once more."

"Do you think so?"

"Yes. It simply makes sense." She nudged him a little more, this time knowing it was the direction his subconscious wanted to go.

Bolack nodded slowly, though his expression remained grave. "Food for thought, certainly."

Margot found the fact Bolack didn't know she was manipulating him deliciously ironic, he being the head of the Void Reborn. No Summus Abbatissa would have allowed Margot into her head, let alone influence her feelings. It proved the point that the top leadership positions in the Order of the Void had to be filled by women with uncommon talent, not men whose abilities were much weaker. And Bolack wouldn't even count as among Lindisfarne's most talented men. His sole claim to head the Void Reborn was an innate flair for politics, though Margot had to admit he was superb at it.

Of course, Margot didn't even try to influence Sister Rianne in the brief time she was on Wyvern. As an abbess in a branch of the Order that had stayed true to the old practices, her talent was strong enough to notice any attempt. Which made Archimandrite Bolack's hold on the Void Reborn even more ludicrous.

But who would replace him in due course? The only Sister she'd met, be it ever so briefly during services at the abbey, who projected both an aura of deep serenity and a powerful talent, was Ardrix, Leading Sister of the Hegemony's Colonial Service. That she wasn't engaged in monastic work and hadn't been for a long time, however, could be a drawback. Still, Margot figured she should befriend her and explore the possibilities.

She and Bolack reached the wall surrounding the orchard and, without a word, turned and walked back toward the abbey on a parallel path.

"You know, it would be difficult to get a curtailment in the powers wielded by men of the Order through the Council of Elders," Bolack said, breaking the silence.

"It need not be. The only thing required is an abdication of those in the positions of abbot, and yours, of course, to be replaced by abbesses and a Magistra Abbatissa to oversee them until such a time as the new Empire has reincorporated Lindisfarne."

"And those abbots will resist, Sister. Only the Council can force them out. But since half the Council consists of former abbots who retired as simple friars, I doubt your notion will receive enough support to make it so.

"You won't have any idea until you present the question to them," Margot replied, feeling gratified that her nudges were yielding something. This was the first time Bolack actually touched on the mechanics of bringing the Void Reborn back under Lindisfarne. "Especially if you announce your retirement and join the Council once your successor has been named."

"My retirement?" Bolack shook his head. "No. Not until the Almighty calls upon me to step down."

"How will you determine when it's the right moment?" Margot asked in a gentle tone, one to inspire confidences.

Bolack shrugged. "Since the Almighty moves in mysterious ways, I simply will."

***

That evening, after services, Margot intercepted Ardrix and proposed a walk around the abbey grounds.

"Tell me, Ardrix, what exactly does the Leading Sister of the Colonial Service do?" The former asked as they strolled out into the orchard beneath a growing carpet of stars, now that night had replaced the long summer twilight. "I'm aware you work with the service's inspector general, Crevan Torma, but that's it. I'm not even sure what General Torma does if truth be told."

Ardrix realized this wasn't an idle query. From the contact she'd had with the three Lindisfarne Sisters since returning to Wyvern, she understood everything they said, every question they asked was geared toward a singular goal, that of bringing the Void Reborn back under the Order's Summus Abbatissa. But she couldn't quite see why Margot asked about her work in the Colonial Service.

"Crevan is the principal staff adviser to the commander-in-chief of the service and can stick his nose into any aspect and every corner of the Colonials. He's the commander's all-seeing eye, his voice, and his executor, you might say." Ardrix gave Margot a brief smile. "My primary role is to act as the liaison between the Service and the Order of the Void Reborn. What that really means is I oversee the Order's activities on colonies for the Archimandrite."

"Ah. So you report directly to Bolack."

"On matters affecting the Order, yes. Otherwise, I report to Crevan."

Margot nodded.

"Who reports to Admiral Godfrey. He, in turn, reports to President Mandus." She returned Ardrix's smile. "I'd say you're directly plugged into the Hegemony's highest levels."

"I suppose so. Although my day-to-day activities are mundane. Reading and commenting on reports from the colonies and their Void Reborn detachments, advising Crevan and Admiral Godfrey on matters pertaining to the Order, that sort of thing. I have a weekly conversation with the Archimandrite for about half an hour, primarily to update him on the few issues regarding the colonial Brethren he should be acquainted with."

"You make yourself sound unimportant, Sister. Yet you were half of the Hegemony's diplomatic mission to Lyonesse, the other sole surviving human polity."

"Brief as it was."

"Through no fault of yours."

Ardrix stopped and turned to face Margot. "What is it you want of me, Sister? Your questions and comments surely don't stem from idle curiosity."

"No, they don't." Margot's gaze was steady and open. "Tell me, Ardrix, what do you think of the Void Reborn returning to orthodoxy under the Summus Abbatissa on Lindisfarne?"

Ardrix tilted her head to one side and returned Margot's stare with an air of curiosity.

"What do you mean by returning to orthodoxy?"

"Appointing the most talented to the top leadership positions."

"You mean replacing abbots with abbesses and Archimandrite Bolack with a female?"

They started walking again and headed back to the abbey, whose windows glowed softly in the darkness.

"We have yet to find a man with the same talent as the top women. I'm sure your experience is the same. For instance, the Archimandrite does not possess a fraction of your abilities."

"And yet the equality between men and women when it comes to occupying the top leadership jobs has served the Void Reborn well over the last two centuries."

"It could be, but the Void Reborn has been confined to four star systems in close subspace communications with each other. It is much different when the distances are such that the leaders of star system head abbeys are essentially alone in making decisions and require much more insight, which is given to them by a strong talent. I'm afraid men just aren't quite up to the task, and as the Hegemony expands, you will soon discover the limitations of the lower-talent minds."

"Yet non-adepts, both men and women, have ruled the widely scattered imperial worlds for over a millennium. How do you explain their success?"

Margot hid a smile at Ardrix's reasoning. She clearly wasn't one to accept explanations meekly from an older and more experienced Sister.

"Ah, but those rulers had only worldly responsibilities. Abbesses have spiritual duties on top of them, as well as more complex non-spiritual obligations. And they cannot allow themselves to have any weaknesses whatsoever. They must remain strong yet humble, exert greater moral influence, and sacrifice themselves on the altar of the common good by abjuring any ambitions other than to serve the community." Margot studied Ardrix's face for a reaction but saw nothing other than polite interest. "I dare say it takes exceptionally strong talents to be and do that."

Ardrix inclined her head, thinking of Bolack's ambitions to make the Void Reborn the sole Order in human space under his leadership. Of course, it didn't mean highly talented women couldn't fall prey to the same aspirations. They were human, after all. But perhaps it was a lot less likely because they possessed a much clearer understanding of their own souls, just as Ardrix did. And she was fully aware that she belonged in the top tier of talented Sisters.

They entered the quadrangle around which lay the abbey's principal buildings, including the dormitories.

"Granted. And now, I shall repeat my question. What is it you want from me?"

Margot stopped and studied Ardrix once more.

"Nothing."

"I find that hard to believe."

"And yet it is true. Good night, Sister."

With that, Margot walked away, headed for the guest wing, leaving a thoughtful Ardrix to stare at her receding back.

Perhaps Margot wanted nothing from Ardrix, not directly, at least. Yet she'd given her more than enough to ponder. And that had to have been her goal all along.

Feeling an unaccustomed disquiet, Ardrix headed for the orchard, deserted at this time of the evening, to meditate while walking among the fragrant trees. Her thoughts were jumbled but instead of struggling to make sense of them, she simply allowed a stream of consciousness to flow through her. Images, ideas, even visions of things that had not yet happened, that might never happen, passed before her inner eye.

Then, like a dam bursting, Ardrix saw everything, the past, the present, and the future intertwined, and she almost gasped as thoughts swirled between her conscious and subconscious mind. Finally, they settled into a recognizable pattern, and with a clarity that took her by surprise, Ardrix understood what she must do. Because she now suspected she was the one who was destined to bring the shards of the Order back together as a whole.

—21—

"The survey report says all forty-eight ships brought back by *Caladrius*, *Strix*, and *Remus* are sound and compatible with the rest of the fleet, sir."

Admiral Sandor Benes, the Hegemony's Chief of Naval Operations, beamed with satisfaction. "That's excellent news, Anton."

"Of course," Vice Admiral Anton Mejik, the Deputy CNO, said in a droll tone, "it's a good thing our shipbuilding techniques haven't changed much since the empire's downfall. Otherwise, we'd face a big integration problem."

"And how do you propose we employ them, considering the anomaly that certain crew reported during wormhole transits? I'd rather not deactivate the AIs just yet. We don't have enough personnel to bring their companies up to full strength."

"I have just the solution for that, sir," Mejik replied, smiling. "Or rather, the operations staff came up with it. We station twelve in each of our core star systems — six cruisers and six frigates — as a local garrison, freeing up existing ships for long-range reconnaissance and patrolling the colonies. Since they'll never be more than a day's travel away from their respective orbital bases, we can use minimum crewing and rely on the AIs for routine tasks. And best of all, no wormhole transits beyond the initial deployment."

"A good plan." Benes nodded slowly as he mentally counted off the various units freed up by the new ships. "It not only increases the fleet by twenty-five percent in one fell swoop but does so while keeping crew demands as low as possible. We should be at parity with Lyonesse now, if not ahead of them. It's too bad General Torma never got a full count of their navy's ships."

"We know they're stretched out much more than us because of the number of star systems they've reclaimed. We, at least, still form a compact yet growing sphere."

"And we'll eventually become just as stretched out. A shame they broke off diplomatic relations, though. It would have been interesting to see just how far cooperation with them could have taken us. Now, we have no choice but enter a race to expand, and we're many decades behind them." Benes sighed. "That new Lyonesse president seems like quite a piece of work based on Torma's report. Suspected of murdering his predecessor to clear the way? So much for democracy."

He shook his head.

Mejik shrugged. "Let's hope we don't go down that road and end up with someone of his ilk."

"Indeed. At least we have had no political assassinations, actual or suspected, since the Hegemony's founding. Nor are Hegemonic supremacists springing up everywhere like bad weeds, unlike the Lyonesse First crowd, which seems to be both xenophobic and zealous about it."

***

"What do you think of Sister Ardrix?" Margot asked Archimandrite Bolack as they took their morning stroll through the abbey orchard.

Bolack gave her a sideways glance, surprise, and curiosity clearly visible in his eyes.

"Why do you ask?"

"I had an interesting talk with her after evening services a few days ago."

"About what?"

A mischievous smile appeared.

"Ah, Archimandrite. I asked first. Answer my question, and I'll answer yours."

"Oh, very well," Bolack grumbled. "Let me see. Ardrix is extremely intelligent — one of the smartest Sisters in the Void Reborn, in fact. She's also blessed with one of the strongest talents, which is why she worked with the State Security Commission, assigned to Brigadier General Crevan Torma — Torma the Taciturn as he's sometimes known — before moving with him over to the Colonial Service."

"Did she now?" It was Margot's turn to show surprise. "And what was she doing with the Commission?"

"Assisting investigators and interrogators whenever the insight and abilities of an empath were required. Among others, she can project images into unshielded minds and release those hiding in their subconsciousness, you see. Vivid ones that help break resistance in criminals."

Margot frowned.

"An unusual manifestation of the talent."

"We have several Sisters with that capacity. They mostly work with State Security's investigators."

"I see. It's not the sort of work the Void traditionally carries out. We use our talent to heal, not coerce."

Bolack gave her a sly smile.

"Don't tell me you never use your talent to gently guide a troubled mind without the individual in question knowing about it. What the Sisters in the Commission do isn't that different. Criminals are, by definition, troubled minds, and the Sisters use their talent to guide them into confessing their crimes, thereby setting them on the path of healing."

"Specious argument, my dear Archimandrite, but very well. Ardrix worked for the State Security Commission because of this interesting twist to her talent. And now she's one of the most highly placed members of the Void Reborn, overseeing the Order's activities beyond the Hegemony's four core worlds on your behalf. And she interacts daily with very senior people, including the head of the Colonial Service and even President Mandus occasionally."

A nod.

"Yes. I had not considered her that way, but she is my right hand in many respects, clearly bridging the secular and the spiritual in a way no one else in the Void Reborn save for me has done. Does that answer your question?"

"It does."

"Now, please answer mine. What did you discuss?"

"Her current duties, who she reports to, the failed diplomatic mission to Lyonesse, and her views on the Void Reborn adopting orthodoxy and submitting to Lindisfarne."

"And her views on the subject were?"

"She expressed a certain amount of skepticism, mainly. We didn't pursue the matter, so I couldn't tell you whether she was leaning more in favor after listening to my arguments. But she seemed thoughtful when we parted."

Bolack stopped and faced Margot.

"Why did you engage her in such a discussion?"

"Because she seems your natural successor when you retire to a life of quiet contemplation, Archimandrite."

He frowned, as much in surprise as in puzzlement.

"I had not considered who would replace me in due course. At least not seriously. But Ardrix's name never bubbled to the surface whenever I thought about it."

"Don't you figure she'd make a splendid Magistra Abbatissa?"

"You mean bowing to Lindisfarne?"

"Yes, that thought had crossed my mind."

"You're being disingenuous, Sister."

"Am I? Still, Ardrix seems a likely candidate to bring about the unification of the Void Reborn with Lindisfarne, don't you think."

Margot mentally nudged Bolack, finding it easier than the previous times. She was getting used to his mind.

After a few moments, Bolack slowly nodded.

"She might be, yes."

Satisfied, Margot changed the subject so Bolack could mull over the idea and let it sink in. Just like she'd done with Ardrix.

***

"Come in, Ardrix." Archimandrite Bolack waved toward the chair facing him across his desk as he pushed aside his tablet. "And how are you today?"

"Well, Archimandrite." She sat, eyes focused on her superior. "And you?"

"Tolerable. What do you have for me this week?"

"The latest reports from the priories on Santa Theresa and Celeste are positive regarding accelerated development. Both target populations are taking giant strides back up the technological ladder. The priory on Novaya Sibir is still establishing itself, but in the absence of a native population, they minister only to the colonists. The expedition to Meiji landed safe and sound. At the time they made their report, they were still scouting for the most suitable site to establish a beachhead. Finally, the expedition to Caledonia is in the last stages of preparation. They should depart in two weeks. And that's all I had. Everything is proceeding as it should."

"Excellent, thank you." Bolack studied her for a few heartbeats with a faintly quizzical air as if trying to decide whether he should broach a different subject. Finally, he said, "I understand from Sister Margot that you two had an interesting conversation covering, among other subjects, the matter of the Void Reborn submitting to Lindisfarne with everything that it implies."

Ardrix inclined her head.

"We did."

"And what are your thoughts on the matter?"

She'd feared that question would arise and composed herself.

"The way I see it is we must make a choice. Either we formally declare ourselves schismatic and chart a course separate from the Old Order, like the Lyonesse branch will undoubtedly do. Or we can replace abbots with abbesses and priors with prioresses when they retire and return to orthodoxy under Lindisfarne. With that option, we reserve the posts of chief administrators exclusively for men, as was done in the past. We must remember the Order of the Void was created almost two thousand years ago to provide a refuge for women with an uncontrolled wild talent. One that troubled their lives and drove many of them mad. Within the Order, they learned to control it and eventually use it for the betterment of the community. Since the talent in men is only a fraction of a woman's, they have never needed the Order to survive and thrive."

"Interesting historical resume, but we've created a situation where men may occupy the highest positions. Taking that away from them will create a lot of ill will."

"Which is why I said we could replace abbots and priors with abbesses and prioresses when the former retire and female chief administrators with men when they retire as well and stick to that configuration going forward."

"Are you proposing we should do so, or was that simply conjecturing?" Bolack half cocked an eyebrow at Ardrix.

"I've thought about it ever since I spoke with Margot and have concluded that it's best for the Order and the Hegemony's future if we submit to Lindisfarne. We will eventually expand our sphere to include it and release the Lindisfarne Brethren into the wider galaxy. The Order and the Hegemony will be stronger if we're united. Especially if we face a hostile Lyonesse, and that consideration alone will push most in the Void Reborn to favor submission."

Bolack let out a deep sigh.

"I'm afraid you're correct, Ardrix, as much as it pains me. At one time, I'd hoped to join the Void Reborn with the Lyonesse Order, but events have far outstripped that dream. Very well. Do you accept becoming the head of the Void Reborn and reuniting us with the Order of the Void?"

Ardrix nodded.

"I think I have no choice in the matter. The Almighty is surely expecting me to do so. I can feel it."

"As I can feel the time to turn the Void Reborn over to you has come. Oh, the Council of Elders will have its say on the matter of making you Magistra Abbatissa. Still, our tradition of the outgoing Archimandrite proposing his or her successor will help. You will become our new leader in due course."

"Why?"

"You mean, why do I agree to step down and reimpose orthodoxy on us?" Bolack stroked his bearded chin with one hand. "Because I believe it's the Almighty's will. Don't ask me how I've come to that conclusion. Simply accept that I have. Besides, I find myself wearying of the burden. I've been Archimandrite for over fifteen years, and it's time I step aside for someone younger and with more energy."

Ardrix, a Sister with a talent stronger than ninety-nine percent of the Void Reborn Brethren, suspected Sister Margot, in whom she'd recognized a kindred adept, had nudged Bolack in the desired direction. After all, his talent was circumscribed, and his ability to shield his mind from outside influences was small. If Margot judged it necessary to manipulate Bolack at a subconscious level, then she must be very sure of the necessity for the sake of their shared future.

"And I accept it." Ardrix bowed her head. "Yours is to decide when the handover happens. I am not in a hurry, nor is the universe. It will be years before Lindisfarne is part of the Hegemony's sphere. Until then, we live a parallel existence while acknowledging the Summus Abbatissa as our leader. Years during which we rearrange ourselves to meet the Order's strictures. But there's no need to mention that until after I've taken over."

"I had no intention of doing so. Yours will be the honor and the difficulties in leading the Void Reborn back to orthodoxy."

—22—

"Our time together might come to an end soon, Crevan." Ardrix took a chair across from Torma's desk at his unspoken invitation when she returned to the Colonial Service's HQ.

"Why? Is it something I did?"

"No. It seems my destiny isn't quite what I expected."

"Oh?" Torma's dark eyebrows shot up in question.

"Archimandrite Bolack is retiring, and I'm his designated successor."

Torma sat up in surprise.

"How did that happen? I mean, you're more than capable of leading the Void Reborn, but still."

"My primary mission will be to subsume the Void Reborn into the Old Order and acknowledge Lindisfarne as the head of the Void."

"Oh!" Torma sat back, his face reflecting the thoughts coursing through his capacious mind as he parsed the implications of

Ardrix's words. "What changed Bolack's mind? I thought he wouldn't bow to Lindisfarne unless they accepted men in the top leadership positions."

Ardrix let out a humorless bark of laughter.

"I suspect Margot changed his mind, and not in a way he noticed."

Torma's eyes widened slightly.

"You mean she messed with his subconscious?"

A nod.

"Yes. And that's a factor in why I agreed with the Lindisfarne Brethren and accepted to succeed Bolack. His mind is average among males of the Order, and even I could enter it without him knowing, let alone a powerful talent like Margot. Since appointing the strongest to the top leadership positions simply makes sense as the Hegemony expands rapidly, it removes men from contention."

"Are you sure Margot didn't influence your mind?"

"I would have felt any attempt, contrary to the Archimandrite. She merely spoke her thoughts, and that was enough to convince me."

Ardrix sounded so sure of herself that Torma shrugged.

"Okay. So when does this blessed event happen, and how will you convince the men they're returning to second class status?"

"Not second class, Crevan. They'll exclusively take over the chief administrator positions again, making them, in effect, second in the order of precedence of any abbey or priory."

"What if you come across a man with the talent of a powerful woman?"

"Then we'll have to readjust. But we'll have to readjust because their kind has never been seen in all the centuries since the Order was founded, meaning they don't exist."

"You'll still have plenty of unhappy friars to contend with."

"Initially, perhaps. However, as the abbots and priors retire, strongly talented women will replace them, and when the female chief administrators retire, men will replace them. No one can argue with the logic that we need those with the most powerful abilities at the top."

"I guess you know what you're doing. But aren't you afraid the unhappy men will simply leave the Order or split off into a schismatic sect?"

"Then we're well rid of them since they will have proved they lack the discipline to take the Order of the Void back to the stars."

Torma let out a soft yet appreciative whistle.

"I always knew you were ruthless, even for a Sister assigned to the State Security Commission."

"As the ancients said needs must when the devil drives," Ardrix replied in an amused voice, right eyebrow cocked.

"So, when do you take over?"

"When Bolack convenes the Council of Elders sometime in the next two weeks. It must accept his resignation and bless my taking over from him."

Torma frowned.

"And what if they don't confirm you as his successor?"

"They will."

Again, Ardrix sounded utterly sure of herself.

"Dare I ask why you're so certain?"

"Because I'm the only candidate being put forward by Bolack."

"What if another Sister, one with a powerful talent, proposes herself as a candidate?"

"No one will do so. They're aware that the successor proposed by the current Head of the Order gets first consideration by the Council. If the Elders reject him or her, then they must find another successor. But they will not reject me since I am the most suitable candidate due to my unique experience in worldly matters at the highest levels.

"It looks like you have it figured out, Sister. Congratulations on becoming the next Archimandrite."

"I won't be taking on that title. Rather, I will become the Magistra Abbatissa, the senior abbess responsible for all Void members in the Hegemony, who will, in due course, report to the Summus Abbatissa on Lindisfarne."

"Why in due course?"

"Because I must permit the abbots and priors to retire voluntarily before bowing to Lindisfarne. Until then, we remain the Void Reborn."

A chuckle.

"Taking it gradually, eh? Wise. Who will replace you here in the Colonial Service? Or will we no longer have a Leading Sister?"

"I don't know just yet. And please don't speak to anyone about this until the Council meets. Not even Admiral Godfrey. Neither Bolack nor I will mention the return to Lindisfarne's rule until after I've replaced him."

"Promised." Torma leaned back in his chair. "You know, no one's ever explained to me why the Void Reborn has men in the top positions when the Order of the Void never had any."

"That's quite simple. During Empress Dendera's final days, she became so paranoid that she ordered the execution of all Sisters of the Order, beginning with the high-ranking ones. When the dust finally settled over the hole in the ground that used to be Draconis, very few Sisters remained, most of them young and undeveloped. But many friars escaped, including the most senior chief administrators. One of them gathered the survivors around him and began rebuilding the Order. Since none of the Sisters was anywhere near ready for positions such as abbess and prioress, he took on the leadership himself, adopting the title Archimandrite. It was used long ago to designate a superior abbot, one who supervised several ordinary abbots and abbeys. In due course, other friars took on the duties of abbot and prior as the Order expanded once more and set up houses on our four core worlds until the first Sisters were ready. By then, having men in the top leadership positions had become accepted by the Sisters, even though it was abnormal."

"And now you seek to correct this."

Ardrix gave Torma a helpless shrug.

"I have no choice. If we're to survive in the long term, we must find our roots again and appoint only the strongest talents as heads of abbeys and priories."

"And the Order itself, or at least the Hegemony's branch of it."

"Just so. I believe it's what the Almighty wants, and so does Archimandrite Bolack."

Torma smirked.

"With a little help from Sister Margot."

***

"Tell us, Ardrix, why should you succeed Archimandrite Bolack as head of the Void Reborn?" Elder Frieda, the head of the Council, asked, examining Ardrix with an emotionless gaze.

Frieda had been Bolack's predecessor as Archimandrite and was known to be severe in her outlook on just about any subject. The remaining Elders, twenty in all, stared at Ardrix through eyes equally devoid of expression. Bolack sat to one side, beyond her immediate field of view, silent, speaking only when asked to do so by the Council. Ardrix was on her own.

They were in the cavernous chapterhouse, where every word spoken could be heard from end to end, although they occupied but a tiny part of it, the front row of seats to one side of the altar.

"Because I'm the most qualified from among the Brethren, Chief Elder. I have extensive experience in secular matters at the highest levels as well as in the religious realm. Since the Archimandrite sits on the Hegemony's Executive Committee, that secular experience, unique among the Sisters of the Order, will be invaluable to the Void Reborn."

She returned Chief Elder Frieda's stare impassively, noting the deep lines in the older woman's wizened face. Like her fellow councilors, Frieda was well over a hundred years old and no longer possessed that ageless look so common among Sisters of the Void. Everything about her but the eyes told of time's fleeting passage. And her voice, which remained strong and resonant.

Ardrix felt many minds attempting to probe hers, but she remained unmoved as her defenses easily brushed them aside. Twenty-one pairs of eyes set in stony faces peering at her silently as she stood before them had no effect either.

"So Archimandrite Bolack claims," Frieda finally said. "Yet we usually select the Head of the Order from among the abbots and abbesses. And while you play a supervisory role over the missions we send out as Leading Sister of the Colonial Service, it's not quite the same."

"Before Archimandrite Bolack, the Head of the Order played no role in the Hegemony's secular governance. Now, he does as a member of the Executive Committee, which means an abbot or abbess whose sole experience is within the Void Reborn will be at a disadvantage compared to me. I put to you that Archimandrite Bolack and I are, in fact, the sole members of the Order qualified to lead it through these tumultuous times."

Frieda's left eyebrow crept up.

"You put to us? Isn't that rather presumptuous, Sister? We are the Council of Elders, the Order of the Void Reborn's supreme authority on matters of governance."

Ardrix inclined her head in a gesture of acknowledgment.

"Certainly. But my words still stand, Chief Elder."

The ghost of a smile crossed Frieda's ancient lips.

"You don't intimidate easily, do you, Sister Ardrix?"

"No, Elder, I don't."

"Good. We need someone strong to lead the Order." Frieda let her eyes roam over her fellow councilors. "Does anyone have questions or comments?"

When all she received in return were shakes of the head, she said, "Then we will vote. Those in favor of Sister Ardrix being named Archimandrite Bolack's successor?"

Fifteen hands rose.

"It is done." Frieda climbed to her feet. "Archimandrite Bolack, please join Ardrix in front of me."

He obeyed, and Frieda said, "The chain of office."

Bolack slipped the necklace with the phoenix orb from his neck and handed it to her. Frieda bowed her head at him, a gesture he returned.

"The Order of the Void Reborn thanks you for your devoted service, Archimandrite Bolack. You now become one of the Elders sitting on the Council."

Then she faced Ardrix.

"On behalf of the Council of Elders, I appoint you to head the Order of the Void Reborn." She placed the chain around Ardrix's neck, and both bowed their head at each other. "Archimandrite Ardrix."

"I shall take the title Magistra Abbatissa, Chief Elder."

Frieda gave her a strange look and hesitated for a fraction of a second before saying, "Then so it shall be, Magistra Abbatissa Ardrix. May your rule be fruitful, and may you lead the Order to greater heights for the glory of the Almighty."

"The Void giveth, the Void taketh away. Blessed be the Void."

"Blessed be the Void," the Elders replied in unison.

"We must speak of your plans soon, but not today," Frieda said with a significant glance at Ardrix. It made the latter wonder whether Sister Margot had cultivated the head of the Council of Elders as well. Frieda would have had nothing but time on her hands and an intellect ready to examine all angles of Margot's logic. If so, it heartened Ardrix because it meant she was on the right track.

"Certainly."

That evening, Ardrix entered the chapterhouse, and under the silent looks of the assembled Brethren, she took what had been Bolack's chair for so long. Before sitting, those present bowed their heads to her and she to them. Then, the service proceeded as usual. No further ceremony attended the change of leadership.

—23—

"I'm surprised Bolack decided to retire so suddenly and turn the job over to you." President Mandus gestured at the sofa arrangement around a low table on one side of her office. "Please sit, Magistra."

Once both faced each other across the table, Mandus studied Ardrix for a few seconds before saying, "Isn't it unusual for someone so young and who hasn't been an abbess to become Head of the Order?"

"Yes, but we live in unusual times and the Order must adapt if it is to survive. I am the best suited for our future as we expand and minister to fallen populations, Madame. If this were still the era of isolation, I wouldn't have been."

"And what are your views on submitting to Lindisfarne? I know Archimandrite Bolack wouldn't consider it unless they accepted men in the top leadership positions."

Ardrix looked Mandus in the eyes.

"We will eventually merge with the Order of the Void, Madame, at the latest once Lindisfarne joins the Hegemony. We cannot afford two separate Orders if the Hegemony will be the Empire's successor, and if that means only Sisters attain the ranks of abbess and prioress, then so be it."

Mandus tilted her head to one side.

"And how do you see us inheriting the Empire's mantle?"

"Not by imitating Lyonesse. Their version of democracy has reached its end, predictably, after just under two hundred and fifty years, which is historically the time span such forms of government get before spiraling into corruption, authoritarianism, and civil strife. The Almighty only knows how it'll end, but it won't be pleasant."

A frown. "So you're saying we shouldn't democratize our politics?"

Ardrix nodded.

"At least not at the interstellar level. There was really nothing wrong with the old Empire's way of doing things, except it, too, had an expiry date, one provoked by Stichus Ruggero when he found a loophole to get around the restrictions on who could become emperor. We're not doing things much differently in the Hegemony. Our leader, whether it be regent or president, is a former military officer of four-star rank elected by the Conclave of senior military and civilian leaders. Replace that Conclave with a Senate whose members represent the imperial worlds and leave those worlds to decide how they're nominated and how to govern themselves and we're back in the golden age of the Empire. Ruggero represented an anomaly who got in because the Empire was tired, somnolent even. A constitution modeled on the old Empire's that provides specific safeguards against a repetition would prevent another Emperor Stichus."

"But would it prevent another collapse?"

"All empires die, eventually. We can but hope the next one's death will be of old age, promising rebirth like the Hegemony's Phoenix, rather than a conflagration that destroys most of our species. But it will live longer than Lyonesse's democracy. I saw signs of the Republic's descent into madness myself. Continue calling it the Hegemony or call it the Second Empire. It doesn't matter. Just as long as we keep the First Empire's constitution suitably amended. And expand aggressively to counteract the coming chaos in Lyonesse space. There can be two human polities existing side-by-side, but we must grow strong enough so we can resist any attempt by Lyonesse gaining the upper hand and threatening us."

A faint grin appeared on Mandus' face.

"So you think I should proclaim us the Second Empire and become Empress Vigdis the First?"

"Empires have been ruled by individuals holding various titles, Madame. You merely need to continue as you are for now. But I would suggest adopting the old imperial constitution with safeguards and perhaps provisions allowing a transition from the Conclave to a Senate as we expand."

"You know, Magistra, this was definitely not the conversation I was expecting us to have. Yet now that we're having it, you've awakened ideas dormant in the back of my mind, and I find myself agreeing with you to a large extent, perhaps even completely."

Ardrix suppressed a smile. Her mentally nudging Mandus was working. Sister Margot wasn't the only one capable of influencing one of the highest in the Hegemony.

"Then I'm gratified, Madame."

"Let's have a fulsome discussion of the issue with Chancellor Conteh at the next Executive Committee meeting. I can see a great debate forming in the Conclave around whether we continue as the Hegemony or assume the mantle of the Second Empire."

"Perhaps, but most Conclave members might see a change in our title as heralding an increased effort to reunite a shattered humanity under our rightful leadership."

"And not that of Lyonesse." Mandus nodded thoughtfully. "We've done a lot in the last few years, but it's still only the beginning of the beginning. It will take generations to accomplish."

"Without a doubt, yet we've started, and, except for the first mission to Celeste, have done well. Ensuring we're on the right track will eventually lead us there. And I believe the right track is recreating the old Empire as it was in its early days. At a thousand years, it was one of the longest-lived, stable polities in human history."

Mandus gave Ardrix a curious look.

"You almost sound like a mystic prophesying a new beginning, Magistra."

"Perhaps I have a touch of mysticism in me, Madame. One reason the Council appointed me as Magistra of the Order was because of my extensive abilities, surpassing those of most Sisters. You could do worse than refer to me as the mystic who called for the founding of a Second Empire when you face the Conclave at some point. I was made the supreme religious leader of the Hegemony for a reason." She shrugged. "In any case, that's not for today or next week. We can remain as we are for a few years yet, until the Order completes the leadership turnover and we add a few more worlds to the Hegemony."

"The time I have as president is limited. Not that I must be the one who transforms the Hegemony into the Second Empire. My successor can do so, and he will be of the same mind as I."

"He?"

"Admiral Sandor Benes will likely take over when my term ends, and he's as much of a realist as I am. You'll find him easy to work with and likely one hundred percent on board with your vision. He's mentioned a few times since your return that he doesn't think going the way of Lyonesse will do the Hegemony any favors considering developments there."

"Good. That's another advantage of our system. No radical changes in policy from one leader to another."

Mandus nodded. "Indeed."

***

"How did the meeting with President Mandus go, Magistra?" Sister Margot fell into step beside Ardrix as the latter took her afternoon walk through the abbey orchard.

"Well. I believe I've convinced her." Ardrix recounted the discussion with Mandus. "Of course, I nudged her a little, but not that much. Her subconscious was already thinking along those lines since Crevan and I returned from Lyonesse with news of events there."

Margot let out a soft chuckle.

"Lyonesse's political leadership really proved itself shortsighted, didn't it? They merely spurred the Hegemony on by deciding on competition rather than cooperation. And this means Wyvern will remain the center of human space after all."

"You think?" Ardrix gave Margot a curious glance.

"I know it will be so. You are bringing the Void Reborn back into the fold, while the Lyonesse Order will continue on its own path, schismatic to the last. They share the arrogance and blind certainty of the Republic's leadership that they are the future, and it will be their downfall." Margot allowed herself a soft smile. "Lyonesse are but children playing at recolonizing the galaxy while we endured throughout the centuries, unchanged and eternal."

PART II – SECOND NIGHT

— 24 —

Mykonos
Republic of Lyonesse

Farrin Norum, Lyonesse's former Chief of the Defense Staff, had the distinct feeling of being observed as he walked along Thera's main street, knapsack on his back. The main settlement on Mykonos' second continent, Karinth, was a sleepy, dusty place at the head of a bay overlooking the Boetian Sea. The area had suffered orbital bombardments during the Great Scouring and this version of Thera was a few kilometers south of the original, now nothing more than a series of overgrown craters.

There was no possibility of getting much further away from interstellar civilization than homesteading in Thera's backcountry, which Norum, desirous to be forgotten, was doing. He'd cashed out his considerable pension and simply vanished from the grid, establishing himself on a large, wooded property fifty kilometers west of town, where he wrote his memoirs, hunted, and farmed a small patch of ground to provide himself with vegetables year-round.

Norum visited Thera every few weeks to pick up supplies and the latest news, spending the rest of his time in isolation or, if truth be told, in hiding. He'd left Lyonesse five years earlier, a few weeks after being fired by President Derik Juska and a step ahead of an assassination squad, or at least so he believed. Juska both hated and feared him, and it was an even bet the president wanted to make sure Norum joined Aurelia Hecht in the Infinite Void.

No one on Mykonos knew him as Farrin Norum. His identity credentials, bought at a substantial cost on Lyonesse, had him by the name of Victor Devaine, and that was how the merchants in Thera addressed him whenever he appeared. But this was the first time in five years he felt watched. Yet Norum saw no one paying him any attention, meaning the observer, if such an individual existed, stood behind a polarized window, invisible from the street.

The Thera Arms hotel and bar dominated that stretch of downtown with its three stories and long facade, and it was a likely spot from which a stranger would be watching. Norum was suddenly conscious of the weight of his blaster, tucked away under his left arm in a shoulder holster. He carried it whenever he left his homestead, and even inside the house, it was always close at hand.

Norum shook his head at the renewed thought of how far he had fallen, thanks to Derik Juska. From the most senior military leader in the Republic and one of the most influential people in the known galaxy to a bearded, shaggy recluse with the almost constant apprehension he lived on borrowed time.

He made his last visit of the trip to the grocery store, where he picked up enough non-perishables to last him until the next time. Then, laden with bags, he headed for his ground car, a battered, old, all-terrain vehicle as dusty as Thera and as uninspiring. With a last look around, he loaded the bags and his knapsack — filled with items he'd bought at the local hardware and clothing stores — and climbed aboard, still sensing eyes on his back.

Norum wasn't taken to flights of fancy. In fact, he was as grounded as they came, and he knew he wasn't mistaken. Like all Norums, he carried shards of his ancestress Marta's talent, and she'd been the most powerful Sister of her age. Someone had been watching him. And that someone could easily deploy a miniature drone to track him back to his home in the woods, unseen and unheard.

Norum started the car's power plant and turned onto the main road leading into the interior, where small settlements dotted the countryside, and hidden homesteads lurked beneath the shade of tall, native trees.

After twenty kilometers, Thera having vanished below the horizon, he stopped and retrieved his portable battlefield sensor from a hidden compartment beneath the car's control panel. It was one of several highly classified items he'd purloined on his way out the door when Juska fired him. Then, he climbed out of the car and aimed the sensor at the sky behind him, eyes on the readout.

The day was sunny and cloudless, as were most days in that part of Karinth, and he squinted at the sky every few seconds as he moved his sensor's pickups in different directions, trying to find evidence of a drone following him. And soon enough, he found it five hundred meters behind him, at an altitude of thirty meters. The thing was no larger than the palm of his hand and covered in a stealth coating, making it essentially invisible to the naked eye and civilian-grade sensors. Even his battlefield version was having a hard time keeping the drone in focus, meaning it was likely government issue.

Juska's minions had finally found him, and if he was right, they undoubtedly belonged to the Lyonesse Office of Inquiry, the Republic's new interstellar law enforcement agency created by President Juska himself four years earlier. But Norum suspected the LOI of enforcing Derik Juska's will and not necessarily the law itself, hence its hasty creation within twelve months of Juska assuming power. And this was despite the Republic not having seen the need to establish such an organization for over two centuries.

What to do now, though? Norum watched the drone hover on his sensor display, wondering whether its operators knew he'd rumbled them. They had to be aware by now. The video pickups on those drones were precise enough to read the tiny serial number on the back of his sensor at half a kilometer.

Ironically, it meant they were now also aware that he'd stolen said sensor from the Navy, which left him open to arrest for theft of classified material.

Still, his isolation meant he had no friends, not even acquaintances, he could fall back on instead of leading the drone users to his home. Nor did he have a weapon precise enough at long range to shoot the drone.

Weariness suddenly overtook him as the last five years of living under a false identity, hidden from the universe, coalesced into an almost unbearable weight on his soul. But with it came a renewed determination. If he couldn't shake his pursuers, then perhaps Norum might balance the scales by preparing to receive them on his turf and under his conditions.

He climbed back into his car and sped off, pursued by the drone.

Why now, he wondered. Why, after five years, did his would-be executioners show up? Because that was the only reason someone was keeping watch on him, to make sure they caught him in an isolated place where he could vanish without a trace.

Perhaps Juska was preparing to force through the constitutional amendments lifting term limits he'd feared were coming and had sent his loyal police to eliminate anyone who might become a nucleus of opposition. The Almighty only knew how many of his foes on Lyonesse he'd dispatched by now. There would certainly have been an epidemic of unexplained cardiac arrest among them over the last few years.

Norum finally reached the turnoff that led to the stabilized earth road running under a lengthy canopy of trees until it ended in the clearing where his house sat, surrounded by the gardens where he grew much of his food. He'd bought the place off the estate of a deceased man who'd turned it into a self-sustaining fortress over time. It seemed the previous owner had been just as paranoid as Norum, or maybe even more so.

Powered by a small, modular fusion reactor, the property had all the modern conveniences — a deep well for water, composting septic reservoirs to take care of waste, a pair of agricultural droids that tended the gardens, and a security system as effective as any short of a military installation. The sprawling house appeared to have only a single story, an innocuous one at that, surrounded by a veranda beneath a low-sloping peaked roof. But it had an underground level that was nothing short of a bunker. A small army equipped with high explosives might have a chance to penetrate it, but just.

Doors made from starship-grade alloy slid aside at Norum's approach, revealing a cavernous garage where he parked his car. It shut behind him, sealing the house from the exterior and any immediate threats. By now, the drone would have revealed his location to its operators, and he could anticipate an attack at any moment, although he assumed they would arrive in the middle of the night. Assassins preferred to work in darkness.

In theory, he had the ability to outlast them. He'd stockpiled enough food for several weeks and doubted they were bringing a small army and high explosives. They'd want to simply make him disappear before vanishing themselves as if neither he nor they had ever existed. And even the best-defended homestead had flaws in its armor. For example, the security system was entirely wireless, although it was encrypted. But government agents would have the means to crack the encryption, given enough time.

No, he'd have to ambush them the moment they appeared while they were still orienting themselves. And then what? If he eliminated them, more would eventually appear, this time unannounced.

Had he reached the end of his life as Victor Devaine on Mykonos? Must he move on? If so, where? It took them a few years to find him. If he should leave for one of the Republic's outer star systems under yet another false identity, how much would that gain him? A few extra years? Norum's mind shied away from the obvious conclusion, and he forced himself to focus on the immediate.

Once inside the house, Norum proceeded directly to the security room in the basement and inspected each element of his array, starting with the passive sensors that covered the outer perimeter and the road in. Then, he ran through the active sensors linked to weapons emplacements hidden in each corner of the building's walls, behind panels that looked like the same fake wood as the rest. The automatic guns were small caliber with limited ammunition, but enough to repel a concerted attack. Yet, Norum felt he should avoid using them so he might draw his pursuers into the house and eliminate them himself, hopefully leaving at least one alive long enough so he could ask a few questions.

Therefore, he shut off the active sensors, leaving no trace of emissions that sophisticated scanners would pick up. He set the front door lock to normal rather than bar it entirely with the retractable interior steel panel like he did the back door.

Then, he made himself supper and settled in his darkened kitchen at the back of the house to wait with a repeater of the security system display panel beside him.

Shortly after oh-one hundred, something triggered the passive sensors. A vehicle with no lights had turned onto his private road and was slowly approaching.

— 25 —

Norum barely had time to make out the car creeping up toward the house when the entire passive sensor network collapsed. And that wasn't an accident. The unknown people aboard the vehicle must have detected the system's carrier wave and jammed it with the greatest of ease. He briefly debated lighting up the active portion of the net — it worked on a different wavelength — but decided against it. If they so quickly deactivated the first layer of security, they'd be equally fast with the second, and they might just decide he was awake and waiting for them. And that would hamper his plan for luring them into the house.

He pulled down his night vision goggles and laid his blaster on his right thigh, aimed at the open doorway to the hall beneath the kitchen table, where it would hopefully not be seen until it was too late. The intruders likely carried the most advanced battlefield sensors and could see where he was through the walls when they got near enough. But the house was so well soundproofed he couldn't hear their car approach. Of course, he could see nothing of the front since the kitchen was at the back, and he'd lowered the blinds there, cutting off any view.

Norum felt the tension stiffen his neck and shoulders, and he slowly rotated his head, eyes glued to the doorway before resting it on his left arm, which lay across the table, so he mimicked a sleeping person. Finally, he heard a faint sound outside, a shuffling on the veranda as at least two pairs of feet slowly made their way around, presumably staring into windows, looking for him without result, trying to match their sensor reading with a visual. Someone tried the back door with an electronic override, yet it didn't work since the lock was virtually impossible to force with the steel panel in place.

The soft footsteps returned to the front where they tried that door, and the lock quickly gave. Norum suddenly sensed the presence of two people in his house with uncanny accuracy. It was almost as if he could see them through the intervening walls. Two men, judging by their breathing patterns.

They slowly made their way into the corridor, which was in total darkness, but the way they appeared to move proved they, too, wore night vision goggles. When a shadow appeared in the doorway, Norum pulled his blaster's trigger, briefly lighting up the kitchen as bright as day, and was rewarded by a thud as the man fell to the ground with a loud death rattle coming from his throat.

Almost immediately, Norum fell off his chair to get out of the corridor's direct line of sight and rolled toward the back door. He heard the twin coughs of a needler fired double-tap style, but the needles passed through the space he'd occupied moments earlier and tinkled against the far wall.

Norum reached up and touched the door's control pad, sending the steel panel into its recess and unlocking it. He jumped up and slid out onto the back veranda in a single movement, then locked the door again and ran to the front of the house, trapping the second man inside — at least for as long as it took him to unlock the back door.

When he reached the main entrance, he opened the panel a small crack and glanced inside, spotting the second man crouching over the first at the far end of the corridor. Norum opened the door and pointed his blaster at him.

"It's over. Drop your weapon, or you'll join your friend in the Infinite Void."

But instead of complying, the man raised his needler and fired. Norum sensed a sudden wave of needles passing by his left cheek as he pulled the trigger of his blaster twice. The intruder dropped his weapon and fell to his knees, wounded.

Norum cautiously approached him, blaster aimed at the center of mass, finger on the trigger, but he merely looked up at Norum through his night vision goggles, his breath a painful rale.

"I'm going to hazard a guess. You're Lyonesse Office of Inquiry agents come to assassinate me."

The man didn't answer.

"Is your friend dead?"

A few heartbeats later, he finally spoke.

"No, but he'll soon be if we don't get him medical help."

"I'm afraid that won't be possible unless you answer my questions."

Norum was betting on the men being former municipal cops recruited by the LOI and not hardened assassins who'd rather die than give up their secrets. One of the good things Lyonesse had developed over the last two centuries was the ability to identify sociopaths in the general population and either cure them or imprison them for life in the Windy Isles. Which meant Norum seriously doubted either of the specimens in front of him suffered from the sort of psychological abnormalities that would make them excessively dangerous.

"Very well."

"Are you LOI?"

"Yes."

"And were you sent to kill me?"

"Yes."

"Why come now?"

The man let out a bitter chuckle, followed by a grunt of pain. He coughed a few times.

"Because it took us the better part of a year to track you. This was a no-fail mission."

"Well, I believe you failed. Why was I being targeted?"

"Orders, that's all I know."

"Are others being targeted?"

"Yes. Pretty much any opponent of the president." The man coughed again. "Listen, I'm feeling faint. Can we wrap this up?"

"Sure." Norum stroked the trigger of his blaster once more, this time aimed at the man's heart. Moments later, he slumped forward without another sound, dead.

Norum anticipated feeling repulsed by the deliberate killing of another human being, but he experienced no emotions whatsoever, not even the gratification of having survived. Perhaps it was due to all the adrenaline coursing through his veins. He quickly went over and knelt beside the first man, looking for a pulse, but the latter had died while he questioned his comrade.

He stood and gazed at the two bodies, wondering what to do with them. Eventually, someone would notice their absence, and if the men had been even slightly professional, they would have left information about his location for their colleagues in case of an emergency. It meant he'd have to leave, and soon. But in the meantime, he dragged their corpses out into the woods one by one and simply left them for predators after emptying their pockets. The needlers, he tossed into their car.

Then, Norum packed what he called his escape bag, a duffel containing spare clothes, ammo, and power packs for his gun, enough ration bars for several days, the means of disguising himself, and a few items of sentimental value along with stacks of untraceable cred chips, most of them hidden in secret compartments.

Ships for Tiryns, on the main continent, left every morning at daybreak, and he'd decided to travel on one of them. It was the most straightforward and anonymous means. He planned on heading for Mykonos' capital, Petras — not the original, but the new city rebuilt a few kilometers south of the ruins — where he could find someone to create a new identity for him. Once he had those credentials in hand, Norum would take a shuttle up to the orbital station and board the first ship headed for the frontier.

He locked the house, climbed aboard his car, and headed back to Thera, where he parked in a lot near the waterfront and spent the rest of the night waiting. At dawn, he left the car, hoisted his duffel over his shoulder, and walked toward Pier One, where the mixed passenger-freight ship *Pride of Boetia* was engaged in final boarding. Norum went up to the gangway, where he met a petty officer who stopped him.

"I'm looking for a berth to Tiryns."

"Single passenger cabin is a hundred and twenty creds."

Norum dug out a few untraceable cred chips from his pocket, counted off the amount, and handed the sum to the man, adding another twenty for his trouble.

"Welcome aboard, sir. Your cabin is number 26."

The *Pride of Boetia* was a typical Mykonos tramp. Three hundred meters long, fifty wide, with a flush deck ending in a four-story structure aft, she carried fifty passengers and stacks of standard freight containers. But at least she was clean, and the crew showed pride in their vessel.

After going up the gangway, Norum entered the aft structure. He found his cabin on the second level, and it was tiny, though it had private heads. There was barely enough space to move beside the cot fixed to the bulkheads, but the trip across the Boetian Sea took only three days. He dumped his duffel and stretched out on the cot, and, to his astonishment, he felt sleepy enough to fade away within minutes, the last of the night's adrenaline dissipating.

He stayed in the cabin most of the time between meals, and, fortunately, what few passengers the *Pride of Boetia* carried on this run kept to themselves. Norum wondered how many of them were fleeing Karinth like he was, preferring the anonymity of a ship's berth bought with untraceable cred chips to the quick ninety-minute shuttle run between Thera and Petras, where one's identity was checked at the gate.

They arrived in Tiryns late in the day and after Norum walked off the ship, he searched for a cheap inn to spend the night before taking the first bus of the day to Petras, an hour inland via the highway. He found one a few streets from the port, in a ramshackle two-story wooden building. The room appeared clean, but the furniture, sheets, and towels had the distinct look of prolonged usage. Still, it was only for one night, which he spent lying on the bed fully clothed. By now, the LOI agents would have been missed, and his escape would have been discovered, which meant that he remained vulnerable until he could change identities, including his appearance.

The next morning, he swallowed a quick breakfast in the inn's dining room and hurried to the downtown bus station, where he paid for a seat and boarded along with two dozen other passengers. No one paid him the slightest bit of attention, and he hadn't used his credentials since leaving home, meaning the chances of his being free from pursuit remained good.

An hour later, Norum alit in the center of rebuilt Petras, which he'd last visited when he arrived on Mykonos five years earlier. He immediately headed for the seedier south side of town and took a room at another inn, this one less clean than that in Tiryns. But it didn't matter. He wouldn't be spending the night here. The room was merely a place to hide until evening fell and where he could change his appearance.

Norum immediately went to work on the latter, trimming his wild beard and long hair until he almost looked respectable. Then, he tinted both to hide his native blond behind dark brown dye. That done, Norum inspected himself in the room's mirror and liked what he saw. Victor Devaine was gone for good, and a casual glance at him wouldn't reveal his former appearance, let alone that of Admiral (retired) Farrin Norum.

Then, he settled down to wait until darkness fell, munching on a ration bar for lunch and supper.

— 26 —

"That's their vehicle," Lyonesse Office of Inquiry Agent Rey Weston said as she and her colleague, Beth Svent, flew over Norum's house at low altitude in a rental aircar they'd picked up from Thera Cars and Things. The two vanished agents had reported back to the Petras field office before going in, leaving their particulars as an insurance policy.

"I don't like this — I'm not picking up any life signs." Svent frowned at her sensor's readout. She was tall, thin, with short brown hair, brown eyes, and a narrow face. "It's been almost four days since they informed us they'd found the target."

"That means they're probably dead." Weston, as tall as her colleague but stockier, with long blond hair framing a full face, sighed. "Let me land this thing."

The aircar settled a few meters from the house, and as the powerplant wound down, Weston and Svent pulled their needlers from shoulder holsters. Then, they climbed out, Svent still holding the battlefield sensor in her left hand, eyes going from its display to their surroundings and back.

"Definitely no life signs, Rey."

Weston walked over to the other car and looked inside.

"Their personal weapons are on the back seat. Let's see if we can get into the house."

The lock proved easy, and both agents cautiously entered, checking room after room.

"This place feels like no one's been here in several days," Svent said once they'd finished exploring the ground level — without finding the door to the basement.

"Seems like the target's car is gone. But where are Goordev and Hakusa? They can't have left with him."

They returned to the veranda and glanced around once more.

"Let's search for a pair of freshly dug graves, shall we?"

A few minutes after they began quartering the grounds surrounding the house, Svent wrinkled her nose and made a gagging sound.

"By the Almighty, I just caught a whiff of something terrible!" She looked around until she saw the faint disturbance in the undergrowth beneath the tree line. "There. Looks like someone dragged something into the woods."

The stench got stronger as they approached, Svent in the lead, ducking under low-hanging branches. Eventually, Svent stopped and retched, pointing at something in front of her.

"Goordev and Hakusa," she said between gasps. "Must be dead for almost four days."

Weston came around her and stopped, then with a suddenness that surprised both of them, she vomited at the sight of the decomposing and partially eaten bodies. Once she'd emptied her stomach and was reduced to dry heaves, Weston backed away from the corpses and turned, heading out of the woods and returning to the open area around the house. Svent, breathing heavily through the mouth, followed her.

"That was disgusting beyond belief," Weston finally said once she regained control of herself. "I'm going to have fucking nightmares for weeks."

"At least we know what happened. The target must have gotten the jump on them," Svent replied in a steady voice. "I saw evidence of blaster entry holes in both torsos. And there's something that really enjoys decomposing human flesh in the area. Did you see the chunks missing?"

"Aw, come on." Weston retched again. "Don't be a sicko."

Svent gave her a wintry smile.

"I can't help it if you're a little sensitive, now can I? What next?"

"I'm sure as hell not going near those bodies again. Let's call it into the field office and let the boss decide."

"He'll want the local crime scene investigators to come and take a look, that's for sure. Let me tell him." She fished her communicator from a tunic pocket and established a satellite link with the office in Petras.

Svent spent a few moments updating the agent in charge, then closed the link.

"He wants us to stay until CSI arrives."

"Meanwhile, the target is on the loose and getting farther and farther away."

She shrugged.

"We won't find any traces of Victor Devaine. He probably took a ship and is in Petras by now, under a new identity and headed for orbit and an outward-bound starship."

Weston gave her a hard glance.

"Keep on being cheerful and optimistic, Beth."

"What can I say? I'm a realist, and realistically, our friend Admiral (retired) Farrin Norum slipped the noose."

"At the very least, we should put out a BOLO on him, last seen as Devaine, probably going under a different name with a modified appearance."

"I'll set up the BOLO. There's only so much he can do to disguise himself anyway."

While Svent returned to her communicator, Weston walked around the property, wishing she had a mint to take away the sour taste of vomit still lingering in the back of her mouth.

She finally sat in their car, kicked her seat back, and closed her eyes. Svent joined her ten minutes later, and they silently waited for the Mykonos Police CSI team to show up. When the investigators finally arrived three hours later, the sun was already low on the horizon, and Svent quickly showed them the bodies before returning to their vehicle.

"Let's go."

"We won't make it back to Petras tonight," Weston said, engaging the power plant.

"It doesn't matter. A hotel in Thera with a bar is what we need right now. I could murder a tall glass of whiskey."

The car lifted off, and Weston pointed it back at the coast and Thera, where they landed fifteen minutes later, returning the vehicle to the rental office before heading to the Thera Arms hotel, where they each took a room for the night. They'd be on the first suborbital shuttle out in the morning, but both needed several drinks in the meantime. The stronger, the better.

"The boss is going to be really unhappy if Norum gets away clean," Weston said, staring into her glass, swirling the vodka tonic around. "Really unhappy, and you know what that means."

Svent shrugged.

"The idiots who let him escape are dead. We're just the insurance."

"And if he's looking for scapegoats, we'll be it since we're the next closest."

She took a healthy swig of her whiskey and soda.

"No point in borrowing worries, Rey. What happens will happen unless you want to leg it like Norum and vanish to some god-forsaken planet on the fringes of civilization."

"Pass. I'll take my chances with the boss not crapping over us."

They sat in a corner of the Thera Arms bar, far from prying ears, but still had their jammers active. The large space facing the street on the ground floor was paneled in dark wood or a reasonable facsimile thereof, but the tables were gleaming copper, as was the bar itself. A mirror ran the length of the room behind it, fronted by glass shelves holding bottles of every description.

"You know Goordev and Hakusa were rank amateurs, right? Lannion City cops who, when they'd been told they had no chances of advancement, joined the LOI and quickly shifted to the Special Operations Division. They had no business going up against a forty-year veteran of the Navy like Norum. You and I would have done better with our eyes closed."

"Which is why we work for a field office rather than Special Ops?" Weston shot her colleague a sardonic gaze. "I don't know about you, but I figured the LOI would give me a nice little job after I did my twenty-five years in Defense Force Security. No wet work, no skirting the legalities for political purposes, just interstellar law enforcement."

Svent let out a bitter laugh.

"And weren't you disappointed to find out even us field office grunts are mired in politics more than law enforcement?"

"Yep." Weston took a big gulp of her drink. "I'm seriously thinking of leaving the LOI. I just can't reconcile myself to some of the unethical crap we do for a living."

"Unethical? Try downright criminal at times. But they won't let you go, Rey. The LOI is like organized crime — once you're in, you're in for life."

Weston snorted.

"It can't be that bad."

"Probably not. But it feels like that sometimes." Svent downed the rest of her drink, then tapped the screen embedded in the middle of their table to order another. "Mind you, I did thirty in the Navy before succumbing to the allure of LOI recruiting and feel dirty most of the time these days. I mean, the tricks we pulled on the Mykonos government to bring them in line with the president's will were something else."

"Ha! Tricks. Nice way to put it. Except those tricks were more in the line of extortion." Weston took another gulp. "Dear LOI. The president's own Praetorian Guard. Too bad we don't have snazzy uniforms to go with the job."

"You mean silver-trimmed black, like the old Imperial Guards Corps created by Stichus Ruggero, the first of the Mad Emperors?"

Weston gave her a speculative look through narrowed eyes.

"Do you think Juska is the first of the mad presidents, perchance?"

"More like the first of the dishonestly elected presidents. Rumor has it he's planning to push through a constitutional amendment removing term limits for elected officials."

"Ouch." Weston winced. "If he makes it a reality, I can name a lot of senators who'll hang on to their seats until the day they die, getting richer every year they remain in office."

"A lot? Try most. Bastards have become inbred, with veritable dynasties holding on to seats for the same families over the last few terms. Removing term limits will simply ensure that those families own their seats outright."

"And Derik Juska owns the presidency."

"Yep." Svent raised her glass in a mock salute. "Here's to history repeating. I wish it was first as a tragedy, then as a farce, but I think this won't end well for the Republic. Once the political elite twist the rules to favor themselves rather than the electorate, it's pretty much over. Let me ask you something, though. You're not a Lyonesse First idiot, right?"

"Do I seem retarded? Of course not. But that's an opinion I keep to myself nowadays. You?"

"Not in a million years."

Weston drained her glass. "You want another one?"

"Is Derik Juska a slimeball?"

"Two more coming right up."

—27—

Just after twenty hundred hours, Norum left the inn via the back way, his duffel slung over his shoulder, and headed deeper into the seedy part of Petras, looking for likely taverns.

The planet had been re-colonized over a hundred years earlier, and the inhabitants had ample time to create a part of Petras that was more or less dominated by an underworld of sorts. Norum figured he'd find a good ID forger somewhere in the area, one who had the contacts to insert the new identity into the Mykonos databases, making it virtually unimpeachable. At least on this world.

Not sure where to begin, he entered the first place he came across and sat at the bar, letting the noise of many conversations wash over him. He looked around in the dim light, but faces were indistinct while shadowed eyes kept moving, many of them passing over him, the newcomer.

Norum ordered a beer from the human bartender, a middle-aged man with black hair and a black beard, both liberally shot with silver, and slipped him a cred chip when he placed the foaming mug down. After taking a long sip, Norum glanced around the room again, trying to identify the clientele by their clothing and demeanor. He figured they were primarily working class, with a few shifty characters among them, and wondered whether he'd find a lead to a forger here.

After a while, he dug another cred chip from his pocket, a twenty, and slowly tapped it against the copper bar top until the bartender approached him, one eyebrow cocked in question. Norum made a gesture asking him to lean over, and he did.

"I've lost my ID credentials and was wondering whether you knew someone who could do up a new set for me?"

The man's eyes shifted from the cred chip to Norum, and he shrugged.

"No idea, my friend."

He walked away, and Norum finished his beer, picked up his duffel, and stepped back into the humid night air. After trying four more taverns, he entered the least salubrious of them, the Frond & Fever, where the patrons mostly didn't look like honest, hard-working citizens, and he sat at the bar there, too, ordering a beer. When it arrived, he asked the bartender — a blowzy blonde woman of indeterminate years this time — the same question while playing with a forty-cred chip.

She briefly glanced at the chip, looked over his shoulder, then back at him, saying in a raspy voice, "Maybe I do. But what tells me you're not some LOI or Petras Police simp looking for trouble?"

Norum shrugged.

"Nothing, I guess."

The woman studied him for a moment, then gestured to someone across the room. Within seconds, a scruffy little man in his late fifties slipped on a barstool next to Norum.

"You summoned me, oh Delightful Deedra?"

She jerked her chin at Norum.

"This gent has lost his ID and is looking for a replacement."

He turned to the retired admiral.

"Is that so? And why aren't you going to the authorities for new credentials?"

"Let's just say they won't find my new identity in their database and leave it at that." Norum pushed the forty-cred chip toward Deedra, who made it disappear almost as if by magic.

"Ah." The man nodded knowingly. "You're an illegal, are you?"

"Something like that."

"You got old credentials?"

"Yes."

He held out his hand.

"Let's take a look at them."

Norum fished the Victor Devaine ID from his inner tunic pocket and handed it over. The man studied it intently for a minute, then looked up at him.

"Nicely crafted. I don't recognize the work, though."

"I got it on Lyonesse."

The man handed the credentials back.

"So, you're on the lam from the capital. Why change now? That ID must be in the Mykonos database."

"I've been made and need to disappear again."

"Care to tell me who you really are?"

Norum grinned at him and said, in an incredulous tone, "No."

A cackle of laughter erupted, and the man stuck out his hand.

"I'm Ahmed, by the way."

Norum took it, and they shook.

"A pleasure."

"Ten thousand."

"Beg your pardon?"

"It'll be ten thousand creds for a new ID, guaranteed to be in the Mykonos database. I presume you have that kind of money since you're looking to replace the old credentials for which you probably paid the same, if not more."

"Sure. Ten grand it is. How do you want to proceed?"

"In good time. Come back here tomorrow evening at twenty-hundred hours and bring the creds."

With that, Ahmed slid off the barstool and vanished.

Norum turned to Deedra.

"Any recommendations on a place to stay? Anonymous, it goes without saying."

"Try the Grandfell Arms next door. They don't ask for a name, just payment up front."

***

"See, if I were Norum, I'd obtain a new identity and then scarper," Rey Weston said as she and Beth Svent walked across the Petras spaceport after disembarking from the suborbital shuttle shortly after noon the next day. "But a good one that'll hold up long enough to get him off Mykonos, now that's the problem."

"Considering Norum is probably in Petras and has been for the last day or two, he'll be looking for someone around here. Who do we know in the local police that could point us at the best forgers in town?"

Weston and Svent exited the terminal and looked for a taxi while thinking about the question.

"I figure we can start with Williams. If she doesn't know, she'll give us the right name." An automated taxi broke from the ranks as Svent raised her arm and stopped in front of them.

"Okay. Williams it is."

They climbed aboard, and Weston gave the address of the LOI field office.

Once there, Weston called Staff Sergeant Quinn Williams of the Petras Police's Major Crimes Division and reached her right away.

"Hey, I heard about your two agents who bought it on Karinth. Tough to take," Williams said the moment she accepted the link. "You have my condolences."

Weston shrugged.

"They were HQ assholes, so no great loss to us. The reason I'm calling is because the guy who did it is probably in Petras by now and shopping around for a new identity. You wouldn't know of any good forgers he might tap?"

Williams smiled at her.

"As a matter of fact, I do." She rattled off four names. "If I had my druthers, I'd go with Ahmed Nouri or whatever he uses as a last name these days. He's not only the best of the bunch but also the most approachable. He has a sixth sense for cops, almost like a Void Sister's talent, so he doesn't mind talking to people looking for what he's offering. The others tend to vet potential customers a lot more using cutouts."

"Why is he still operating if you know so much about his business?"

Williams let out a chuckle.

"That's because we've never been able to pin anything on him. His sixth sense sees to that. He's never caught with his gear, and his contacts within the local administration are impossible to find because he pays them well. Do you know what name your perp is under? Because I'm assuming he's not advertising his real identity."

"He's known as Victor Devaine. We put a BOLO out on him yesterday, but he'll have changed his appearance and be hanging out in places where they don't want your name, let alone your ID."

"You can try Ahmed, but I don't think he'll be talking about any of his clients.

"Not voluntarily, no. Where does he hang out?"

"In a few places." She named them. "But mostly the Frond & Fever Tavern."

"Thanks for the tips, Quinn. I owe you one. Can you give me a quick description of this Ahmed character?"

"Sure."

When she was done, Weston said goodbye and cut the link. She then sat back and looked at Svent.

"How would you like to go bar hopping tonight?"

"I wouldn't particularly. Those bars named by Williams aren't in the pleasant part of town."

"Which is why we won't dress for success like the good little coppers we are. We'll wear downmarket togs."

Svent wrinkled her nose.

"How downmarket?"

Weston beamed at her.

"Very."

***

That evening, Norum returned to the tavern and was quickly waved into a back room by Deedra. There, he found Ahmed with a closed case, sitting on a bare wooden table in the center of the space. Boxes lined the windowless walls, most of them dusty, their contents unidentifiable, though the lighting was harsh and outlined a second door opposite the one he'd come through.

Ahmed bowed his head.

"Welcome, welcome."

"I have the creds if you're ready."

"Let's see them."

Norum pulled a set of cred chips from his pocket and placed them on the table. "Ten thousand."

Ahmed quickly counted them, then nodded.

"As agreed."

He opened the case and pulled out a scanner.

"You're about to become Ian Harter, a native of Mykonos born sixty-one years ago. Let me take your biometric data."

"And what'll happen to Victor Devaine's biometrics? Doesn't Mykonos run regular checks of the database to detect duplications?"

"When I slip Ian Harter in, I'll change Devaine's. And no, I won't tell you how I get access. Now stand still and keep your eyes open."

Ahmed held the scanner up to Norum's face, taking a retina imprint and his picture, then scanned the rest of his body. After a bit, he stared at the machine's display and grunted.

"It'll do." He connected the scanner to another instrument in the case and waited. After a minute, the black box extruded a small card bearing Norum's face with the name Ian Harter and a fake birthday. Ahmed handed the card to Norum.

"There you go, my good sir. The embedded chip has your biometrics, which will be in the Mykonos database by tomorrow morning, so don't use it until then."

Norum examined the ID closely but couldn't spot any differences from those issued by the government and said so.

"Of course," Ahmed replied. "I'm one of the best forgers in this star system."

"Do you forge things other than credentials?"

A smile appeared on the man's narrow face.

"Yes, and I'm not telling you what they are. I believe this concludes our business." He closed his case and picked it up. "A pleasure, Mister Harter."

Then, Ahmed left the room via the other door, presumably leading to a back entrance. Moments later, Deedra appeared.

"Done? How about a beer on the house?"

"Sure." He followed her back into the taproom.

And tomorrow, he would look for a starship headed to the far frontiers.

—28—

Norum raised the foaming mug to his lips when a tall, muscular woman with long blond hair leaned against the bar beside him. A second, thinner woman with short brown hair, brown eyes, and a narrow face joined her moments later. Both wore casual attire, the kind people typically wear on weekends while doing chores around the house.

The first woman attracted Deedra's attention, and she approached them.

"What can I get you?"

"Two beers and some information."

"Right. Two beers coming up." Deedra filled a pair of mugs and placed them in front of the woman and her companion. "Now, what do you want to know?"

The woman tossed a cred chip on the bar, then raised her mug for a sip.

"Nice. We're looking for a guy who goes by the name Ahmed Nouri."

Deedra's gaze hardened.

"Why?"

"We need some information from him."

"Well, he isn't here right now."

"Where can we find him?"

A shrug.

"No idea."

"Ever heard of a guy called Victor Devaine?"

Norum, startled, felt his heart beat faster as he kept his eyes on his beer. Deedra must have glimpsed the name on his previous ID when Ahmed examined it, but she didn't react.

"Nope. You cops or something, with your questions?"

The woman smiled.

"Or something. We're looking for this Devaine guy and figure Ahmed may have given him a new identity."

Lyonesse Office of Inquiry, Norum thought. The backup to the team he'd killed.

"I can't help you with that, sorry."

She picked up the cred chip and walked away, not even glancing at Norum, who wondered whether he should simply drain his mug and leave now or wait for the two LOI agents to go.

The woman nudged Norum.

"Hey, buddy. You wouldn't happen to know where Ahmed is?"

Norum shook his head, eyes still on his beer.

"No. Sorry."

"You a regular here?"

"Yep."

"Can you tell me whether Ahmed is here regularly, and if so, when?"

"Dunno. He's here most evenings, leastwise whenever I'm in. But he doesn't keep to a schedule."

"But not tonight."

Norum shrugged.

"If he ain't here, then he ain't."

"Can you tell me where we might find him?"

"No. It's not like we're friends or anything. Not even nodding acquaintances. I know who he is. He doesn't know me from squat."

The woman raised a hand to signal Deedra.

"Give this guy another of what he's drinking."

She turned to Norum again.

"Thanks."

After paying for the beer, she and her companion took their drinks and headed for a vacant table in one corner, evidently willing to wait for Ahmed. But Norum doubted the forger would reappear in the Frond & Fever that evening. He finished the second beer, picked up his duffel bag, and left the tavern after a wave at Deedra, knowing he'd never return.

***

"Funny that," Weston said, staring at the door that had just closed on the man with whom she'd spoken at the bar. "Why would a regular carry a big old bag that looks like it contains everything he owns?"

"Because he's homeless?" Svent replied with a shrug. "He certainly looked a bit on the rough side."

"No. Homeless folk don't hang out in bars, not even dives like this one." Weston's eyes narrowed. She climbed to her feet and headed for Deedra.

"Excuse me, but the man who I bought a beer, what's his name?"

"Ian Harter."

"He says he's a regular here."

"Sure." Deedra nodded.

"Does he always carry a duffel bag like he did tonight?"

She made a face.

"Not that I notice. Maybe he's between flop houses."

"Thanks." Weston returned to her table and sat with a sigh. "You know what, Beth? I'm not even sure I want to be doing this. Admiral Norum was a great Chief of the Defense Staff, an honest man who had his head screwed on straight and his heart in the right place."

"He killed two men, LOI agents."

"Special ops assholes whose opinion of themselves was way higher than anything supported by reality. Besides, Norum was acting in self-defense. They were there to kill him."

Svent made a face.

"Granted. But we still have a mission."

"And I'm questioning it. Oh, not the legality. Murder is illegal as hell, even if it's done on the orders of the government."

"It's not really murder if you do it on the government's orders. More like an extra-judicial execution."

"Potato, potahto." She took a sip of her beer, then speared Svent with her gaze. "Tell me you'd kill Admiral Norum in cold blood. Go ahead."

Svent met Weston's eyes, then looked at the scarred tabletop.

"I couldn't. I'm not a Special ops jerk. Damn it, I'm a cop, not a killer."

"So, what do we do? They assigned us as backups for Goordev and Hakusa. If we don't get Norum, our ass is grass as far as HQ is concerned."

"A little over dramatic, no? We'll get a reprimand and move on to other things."

"You think? How about the bosses don't want two mooks wandering around knowing they were ordered to murder a retired CDS? At least if we succeed, we've got every reason to keep our mouths shut. If we don't do it, we're a liability."

Svent looked up at Weston.

"Oops."

"Yeah, oops indeed." She took another swig of her drink. "So, to repeat, what do we do?"

"Is it wrong for me to wish Goordev and Hakusa had succeeded? Then, we would have never discovered that Admiral Norum was a target, let alone been assigned to eliminate him.

"Or that the field office read another team into the operation and sent them in our stead." Weston shrugged. "It doesn't matter. We're in it up to our necks. If you're willing to kill Norum, then let's find him and do so. Otherwise, we might start thinking about taking early retirement from the LOI and disappearing ourselves."

Svent let out a bark of bitter laughter.

"I'm not willing to murder a man just because the government wants him gone. But neither am I willing to simply disappear."

"The way I see it, we either vanish on our own, or the LOI makes us vanish. Or we keep looking for Norum, and when we find him…" Weston made a cutting gesture across her throat.

"Let's keep looking for Norum and figure out what to do when we find him." When Weston made to protest, Svent raised one hand. "Yeah, it's temporizing, but could be we'll figure something out in the meantime."

"Okay." Weston drained her mug. "Do you want to wait around for Ahmed or call it a night?"

"Let's go. We can always return tomorrow." Svent also finished her beer, and a thoughtful Deedra watched them leave the tavern.

Cops looking for Ahmed wasn't unusual, but they never found him, at least not in the Frond & Fever.

***

Norum checked into a slightly better hotel than the Grandfell Arms, but still in the wrong part of Petras, and after settling in, he searched for an outbound ship using his communicator. Unfortunately, there were none in orbit or on the ground at the moment, and the only ones due in the next week were headed for Yotai, Arietis, and Lyonesse, the opposite direction of where he wanted to go. Was the universe sending him a subtle hint that he shouldn't run away from his troubles but toward them?

To do what? President Juska's own law enforcement arm was targeting him. He'd be finished the moment he raised his head above the masses. Besides, Juska's takeover of the government was proceeding with no serious objections from the citizenry or their elected representatives. In fact, many of them were cheering him on as he destroyed over two hundred years of democracy in the name of Lyonesse First zealotry.

No, there was nothing to be gained by heading back to Lyonesse and attempting to foment opposition. He wouldn't last more than a few days if that. Since he was slated for murder by the LOI a year ago and stayed alive this long by hiding, it was a given that other potential opposition members had been killed by now.

His choices were stark. Find another world to settle on and pray they wouldn't discover him again or leave the Republic altogether, meaning head for the Wyvern Hegemony and request political asylum. But in the meantime, he had to keep a low profile. Who knew what kind of persuasiveness the LOI agents he'd met in the Frond & Fever could exercise on Ahmed and obtain Norum's new identity.

And so, he hunkered down in the Hyan Hotel, opting to pay by the week, leaving only for mealtimes and in the evenings to prowl the surrounding pubs. He was mainly looking for the two obvious LOI agents interested in Ahmed and a bit of time around other human beings. He found the former quickly. Or rather, they found him.

Norum sat at the bar of the Probity Pub, a rundown establishment on the fringes of Petras' rough quarter, nursing his beer, when the agents entered. They scanned the room like the pros they were, and the blonde woman's eyes rested on him, recognition writ large in the mirror over the bar, reflecting both Norum's face and those of the LOI operatives.

They approached Norum, and the blond slapped him on the shoulder. "Ian Harter, isn't it?"

"Who wants to know?"

"You're not carrying the duffel with everything you own tonight."

"Could be I've stored it in the back room. You got my name. What the hell are yours, chum?" Norum asked, their eyes meeting in the mirror.

"I'm Rey Weston, and this is Beth Svent." She jerked her thumb at the other woman.

"Well, Rey, I'm a solitary man, so I'd be thrilled if you fucked off."

Norum's gaze turned back to the bottom of his beer mug, fearful they might recognize him even through his disguise or at least get a vague impression of familiarity that might make them dig further.

"You wouldn't happen to have seen Ahmed Nouri, the forger, recently, would you?"

"Nope."

Norum glanced up to see Weston studying him intently, a slight frown creasing her forehead.

"You still here? I thought I said I enjoyed being alone."

"It's a free Republic."

"Not so much anymore."

The words were out before Norum realized he sounded like a malcontent, just the sort who'd attract the Lyonesse Office of Inquiry's attention. But he'd played his hand and might as well go with it.

"What do you mean?" Weston asked absently as she nodded at the bartender, and then the beer pulls, raising three fingers.

"That since Derik Juska became president, the Republic ain't so free anymore. And it's getting less free by the day, what with the damned LOI sticking its fingers into all sorts of stuff that used to be private. But what do I know?" Norum shrugged and took a sip of his beer. "I'm just an unemployed drifter."

"Not a fan, are you?"

"Of what? The president? No. Only complete idiots support the direction Juska's taking our once blessed Republic." Norum drained his mug. "And now, if you'll excuse me."

He made to stand just as the bartender shoved three glasses of beer in front of Weston, who handed one to Svent and pushed the other toward Norum.

“Here, pal. A little something to make up for my annoying you.” Weston squinted at Norum as she pulled her right hand from her trouser pocket and clapped a hand on the latter’s shoulder. “It’s interesting. The more I look at you, the more I’m reminded of someone, but I can’t remember who.”

“I’ve often been told I got a pretty common face.” Norum took the glass of beer and drank deeply from it as he shrugged off Weston’s hand. “Thanks for the drink. But it won’t make me like you any better.”

Once he’d emptied the glass, Norum stood and left the pub without another word. Weston watched him leave, a thoughtful air on her face.

She turned to Svent.

“That man definitely reminds me of someone, and I’ll wager the face he’s wearing isn’t his own. Let’s grab something to eat while we’re here.”

Both sat in a booth at the back of the pub, enjoying their beers and were soon eating simple meals that were tolerably tasty — pea soup and ham sandwiches.

“You got him?” Svent asked as Weston stared at her communicator.

“Yeah. Looks like he’s stopped. Could be where he’s holed up.”

Weston had stuck a miniature quasi-invisible tracking device to Norum’s shoulder when she slapped it, figuring to keep track of the vaguely familiar man. Since this Ian Harter reminded Weston of someone, it would eventually come to her. Of that, she was sure.

“Want to go check tonight?”

"We should in passing. Then we'll keep a low-level lookout for him. At least until I decide he's no longer worth watching."

Weston polished off her plate, finished her beer, and then waited for Svent to do likewise. When she was done, both stood and left the pub. Weston doubted they'd ever return. Once outside, she consulted her communicator's virtual display and nodded to the right.

"He went that way."

They walked along a dimly lit street, Weston glancing discretely from time to time at the communicator she loosely held in her left hand and eventually passed in front of a tired-looking hotel. It seemed like a relic of the Empire's fall, even though no structures survived the Retribution Fleet in Petras, and she said, without missing a step, "Harter is in this rattrap."

"Noted."

Neither gave the hotel so much as a sideways look and soon they turned a street corner and vanished into the night.

—29—

"I'm willing to bet Ian Harter isn't the man's real name," Weston said by way of greeting early the next day when she entered the office she shared with Svent in the Petras LOI headquarters.

"Good morning to you, too." Svent smirked at her. "Aren't you getting a little obsessed with the man?"

"I keep repeating — he reminds me of someone, and until I figure that out, he'll be on my mind." Weston dropped in her chair across from the wide desk they shared. "Before going to sleep last night, I stared at the image we took of him for a while and I'm getting convinced I remember him from somewhere. He's wearing a disguise, that's almost certain. Time to do an in-depth search on Harter, Ian, and see what we come up with."

"Okay." Svent called up a virtual display and entered the name. A few moments later, she said, "There are three Harter, Ian, in the Mykonos database, including our guy. According to it, he's a

Petras native in his early sixties, of no fixed address, with no family. Not much else about him in the database."

"When was the last update to his record?"

"A few years ago, according to the timestamp, but those can easily be falsified."

Weston tapped the desktop with her fingertips, frowning.

"Pull up Devaine, Victor, and show me both faces side-by-side. Then, compare his biometrics to Harter's."

"Do you believe Harter is Norum?"

"Could be. He made us as LOI agents, that's for sure."

Devaine and Harter's faces appeared in midair over the desk, and Weston studied them, her frown deepening.

"The biometrics are different," Svent said. "Not by much, but enough to mark them as separate identities."

"Those can be faked as well. Still, compare both to Norum's."

After a bit, Svent shook her head.

"Different as well, but like you said, the entries in the database can be faked."

"Sure. Yet I'm willing to bet that if we hauled Harter in and subjected him to a full scan, we'd find his actual biometrics don't exactly mirror what's in the database. They'll match at the superficial level, enough to pass standard checks, but that's it."

"We have no reason to arrest him and subject him to a full scan."

"We're the LOI and don't need a reason, so long as we release him within twenty-four hours with our excuses. Heck, we don't even need to do that since he's a drifter with no known family. We could make him disappear if we wanted to." Weston grimaced. "Not that I'm considering such gross abuse of our powers. But some in the office would."

"Many would," Svent replied in a soft tone. "Judging by the company we're keeping these days."

"Yeah. More's the pity. Quietly resigning and heading off to parts unknown is sounding a lot better." Weston glanced at the faces floating above the desk. "They could be related for all we know. There are enough points of similarity to indicate that they are not complete strangers. Maybe they're even one and the same.

"Meaning we definitely want to think about it before bringing him in because the moment we do that, we'll lose control over the investigation, and we both know what'll happen, especially if he is Norum."

"Yeah. They'll order us to execute him. And doing so is something I cannot wrap my head around."

"Neither can I."

Weston gave her partner a helpless shrug.

"We need to make up our minds soon."

"I believe mine is already made up. I'd rather chuck this job and vanish than kill an innocent man in cold blood."

"What about your pension?"

"Already cashed it in. You?"

"Same." Weston tapped the desktop again. "Okay, we don't take Harter in. But I'd still like to find out who he is."

"How about we ask him?"

A bark of laughter escaped Weston's throat.

"Just like that?"

"Yep. Just like that. If he isn't, we make our way out to the stars on the next available ship using false IDs."

"And if he is?"

"We take him with us. Or if he has an escape plan, he takes us with him."

Weston shook her head.

"I can't believe we're talking about deserting."

"We'd simply be abandoning our posts, which carries no penalties other than forfeiture of pay and allowances. The LOI isn't under military discipline."

"Except because of what we know, they'll go after us if we run."

"Human space is big, and the LOI isn't all-seeing and all-knowing. If you want proof, look at how long it's been taking to find one man who doesn't want to be found."

"True. So, do we visit Harter?"

"We have nothing better on offer." Weston stood. "Let's go."

They easily tracked their quarry to a dingy diner close to his hotel. He was alone in a booth nursing a cup of tea, and before he could react, they slipped in with him, one on each side.

"Hey, Ian. How are they hanging?" Weston gave Norum a friendly grin. "You remember my colleague, Beth?"

Norum gave her a wary look.

"What do you want? I haven't seen Ahmed and still don't know this Devine guy."

"It's Devaine, actually. But we're not here to ask about them." The grin widened. "We're here to talk about you, my friend."

"I'm not interested."

"But we are, and since we carry LOI credentials, it might be wise for you to pay attention."

"Take your LOI credentials and shove them down a black hole." Norum raised the mug of tea to his lips, glad his hand remained steady.

"I don't get your hostility, Ian. I merely want a friendly talk about identities and escape routes."

Norum's eyes hardened.

"I don't, so go away."

"You see, we figure that behind the fake ID and disguise, you're a certain retired Navy officer who some nasty people want to terminate. And you're looking to get off Mykonos, except no ships are heading in the right direction."

"If that's what you think, why don't you take me in for enhanced interrogation?"

Weston grimaced.

"We can't because it could mean your death. Beth and I don't really fit in with most LOI agents — we have morals, ethics, and a sense of honor. We're former career Defense Force personnel who thought the LOI might make an interesting post-military career. Considering the degree of lawlessness in how the agency carries out President Juska's directives, we're now looking at other career choices. Except since we were read into the operation to terminate the retired Navy officer I mentioned, we can't quit without carrying it out. Otherwise, we know about it, but the agency has no leverage over us. Yet we don't want to murder an innocent man in cold blood."

Norum glanced at Weston with a perfectly blank expression.

"I'd say you're in a bad position."

"Yeah. We discovered having a conscience instead of being a sociopath isn't conducive to a long life serving the Republic as an LOI agent." Weston met Norum's eyes. "So, we wondered whether the retired Navy officer might have an escape plan and would let us tag along. We can both procure fake IDs that'll pass muster and cashed out our pensions so we can live off unmarked cred chips for a long time."

Norum saw no deception in Weston's gaze. Yet he'd survived this long by being suspicious of everyone and everything.

"You can always ask your retired spacer whenever you meet him."

Weston took a stab.

"We're asking you, Admiral Norum."

The man's eyes narrowed in annoyance just enough to be noticeable, and Weston was convinced she was right.

"I'm not sure why you assume that's who I am, but you're mistaken."

"Fair enough. But I'd like to point out we can be useful to anyone escaping Mykonos for a destination far from the Republic's core." Weston glanced at Svent. "Let's go, Beth. Our friend here can mull things over and decide whether to trust us."

They stood, and Weston said, "We'll find you in a few days."

Then, they left the diner, and a rather pensive Norum stared at the door. He was sure Weston had been telling the unvarnished truth. There was also a soothsayer streak in his family lineage, going all the way back to his illustrious forbear Marta Norum.

But what to do with Weston's declarations? Norum had been traveling alone for the last five years, and by now, he preferred not to rely on anyone. He emptied his tea mug and held it up, a signal to the server that he wanted another.

***

"That was Norum for sure," Weston said once they were back on the street. "I finally recognized his face beneath the disguise. Besides, he was too cool by half for a civilian drifter."

"You realize he could always shop us to our bosses for having called the LOI a den of sociopaths we're keen on leaving at the next opportunity. Or words to that effect."

Weston shrugged.

"Even if he is Ian Harter, of no fixed address, he'll stay a million klicks away from the agency. Guys like him avoid the authorities like the plague. Besides, what proof would he have? No, we'll let him stew for a while."

They returned to the office in silence, each lost in their own thoughts.

"How do you propose we vanish?" Svent asked once they were behind closed doors.

"I figure we tell the boss we're hot on Norum's tail and need to go undercover so we have plausible deniability when we finally whack him."

Svent smiled as she raised both eyebrows.

"Sneaky. I like it."

"And then, weeks, maybe even months later, when he realizes he hasn't heard from us ever since we went undercover, we're hundreds of light years away, living under new identities."

"Okay. Agreed. The only remaining question is, do we keep on trying to convince Norum we're the good guys, or do we strike out on our own?"

"We keep trying with Norum. He's a really smart guy — otherwise, he'd never have become Chief of the Defense Staff — and he has plenty of experience vanishing. I'd say right now, he has a plan and is merely waiting for a ship headed in the right direction. Besides, I figure we've decided to protect him, right?"

Svent made a face.

"I suppose so. It's better than trying to murder him."

"Aye, that it is. In spades."

They fell silent and eventually busied themselves with routine matters until the workstation let out a soft bleep. Svent glanced at its virtual display.

"An unscheduled ship dropped out at the heliopause from Yotai bound for Hatshepsut. I set up a search program to warn me of anything headed outward from the Coalsack, just in case."

"In case of what? That Norum might jump on it, or that we would?" Weston cocked an ironic eyebrow at her. "Let's find him again and let him know. That ship will be here in twelve hours, so there's no time to lose."

"What about our undercover IDs? It'll take longer than that to get them."

"If we go the private route. But needs must when the devil drives. We'll get them from the quartermaster after I brief the boss on our plan. That'll restrict those aware of them to him, the QM, and no one else. And we'll make it somewhere we can get new IDs well before they twig."

—30—

Rey Weston, now carrying the identity of a woman named Gail Benett, and Beth Svent, whose credentials had her as Vera Jakkari, found Norum in a different diner from the one they'd visited earlier. He was eating his evening meal in a quiet corner booth and put down his fork when he saw them approach.

"How is it you always seem to know where I am?"

Weston and Svent slipped into the booth with him, the former smiling.

"Let's just say we have an instinct for tracking people."

"Or you planted something on me. What do you want now? Twice in one day, it must be urgent." Norum picked up his fork again, speared a chunk of chicken breast in a sticky orange sauce, and popped it in his mouth.

"There's an unscheduled ship inbound. It's arriving from Yotai and is headed for the frontier — terminus at Hatshepsut. It'll land at the Petras spaceport early tomorrow morning. We plan on being aboard, under new identities." Weston briefly explained their scheme. "Are you coming with us, Admiral?"

Norum eyed her.

"What's the ship called?"

"The *Dragon's Hoard.* She's an independent, a free trader."

"I know her — a former Navy corvette that used to be named *Teekon* sold to the private sector and refitted after being decommissioned. She's old but solid and goes places the liners don't."

"That's good to know. Look, you need to leave Mykonos and head for someplace where you can simply vanish. So do we. While we're working undercover, we can do things to help you that no one else can."

"How about if I decide to head for the Hegemony?"

Weston shrugged.

"We can do that. The Republic is turning into something I don't recognize anymore. At least if we head for the Hegemony, we won't have to live under assumed names for the rest of our lives, constantly looking over our shoulders. Our bosses will eventually figure out we've run, and they might take exception to that, considering what we know about the order to have you terminated."

Norum knew instinctively, once again, that Weston was telling the truth.

The latter withdrew her undercover credentials and showed them to Norum.

"There, that's the name I'll be traveling under. These are as good as the real thing, and only my boss and the field office quartermaster know this is me. Beth has the same. Basically, we can go anywhere in the Republic, no questions asked. So, what do you say?"

"Tomorrow in the wee hours at the spaceport?" Norum cocked an eyebrow at Weston. "Okay. I'll take my chances with you two. If you were going to arrest me, you wouldn't have gone through all this. But I'm not Farrin Norum." He gave Weston and Svent a hard glare. "I'm Ian Harter. Understood?"

Both nodded. "Understood."

"Then I suggest you go stuff your lives into a single kit bag and wish whatever doesn't fit a fond farewell. Ask me how I know. Or better yet, don't. See you in the morning." Norum resumed eating, eyes on his plate. "Oh, and we'll meet for the first time aboard the ship."

After a brief glance at each other, sensing they'd just been dismissed, Weston and Svent stood and left the diner without speaking another word.

***

A pink band outlined the hills east of Petras the following morning when an autotaxi deposited Norum in front of the spaceport terminal. He climbed out, hoisted his kitbag over his shoulder, and entered the sprawling two-story structure. Though brightly lit, it felt abandoned at this hour of the day, and he briefly stopped inside the door and oriented himself.

He spotted the automatic terminals and went up to one. There, he entered the name *Dragon's Hoard* and found she still had open berths. He produced his Ian Harter credentials to reserve one. The biometric scan quickly checked and accepted them. He then fed several unmarked cred chips he carried into the slot provided to pay for it. In return, the machine spat out a small card that provided instructions on where she was docked. He would present the card at the main airlock as proof of purchase.

Norum made his way down the empty concourse, not meeting any other living soul along the way. But he found *Dragon's Hoard* in docking bay E14 as advertised, her main airlock connected to the terminal by a short, flexible tube. He could see activity on her other side and glimpsed containers being loaded into her cargo bays.

A middle-aged woman of average height with short gray hair stood on the terminal side of the boarding tube, a bored expression on her face. She wore faded gray coveralls tucked into calf-high black boots and held a small reader in her hand.

"Good morning," Norum said, giving her a pleasant smile and holding out the card.

"Mornin', sir," she replied in a raspy voice. "Thanks."

She scanned the card with her reader and nodded.

"Welcome, Mister Harter. You'll find the passenger accommodations forward of the airlock on the same deck. That'll be to your right when you get aboard. You're in cabin 9C. It's a shared space — four bunks. Two of them are already occupied by folks who came aboard fifteen minutes ago. The fourth will remain empty on the upcoming leg to Tyson's World. By the way, I'm the purser, Petty Officer Redfern, but everybody calls me Red."

"Thank you, Red."

She stepped aside and waved him into the tube.

Norum had served as an ensign aboard *Dragon's Hoard* when she was the corvette *Teekon* more than forty years earlier and quickly found his way to what had been the main accommodations block. As a civilian tramp freighter, she carried a fraction of her former naval crew and most of the cabins were now devoted to paying passengers, while her former missile and main gun compartments had been transformed into extra cargo bays.

The door to cabin 9C stood open, and he heard familiar voices coming from within. Norum entered and stopped on the threshold.

"I guess I'm joining you folks. My name's Ian Harter."

Weston, who was sprawled on one of the four beds, sat up and said, "Gail Benett."

Svent, sitting on another bed across the compartment, stood and held out her hand.

"Vera Jakkari. Where are you headed, Ian?"

"Hatshepsut. You?"

"Same. Gonna look at making our fortune on an up-and-coming new world," Weston replied. "Me and Vera, we're old pals. Known each other for longer than either of us cares to remember. Grab yourself a bunk and stand easy, Ian."

The cabin still had its standard navy configuration. Four bunks in a single layer built into the bulkhead, two on each side, sitting high off the deck, with privacy curtains and storage space both beneath and above them. A table and four chairs occupied the center, while a door at the far end led to the heads and shower. It was cozy and designed for crews on short patrols, not lengthy expeditions.

Norum dropped his kit bag on one of the two remaining bunks and shrugged off his jacket.

"Any idea where the saloon is? I wouldn't mind a cup of tea and something to eat. It's a bit early for the usual diners in town to be open, and I'm hungry."

"It's forward of where we are, just past the next airtight doors. Vera and I scouted it out when we came aboard but decided we'd wait in the cabin to see who else showed up before sitting down to breakfast."

Norum, who'd figured the crew mess had been transformed into a saloon and the wardroom into the much-reduced crew mess, nodded.

"We're it at least until the next stop, according to the purser. Unless someone else shows up at the last minute. Any idea how many passengers are aboard?"

Weston shook her head. "No, but based on what we saw in the saloon, there must be at least fifty or sixty."

Which made sense to Norum. Corvettes of *Teekon*'s class carried ninety crew members, and now that it was a lightly armed freighter, that total would be twenty at most, leaving seventy berths for passengers. Which explained why they filled the cabins to capacity or nearly so.

"Well, I'm off to the saloon. You guys coming?"

Weston climbed to her feet.

"Yep. We didn't have breakfast either. By the way, I was amazed at how easy it is to winnow down your personal possessions until everything fits in one duffel bag when you're emigrating to the outer edges of Lyonesse space."

"Traveling light is a fine thing, Gail."

The saloon was at least three-quarters full of people seated around tables, talking quietly among themselves. A buffet table at one end, with a samovar chugging away, offered standard breakfast fare — muesli, rice, various steamed or fried vegetables, eggs, ham, and other meats, along with plenty of fresh fruit.

They picked up trays, plates, cups, and utensils and helped themselves, then sat at one of the few remaining tables.

"A decent spread," Weston commented before taking an appreciative sip of the black tea she'd drawn from the samovar. "And a strong brew. I think this ship will do us."

"Since it's the only one out of Mykonos headed for the frontier, it'll have to," Norum said in a faintly sarcastic tone.

Weston raised a hand in surrender.

"True. But it's still nice that breakfast is as good as any aboard a Navy ship. Let's dig in."

They ate in silence, shoveling food into their mouths. Then, pushing his empty plate away, Norum gave Weston a curious look.

"You seem awfully chipper this morning."

"There's something liberating about leaving everything behind, isn't it Vera?"

Svent nodded. "Yep. We were meant to do it. Working for our old mob turned sour on us, and this is the only way out. Though I'll be happier once we're FTL outbound. Or rather more relaxed."

Norum let out a soft chuckle.

"Leaving your jobs is like leaving organized crime — you can only do it by disappearing. One more of the many things that organization has in common with OCGs."

A nod from Weston.

"It took us a while to figure it out, but the agency attracts the wrong sort of people. And we didn't fit. Anyway, it's the grand adventure for us now. They say travel broadens the mind, and I'm ready to have mine broadened."

They were on their second mug of tea when the public address system came to life.

"All passengers, now hear this. Liftoff is in ten minutes. The airlocks are shut and barred, so it's too late if you have a last-minute change of heart. Please proceed to your cabins and lie on your bunks. That is all."

Norum, Weston, and Svent glanced at each other as they drank the rest of their tea. They had successfully passed the first hurdle and were aboard a ship bound for the frontier, as anonymous as the rest of their fellow passengers.

—31—

Hatshepsut
Republic of Lyonesse

Currag DeCarde wasn't a happy man. The former Lyonesse ambassador to the Wyvern Hegemony glared at the recently appointed chief of staff of the Theban Defense Force — soon to become the Hatshepsut National Guard — as he bit back a sarcastic reply.

"Don't look at me like that, *Colonel*." Brigadier General Edward Estevan made DeCarde's former rank sound like an insult. Stocky and bald, with a lantern jaw, hooded dark eyes, and a silver goatee, he gave off an aura of toughness and competence. But that was an illusion, as DeCarde knew only too well.

"And how, pray tell, am I looking at you, E.E.?" The latter asked in an innocent tone, using a nickname bestowed on Estevan by troops who were none too fond of him when he was a company commander under then Lieutenant Colonel Currag DeCarde. Everyone in the 3rd Battalion, 21st Pathfinder Regiment, knew that Estevan loathed the nickname because he understood it wasn't given out of respect. On the contrary.

"You know I don't like being called E.E., Currag," Estevan growled, frowning. "And you were staring at me the same way one does at a recruit who stepped in it."

"Perhaps it's because you're about to screw things up beyond all recognition, Eddie. I know President Juska is in a hurry to consolidate his power over the Republic's far-flung star systems. But you stomping around Hatshepsut in your big boots, upsetting everyone and his dog, is going to be utterly counterproductive. Just the fact that Lyonesse imposed an offworld chief of staff on Thebes has already caused a lot of damage to our relationship with the people around here."

"That's not my problem. I've been sent here to establish the Hatshepsut National Guard, which encompasses more than just the Theban Defense Force."

DeCarde let out a humorless chuckle.

"The Thebans are the only game on this world. You don't seriously expect any of the Aksumite cities to put up functioning units, do you? What they have right now is just one step above armed mobs barely kept in check by the current bosses. They're useless and will be nothing else. If you're looking to recruit in Aksum, you'll have to start from scratch. But that's beside the point."

He sighed. Estevan should never have gone beyond the rank of major. The man simply lacked leadership abilities, intelligence, and acumen. But he was politically connected and now part of the coterie of senior officers beholden to a president whose naked ambitions they served without question.

DeCarde, on the other hand, was living in internal exile on Hatshepsut thanks to that same president stripping him of his job and reserve commission after he told the latter what he thought about cutting diplomatic ties with the Hegemony. Of course, DeCarde had already made up his mind to leave Lyonesse service and relocate far away from the capital, like his old friend Farrin Norum, when he spoke to the president.

And for the last five years, he'd been the senior adviser on military matters to the Theban government, guiding them in developing and implementing a modern defense policy and helping the Theban military leadership mature.

"What's beside the point, Currag, is you. With my arrival here, you are no longer of any use. I have my orders and will fulfill them to the best of my abilities."

DeCarde forcefully restrained himself from commenting on Estevan's skills or lack thereof as a senior officer.

"Whether I remain useful is for the Thebans to decide, Eddie. Not you. I'm an employee of the Theban government and answer to the minister of defense. And I'll go on record saying the minister and the Theban president both have their heads screwed on straight. They know what they face and are going about it the right way."

The irony of that statement didn't escape DeCarde. He'd been sent as ambassador of the Republic in Thebes before his mission changed to representing Lyonesse on Wyvern. But that job had been more than merely diplomatic. He was to act like a proconsul who'd essentially impose the Republic's will — gently, of course

— on the Thebans with the goal of pushing Hatshepsut up the technological ladder as fast as possible.

"Sure. Yet Lyonesse will set the defense policy and oversee its implementation, and the Hatshepsut National Guard will become the local arm of the Lyonesse Defense Force. There no longer is any role for you or the minister. I'm the top Ground Forces leader in this star system, and I answer to the Lyonesse Secretary of Defense."

DeCarde let his eyes slip to one side until they stared out the window at the parade ground. They were in the office Estevan had taken over on Marine Corps Base Hatshepsut, next to that of the commanding officer, 1st Battalion, 21st Pathfinder Regiment. Estevan, as a brigadier general in the Lyonesse Defense Force as well as the Theban armed forces' chief of staff, could have installed himself anywhere.

The Defense Ministry, for example, an option DeCarde would have found less objectionable than isolating himself at the heart of the Lyonesse contingent, far from the Thebans he purported to command. But that was E.E. — no sense of discernment.

"And here I thought National Guards answered to the star system's head of government unless they were federalized."

"That's no longer the case. The sole difference between them and the Army is they can't be deployed from their world of origin."

"President Juska's policies are really making it hard for worlds such as Hatshepsut to be enthusiastic about joining the Republic."

"With the Wyvern Hegemony threatening us at every turn, those policies are necessary, Currag."

DeCarde blew a raspberry, knowing Estevan's comment encapsulated what passed as the Lyonesse First movement's political philosophy.

"The Hegemony isn't a threat to anyone. They're decades behind us, a dozen or more star systems away from Hatshepsut via the wormhole network, and uninterested in fighting the Republic."

"That may be your opinion, but it's neither mine nor anyone else's back on Lyonesse. The Hegemony represents an existential threat to us."

"Spare me the Lyonesse First bullshit, Eddie. We would have been better maintaining diplomatic relations and building on the spirit of cooperation shown by Al Jecks and his Hegemony counterpart when they met in Earth orbit."

Estevan gave DeCarde a hard look as he leaned forward, hands on the edge of his desk.

"Your words are verging on treasonous, Currag. And if you spoke them to President Juska after your return from the Hegemony, I'm not surprised he fired you and terminated your reserve commission."

DeCarde let out a bark of laughter.

"Treasonous? I thought we enjoyed freedom of speech in the Republic."

"Up to a point."

"Oh, really? And what would that be?"

"When that speech can cause active harm to the Republic's interests."

"And my downplaying the Hegemony as a menace is harmful?"

"Yes, because it might induce others into underestimating them when they clearly threaten us. Speak out of turn like that in public, and you might get a visit from the Lyonesse Office of Inquiry."

A disbelieving DeCarde shook his head.

"This is beginning to sound unreal. When did the Republic turn into a police state?"

"A lot of things have changed in the last five years. You won't have noticed, buried in this backwater, but President Juska's reforms are transforming the Republic into an entity capable of challenging the Hegemony and recovering what used to be human space under the old Empire."

"And jettisoning the values upon which the Republic was founded in favor of what? A much darker version of the future than Jonas Morane could ever have envisioned for his creation?" DeCarde tilted his head to one side as he studied an increasingly irritated Estevan. "There's an ancient political philosophy dating back to the twentieth century called fascism. Ever heard of it?"

Estevan returned DeCarde's stare.

"No."

"I'm not surprised. It fell out of favor long before the Empire's founding. Briefly told, fascism is a political system marked by centralization of control under an authoritarian leader, an economy subject to stringent governmental controls, suppression of the opposition, sometimes violently, and typically a policy of belligerent nationalism. Perhaps it's being revived by Derik Juska. Think about that, Eddie. A philosophy that was suppressed over eighteen hundred years ago because it was deemed utterly unsuitable to organize human societies is rearing its ugly head in the Republic of Lyonesse, of all places."

DeCarde shrugged.

"I suppose we've had a good run — over two centuries of peaceful democratic existence — but it appears to be over. Still, looking back at history, two hundred years is the average length of time democracies exist before they turn into something less palatable or collapse altogether. The major flaw in the democratic system is that professional politicians, people who've done nothing else in their lives, eventually take over the government permanently, installing themselves as elites. And they end up running the state for their own benefit rather than the citizenry at large. You know, people like Derik Juska. Once that happens, the electorate no longer has a voice, and our old friend fascism or its fraternal twin, socialism, surfaces."

"Thanks for the ancient political science lecture, Currag." Estevan's tone dripped with sarcasm, and DeCarde knew the man's patience with him was at an end. "But I happen to think the Republic needs a strong, unifying president to face the Hegemony. If Aurelia Hecht hadn't died, we'd be in dire peril right now because she was weak and incapable of taking the steps to secure our future."

"Aurelia was many things, but weak wasn't one of them, both mentally and physically. Which makes her death all the more suspiciously convenient."

Estevan's eyes narrowed.

"What are you insinuating?"

DeCarde belatedly realized he might have gone a step too far and made a face.

"Nothing."

After a long glare, Estevan sat back in his chair.

"I believe we've said everything we have to say to each other. Stay on the Theban government's payroll, if you like, but you're effectively out of a job, and so is the minister. And watch your mouth. It might end up getting you in trouble."

Understanding he'd been dismissed, DeCarde stood.

"You may wish to look over your shoulder as well, Eddie. History has shown that under the form of government we're seeing develop on Lyonesse, even the most loyal are vulnerable to the leader's impulses, and those impulses will get more paranoid the longer he's in power. Sudden death by cardiac arrest then becomes a distinct possibility. You know, like what happened to Aurelia Hecht."

— 32 —

Brigadier General Edward Estevan, Republic of Lyonesse Marine Corps, stared at the empty office door as his former commanding officer's footsteps faded away. He remembered Currag DeCarde only too well and knew the latter believed he should never have been promoted beyond major. That alone colored his feelings about DeCarde, who, had he stayed in the Corps, would surely have ended as Commandant, like so many of his forbears.

But give the devil his due. DeCarde was more intelligent than most officers and possessed a natural leadership style that had the troops willing to follow him through hell and back, something Estevan wished he could inspire. Still, he'd made brigadier general and was chief of staff of the nascent Hatshepsut National Guard while DeCarde faced obscurity as a man with nothing left in life.

Yet Estevan felt no pity for him even though his anger and jealousy at DeCarde had burned themselves out long ago. DeCarde's opposition to President Juska's plans for Lyonesse's future made him an enemy, not of Estevan, but of the Republic itself. Perhaps he should warn the local LOI station chief about him and his treasonous opinions. Yes, that's what he would do.

***

"It's as I suspected," DeCarde said when he dropped into the chair facing the minister of defense's desk in Government House, a sprawling complex home to senior officials. "Edward Estevan has orders to create the Hatshepsut National Guard based on the Theban Defense Force and remove it from Theban oversight. The Guard will take its orders from Lyonesse, not from you."

The minister, Jabari Olonga, a dark-complexioned man in his mid-fifties with gray hair and a gray beard framing an intelligent face, grimaced.

"Damn."

"Yep. And there's nothing you can do about it. The Defense Force is Lyonesse trained, organized, and equipped. They'd never resist the transfer. If necessary, I'm sure Estevan will use the 1/21st as his enforcement arm."

"But why take away our control?"

A weary shrug.

"It's part of President Juska's plan to exert Lyonesse domination over the Republic's various star systems rather than treat them as sovereign worlds within a federal system as the constitution requires. You do that best by exercising complete control over the local military. The other worlds with defense forces will likely face the same situation. You and I are effectively out of a job, Jabari. And all because of this Lyonesse First nonsense, which, in the final analysis, is nothing more than a cover for Juska's machinations. He doesn't believe in the ideology but is gleefully using it to advance his own agenda."

Olonga shook his head.

"My, but you've become cynical, Currag."

"I've always been cynical. But I'm no longer hiding it. Why bother? The last five years have proved me right on so many levels when it comes to the Republic's bleak future as a democracy under Derik Juska."

"It can't be so bad, surely?"

DeCarde nodded.

"Oh, yes, it is. Take the Lyonesse Office of Inquiry, for example. They pretend to be an interstellar police force, but they're political enforcers for Juska, nothing more. The LOI will pursue opponents of his regime while ignoring corruption and malfeasance done in support of it. Hell, the Hegemony's State Security Commission, which is portrayed by the Republic's propagandists as a political police organization, is more honest, more disciplined, and much, much more professional. They are a uniformed, interstellar law enforcement agency, not personal security for the supreme leader."

Olonga gave DeCarde a curious look.

"You really don't like President Juska, do you?"

"That would be an understatement. He's a smarmy, power-hungry sonuvabitch who, unfortunately, is an extremely plausible orator. Juska can bamboozle the average citizen with the greatest of ease, and he's got enough of his supporters in the Senate to ensure he gets everything he desires."

"And what does he want?"

"Absolute power so he can implement his vision — a dictatorship in everything but name where he alone calls the shots, and any opposition is eliminated, with extreme prejudice if necessary. In fact, I suspect he's responsible for President Hecht's untimely death, but no one will ever find the slightest hint of proof."

An air of astonishment overtook Olonga's earlier expression. "Really?"

"Yes, and I'm not the only one. Derik Juska is a nasty piece of work, a lifelong politician without scruples, morals, or any other redeeming features, let alone a shred of empathy. A true sociopath if there ever was one."

***

Currag DeCarde stepped out through Government House's side door into the late afternoon sunshine. He stopped and stretched, wondering what he would do now. Then, he ambled off toward the main gate and the city of Thebes beyond. In his five years here, he'd acquired a tan deep enough to pass as a native, and he wore the loose, white shirt and trousers favored by the locals, making him virtually indistinguishable from the Thebans.

A faint rumbling that grew rapidly made him stop in his tracks, and, hooding his eyes with one hand, DeCarde looked up into the clear blue sky, dotted here and there with white cloud puffs. It sounded a lot deeper than that of a shuttle, and there was only one ship due today, the *Dragon's Hoard.* DeCarde always enjoyed seeing who got off that particular vessel.

It was a frontier tramp that carried all manner of people, weighed heavily toward adventurers coming to seek their fortune on the Republic's most distant world, and they tended to vary between honest but clueless and roguish to the nth degree. And sometimes, those included people on the run from the government whose only crime was opposing Derik Juska.

DeCarde hopped aboard a bus passing in front of Government House and headed for the spaceport, arriving just moments before the *Dragon's Hoard* touched down. He climbed onto the spaceport terminal's roof terrace — it was a single-story building, which meant the ship, still ticking and pinging from re-entry, towered over him — and stood under a canvas awning.

The belly ramp dropped, and moments later, the first passengers disembarked. They stopped as soon as they came out of the ship's shadow, blinking in the harsh sunlight, before getting their bearings and heading for the terminal's main tarmac-side doors. There was something faintly familiar about the three — two women and a man — in how they looked around, carried their bags, and moved, and he figured them for ex-military. Interesting. Hatshepsut got its share of former service personnel, but they rarely rode on ships like the *Dragon's Hoard*, preferring to take the regular liners and supply runs.

The man caught his attention for some reason, and DeCarde squinted at him, wondering what it was. He felt as if he knew him. Not by his outward appearance but by the structure of his facial features, his movements, and especially his eyes, which were never still. DeCarde decided to intercept the three and welcome them to Hatshepsut and left the rooftop terrace.

***

Norum knew the easy part of his perilous passage was over. Hatshepsut represented the end of the line in the Republic of Lyonesse. How he and his two companions would get from here to Wyvern, he didn't know. But this place was still safer for him than Mykonos. For now.

They entered the terminal, a simple, airy box made with local materials — wood and adobe — and sporting wide openings instead of windows to improve the airflow in this tropical climate. There, they joined the line at the immigration counter staffed by a dark-complexioned woman of indeterminate age wearing a simple white uniform.

Since Hatshepsut wasn't integrated into the Republic's identity tracking system, she simply scanned their IDs, checked to make sure the image matched the person, and waved them through with a bored welcome. And since the vast majority of the star system's inhabitants didn't carry any identification whatsoever, Norum figured they'd be safe for as long as it took to find passage on a trader headed for the Hegemony.

His restless gaze suddenly spotted a familiar face standing by the exit. The sandy blond hair was long, as was the beard, but the deep blue eyes were the same, and they scrutinized him with an intensity he remembered from his days at the Academy long ago. Currag DeCarde, looking as if he'd gone native. Both had been in the same class and had followed parallel careers, Currag in the Marines, he in the Navy, until Currag had decided to retire from active service.

Norum saw a hint of recognition on DeCarde's face as if he thought he knew him but couldn't remember from where. They'd last seen each other five years earlier, just after DeCarde had returned from Wyvern to be fired by the president and before Norum moved to Mykonos and had commiserated on the direction the Republic was taking under Derik Juska.

He had to make up his mind quickly on whether to acknowledge his old friend or avoid him. But DeCarde didn't give them that option. He intercepted Norum and the other two before they made it to the exit.

"Hello, folks," DeCarde said with a smile. "Welcome to Hatshepsut. You three wouldn't be ex-service members, would you?"

"Why do you ask?" Norum frowned suspiciously.

"Because you have that air about you. I'm Currag DeCarde, late of the 21st Pathfinders and currently employed by the Theban Ministry of Defense. I often come to watch new arrivals and see if there are former military among them. The ministry is very interested in recruiting people with experience." He speared Norum with his keen eyes. "Even those who were in the Navy."

"We don't plan on staying long enough to pick up work, Mister DeCarde," Norum replied. "Our intention is taking a ship into the Hegemony."

DeCarde cocked a questioning eyebrow.

"Are you, perchance, looking to get away from everything?"

"You could say that."

"Tell you what? I live in a big house by myself. How about I do you three a good turn and invite you to stay with me a few days or until that ship for the Hegemony shows up?"

"I don't know about that," Weston started to say, grimacing.

But Norum, who was convinced his old friend had recognized him by now, nodded.

"We'll take you up on that. The name's Harter, Ian Harter, by the way." Norum held out his hand. "And they're Gail Benett and Vera Jakkari," he added, nodding at them while he and DeCarde shook.

"Could we speak in private for a few moments, Ian?" Weston asked.

"No need, Gail. Colonel DeCarde is an honorable man who we can trust."

Weston and Svent exchanged a quick glance, and then the former shrugged. "Your call."

"Okay," DeCarde dipped his head once. "If you've got your things, let's hop on the next bus and head into the city."

— 33 —

Two bus rides and a walk up a steep hill to where DeCarde's house sat in a row of similar homes had them sweating, but the sun was kissing the horizon, and the heat of the day would soon dissipate. Surprising DeCarde, two men wearing relaxed business clothes of the type preferred by federal officials waited for him, seated on his front porch bench.

Both rose when DeCarde and his guests filed through the front gate. The former stopped dead in his tracks, face hardening.

"What the hell do you want, Nieman?" He glanced over his shoulder and Norum. "Quimper Nieman is the local LOI head honcho, and the goon with him is his evil shadow, Rolo Ghanis."

"We just want to have a talk with you, DeCarde."

"Well, I don't intend to waste my time with you, Neiman, so fuck off."

"I could haul you into the field office."

"You have no jurisdiction here, so get off my property before I have you arrested by the Theban police for trespassing."

"Okay, then listen up, wise guy. We hear you've been speaking against the Republic's government policies. Take care you don't utter any treasonous words in public because that will fall under my jurisdiction, and I will drag your ass in."

"I'll bet that prick Estevan asked you to harass me. I'll tell you what I told him. Last time I checked, the Republic still has freedom of speech. Now, was that everything? If so, leave and don't ever come back."

"Consider yourself warned, DeCarde. What you consider freedom of speech can easily cross the line, and when you do..." Nieman jerked his thumb across his throat. He then glanced at Ghanis and nodded toward the street. "Let's go."

"Hang on a moment, boss." Ghanis studied Norum, Weston, and Svent. "Who are these three, DeCarde? Looks like they haven't been here very long."

"Friends, and that's all you'll find out."

"What are your names, friends of DeCarde?"

"Harter," Norum said, then he jerked his thumb over his shoulder. "Those two are Benett and Jakkari."

"You just get off a ship?"

"Yeah. What's it to you?"

"Why did you come to Hatshepsut at the ass end of the Republic?"

"None of your business."

A slow smile spread across Ghanis' face.

"I can see why you're friends with DeCarde. You've got the same shitty attitude. Take care you don't cross any lines either."

"What lines would those be? As far as I'm concerned, as a citizen of the Republic, I'm free to speak my mind."

"You just keep on thinking that, bub."

Then, they brushed by DeCarde and the others and vanished down the street while DeCarde led the way into the house.

"Wasn't that fun?" Weston said, looking around the spacious, tiled foyer. "They're probably ex-city police bastards who had no chance of advancement in the force and joined the LOI instead."

DeCarde glanced at her, then at Norum as he ushered them into the living room.

"Your friend seems knowledgeable about the Office of Inquiry. Anything I should know?"

"Rey and Beth — Weston and Svent, to use their real last names — are LOI and ostensibly on the hunt for me, Currag. I'm supposed to be terminated with extreme prejudice. But since both are former service, they're not the usual sociopaths that gravitate to the LOI and can't go through with cold-blooded murder. So, they deserted their posts and came with me to find refuge in the Hegemony."

DeCarde shook his head.

"Damn Derik Juska to hell. So, it's as I suspected. The untimely deaths of so many opposition figures were terminations."

Norum nodded.

"Yes. I'd kept my head down since leaving Lyonesse, living under a new identity, but they spent a lot of time and effort trying to find me. I don't know whether it's because Juska considers me a threat to his regime or whether it's personal. He and I never got along, and I do believe he developed a visceral hatred for me. It's a small step from eliminating your opponents to having those who don't present a threat, but you merely dislike murdered."

DeCarde handed out cold bottles of beer as they sat around a low table, and Norum told him about the assassination attempt and how he met Weston and Svent.

"Pretty ingenious, pretending to go undercover so you can more effectively hunt Farrin," DeCarde said once Norum fell silent. "But they'll eventually track your cover identities to Hatshepsut."

"We hope to be in the Hegemony by then," Weston replied. "Which reminds me, we need to exchange our Lyonesse creds for portable wealth — precious metals and gems — so we have something to live on in the Hegemony."

"There won't be any problems with that on Hatshepsut. The locals are hungry for creds to buy offworld goods, and they have plenty of portable wealth that was saved up during the centuries of darkness." DeCarde finished his beer and sat back. "Getting a ship will be hit or miss. There are no regular runs. We find out about an arrival when they emerge at the wormhole terminus and ping the orbital station. They're mostly tramp traders, although the odd company freighter shows up from time to time. But it's only a matter of when, not if, before Juska forbids any Hegemony vessel from approaching Hatshepsut. And the Navy will enforce it."

DeCarde sighed.

"Your old service has changed a lot in the last five years, Farrin. Officers loyal to Juska have replaced the good guys. I've seen the same in the Marine Corps, although it hasn't gotten down to battalion commanders yet. The 1st of the 21st, which is the current garrison here, is still under one of the apolitical lieutenant colonels whose oath is truly to the constitution. But higher than that?"

He briefly described Edward Estevan, and Norum nodded.

"I vaguely remember him. Not an impressive officer, from what I recall."

"No, on the contrary, but he's politically reliable, and that's the sort taking over the Defense Force. Thankfully, Al Jecks still commands the Hatshepsut Squadron, and he doesn't have a political bone in his body. But his replacement will be a Lyonesse First jerk. You can be sure of that."

Norum scowled before taking another sip of his beer. Then, he said, "Juska is destroying everything."

"May I ask a question, Colonel?" Weston said in the ensuing pause.

"Sure."

"How did you recognize Admiral Norum when the LOI, us included, couldn't identify him?"

DeCarde chuckled.

"I've known Farrin for over forty years. We were classmates at the Academy and pretty close throughout our four years there and afterward as officers. The eyes did it for me. The eyes and the way he moved, his mannerisms. Things you'd have a hard time disguising, no matter how well you tried."

What DeCarde didn't add was his preternatural ability to see through disguises, falsehoods, and other forms of dissimulation. Family tradition had it go back to the distant Ancestor who founded his lineage, but DeCarde didn't know either way. He merely accepted his skill and used it judiciously.

Weston inclined her head, acknowledging DeCarde's explanation. Whether she believed it, no one could tell.

"That certainly makes sense, sir. Still, you're an excellent observer. Will the LOI idiots give you any trouble?"

A frown spread over DeCarde's face.

"Probably. They really hate people who stand up to them and will try me on — again. Not that they've succeeded so far, seeing as how I'm the Minister of Defense's senior adviser for now. But the LOI is intruding into Theban affairs more and more these days. Still, I can't help myself with them. The slimy cretins bring out the worst in me."

"You just said, for now, Currag. Does that mean you'll soon be out of a job?"

DeCarde nodded.

"Me and the minister."

He explained about the creation of the Hatshepsut National Guard under Lyonesse's control using the Theban troops.

"That's not a National Guard," Norum said in a tone of disgust. "That's a local extension of the army. Let me guess — Juska is doing it so he has troops he can use to convince the star system government that obeying his orders is the better part of valor."

"Got it in one."

"And what will you do when you're no longer employed by the Thebans?"

"I haven't thought about it yet. But now that I am, I figure it's either head for Axsum and find a job in one of the cities there or leave Hatshepsut altogether. If I stay in Thebes, I'll probably end up in the LOI's dungeon."

"Come into exile with us, Currag," Norum suggested. "If you haven't made Juska's termination list yet, you will soon enough."

"And do what?"

"Stay alive. Ride out the insanity that is Derik Juska's government."

"What makes you think we can ride it out? If Juska gets what he wants, he'll simply ensure his successor continues in the same vein. Barring a miracle, the Republic as we knew it is finished, and I don't believe in miracles. Hell, it's Stichus Ruggero all over again, but without the charm. Except this time, it didn't take nearly as long for his type to appear, thanks to a glaring but overlooked weakness in the Republic's version of democracy. And that's the fact we don't demand certain qualifications of our president as proof of competence and integrity, such as prior military service."

Norum pulled up one side of his mouth in a half grimace.

"Granted. Although I'm much less plugged into the politics of the day and what's happening on Lyonesse. A result of isolated living in the countryside far from other humans, fat and happy, until the LOI found me."

DeCarde snorted.

"I thought I'd be okay too, living on the ass end of the Republic, to quote Ghanis. But it looks like Lyonesse politics have caught up with me as well. I think maybe I'll join you in exile since it could be the prudent thing to do. It's not like I have anything holding me here or anywhere else." He winked at Norum. "Besides, I know people on Wyvern."

"Do you think they'll take us in?"

A nod.

"Without question. The Hegemony has its quirks, but they seem to be much closer to the honorable ideal than we are nowadays. Which isn't saying much since the Republic is shedding its virtue at hyperspeed."

"That's good to know."

"Yep. And now, can I offer you a meal? It won't be much in terms of variety, but it'll be nourishing and satisfying." DeCarde climbed to his feet without waiting for an answer. "Theban food is usually quite spicy, but I prefer a more subdued version."

***

"You know what, boss?" Rolo Ghanis said. "I figure there's something fishy about the three mooks DeCarde brought home from the spaceport."

They were walking down the hill from the residential quarter and back to the Lyonesse High Commission, near Thebes' Government House, where the Hatshepsut LOI detachment had its field office.

"Cop's instinct?"

Ghanis nodded.

"Yeah. Maybe we ought to check them out. They'll have come in on the *Dragon's Hoard*. It's the only ship that landed today."

"Okay, sure. Let's do that." They turned a corner as they reached the bottom of the hill and Nieman asked, "Tell me, though, what about them caught your attention?"

"The eyes. They were watchful, more so than you'd expect from your average civilian. Almost as if they were measuring us up, fitting us for an intervention, if you know what I mean. The two who didn't speak, Benett and Jakkari, in particular. The other clown, Harter, sounded like he was some high mucketymuck."

Nieman trusted Ghanis' instincts because they were rarely wrong. They'd spent twenty years as cops together in Lena, Yotai's capital, the last ten as detectives, before moving over to the LOI when it was clear they were no longer wanted by the Lena police service. That their sometimes-questionable methods might have had something to do with it never crossed their minds.

Once back in the office, Ghanis called up the immigration files on the system Lyonesse had installed for the Thebans — like all of Lyonesse's gifts, it had stayed under the Republic's control — and quickly found Harter, Benett, and Jakkari. They were among the two dozen passengers who'd disembarked earlier that afternoon.

"Says here they got aboard the *Dragon's Hoard* on Mykonos. They also received their credentials there."

"Then let's message the Mykonos field office with copies of their IDs and see what they can tell us."

—34—

For the next two days, Norum, Weston, and Svent wandered through Thebes, sightseeing, while DeCarde wrapped things up at work before he disappeared. Of course, he didn't tell anyone he was leaving Hatshepsut, not even Jabari Olonga, with whom he'd developed a fairly close relationship over the past few years. DeCarde had decided to simply vanish.

He ran across Abbess Rianne the second afternoon while crossing Government House's inner quadrangle. She'd been spending a lot of time behind closed doors with President Jorg Freeman lately, meetings that not even the latter's closest advisers attended. DeCarde suspected Rianne was preparing Freeman for his assumption of the Hatshepsut presidency under close Lyonesse control. The Void Brethren had been increasingly meddling in secular affairs and promoting the Republic government's policies, a strange turn of events if there ever was one.

"Colonel." Rianne bowed her head slightly, watchful eyes meeting his. "I trust everything is well with you?"

"As well as can be expected, Abbess. Going to see President Freeman?"

As always around her and the other Brethren, DeCarde instinctively raised his mental barriers, only vaguely aware he'd done so. He also had the familial distrust of the Order, which went back to the Ancestor, who'd lived before the Empire's founding and during its early years. That it was because he had more than a smidgen of talent — which made him such a good diplomat — didn't register.

"Actually, I'm here to see you first, then the president."

"Oh?" DeCarde cocked a questioning eyebrow at Rianne. "Well, you're seeing me. How can I help you?"

"It's more a case of how I can help you. I understand from General Estevan that you'll soon be out of a job."

"Perhaps."

"We may have employment to offer you, Colonel. As you know, we're establishing a priory in Mazaber very soon and could use your services as a diplomat to smooth the relationship between the prioress and the Mazaber authorities. Thebes isn't quite ready to assert full control over Aksum's primary cities just yet, and the political situation will remain a tad unsettled for a while."

DeCarde studied Rianne for a few seconds. While the Order did use non-Brethren for certain specialized tasks, Mazaber had calmed down significantly in the last four or five years and he didn't quite see the necessity for one with his skills. Besides, the

Theban Army — much more modern than anything in Mazaber by far — would accompany the priory's personnel.

He had what he called finely tuned bullshit detectors, and they were tingling right now. The reason she gave him wasn't the real reason.

"For how long would that be?" He asked, temporizing while he decided whether to challenge Rianne.

"A few months, perhaps longer. Then we'll seek to establish priories in Ladak, Adaba, and Tikon, potentially giving you employment for a few years."

And keeping him conveniently away from Thebes, the capital, while Estevan and Rianne transformed Hatshepsut into one of Juska's satrapies instead of a sovereign member of the Republic's confederation, with the right to self-governance. DeCarde must seem a more significant threat to the established order than he truly was. Why not simply kill him? Or could it be that Rianne was attempting to save his life by getting him out of sight? Possibly. While the Order of the Void supported government policies, it surely didn't condone political assassination.

"I'm honored that you consider me worthy of the task, Abbess." DeCarde inclined his head. "I accept, although my responsibilities to the minister of defense aren't quite over yet."

"It'll wait a few weeks, Colonel. Thank you, and enjoy the rest of your day." With that, Rianne continued across the quadrangle toward the wing with the president's office.

DeCarde watched her go, hoping a ship headed into the Hegemony would show up while he could still claim work in Thebes. Once he was in Mazaber, getting away might be much more difficult, if not impossible.

***

"We got an answer from the Mykonos field office, boss," Rolo Ghanis stuck his head into Nieman's office. "And guess what? Benett and Jakkari are two of ours, on an undercover mission. They asked us to extend them every assistance, if needed. Otherwise, we should ignore them."

"Did they say what mission?"

Ghanis shook his head. "Classified top secret need-to-know."

"What about Harter?"

"That's where it gets even more interesting. They think Harter's ID is fake but can't prove it so far. His background in the Mykonos database seems a bit sketchy."

"Do they have any idea why this Harter character, whose real name might be something entirely different, is traveling with two undercover LOI officers?"

"If they do, they didn't say."

Nieman sat back in his chair, fingers tapping on its arms.

"I don't like it, and I intend to find out what that is. There's something wrong with the entire setup. For instance, why are Harter and the officers staying with DeCarde, someone known to criticize the government? We carefully vet every prospective LOI member for loyalty before hiring them."

"The Mykonos field office doesn't want us to interfere."

Nieman banged his fists on the chair's arms.

"Fuck 'em. This is Hatshepsut. I'm in charge here. We're checking them out."

Ghanis raised both hands in surrender.

"You're the boss."

"Yes, I am. And tomorrow morning, bright and early, we'll pay DeCarde's place a little visit to chat with his three guests."

But when they knocked on the door the next day, DeCarde opened it and told them to leave the property immediately or show him a warrant. They walked away but slipped into the shadows beneath a nearby tree and sat on an old wooden bench half hidden by bushes to wait.

Not long afterward, DeCarde, dressed for work, emerged from the house and headed down the hill. He appeared lost in thought and didn't spot the lurking LOI agents. About half an hour later, two figures came through the front door — Benett and Jakkari. They leisurely strolled toward where Neiman and Ghanis sat, and the agents stood.

"Remember us?" Nieman asked, pulling out his credentials, imitated by Ghanis.

"Yes," Weston said in a wary tone. "What do you want?"

"Just to have a little chat between friends."

"And what if we don't want to?"

"That would be a shame. Your boss on Mykonos told us to offer you every bit of assistance possible in the pursuit of your case." A knowing smile spread across Nieman's face. "Colleagues."

When Weston gave him a hard stare, Nieman chuckled.

"We followed up on you the other day and found out from Theban immigration that you originated on Mykonos, so we sent a message to the field office there asking if you were known to them. Lo and behold, we received a response telling us you two were LOI agents operating undercover on a classified, need-to-know mission."

Weston groaned inwardly. That was precisely the sort of stupid crap the agent in charge of the Mykonos field office would pull instead of simply confirming their identities as legitimate.

"And what if we are?"

"Well, your friend Harter came back as sketchy, unknown to your boss, so we were wondering who he really is and what his connection to you might be."

"Sorry. Can't tell you. It comes under the classified heading. Now, if that was everything you wanted, good day."

Weston made to step around Nieman, but he held out his arm.

"Look, you're operating on my patch without my knowledge. That just isn't on. I'm the agent in charge here in the Hatshepsut system and, therefore, your superior. I can invoke the disciplinary process to make you tell me. Who is Harter, and what is he doing with you?"

Weston bit her lower lip as she put on an air of indecision while parsing the possible answers. Finally, she shrugged.

"Okay. Since neither of you looks like a Hegemonist, here's how it is. Harter isn't his real name. It isn't even the name my boss back on Mykonos knows him under. He's a spy who's off to Wyvern on a mission we know nothing about. Our job is to see him on a ship headed for the Hegemony and protect him while he's waiting. Satisfied?"

"Hang on for a minute. First of all, which organization does he belong to? Last I heard, the Republic didn't have a spy agency. And second, why doesn't your boss know him under Harter?"

"That's easy," Weston replied, pleased her little fabrication was coming to life. "He's an LOI agent. The office established an intelligence group a while back. Very hush-hush. Need-to-know only. And my boss knows him under another name because Harter assumed his current identity just before we left Mykonos and didn't tell anyone but us, his guardians. He's a touch paranoid if you must know. Apparently, it's a good trait for an intelligence operative to have. In effect, his trail stops cold on Mykonos."

Weston gave Nieman a hard stare.

"And if any of this gets out, I'm personally terminating you and your sidekick."

Nieman raised both hands, palms facing outward.

"Whoa there, friend. No need to make threats. Rolo and I get it. We won't speak of this to another soul."

"Make sure you don't." With that, Weston and Svent turned around and headed back to DeCarde's house, watched by a thoughtful Nieman.

"You buy what they just tried to sell us, boss?" Ghanis asked.

"Not for a frigging minute. But she's plausible. I'll give her that."

"So now what?"

"We talk to Harter." Nieman fished a tiny video pickup from his trouser pocket and stuck it on the tree trunk facing the house. "Let's get back to the office. When we spot Harter leave, we'll try to intercept him in town."

***

Weston told Norum about their encounter with Nieman and Ghanis. When she was done, Norum gave her a crooked smile.

"Good thinking under pressure, Rey, but do you figure he bought it?"

"Probably not," Weston admitted after a moment. "Still, it might be enough to throw him off the scent until a ship headed for the Hegemony shows up."

"And that's all we need," Svent said.

"Yep." Norum paced DeCarde's kitchen, where the three enjoyed a second cup of morning tea. "Yet we need to prepare for more drastic measures, such as eliminating Nieman and Ghanis if they get too nosy."

"I'm not sure I'd be comfortable with that, sir." Weston made a face.

"Neither would I, normally." Norum gave her a half smile. "But I've already killed two LOI agents who were coming to assassinate me. It gets easier after the first few, especially if the goal is staying alive."

"We'll do as you want." Weston frowned. "Mind you, I think they gave up too easily, whether or not they believed my story even a bit."

"You figure they've left something behind?"

Weston nodded.

"Surveillance. You'd be amazed at how small sensors are these days."

"So why don't I just walk out the front door in an hour or two and see what that gets me? It's not like they'll try anything stupid in the middle of the day in the better part of Thebes."

"You sure you want to risk it?"

"They'll keep on us. Why not give them something to play with while we wait for a ship?" Norum tilted his head to one side in question. "Besides, it could be fun."

—35—

"Ian Harter." Agent in Charge Quimper Nieman dropped into the chair across from Norum, who sat beneath an umbrella on the terrace of a café overlooking the harbor. Ghanis took the one beside Nieman. Both were studying Norum from behind sunglasses.

Norum didn't immediately acknowledge them, his eyes focused on a steamship docking at one of the commercial piers.

"What do you want, Nieman?" He finally asked.

"To have a little chat about you and your reason for being on Hatshepsut."

"I thought Benett cleared that up with you earlier today." Norum still didn't look at either of his unwanted guests. "Not that she had any reason to do so, seeing as how it could jeopardize my mission."

"Yeah, well, see — we're not actually sure we believe Benett's story."

Norum shrugged and gazed at Nieman for the first time.

"Suit yourselves. Now leave me alone."

"You're an LOI intelligence agent?"

"If that's what Benett said, then sure."

"You know what's funny? We've never heard of the LOI having a covert intelligence branch."

"That means operational security is still holding." Norum picked up his teacup and had a sip. "Look, I'll be gone soon in the direction of Wyvern, and Benett and Jakkari will return to Mykonos. So just leave us to do our thing."

"Can't. Something about you and Benett's story stinks to high heaven."

Norum gave himself a sniff.

"If anything reeks around here, it isn't me. Did either of you forget to shower this morning?"

"Ha, ha. Hilarious."

Norum shrugged again.

"I'm an LOI operative, not a comedian." He finished his tea and stood. "If you'll excuse me, I need to get some fresh air. The one at this table is turning rather stale. You really ought to wash more often, you know."

With that, Norum wandered off into the direction of the port and its warren of warehouses and cranes, wondering if they would follow him. He carried his blaster in a hip holster, invisible beneath the shirt hanging loosely over his trousers. Perhaps he could terminate them in the dark corner of an abandoned shed on the water's edge.

They obviously didn't buy what Weston had told them, and it was only a matter of time before they figured out he was a wanted man. And if the Mykonos field office ended up telling Nieman that Weston and Svent were hunting Admiral Norum, retired, things could spin out of control rapidly.

But the last glimpse he caught of Nieman and Ghanis was them heading back downtown. Maybe they wouldn't be such a big problem after all.

***

"What now, boss?"

"Now? We ask the Mykonos agent in charge about the story Benett spun for us."

"Do you think he'll tell us if Harter is really an LOI intelligence operative?"

Nieman grinned at his sidekick.

"He told us that Benett and Jakkari were undercover LOI agents when I wouldn't have in his place. I'd have simply confirmed that the IDs were real."

Ghanis nodded.

"Right."

The answer came back from Mykonos more quickly this time. There was no LOI intelligence operative being escorted to Hatshepsut by members of the Mykonos field office.

"Well, ain't that a kicker?" Ghanis sat back in his chair as Nieman read him the reply. "So Benett, or whatever her real name is, told porkies."

"It gets better." Nieman glanced at the display hovering over his desk. "The actual mission Benett and Jakkari — or rather Rey Weston and Beth Svent — are on is finding Admiral Norum. I checked them out in the agency's database, and both are former Defense Force. Weston did twenty-five years, and Svent did thirty. Now Harter is definitely a fake identity, real name unknown so far."

Nieman paused and gave Ghanis a sly look.

"Are you thinking what I'm thinking?"

"That Harter is Norum, and they're trying to help him get away, seeing as how he's the former Chief of the Defense Staff and would have been their top boss while they were in the service?"

Nieman raised a knowing eyebrow and nodded.

"You're a fine detective, Rolo. Among the best. But it means Weston and Svent are traitors, something the Mykonos field office should figure out any moment now if they haven't already."

"You know, Harter being Admiral Norum would explain the vibe I got from him. What are we going to do with this information?"

Nieman's display chimed for attention, and he glanced at it.

"Act, but quickly. A Hegemony ship just popped out of the wormhole and signaled Hatshepsut Control. It'll be here in twelve hours and gone again in twenty-four."

***

DeCarde got home with news of an inbound Hegemony ship.

"And not a moment too soon," he said. "If Nieman pinged the Mykonos field office with a further query after you spoke with him the other day, he'd have received an answer by now, which might jeopardize you, and he must surely be aware of the Hegemony ship arriving within the next twelve hours. That means we need to lie low until just before it leaves again. Give me your creds now and I'll exchange them for portable wealth.

Once I'm back, we're relocating somewhere the LOI won't find us."

They passed over their cred chips and packed their meager belongings while DeCarde vanished into Thebe's less salubrious quarter, seeking his trusted money changer.

He returned just before twenty hundred hours and distributed slips of precious alloys and other valuable small items before packing his own bag and leading them down the hill to an unregistered flophouse whose owner asked no questions and never discussed her customers with anyone.

When Nieman, Ghanis, and the two dozen LOI agents stationed on Hatshepsut raided DeCarde's residence shortly after midnight, they came up with nothing.

"The bastards figured we were onto them," Ghanis said once they'd regrouped in a living room as cold and empty as the rest of the house.

"Doesn't matter," Nieman replied. "If they're looking to flee in the Hegemony ship, we'll catch them at the spaceport."

***

"If they're on to us, they'll be watching the ship from the moment it lands until it lifts off again," Weston said once they were in a dingy room lit by candles since the flophouse hadn't been connected to the electric grid yet, like so many places in Thebes' lower quarter. "That might make it difficult to get aboard."

DeCarde chuckled.

"Believe it or not, we're far from the first to escape Hatshepsut for the Hegemony with the authorities on our tails. Any number of people on the run are assumed to have vanished somewhere on Axsum when they really took a starship out of the Republic. And that means the people smugglers have ways of getting us aboard *Lara* — the inbound Hegemony freighter — unseen by anyone on the ground."

"You seem to speak from experience, Currag," Norum said.

A bitter grin spread across DeCarde's face.

"You could say I helped a few good people who were being persecuted by the Republic's government to escape. Some aboard the very same *Lara* we're taking."

Norum cocked an eyebrow at his friend.

"And why didn't you mention this before now?"

"I wasn't going to say anything at all if we'd gotten away without the LOI interfering. Some things are better taken to the grave. And no, I won't give you any names. Just take it as a given that folks who you might believe were killed by the government are alive and well in the Hegemony. Not many, but enough to give Derik Juska heartburn if he knew about them."

"You're a man full of surprises, Currag DeCarde."

"I'm also a man of honor, and Juska is taking Lyonesse down a thoroughly dishonorable path. So, I do what I can to frustrate his plans, little as that may be. But now it's time for me to take a final bow and leave the same way I helped so many others quit the Republic."

"And that would be how?"

"Simple. We climb aboard a container that bears specific markings and get loaded aboard *Lara* with the rest of the cargo. Once the ship is sealed, just before liftoff, the crew frees us from the container, and we settle in a cabin on the accommodations deck."

"Aren't you afraid the LOI will scan the containers for life signs?"

"The one we'll be using is lined with lead — nothing can penetrate it. And it has an autonomous oxygen scrubber that'll last us several days. I had it prepared the moment I heard *Lara* had come through the wormhole. In fourteen hours from now, we'll head to one of the warehouses in the port where it's waiting."

Norum nodded.

"A sophisticated setup."

"We've had to use it fairly often, especially since the Republic's government forced the Thebans to implement exit controls. *Lara* and a few of the other ships on the Hegemony-Hatshepsut run bring the empty containers back for reuse."

The next morning, shortly after daybreak, they heard a faint rumble. It grew rapidly, reached a crescendo, and then died away to nothing. *Lara* had landed.

A few hours later, DeCarde led them through a warren of narrow streets and alleys in the old part of the Port of Thebes and entered a dilapidated warehouse. Inside, they found a standard, off-white container showing heavy use sitting on a low-bed trailer hitched to a primitive-looking hauler. A man, presumably a Theban by his black hair and deep tan, appeared as they entered.

"Everything is ready for your passengers, Currag," he said in the local accent, proving he was Theban. Then he noticed DeCarde carrying a duffel bag. "Don't tell me you're leaving, my friend."

"I'm afraid so, Joshua. The LOI is getting a bit too close."

"Bugger the LOI." Joshua spat on the rammed earth floor. "Damn motherless bastards. I'm sorry to see you go. Who will pick up the slack with this?" He jerked his thumb over his shoulder at the container.

"Someone will contact you whenever a passenger for the Hegemony shows up and needs to board unseen."

"Okay. Climb in."

They entered through the open door, which slammed shut behind them. Soft lighting came on, and the gentle murmur of an air scrubber made itself heard. The interior wasn't much. Benches ran along either side while the powerpack and scrubber sat at the far end, and that was it. DeCarde dropped his bag and sat.

"I suggest you join me. It'll get shaky when we begin to move."

The others followed with alacrity seconds before the entire container jerked beneath them. Then, they felt it run over bumps and through dips.

***

"Still nothing," Rolo Ghanis reported after tucking his communicator back into his shirt pocket.

He and Quimper Nieman stood on the roof of the spaceport terminal, watching *Lara* load. LOI agents standing beside Theban immigration officers scrutinized every single person going aboard. They even scanned containers for life signs before allowing them to be loaded.

"That was the last of the passengers." Nieman exhaled loudly in frustration. "And that looks like the final container."

He nodded at a dinged, off-white rectangular capsule sitting on a trailer hauled by a crudely built truck passing through the gauntlet of LOI agents armed with handheld sensors. They obviously didn't pick up any life signs because they let it continue toward the ship's open belly ramp. There, the truck driver positioned the container beneath a mobile gantry hanging through the opening and climbed out to release the catches holding it to the trailer.

An unseen operator lowered claws and picked up the container. Moments later, it vanished into *Lara*'s hold, and the truck drove away again. Then, the gantry was retracted, and the belly ramp rose to seal the ship's hull.

"Well, that's it," Ghanis said. "Our targets aren't taking this one, which means they're still loose in Thebes or the islands."

"Recall the team, and let's head back to the barn. But we'll figure out where they went, mark my words."

— 36 —

A rattle sounded from outside the container, and the door swung open. Moments later, a curious face peered in.

"Ah, four of you this time." Then, the man's eyes widened. "Mister DeCarde? Why are you taking the special travel arrangements?"

"Hi, Benny." DeCarde climbed to his feet. "Things were heating up on Hatshepsut, and I figured it was time to wander. I suppose *Lara* is buttoned up?"

"Yes, sir." At that moment, vibrations ran through the ship's hull. "And we'd better get you and your friends to bunks, stat. Fortunately, we're not taking any passengers other than yourselves on this trip, so there's a cabin for each of you."

They exited the container to find themselves in a cavernous cargo hold filled with similar pods, stacked and tied down. Benny led them through a warren of narrow passages between the stacks and through an airlock into the habitable part of the ship. There, he took them along a narrow corridor whose bulkheads were pierced by open doors at regular intervals.

"Pick whichever one you like, but do it quickly."

As if to underscore his words, a klaxon sounded, followed by a male voice announcing liftoff in one minute. Benny hurried away to his own station.

The four glanced at each other, and Norum shrugged. "I'll take this one," he said, pointing at the nearest door.

When the klaxon sounded again as the vibrations reached a climax, they were flat on their backs in their chosen cabins' bunks. Then, immense hands pressed on their prone bodies as the ship lifted vertically under the impulse of its belly thrusters.

After a while, the pressure abated, and they felt a moment of quasi-weightlessness before the artificial gravity kicked in. They were in Hatshepsut orbit.

Norum, driven by an impulse to say farewell to the Republic of Lyonesse, was the first in the corridor, looking for the passenger saloon and a display repeating the view from the bridge. He found it behind a door appropriately marked as such, and there was a large screen showing the planet below them.

Just as he settled in a chair and the other three joined him, the view changed, indicating *Lara* was breaking away from the planet. It soon shrank as the ship sped up toward its hyperlimit.

"Adieu," Norum murmured in a wistful tone.

DeCarde looked at him with a curious frown.

"What?"

Norum turned his head and gave DeCarde a sad smile.

"Just making my goodbyes with the Republic."

"You don't expect us to ever return, do you, sir?" Weston asked.

"No." Norum's tone held such a note of finality that she grimaced. "And it's Farrin from now on. I don't want anyone to call me sir anymore. I've left my former rank in the Republic. It's the only way I can contemplate exile in a star nation that might soon be in conflict with the one which formerly held my allegiance."

DeCarde glanced at Weston and Svent and nodded.

"The same goes for me. I'm Currag, nothing more."

Both women looked at each other and shrugged.

"Okay, Farrin and Currag, it is." Weston waved at the display where Hatshepsut was reduced to a blue-green marble wreathed in streaks of white. "And goodbye to the Republic. It's been a treat serving you, but you've become something we can't honor anymore."

She stood.

"Anyone want a drink? I see a dispenser in the corner."

"Sure," Norum said. "Anything alcoholic will do. I think I need to drown my sorrows. By the way, Currag, how and when do we pay for our passage?"

"It's already done. I have an arrangement with the captain. I prepay for supplies in Republic creds at the chandler he uses when he's in port and simply selects whatever he wants up to the given amount. That also notifies him the special container will get loaded and with how many passengers. The booze, food, and everything else is paid for."

Norum raised his eyebrows.

"You really had a sweet system to evacuate people going on."

"Yep. I just hope it continues even without me. Plenty more folks will be looking to escape Derik Juska's Lyonesse First paradise."

Weston returned and plunked beer bulbs in front of everyone.

"There's harder stuff available, but I figure we might as well start off with some suds."

She sat and opened her bulb, imitated by the others.

"So, to what do we drink?"

Norum thought for a second, then said, "To the Republic. It was nice while it lasted."

"The Republic."

They took big gulps of their beer, and DeCarde sighed.

"What do you intend to do when we reach Wyvern, Farrin?"

"Talk to the one man I know there — Crevan Torma. I figure we have enough of a rapport that I can ask him for help to see us through the first few weeks. We got along rather well when I was CDS, and he was the Hegemony's ambassador. After that? Who knows? I suppose it'll be one day at a time. Historically, exiles tend to live marginal lives."

"You wouldn't sell your services to the Hegemony based on your knowledge of the Republic?" DeCarde asked.

Norum shook his head.

"No. Despite what Juska is doing to the Republic, I couldn't turn against it by selling its secrets. Not that anything I know is current after more than five years."

"How about helping the Hegemony with its colonial projects? It would allow us to use our talents in an area we know without touching on Lyonesse's confidential matters."

After thinking about it for a few heartbeats, Norum said, "Perhaps."

"We need to find something useful once we get there, for our long-term survival more than anything else. Our portable wealth will only last us for a few years at best, and I doubt the Hegemony's government will grant us a stipend for as long as we live simply because we're refugees from Juska's regime. They're not the type to be that generous, although I'd call them more inclined to being utilitarian than anything else, surprisingly enough. It's what let them wallow in isolation, with no ambition to reclaim human worlds for two centuries."

"I thought I'd find you here." A tall, thin woman with short gray hair above a seamed face stood in the doorway, smiling. "Benny told me Hatshepsut had gotten too hot for you, Mister DeCarde."

The latter stood and smiled back.

"Indeed, Captain. Let me introduce my companions — Farrin Norum, Rey Weston, and Beth Svent." They each climbed to their feet and nodded politely upon hearing their names. "And this is Captain Alcina Goodner, master of the *Lara*."

"A pleasure to have you aboard. Otherwise, my passenger compartment would have been empty for the trip back to Wyvern. Again." Goodner grimaced. "The number of folks visiting the Hegemony has dropped to nothing in the last year. If it weren't for the occasional refugees, I'd consider converting the cabins to cargo holds. But that may be about to change as well. I heard from my business contacts in Thebes that the Republic's government will be imposing a trade embargo on the Hegemony, and I'm not inclined to smuggle goods across the border. There's no profit in it, considering the risks. So this could be my last run to Hatshepsut, anyway. Besides, I hear pirates are appearing in the lawless star systems between here and the Hegemony, renegades from the Republic based on their ship configuration."

Norum's tilted his head to one side.

"Really? There have been none of those around for a long time."

"Attackers targeted merchant ships just after they emerged from wormhole termini in the last couple of months. Thankfully, they managed to escape relatively unscathed. But it's only a matter of time."

Norum and DeCarde exchanged glances.

"Did Derik Juska's administration encourage them to prey on Hegemony shipping as privateers?" The former asked.

"Quite possibly. I wouldn't put anything past the man, even trying to goad the Hegemony into taking rash actions."

"Hell, they could be regular Navy units disguised as pirates, for all we know." Norum shrugged. "Just as long as we don't run across any."

"*Lara*'s a pretty fast ship. If someone's waiting to ambush us at a wormhole terminus, we'll be FTL before they can range their weapons," Goodner said. "And on that note, I'd better head for the bridge. We're jumping soon."

The four sat again and finished their beers. Norum smacked his lips and said, "This stuff the Hegemony brews is actually pretty damn good. It beats the pants off anything produced by Lannion Ales, let alone the swill they make on Mykonos."

"Then you're going to love their wine and spirits. Especially the red, which is made from the grapes grown south of New Draconis. And they distill many fine whiskeys."

Norum chuckled.

"Looks like we got at least the boozy part of our new lives covered."

They were mostly through their second beer when the jump klaxon sounded, and Norum gave Hatshepsut's tiny disc on the saloon display one last glance. Then, the universe shifted, inducing a momentary bout of nausea, and the display went blank. They were in hyperspace, moving away from the Republic's last outpost at a speed faster-than-light.

"Well, that's it." Norum finished his bulb. "And now to find something entertaining to while away the idle days awaiting us."

"If anyone's brought a deck of cards, we could always play poker," Weston said.

"And what would we play for? Bragging rights?"

She had a vaguely libidinous glint in her eye when she replied, "How about strip poker?"

Norum returned her gaze with a wolfish smile.

"I prefer playing that sort of game one-on-one behind closed doors."

"So do I, for that matter." She returned his smile with a hungry one of her own.

Svent and DeCarde exchanged amused glances at the repartee.

"Feel free to go ahead and play according to your, em — desires," the latter said, grinning broadly. "Beth and I will find something to amuse ourselves."

—37—

Lannion
Republic of Lyonesse

"What do you mean your agents had Norum and then lost him?" A furious Derik Juska glared at his Director of the Lyonesse Office of Inquiry, Helga Pelky.

"He killed the agents who were tasked with taking him on Mykonos and then simply vanished. Two more of my people found their bodies and tried to trace Norum but without result. They've now disappeared as well. We know they reached Hatshepsut along with someone we believe could be Norum, but there, the trail runs cold."

"Damn it, Helga. Farrin Norum is the most important member of the previous government still on the loose. We need to track him down and make sure he cannot interfere with my program."

"It took my now deceased agents the better part of a year to find him in the first place, sir. If he reached Hatshepsut as we think, then he could be anywhere by now."

"Even back on Lyonesse?"

She shook her head.

"No. Our entry controls are a lot tighter these days. Fake IDs won't work here."

"Unless he's landed at an out-of-the-way place."

"No more of that either, sir. Every craft entering the atmosphere has to land at an approved location and are tracked until they do."

"Well, thank the Almighty for that." Juska didn't bother hiding the sarcastic edge to his words.

He wondered once again whether appointing Pelky as Director of the LOI had been a mistake. Sure, she was an ardent Lyonesse First supporter, which got her in trouble with her Defense Force superiors back when she was a colonel in Security. But she'd proved shallower, intellectually speaking, than Juska had expected.

"Norum's the only one on the list we haven't caught yet, sir. The others have been taken care of. I think the risk he represents is negligible, seeing as how he's staying below the sensor grid and has for the last five years."

Juska rubbed his chin with one hand.

"I suppose you might be right. Still, keep on trying to find him."

"Yes, sir. You might also be interested in knowing former ambassador Currag DeCarde, who we were watching, has also vanished. He was on Hatshepsut as well, and there may be a connection with Norum and our missing agents. He and Norum were classmates at the Academy and lifelong friends."

"That's annoying. DeCarde also has the potential to cause trouble. No idea where he might have gone?"

"No."

"Was that everything?" When she nodded, he said, "Thanks for coming by and letting me know."

Pelky left Juska's office at the heart of Government House. Almost immediately, Juska's chief of staff entered.

"Are we going ahead without knowing Norum's fate, Mister President?"

"We can no longer delay. Everything is ready."

In a few weeks, the Senate would vote, with a two-thirds majority, to abolish term limits for both the senators and the president. Juska had made sure of that. And once that amendment to the constitution became law, he'd ensure the Republic of Lyonesse became what it should be — a mighty military power under a ruler capable of taking the long view because he would be in office for a long time.

"Very well, sir. And Sister Elana is here."

"Please send her in."

Juska enjoyed his interactions with the Order's new Summus Abbatissa, who'd taken over from Gwendolyn four years earlier, much more than those with the latter. Elana was a woman after his own heart. Not a Lyonesse First zealot, of course. The Brethren professed no politics.

But Elana, a mystic and visionary, led a large faction of the Order, which believed their version of it was the only legitimate one. The Void Reborn were schismatics who would either be absorbed or dissolved, and Lindisfarne had abandoned all pretense at leadership after isolating itself for more than two centuries — it no longer counted.

That belief made Elana a precious ally because she saw his vision as being one to advance the Order's purpose and, more importantly, its power throughout human space. And that was the only thing that counted in Juska's mind. Power. Elana wanted spiritual power, and he wanted everything else. It was a match made in heaven.

She entered his office in a sweep of black robes, her thin, ascetic features impassive beneath a cap of long, blond hair. With intense blue eyes set in a narrow face, Elana reminded Juska of nothing so much as a watchful bird of prey seeking its next victim.

"Mister President."

"Sister. Please sit." Juska gestured at the chairs in front of his desk. Once she'd done so, he asked, "And how is the Order of the Void?"

"Settling nicely in the new role I devised."

Elana had recently steered the Void on an aggressive path to expand its reach and pushed for abbesses and prioresses to get more deeply involved in the secular matters of planetary administration. All in the name of supporting the Republic government's goals because they coincided with hers.

"Good. You and I will elevate Lyonesse to her rightful place in the galaxy."

She gave Juska a faint smile.

"Does that mean you're ready to push through the removal of term limits?"

"Yes. Although the last potential obstacle, Admiral Norum, has vanished, whereabouts unknown, I can no longer delay. As Helga Pelky said just before you arrived, the risk he represents has become rather small."

"Excellent. So long as you keep the Senate in your pocket, you should rule for a long time, long enough to guarantee the changes we are making to the Republic's very fabric become irreversible."

"Don't worry about our dear senators. They'll stay onside for as long as I need them. And since the star systems beyond Lyonesse will never have representation in the Senate, I have ensured that no potentially dissenting voices will be added in the future.

"It's almost as if you're creating a new Empire."

Juska inclined his head.

"That is my intent, but I shall make it much better than the version which died in fire and blood. We will have a strong Lyonesse with no pesky retail politics to keep the Republic from achieving greatness under my leadership."

PART III – FIRST LIGHT

—38—

New Draconis
Wyvern Hegemony

Crevan Torma sat back, a look of astonishment on his normally impassive features, though his eyes remained on the virtual display hovering above his desk. Maryam, who'd taken over the job of Leading Sister for the Colonial Service five years earlier when Ardrix became Magistra Abbatissa, poked her head through the open office door at that moment and caught sight of Torma's expression.

"What's the matter, Crevan?"

"I've just received the most astonishing message from a civilian ship called *Lara,* which does the run to Hatshepsut in the Republic of Lyonesse. They sent it shortly after dropping out of the wormhole before going FTL to Wyvern." Torma gave her a crooked smile. "It's from an old acquaintance. Two old acquaintances, in fact. Admiral Farrin Norum, retired, the former Lyonesse Chief of the Defense Staff and former Lyonesse Ambassador Currag DeCarde. They and two police officers with them are requesting political asylum in the Hegemony."

Maryam's eyebrows crept up.

"Political asylum? How extraordinary! Why did they contact you in particular?"

He let out a humorless chuckle.

"Probably because I'm the highest-ranking Hegemony official they know."

"But since we don't have an extradition treaty — nor any other accord — with the Republic, they do not need to request asylum. They're welcome to land on Wyvern or any other Hegemony world and live in peace."

Torma raised a finger.

"I think they're telling me they are fleeing the Republic because of problems with President Juska's government. Serious problems which might include threats of imprisonment or even to their lives. And they rightly suspect I'd be very interested in hearing what those are and why, especially since I spent time on Lyonesse as the Hegemony's ambassador." A smile briefly softened his severe expression. "Besides, they're probably looking for someone willing to lodge them or help them find a place where they can stay."

"Do you intend to do so?"

"Certainly. There's a fully furnished vacant unit in my apartment building. A two bedroom. They can share."

"Along with the police officers?"

"Yes. Both — a Rey Weston and a Beth Svent — belong to the Lyonesse Office of Inquiry. Or belonged, rather. I'm sure there's quite a story behind them joining DeCarde and Norum in exile." Torma suddenly frowned. "I suppose I should warn President Mandus of Admiral Norum and Ambassador DeCarde's unexpected arrival."

***

The following day, Crevan Torma, wearing his high-collared black State Security Commission uniform with a black beret bearing the Commission's insignia, entered the New Draconis spaceport and headed for the arrivals area. *Lara* had disgorged its passengers and cargo at the orbital station and the former were coming down aboard the regular shuttle run.

A disembodied voice announced the shuttle's arrival at Gate 21, and Torma made his way there, dodging a constant stream of people headed in every direction. He arrived just as the first passengers came through the gangway tube and stood to one side, eyes on the open doors.

Norum and Torma spotted each other at the same time, the former having shed his disguise during the trip. DeCarde was right behind him, followed by two fit-looking middle-aged women, both tall and with watchful eyes.

"Admiral." Torma inclined his head by way of greeting when Norum approached him.

"Crevan. Those two stars on your collar look good. When were you promoted? And it's Farrin. I've not been an admiral for over five years."

They shook hands, and Torma said, "I got my second star three years ago, but I'm still inspector general of the Colonial Service. I doubt I'll ever return to serve in the Commission."

He turned to DeCarde.

"Ambassador, it's got to see you again."

They shook as well.

"I haven't been anything in the last five years, Crevan, so please call me Currag."

"Very well." Torma turned to the two former LOI agents. "And you must be Rey Weston and Beth Svent."

"I'm Rey," Weston said. She jerked her thumb at Svent. "And that's Beth. Glad to make your acquaintance, General Torma. Farrin told us a lot about you. And no, we won't use your first name," Weston added, grinning. "Call it the habit of a lifetime. We're both ex-Defense Force senior noncoms."

"Welcome to Wyvern." Torma glanced at Norum. "I took the liberty of arranging for an apartment in the building where I live, downtown within walking distance of the Palace, all the ministries, and pretty much every amenity. It only has two bedrooms, but it is fully furnished because the area mainly attracts military and civilian bureaucrats who are in the capital during the week and have houses in the countryside."

"That's very considerate of you, Crevan. Two bedrooms will suffice." Norum's eyes briefly went to Rey Weston, which Torma, ever the police officer, didn't miss, and he wondered whether something had developed between them during their trip.

"In that case, my staff car is waiting outside. Let's get you to your apartment. Then, if you're feeling up to it, President Mandus and her closest advisers would like a bit of your time. Everyone is extremely curious about your requesting political asylum."

"Since *Lara* kept New Draconis time, we're well rested and willing to face the day. I assume Rey and Beth aren't required?"

"No. Just you and Currag."

Torma guided them through the terminal and out the front door, where they found a black staff car parked in the official vehicle section closest to the main entrance. They tossed their duffel bags in the back and climbed into the passenger compartment, Torma behind the controls, and sped off toward downtown New Draconis.

The four newcomers craned their necks, studying their surroundings as Torma drove into the heart of the city, occasionally commenting on sights of importance. They stopped in front of a ten-story glass and steel building with balconies dotting the sides.

"This is it. The Raijin Arms. Your apartment is on the fifth floor. I'm on the seventh."

They retrieved their bags and entered, Torma taking them through the security doors.

"We'll get your biometrics scanned right away so the building recognizes you."

He took them to a small alcove just inside the door, stared at a display, then entered data on the virtual screen.

"Please stand in front of the screen until it blinks green."

The four of them did so, and Torma said, "There. You can come and go as you please. The apartment door works on the same principle. It's unit 503, by the way. I'm in 701."

Once in the apartment, Torma stood on the threshold and let them get organized. As he suspected, Norum and Weston took one bedroom, and DeCarde and Svent took the other.

"We're not exactly dressed for the Wyvern Palace, Crevan," Norum said. "And these are our best clothes."

Torma waved away his concerns.

"They're fine for today's meeting. Can I assume you brought portable wealth that will allow you to shop?"

"We did."

"Then, after the meeting, I'll take you to the Wyvern Interstellar Bank, where you can exchange it for Hegemony creds."

"I don't quite know how to thank you."

Torma cocked an amused eyebrow.

"Is it not something friends do for each other?"

A smile appeared on Norum's lips.

"I suppose it is."

"All right then. Let us head for the Palace. You'll be okay on your own for a bit, Rey and Beth?"

Both nodded.

"We will. I think we might wander around the area, exploring."

"Enjoy." Torma turned to Norum and DeCarde. "Shall we?"

During the brief trip to the Palace, or more precisely the Blue Annex, where Torma parked the car, he didn't ask a single question, and when Norum mentioned it, Torma gave him his usual enigmatic smile.

"Why make you repeat your story? I can wait until you tell it to the president and her advisers."

He led the way from the Blue Annex to the Palace proper, passing them through the guard post at the rear of the building and then along corridors paneled in cream colors, their walls decorated with paintings showing ancient war scenes and a few peaceful ones.

They arrived at a subdued doorway guarded by a single man in a severe Wyvern-style business suit, charcoal gray, with an open jacket that didn't quite conceal the bulge of a weapon beneath his left arm.

"General Torma." He nodded once. "Madame President is waiting for you and your guests."

He opened the door and stepped aside to allow them through, and the three people seated around the low coffee table stood.

"Welcome," President Mandus smiled. She held out her hand. "You must be Admiral Norum."

"Madame President." Norum inclined his head as they shook.

Mandus turned her attention to DeCarde.

"It's good to see you again, Ambassador."

"Likewise, Madame." DeCarde, too, bowed his head as they shook hands.

"I'm sure both of you remember Sister Ardrix, who now heads the Order of the Void Reborn as Magistra Abbatissa."

"Sister." Norum and DeCarde both nodded politely. "Congratulations on the promotion."

Ardrix returned the nod with the ghost of a smile playing on her lips.

"Thank you, Admiral, Ambassador."

"I'm Sandor Benes." The man in navy blue with the five stars of a Grand Admiral at the collar held out his hand to Norum.

"Sandor commands the Hegemony's Armed Forces," Mandus said. "But he's here with us because he's the president-designate who'll replace me at the end of my term in a few months."

Benes turned to DeCarde.

"Currag, welcome back. I wish it could have been under better circumstances."

"So do I. When did they make you a Grand Admiral?"

"Two years after you left. The president decided she would no longer be commander-in-chief of the Armed Forces as well as head of state and separated both offices. Anton Mejik, who used to be my deputy, is now the CNO."

"Please sit." Mandus indicated the sofas on either side of the table and returned to her chair at its head. "Now tell us why you ask for political asylum — not that we have an extradition treaty with the Republic in any case."

Norum and DeCarde glanced at each other, and the latter made a go-ahead gesture.

"You see, Madame President," Norum said, "I am being targeted for assassination by the Lyonesse government, and Currag will soon be as well."

"What?" Astonishment was writ large on Mandus and Benes' faces. Even Ardrix raised an eyebrow. "That makes little sense. Why would President Juska wish to have a former Chief of the Defense Staff and a former ambassador killed?"

"Because he believes we present a threat to his vision of the Republic as a strong, expansionist polity under an autocratic president, one who serves without term limits and without the moderating influence of a powerful legislature. And a plurality, if not a majority, of the citizens support him. It's the Lyonesse First creed taken to its logical extreme, of course."

Norum recounted his going into hiding after being dismissed by Juska because he feared he'd end up like President Aurelia Hecht. He mentioned the long animosity between him and Juska as a primary driver. Then, he described his brush with death at the hands of an LOI hit team, his salvation via Weston and Svent, and his joining forces with DeCarde on Hatshepsut. When he was done, Norum turned the conversation over to DeCarde.

"I think what we're seeing in the Republic is a resurgence of an ancient political philosophy known as fascism," DeCarde said after discussing the disappearance of influential people who objected to the government's direction and the growing influence the Order of the Void had over secular affairs. "Juska's program bears all the hallmarks, even though I doubt he's aware of it."

"But why?" Mandus asked.

"Probably because the discovery of another spacefaring human polity pushed the Lyonesse First movement, a marginal group at first, into prominence. After more than two centuries of believing themselves to be human civilization's saviors, the knowledge that Lyonesse's sacred mission — and I use the term deliberately — isn't quite as sacred, let alone unique, came as a shock to the body politic. But I'm sure Lyonesse would eventually have ended up where it is now anyway if we hadn't encountered the Hegemony, except it would have taken longer, that's all. Our founders were too optimistic about human nature when they drafted the Republic's constitution. It has holes that weren't glaringly apparent until now."

Benes nodded.

"So Derik Juska is another Stichus Ruggero."

"In essence. He's a career politician who maneuvered his way to the top through means mostly foul. I believe his next step will be to remove term limits on the president and the senators, and he'll have the necessary two-thirds majority in the Senate to do so. The Lyonesse First adherents among the citizenry will applaud that move most vociferously. And the day it happens will be the day the Republic of Lyonesse is officially dead."

President Mandus shook her head.

"I don't quite know what to say."

"There really is nothing you *can* say, Madame, except perhaps pray for the future of Lyonesse if you're so inclined."

—39—

"It's much worse than what our agents on Lyonesse reported." President Mandus stood to pace in front of her desk once Torma, Norum, and DeCarde had left her office. "Juska making his enemies simply disappear or die of so-called natural causes? He's using political assassination as a tool of statecraft. And he's appointing Lyonesse First fanatics to the most senior positions in the military and civilian hierarchies. Historically, it means a descent into tyranny is imminent, cheered on by a significant segment of the population."

"It also means the Republic will soon become a genuine threat to us, Madame," Benes said. "Perhaps not in the next few months, but in a few years from now."

Mandus stopped and turned her eyes on Ardrix.

"And you, Magistra. What's your estimate of the situation?"

"Considering the increased meddling of the Lyonesse Order in secular affairs — which our agents also reported — I'd say Admiral Benes is right. There will be a growing synergy between the Order and President Juska's regime, making the Republic more aggressive and expansionist."

"Why would the Lyonesse Order be part of such a development?"

"Because they believe themselves the sole and true heirs of the Order of the Void and must absorb or dissolve the other versions. They're as much supremacists as the Lyonesse First movement."

Benes let out a humorless chuckle.

"Proving even something as noble as the Order of the Void can be perverted given the right circumstances."

Ardrix nodded.

"Unfortunately, human nature will always trump noble ideals."

"What now?" Mandus took her seat again.

"We continue as before." Benes shrugged. "There's not much else we can do."

"Except take the next step in establishing our legitimacy as the true heirs of the old Empire," Ardrix said. "The Void Reborn is just about ready to re-enter into communion with Lindisfarne, especially now that we have regular contact via subspace radio relays along with naval patrols and merchant ships visiting the star system. Once we declare ourselves the direct successors to the First Empire, Lindisfarne will join us as a member world. That I know already. After over two centuries of isolation, they are as keen as we are to join with the rest of humanity and expand once more."

Mandus frowned.

"Why only once we declare ourselves?"

"The Summus Abbatissa will not commit to the Hegemony since she considers it small and limited, having outlived its purpose to give humanity breathing space after the Great Scouring so it could recover."

"You've had those conversations with her?"

"Yes, during my visit to Lindisfarne last year."

"And why am I just hearing about this now?"

A mischievous smile appeared on Ardrix's lips.

"Because the time is finally right."

Mandus shook her head.

"And yet another sibylline statement from our Magistra Abbatissa. You'll never change, will you?"

Ardrix's smile broadened.

"No."

"I suppose I knew this day would come. So be it. I'll summon the Conclave and put the proposal before them."

"And what will you call yourself? Empress Vigdis the First?" Benes asked with a faint smirk.

"No. I will remain President Mandus, except I will govern the Second Empire rather than the Wyvern Hegemony. At least for a few more months. Then it'll be your turn, Sandor."

Benes scoffed.

"Don't remind me."

"Oh, come now, surely you're looking forward to the ultimate step in your career."

"True. But with some trepidation. I fear I'll face greater difficulties than you did."

"Of course, you will. Still, you're the best individual for the job, bar none." Mandus smiled at Benes and Ardrix. "Unless there's more you'd like to discuss, I'll let you get on with your day."

As she left the president's office, Sister Ardrix allowed herself a feeling of pleasure that the plan, five years in the making, was finally about to culminate. In a few weeks, Abbot Fenris of the Romerth Abbey, on Wyvern's second largest continent, would retire, leaving the senior leadership of the Void Reborn entirely to abbesses and prioresses. On that day, Ardrix would send a message to Lindisfarne submitting to the Order of the Void's Summus Abbatissa, effectively merging the Void Reborn with the Old Order and paving the way for the birth of the Second Empire. And this time around, the Order would have a much more significant influence over humanity's future. Ardrix would see to that.

***

"A pretty bleak assessment of the Republic's situation, if you don't mind me saying so." Crevan Torma led Norum and DeCarde to the Blue Annex and his office. "We have agents reporting back to us about general conditions, but they didn't paint such a somber picture."

"Yet that's the way it is, buddy," Norum said, grimacing at Torma. "Derik Juska is setting himself up as the modern Stichus Ruggero and a fair proportion of the citizenry is cheering him on. The madness of the crowds, if you will. Low-information voters influenced by the latest and greatest slogans. As long as Juska hides his actions beneath a veneer of respectable democracy, he can do whatever he wants. After all, Lyonesse has a sacred mission, and nothing can interfere with it." Norum's tone dripped with sarcasm as he spoke those words.

"Mass delusion is a frightening thing, Crevan," DeCarde said. "The Republic is falling victim to groupthink in a big way, and any dissenting voices are being drowned out, if not eliminated outright."

"But how could this happen so quickly?" Torma ushered them into his office and indicated they should sit around the low coffee table to one side of the room. "When I was there, just under six years ago, Lyonesse was a thriving democracy."

"It was already sick back then. The shock most citizens felt when we encountered the Hegemony and realized that our sacred mission was nothing of the sort irreversibly scarred the psyche of the public after over two hundred years of fervent belief that we alone were destined to repopulate human space."

"Yet you and Farrin appear untouched by this mental scarring."

"The military mind is generally more flexible than that of the average civilian. We're trained to adapt and overcome, no matter what. Have the Republic's circumstances changed? Fine. Let's go with the new paradigm."

Torma nodded. "That's quite true."

"It doesn't mean every one of our former Defense Force colleagues thinks as we do. On the contrary, the Hegemony's appearance shocked plenty of them, and they adopted the Lyonesse First mindset. Mainly the less imaginative, less intelligent, and less flexible, to be sure, but still in sufficient quantity for Derik Juska's purposes. He's appointing them to key positions, which means the Defense Force is quickly mirroring the Republic's paranoid political posture. Of course, appointing less able officers weakens Lyonesse's military capabilities, but Juska's good with that, so long as the military leadership is loyal to his regime."

"It's such a shame. We were actually looking at the Republic as a model to emulate. But I think that idea is dead, based on what Ardrix tells me when we occasionally meet."

Norum cocked his head to one side.

"Speaking of which, did you receive a replacement for her?"

"Yes. Maryam. She was the Leading Sister of the second attempt at bringing Celeste back into the fold. Since that is progressing better than we could have ever hoped, they brought Maryam back to become the Colonial Service's Leading Sister at Ardrix's recommendation. A small smile relaxed Torma's normally severe features. "Maryam should show up any minute now. She's as inquisitive as Ardrix and must know I'm entertaining guests."

As if on cue, a tall, slender woman with long dark hair framing a smooth, slightly rounded face dominated by dark eyes appeared in the doorway. She wore the black robes of the Void and a necklace on which hung an orb bearing a phoenix at its heart.

"Maryam, please join us." Torma made a come-in gesture. "I'd like to present Ambassador Currag DeCarde and Admiral Farrin Norum."

Both stood as she approached.

"I'm Farrin, and that's Currag," Norum said. "We left our former titles back in the Republic of Lyonesse."

"A pleasure," Maryam replied in a melodic alto as she inclined her head. "Welcome to Wyvern."

"Thank you."

Maryam took a seat opposite them.

"We were just discussing the Republic's precipitous descent into darkness," Torma said.

"Please do tell."

Norum gave her a thumbnail sketch of the situation, and when he was done, Maryam shook her head.

"How sad. It's amazing that one person can twist an entire nation."

"But not that rare." DeCarde shrugged. "There are many historical examples, the most recent being Stichus Ruggero. It happens when societies become too comfortable, too disengaged from their actual governance and allow those with evil intent to seize the levers of power because the checks and balances no longer work."

"I see." Maryam frowned just a little. "Does it mean you and Farrin are here permanently?"

DeCarde nodded.

"Probably. I can't foresee conditions changing any time soon, possibly not even in our lifetimes.

"And what will you do if you settle on Wyvern?"

Norum glanced at Torma.

"We're hoping Crevan can help with that."

The latter cocked an eyebrow at him.

"Perhaps. Two experienced former officers like you could surely be useful."

"There's only one condition," Norum said. "We won't participate in anything that could be used against the Republic. We may have fled it, but a lifetime of service means we're still loyal to its ideals even though Derik Juska is doing his best to erase them."

"Understood."

"And we'd also need to find something for Rey and Beth. They're solid investigators, both on the military and civilian sides."

Torma inclined his head.

"Of course. I'll give it some thought, but I figure I could find employment for the four of you in the Colonial Service's Inspectorate. Your backgrounds would serve me well."

As he brought them back to the apartment later, Torma asked, "Pardon me for being indelicate, but is there something more than just a friendly relationship between you and Rey Weston, Farrin?"

Norum chuckled.

"Guilty as charged. During the long run from Hatshepsut, we became rather intimate and found we enjoyed each other's company. Same for Currag and Beth."

Torma gave DeCarde an amused glance.

"How convenient."

"Quite," DeCarde replied in a dry tone, but a small smile played on his lips nonetheless.

—40—

Over the following days, Norum, DeCarde, Weston, and Svent spent some of their newly acquired Hegemony creds rebuilding a wardrobe and stocking the apartment. By the end of the week, Torma offered all four jobs with the Colonial Service Inspectorate's newly created Special Projects Division. He provided them with a large office in the Blue Annex, credentials that granted them access, and network accounts.

"What exactly does the Special Projects Division do?" Norum asked once they settled around the low table in Torma's office, coffee cups in hand. He'd quickly gotten used to the bitter, caffeinated drink, so different from the teas of his native Lyonesse, where coffee couldn't grow.

"Whatever I need it to." The slight smile on Torma's lips gave lie to his obtuse reply.

"We don't want charity jobs."

"Oh, you'll earn your keep. I have many questions plaguing me but no time to ferret out answers. Your arrival is a dream come true. Or near enough. There will even be some travel involved. You'll get to visit our newest colonies in pursuit of those answers."

"And what might the questions be?"

"Varied. For example, why did a colony's expenses suddenly increase by fifty percent, or why did its use of consumables double? Or why did relations with the natives suddenly worsen? Those sorts of things. I already have six files for you to work on, matters I couldn't handle because of higher priorities. I'll let you get familiar with them, how the Colonial Service and the Hegemony work, and how I run the Inspectorate, tiny as it is — there are only a dozen of us, plus you four now. Then, we can discuss the files. There's no hurry, seeing as how they've waited this long. Take your time."

"Okay, Crevan. And thank you."

Torma waved Norum's thanks away.

"I'm sure you'd have found me gainful employment if our positions were reversed."

"Definitely."

"Oh, and before I forget, another apartment in our building has become available. Since I assumed you'd be glad for a bit more privacy, I reserved it. It's on the fourth floor."

Norum and DeCarde looked at each other, then at the two women.

"Absolutely. Rey and I will move into it this afternoon."

"Then it's settled."

***

"Aren't those two Admiral Norum and Colonel DeCarde?" The Lyonesse agent turned his head toward the pair, who were strolling along New Draconis' principal shopping street, one closed to ground vehicles, along with two women.

His partner's eyes shifted behind sunglasses, and he nodded after a few moments.

"Yep. I figure they're with former LOI officers Weston and Svent."

Several weeks had passed since the four started working at the Colonial Office, and they were enjoying a sunny Saturday afternoon among the crowds filling the downtown pedestrian district. None of them suspected the Republic had sent spies to Wyvern aboard merchant vessels.

"There's a kill order out on all of them," the first agent murmured before taking a sip of coffee. Both sat at a small, wrought iron outdoor café table, enjoying a day off like everyone else. "And I now can see why. They betrayed the Republic by defecting to the Hegemony."

Both were members of the Defense Force Intelligence Group's Special Operations Division, which had branched out into intelligence gathering in the Hegemony during the last five years. The first agent, who went under the assumed name of Sallo Drea, was an Army senior master sergeant. The other, whose cover identity was that of one Yvanos Mardin, was a Marine Corps centurion commissioned from the ranks.

"We'll follow them to find out where they live," Mardin said before draining his coffee cup. "And then we'll see about carrying out the order."

"Won't that risk our cover?"

Mardin scoffed.

"We're not getting much actionable intelligence around here, and our time is almost up. Might as well terminate a few enemies of the Republic before jumping on a ship home."

Both men stood and separated, Mardin following Norum and the others while Drea followed Mardin, weaving in and out of the stream of people ambling along. When their quarry stopped to gaze through shop windows, Mardin continued for another fifty meters and entered a store, where he remained near the door, watching the street while Drea took up the trail. He left the store once the latter had passed and followed at a distance until the targets stopped again, and Drea went past them.

They continued in that manner for most of the afternoon until Norum and his companions left the shopping district. With the crowds thinning, they increased their distance but remained separate. Finally, shortly after sixteen hundred hours, the targets entered an apartment building called the Raijin Arms. Drea and Mardin walked past it without slowing, let alone stopping, and vanished around the next street corner, where they regrouped.

"Let's confirm they actually live there by consulting the directory," Mardin said. He fished a Hegemony-built communicator from his tunic pocket and searched for Norum and DeCarde. "Yep. Raijin Arms is the place. They're not using any cover identities, and no one else has those names in New Draconis. Gotta love the Hegemony's efficiency in keeping track of people."

"So now that we know where they live, how are we going to scrag them?"

"Let's give it some thought. We have plenty of time. Meanwhile, you still need to work on that lass from the chancellor's office."

Drea grimaced.

"Don't remind me. The only reason I've got an in with Darla is because she can't attract anyone else thanks to her toxic personality."

Mardin laughed as he patted his companion on the shoulder.

"Consider seducing her part of the sacrifices we must make to protect the Republic."

***

"You know, I've had a strange sensation of being watched for the last two hours, but it suddenly stopped the moment we entered the building," Norum remarked as they waited for the lift.

"Why wait until now to say something?" DeCarde asked.

"Because as much as I tried, I couldn't spot anyone tailing us."

Weston nodded.

"So that's why you were looking around more than usual."

Norum gave her a crooked grin.

"I was trying to be unobtrusive."

"You were, but I know you better than most people around here." She winked at him. "How sure are you about that feeling?"

"Pretty much one hundred percent. My great-grandmother several times removed was the most talented Sister of her era, if not of all times, and we Norums carry a shard of that talent. As a result, I've learned to listen to my gut instincts over the years because they're almost always right."

"It could be State Security keeping tabs on us," DeCarde said as they got into the lift. "I wonder if Crevan can get us access to any surveillance sensors covering the front of the building."

"Why don't we go ask him right now?"

They got off on the seventh floor and headed for Torma's apartment. Norum touched the call pad and stepped back. Within moments, the door opened.

"I hear you run an illegal bar, General." Norum grinned at Torma. "And I wanted to inspect the place for health and safety violations."

"You're looking for alcoholic drinks, is that it? Well, I'm sure I can find something palatable." Torma waved them into the small foyer, then led them into his living room. "What can I serve you?"

"I think we're in the mood for gin and tonic," Norum said, glancing at the others, who nodded as they sat.

"Then I'll make a jug." While Torma busied himself at a sideboard, he asked, "Not that I mind thirsty friends visiting me on a Saturday afternoon, but to what do I owe this unexpected pleasure?"

"We want to know if you can access any surveillance cameras facing the front of this building."

Torma gave Norum a surprised glance over his shoulder. Norum chuckled and explained why. After finishing, Torma distributed full glasses and took a seat.

"Someone watching you? Interesting. It wouldn't be the Commission. They don't have the resources to follow people who've already been vetted by the government, like you four. But that being said, it's not impossible one of my colleagues doesn't believe said vetting and is looking for evidence that you're not trustworthy. But I can obtain copies of the surveillance records without problems. A Commission major general gets pretty much anything lawful he asks for. If you'll pardon me."

Torma put his glass down and picked up his communicator, which sat on the table next to his chair. He touched the display, and moments later, a voice asked, "What can I do for you, General?"

"I need the surveillance records for the Raijin Arms covering the last half hour. Can you do that for me?"

"Certainly, sir. Give me five minutes, tops."

"Just send it to my communicator address. Torma, out."

He glanced at Norum.

"That was the Commission's New Draconis operations center. They can access public surveillance sensor data."

"There are advantages to a police state, after all," Norum said in an ironic tone.

"We're hardly that bad, Farrin."

"I know. I was just teasing you."

At that moment, Torma's communicator chimed.

"I believe we have the recording. Let me project it to my living room screen."

He touched the communicator's display once again, and the large monitor came to life with a view of the street in front of the Raijin Arms and a time notation in the lower right corner. Torma fast-forwarded the recording until Norum and his companions appeared.

"Okay, let's study everyone who comes up behind us."

A dozen people appeared, crossed the video pickup's field of view, and vanished again. Nothing distinguished them, and none gave the Raijin Arms so much as a glance — as far as they could tell. Several wore sunglasses and could easily be eying the building, with no one being the wiser.

"Please replay it, Crevan."

As he did so, Norum sat back, eyes narrowed. While he watched, he searched through his memories of the afternoon when he surreptitiously looked for anyone paying him more than passing attention. After the third replay, it finally clicked.

"Him." Norum pointed at the sunglasses-wearing, stocky man with short, dark hair and a square face. "I remember seeing him several times in downtown's pedestrian zone."

Torma froze the video and zoomed in on the man.

"Could just be a coincidence. We're not very far from the shopping district," DeCarde said.

"Keep it running."

A few seconds later, Norum said, "Stop. Him as well."

This time, Torma zoomed in on a tall, thin man with short blond hair, a narrow face, and a gray beard. He, too, wore sunglasses and casual clothes.

"Notice something about both of them? Replay the sequence from the beginning, please, Crevan."

After the second time, Rey Weston said, "They both move like long-service military men — with assurance, deliberation, and energy. That alone sets them apart from the rest of the people we see."

Norum pointed at her.

"Give the lady another glass of gin and tonic. She earned it."

"It could still be a coincidence."

Norum turned to DeCarde.

"Perhaps, but those are the only two I can remember seeing earlier. None of the others passing the Raijin Arms rang a bell. And the more I think about it, the more I'm convinced we were under observation for the latter part of our stroll until we entered the building. As I may have mentioned, I'm rarely wrong about this sort of thing."

"Okay, assuming it was them, what now?" DeCarde glanced at Torma. "Can you feed their faces into your surveillance state apparatus and get us identities?"

"I can try, but don't expect much. Like I said, the Hegemony isn't a police state, and we don't keep tabs on everyone. There's no giant database of biometric information on every living human being. Chances are we won't find anything about them."

Torma marked off the two men on the video and sent it back to the operations center with a request that they search for their identities. If those weren't on file, then for any other sightings of them,

—41—

"The operations center drew a blank on your two watchers," Torma said, entering the Special Projects office the following Monday. "They're not known to the Commission or to local police. They've appeared on surveillance video now and then in public places, but then, so have we."

"Anything from immigration?" Norum asked, causing Torma to chuckle.

"We don't have an immigration service, let alone stringent entry controls, as you might remember from your arrival on Wyvern. So, we'll not have any visual records of them landing on this world, nor will we know if they're from elsewhere. Not much of a police state, right?"

"Basically, you're saying we're out of luck trying to identify both men?"

"Indeed."

"And what if they're up to no good?"

"Then we must wait for them to act."

"Damn." Norum shrugged. "Oh, well. Onwards and upwards, as my grandmother always used to say. Thanks for informing us.

"You are most welcome." I do suggest you take extra precautions from now on when you are out and about."

With that, Torma turned on his heels and disappeared down the corridor.

The four exchanged looks, then resumed working without uttering another word.

Shortly after lunch, Sister Maryam popped her head through the office door.

"We've just received the latest intelligence digest from Lyonesse. Since you might be interested, especially by one item in particular, I've forwarded it to your queues."

Norum grinned at her.

"Thank you, Sister."

"Don't mention it." She vanished after briefly returning his smile.

He opened his queue and called up the digest. After skimming over its various items, Norum let out a low whistle.

"He's finally done it."

"Who and what?" DeCarde asked.

"Juska. He's rammed a motion through the Senate removing term limits, with seventy-five percent of the senators voting in favor."

"They would, the swine. It promises them lifetime places at the trough."

"And as long as he keeps the honorable senators happy, Juska is president for life. It says that public reaction to the move seems generally favorable. I wonder how he brainwashed the population to see it as positive."

"Juska's a skilled orator. Probably the best in Lyonesse history. He can wrap anything in rhetoric so convincing he'd have them vote to abolish the Republic." DeCarde gave Norum a sad smile. "Which they did when they elected the current crop of senators, though they knew it not."

"A shame," Weston said.

Norum nodded.

"That it is. But there's nothing we can do about it. And since it's unlikely we'll ever set foot on a Lyonesse-owned world again, we might as well observe the unfolding disaster from afar as disinterested parties while enjoying a bulb of beer and some snacks. Otherwise, we might get a permanent case of heartburn. And now, back to work. Otherwise, we'll never solve the mystery of the increased expenditure of consumables by the mission on Santa Theresa."

"I think we're going to end up visiting the place so we can interview the mission's leader and quartermaster," DeCarde said.

"Suits me." Norum shrugged. "We might as well get familiar with the colonies first-hand if we're going to be an effective special projects team for the service's Inspectorate."

DeCarde grinned at his friend.

"That's the spirit!"

***

Mardin and Drea watched the foursome leave the Raijin Arms, head for the Blue Annex several mornings in a row, and return from the Blue Annex to the Raijin Arms late in the afternoon. They rode aboard an automated staff car that picked them up and deposited them right in front of the apartment block's front doors, leaving only seconds of exposure to any putative sniper.

And the agents were both aware that neither possessed the skills to eliminate four targets within the limited time they would have.

As to area weapons capable of sending them into the Infinite Void, those just weren't accessible to anyone outside the Hegemony military. The government had made sure of that.

The Raijin Arms was equally inaccessible, being promoted as a protected building for senior government officials. Its entrance was essentially a secure airlock between the outer and inner doors, capable of trapping unauthorized visitors so the New Draconis police could pick them up if necessary. Mardin was aware that if they attempted to gain admittance, they would be in the custody of the police within minutes. Besides, like most residential buildings in New Draconis, it had surveillance sensors covering every entrance. As a result, both only approached the apartment block while disguised and had placed an almost invisible video pickup across the street covering the front door.

"We'll have to wait until they're out and about when off-duty," Mardin said a week after they first spotted Norum and the others. "As to how I don't have a clue."

"Poison," Drea suggested. "Brush by them and nail Norum and DeCarde with poison darts or needles. The two LOI officers aren't important enough to worry about."

"It's a possibility. We certainly don't want to shoot them at high noon on a Saturday in the shopping district."

"Unless they go for a nature hike, and we corner them on a deserted woodland trail. In that case, blasters blazing will be a fine thing."

"Although I don't know that they own a ground vehicle if they get driven to and from work in a Colonial Service car. It might limit their weekend outings."

"The only thing we can do is watch them via the video feed and get a sense of their movements."

It proved to be a tedious task, skimming through the feed to catch a glimpse of their targets, but by the third week, they began to see a pattern emerge. For instance, they went out to eat the evening meal at various restaurants twice a week, walking to and from the pedestrian district.

Mardin and Drea, who'd moved to an apartment near the Raijin Arms, followed them — in disguise, a different one each time — and watched them enjoy their evenings. But they still couldn't figure out how to assassinate Norum and DeCarde and escape unscathed.

—42—

Lannion
Republic of Lyonesse

"General reaction among the citizenry to the news the Senate had abolished term limits appears positive, Mister President." Antony Geffen, the Secretary for Public Affairs, said, wearing a pleased expression. "Our education push over the last few months has been effective."

The remaining cabinet members around the table suppressed a smile at his euphemism for indoctrination. In actuality, the Department for Public Affairs disseminated propaganda supporting Derik Juska's regime. It determined what was true and what wasn't and was quietly rewriting some of the Republic's history to make Juska's presidency appear inevitable.

The president nodded once.

"I expected no less, Antony."

Geffen was one of his more inspired choices as cabinet secretary. He'd proved to be superlative in creating effective propaganda and molding public opinion just the way Juska wanted.

"Anything else?"

"No, sir."

Juska turned his eyes on the Secretary of Defense.

"Your turn."

"I have only one item, sir. Our agents on Wyvern have spotted Admiral Norum, Ambassador DeCarde, and the two LOI officers who vanished. All four are apparently working with the Hegemony's Colonial Service."

Juska's face hardened.

"Damn traitors. I trust the agents will do their utmost to eliminate them?"

"They will, sir. Count on it. Both are long-serving members of military intelligence, highly capable and utterly ruthless. They were specially selected with the help of the Sisters for their mission."

President Juska nodded. He knew about Summus Abbatissa Elana's program to find those high on the psychopathy spectrum for special missions. A small number of her Sisters were skilled in identifying them, and she encouraged those.

"Just make sure they die."

When the weekly cabinet meeting — increasingly useless, in Juska's opinion — ended, he left the cabinet room, making no small talk with his secretaries, and returned to his office. Once behind closed doors, he allowed himself a few moments of rage at Norum and DeCarde escaping to the Hegemony.

But then another thought asserted itself. Too many senior Republic officials had vanished in the last two or three years, and not at the hands of his entirely loyal LOI. Could they have ended up on Wyvern, smuggled out of the Republic via Hatshepsut?

And if so, would they form the nucleus of an opposition movement to his regime, perhaps encouraged by a Hegemony government desirous to destabilize the Republic? Maybe he should increase the number of agents in the Hegemony and give them the task of finding and killing traitors. Juska called back the Secretary of Defense, who, fortunately, was still inside Government House.

"What can I do for you, Mister President?" Ty Beelen, the SecDef, asked as he sat across the desk from Juska.

"Ty, it occurs to me that many of the dissidents who slipped through the fingers of the LOI might have relocated to the Hegemony, where they could form the core of a rebel group aided and abetted by Wyvern."

"Indeed, a distinct possibility, sir."

Juska explained what he wanted, and Beelen nodded. "Can do, sir. But we'll need to push back the anticipated total embargo on any starship contact between Hatshepsut and the Hegemony so we can insert and extract our agents under cover of commercial visits."

"Very well. Consider the embargo plans suspended until further notice. How soon can you infiltrate the extra operatives?"

"Not for a few weeks. We need the Sisters to help us select the most appropriate candidates first, then we have to train them so they can pass as Hegemony citizens, and finally, they face the long trip to Wyvern."

"Try to make it as fast as possible. Send teams as soon as they're ready. Don't wait until you assemble a full strike force. The sooner those dissidents merge with the Infinite Void, the better."

"Yes, sir."

"You may go."

Now that Juska had made a decision on the dissidents, he felt better. Good enough to summon his secretary and take her into his private chambers for some relaxation.

Ty Beelen didn't need weeks to find his first assassination team. When he asked the head of military intelligence, he found out that the organization already ran several of them to take out people deemed a security risk to the Republic. Beelen was smart enough not to ask why he hadn't been told about this before. He merely gave the general his marching orders.

Since one of the better teams was between assignments, it was quickly primed to operate in the Hegemony and dispatched to Hatshepsut, where it would find berths aboard a merchant ship headed for Wyvern.

—43—

New Draconis
Wyvern Hegemony

"I get the feeling we're being followed again," Norum whispered out of the corner of his mouth. He, DeCarde, Weston, and Svent were strolling along a downtown pedestrian street, digesting a fine evening meal taken at one of their favorite bistros.

"That's how many times now?"

"Pretty much every time we've been outside the apartment, except when we're at work. But whoever it is must be wearing different disguises every time. I can't recognize anyone."

They stopped in front of a store window, and Norum scanned the reflection of the crowd behind them to see if anyone was acting suspiciously. He thought he'd seen a man look away too quickly when their eyes were about to meet, but he couldn't make him out.

DeCarde saw his friend's reaction and asked, "Did you spot someone?"

"Maybe."

"Persistent little bastards."

"Their parents might have been married, Currag." He grimaced. "I'm getting mightily tired of this. Don't you think it's about time we confront them?"

"And how would we do that?"

"Lead them into an empty alley, a parking garage, something isolated where they'll get a chance at us. Except we'll be expecting them. Everyone is armed, yes?"

All three nodded.

"Good. So am I. There can't be more of them than there are of us in the first place. I figure a team of two is the most likely scenario. Are you game?"

"Yes. Let's see what we've got," Weston said. "And I think I know the perfect place to ambush them."

Norum made a sweeping gesture with his hand. "Lead on, my dear."

Weston turned left, off the main street three blocks down, and then left again, and they found themselves in a poorly lit alley running behind the stores fronting the pedestrian zone. It was lined with large waste disposal receptacles at regular intervals. They created zones of darkness interspersed with light coming from the back of the buildings.

"How did you find out about this place?" Norum asked in a low voice.

"I didn't, but figured there would be an alley behind the storefronts, someplace empty at this time of night." She grinned at him. "Now, how about we make out and see if that draws in our tail."

Weston wrapped her arms around Norum's neck as she pulled him halfway into the shadows of a garbage bin, and he pulled out his weapon, keeping it hidden between them. After a few moments, DeCarde and Svent did likewise across the alley.

Norum kept his eyes on the alley's mouth as he and Weston kissed, and sure enough, after less than a minute, two figures appeared. As they passed beneath the last streetlamp before the alley, he recognized both as faces he'd spotted earlier without knowing they were following them. Weston, whose back was to the interlopers, knew they'd appeared when Norum stiffened.

He didn't look at them directly but kept watch out of the corner of his eyes and tried to appear totally captivated by Weston as they crept into the alley, moving from shadow to shadow. As they neared, the men split up, one headed for Norum and Weston, the other for DeCarde and Svent.

Suddenly, weapons appeared in their hands, and they adopted a firing stance.

"Now," Norum shouted. Weston and Svent dropped to the ground as he and DeCarde, partially masked by garbage bins, pointed their guns at the two men. Within moments, both women had pulled out their pieces and were also pointing at them.

"Drop your weapons," Norum said. "Drop them now!"

When they seemed frozen in place, he shot once over their heads, the blaster round a streak of light that splashed the rear wall of a store, burning a divot in the stone.

The men looked at each other and slowly bent over to place their guns on the ground, and then they straightened.

"Put your hands on top of your heads, then drop to your knees."

Both complied, and, with Weston and Svent covering them, Norum and DeCarde stepped forward to retrieve the men's weapons.

"Needlers," DeCarde said, examining the one he picked up. He ejected the magazine and let out a low whistle once he saw the contents. "Deadly poison darts. Nasty stuff. You asshats were looking to kill us, weren't you?"

When neither of them replied, although they glared at him, DeCarde shrugged. "Have it your way, although I'm sure the State Security Commission has folks skilled in loosening tongues. Speaking of which, I suppose we should call Crevan."

"Already on it," Norum said. He'd tucked the needler in his waistband but still held his blaster while he fished his communicator from a shirt pocket. "Ah, Crevan. Sorry to disturb you so late in the evening, but we caught the two people who've been following us. At least, I suppose they're the same ones. They pulled needlers loaded with lethal darts on us, but we turned the tables. Could you call the right folks to come and pick them up?"

"Certainly. Where are you?"

"Wait one." Norum activated his communicator's positioning system and hit transmit. "You got it?"

"You're in an alley off Freedonia Street. Let me guess — you entrapped them."

"Yep."

"Stand by. I'll have the Commission's Wyvern Group send someone stat."

"Thanks."

"Torma, out."

One of the men moved his hands, and DeCarde aimed his blaster at him. "Don't even think about it, my friend, or I'll wing you. Of course, I might miss and kill you instead. It doesn't matter to me what happens, although it might matter to you."

Fifteen minutes passed before a large, unmarked ground car turned into the alley and stopped. It disgorged four black-uniformed Commission troopers, led by a major who walked up to Norum. He was stocky, with a lantern jaw and intelligent, deep-set eyes beneath bushy black brows.

"Sir, I'm Major Alsten Durron. You're Admiral Norum, the one who called General Torma?"

"Yes, I am." Norum gestured at the two kneeling men. "They attempted to kill us, but fortunately didn't get off a shot."

"I understand from the general that they'd been following you for a while. Any idea who they might be working for?"

"Probably the Republic of Lyonesse. There's a price on my head, and I presume that of Ambassador DeCarde." Norum pulled out the needler and held it out, handgrip first. "They carried needlers with lethal loads."

Durron tsked as he shook his head. "Highly illegal."

He gestured at one of his troopers, who took both weapons, then oversaw their former owners being shackled and dragged to the car.

"I'll interrogate them in the morning, say, around ten. You're both welcome to attend. I'm sure General Torma will as well, and he can get you into the Wyvern Group's headquarters. If not, just call the HQ information center tomorrow and ask for me."

"Thank you, Major. I believe we will join you. It'll be interesting to watch how the Commission interrogates prisoners."

Durron drew himself to attention. "Until tomorrow, sir."

Then, he turned on his heels and climbed aboard the car, which backed out of the alley and vanished down Freedonia Street.

Norum slipped his blaster back into its holster and sighed while Weston and Svent climbed to their feet.

"This wasn't how I expected my evening to end, but it's good that we finally caught them."

"Let's hope they're the only ones after us," DeCarde said.

"I should find out soon enough because my sixth sense for being followed will tell me."

"Hurrah for your sixth sense." Weston wrapped her arm around Norum's and looked fondly at him. "How about we go home. All this excitement has put me in the mood."

He grinned at her. "So that's what it takes, eh?"

—44—

Norum studied both prisoners on the split screen display dominating one wall of the observation gallery. The basement of the New Draconis State Security Commission headquarters seemed cold and impersonal, just the right sort of atmosphere to leech hope from detainees, such as the two in front of him, sitting in separate interview rooms. Their hands were shackled to a staple set in the middle of the metal table, which, along with two metal chairs, were the sole spot of brightness in an otherwise small, drab, windowless space.

Neither of them showed so much as a shred of emotion. They appeared to be in a semi-meditative trance, eyes unfocused, staring straight ahead, their breathing deep and regular, if slow, and Norum felt a sneaking admiration for their stoic calm.

"Neither of them seems fussed," Currag DeCarde remarked. "The sign of professionals."

"Indeed." Torma nodded.

"I understand that they've been on Wyvern for almost two years. Or at least their current identities arrived here almost two years ago," Norum said.

"That is correct. Of course, the identities are false, although the credentials appear genuine enough. Neither has a history on any of the Hegemony's four core worlds." Movement on one side of the split screen attracted Torma's attention. "Here we go. Major Durron is one of the best interrogators in the Wyvern Group."

They watched as Durron sat across from Mardin and considered him in silence for almost a minute while the latter ignored the Commission officer.

"Yvanos Mardin. Not your real name, of course. Are you conditioned against interrogation?"

Mardin's eyes suddenly focused on Durron as he woke from his trance.

"Yes."

"Why?"

"Meaning, why am I conditioned? So I can't reveal anything, obviously."

A cold smile appeared on Durron's lips.

"Funny guy, aren't you? We have ways of bypassing conditioning. They're ugly, especially for the one being interrogated. Apparently, it leaves lifelong mental scars. That's if you don't go insane by the end of it."

Mardin shrugged but didn't say a word. His eyes remained as expressionless as ever.

"Okay. Why did you try to kill Farrin Norum, Currag DeCarde, Rey Weston, and Beth Svent?" When Mardin didn't reply, Durron asked, "Who do you work for?"

Still no answer.

"What's your real name, and where do you come from?"

Mardin remained just as silent as before.

"Want to know what I think? I figure you're a spy from the Republic of Lyonesse."

Did Norum see a slight twitch around Mardin's eyes?

"And you received orders to assassinate those four filthy defectors." An icy grin spread across Durron's broad face as he saw the same thing. "Yes, that's it. Well, you're in luck. We don't execute people for attempted murder. Or espionage, for that matter. At least not in peacetime, and right now, we're not at war with the Republic. I assume you keep in touch with your spymasters via the traders operating between the Hegemony and Hatshepsut."

Mardin's eyes slid over Durron's shoulder and stared at a point on the blank wall behind him.

"Is there a particular trader who carries your messages, or do you use anyone headed for Hatshepsut? I assume you encode communications, of course, but we found nothing that looked like an encryption algorithm when we tossed your apartment. Why is that?"

Durron stared at Mardin, who avoided his gaze.

"What sort of intelligence are you gathering and passing on to Lyonesse? It can't be top secret stuff. You have no access."

Unexpectedly, Durron stood.

"I'll let you think about our little one-sided conversation. Cooperate by telling me everything I want to know, and we'll ship you home unharmed."

Then, he left Mardin, who closed his eyes and fell back into his semi-meditative trance. Or so it seemed. But his breathing wasn't quite as slow and deep as before.

Durron entered the second interview room and sat in front of the other agent.

"Sallo Drea. Not your real name, of course."

He asked Drea the same questions as Mardin and got the same non-answers, though Drea didn't so much as blink where Mardin had shown that slight twitch. Durron left Drea with the same words and vanished from the display. Moments later, he entered the gallery.

"That's it for the opening round, General Torma. We'll subject them to the disorientation protocols for the next seventy-two hours and get at it again."

"I beg your pardon, Major," Norum said, "but what are these disorientation protocols?"

Durron turned to him.

"We'll put them in cells lit up day and night, feed them meals at irregular times, and take them out to exercise at irregular times. That'll make them lose complete track of time while depriving them of sleep. It makes them more susceptible to questioning. And if I figure we need to bring in a Sister, she'll find it easier to prod their emotions and make them experience the sort of debilitating fear that loosens tongues without triggering the conditioning."

Norum and DeCarde glanced at each other in surprise.

"You use Sisters to help interrogate suspects?" The former asked.

"Yes. It's more humane than any other form of coercion. Doesn't the Republic?"

"No. Our version of the Void stays well away from police matters, let alone mind meddling."

Durron frowned as he nodded.

"Interesting. I knew there were differences between the Void Reborn and the Republic's version, but not so fundamental ones. In any case, we'll try again in seventy-two hours if you'd like to watch. I'll give you the exact time on the day of." He turned to Torma again. "With your permission, General?"

"You may go, Major. And thank you."

Durron saluted, turned on his heels, and left the observation gallery.

"You use Sisters?" Norum asked in an incredulous tone.

"We do and have for a long time. Ardrix helped me interrogate many suspects before we were seconded to the Colonial Office. But don't worry. I haven't yet witnessed or heard of anyone going insane under a Sister's gentle ministering. And besides, we only use them on those who we know are guilty."

DeCarde gave Torma an ironic look.

"Not a police state, eh?"

Without losing his sober expression, Torma arched an equally ironic eyebrow at him.

"Why not use all the resources at one's disposal? As Major Durron said, it's more humane than any other form of coercion." He gestured at the door. "Shall we?"

***

Three days later, just after lunch, Torma led them back into the Commission HQ's basement, but not to the same observation gallery as before. Instead, this one opened on either side, via one-way windows, onto what looked almost like surgical suites. Mardin and Drea were strapped to upright steel racks — feet, legs, torso, arms, and head — so they couldn't move.

When Norum asked, Torma said, "It's to prevent them from injuring themselves under the impulse of the Sister's intervention. As I said before, this is a humane procedure."

"A question for you." DeCarde glanced at Torma. "If your Sisters mind-meddle, why do they not simply nudge the suspects into admitting everything? Why inject their thoughts with fear?"

"Conditioning prevents them from speaking even under a Sister's empathic influence. But we found that debilitating fear will break through."

"I see."

"Only a few Sisters can do so, however. I believe Major Durron will use Sister Valery today — if neither of them will speak."

"They certainly look frazzled." Norum jerked his chin at Mardin.

"Sleep deprivation and confusion about time will do that. Right now, both believe six days have passed, not three, and it's weighing heavily on their minds and bodies." At that moment, Durron entered the room with Mardin in it.

"Good evening, Yvanos. You don't mind if I call you by your first name, do you? I just feel like we know each other well enough by now."

Mardin gave him a bleary-eyed stare but didn't make a sound.

"You're probably wondering why I've had you tied up to the rack. It's for your own protection, in case I have to use special means to get your cooperation. I wouldn't want you flailing around and hurting yourself, seeing as how I intend to send you home once we're done here. Now, shall we begin? What is your real name and world of origin?"

"Fuck you." The words came out as a croak.

"Ah, you've regained the ability to speak. Excellent." Durron paced around the rack, slipping from Mardin's field of vision. "Now, are you an agent of the Lyonesse government?"

No reply.

"How long have you been on Wyvern, and what is your mission here? Surely, it's not simply to execute four defectors. You stumbled upon them by accident."

Durron stopped in front of Mardin and repeated the same questions he'd asked three days earlier but to no avail. Mardin remained as silent as the grave. Durron resumed pacing and repeated his questions, beginning with the first one, asking for Mardin's real name. But the latter didn't make a sound.

"Very well, Yvanos. I'll have to use Sister Valery's talent to get the information I need from you."

That got a reaction from Mardin. His eyes fixed on Durron.

"What do you mean by using this Sister's talent?"

Durron smiled. "You'll see shortly."

He walked over to the door and opened it. A short, round-faced woman with curly black hair framing an aquiline nose and impassive brown eyes entered. She wore the black robes of the Void with a phoenix orb dangling from a silver chain around her neck.

"Mister Mardin refuses to cooperate, Sister. If you could convince him otherwise, I'd be grateful."

Sister Valery walked over to Mardin's rack and stopped one pace before him. Her eyes met his, and she held his gaze for what seemed like a long time.

"It should be easy, Major," Valery finally said. "His mental barriers are weak, and his subconscious is filled with all manner of horrors. He's obviously lived a hard life — both for him and those with whom he came into contact. I will begin now."

Within seconds, Mardin's eyes widened in fear, and his mouth opened, but no sound came out. His entire body trembled, and he struggled against the restraints. Moments later, he slumped as far as his fetters allowed him, panting loudly.

"What the—" He gasped, a wild look on his face.

"Are you ready to answer me, Yvanos?" Durron asked. "Or do I ask Sister Valery to enter your mind again?"

"You're nuts. Crazy. Certifiable. And you, Sister, you're a fucking abomination." Mardin's voice quivered.

"Perhaps. But antagonizing the Sister by calling her an abomination?" He tsked. "A terrible choice of words, Yvanos. You ought to be careful since you've experienced what she can do. Now I'll ask again. What is your real name and your world of origin?"

When Mardin didn't answer, Durron nodded at Valery. "Give him another taste."

This time, he screamed.

"V59 726 748, Forrester, Harold, Centurion, born on Yotai," Mardin said once Sister Valery withdrew from his mind, panting as he spat out serial number, name, rank, and planet of origin. "Republic of Lyonesse Marine Corps, detailed to military intelligence."

— 45 —

"Centurion Forrester, pleased to make your acquaintance. Yotai, is it? One of Lyonesse's reclaimed worlds. A former imperial sector capital, if I'm not mistaken. Your forebears must have come from Lyonesse, then. Sector capitals were wiped clean of life during the Great Scouring." Durron glanced at the two-way mirror hiding his audience in the observation gallery before turning his eyes back on the prisoner. "So, tell me, which traders do you use to transmit messages?"

When Forrester didn't immediately reply, Durron said, "Sister, I believe the good centurion needs another meeting with the monsters lurking in his subconscious."

Almost immediately, Forrester rattled off a series of names in a shaky voice, then added, "None of them know anything about the contents of the communications. They're merely paid to enter the message into the subspace queue on Hatshepsut and pick up anything addressed to us like they do for everyone else conducting legitimate business between the Republic and the Hegemony."

"Thank you, Centurion. Why did you try to kill Farrin Norum, Currag DeCarde, Rey Weston, and Beth Svent?"

"Because there's an execution order out on them. They betrayed the Republic. It was mentioned in our last message from home."

"And you saw nothing wrong with killing innocent people who'd found refuge on Wyvern?"

Forrester made a face. "No. Treason is treason, and orders are orders. I serve the Lyonesse government and will do whatever it requires."

"What sort of intelligence have you gathered?"

"Nothing top secret," Forrester admitted after a moment of silence. "Most of it was from public sources. We collated the information and sent it home. We're still working on developing humint."

"Could you give me examples of the publicly sourced intelligence you sent to Lyonesse?"

Forrester let out a bark of bitter laughter.

"I've got plenty. You people aren't exactly particular regarding data protection, probably because you haven't met an adversary in two hundred years."

"And the Republic is?"

"Better than you lot. For example, we pieced together the size and composition of your armed forces down to the last ship simply from reading publications, listening to the newsnets, and talking to off-duty military personnel in various drinking establishments. Nicely done, recovering those forty-eight ships from Cascadia, by the way. Putting them on internal security duties allowed you to send your modern ships out into the big bad galaxy."

Durron nodded appreciatively.

"Okay, a good example. Got any more?"

"Sure. We recently sent a comprehensive economic assessment and forecast back home, created from open-source publications. Your economy is working at full speed, and certain sectors, such as shipbuilding, are experiencing workforce shortages. Some in your government are worried that the Hegemony is expanding much too fast and could experience even greater shortages across most areas of endeavor. But the economic expansion is driven by politics, namely competition with the Republic, rather than organically."

"Very good, Centurion. We'll review everything you've sent to your masters on Lyonesse over the coming days. In the meantime, we'll give you better accommodations and living conditions."

"And then?"

"Once you've told us everything, we'll ship you home unharmed." Durron's smile didn't reach his eyes. "Since you didn't get a shot at Admiral Norum and his friends, there's no point in prosecuting you for attempted murder. And your intelligence-gathering activities are hardly worthy of incarceration since you merely took advantage of our laxness."

"Gee, thanks." Forrester must have been feeling better because his reply oozed with sarcasm.

"By the way, your companion Sallo Drea, or whatever his real name is—"

"Jon Sexton, master sergeant, Lyonesse Army."

"Has been watching every moment of your interrogation from the room next door, where he's also strapped to a rack, just like you are. Of course, he couldn't hear you since I plan on asking him a few questions as well. But perhaps Sister Valery's intervention won't be necessary." Durron touched a control. "He can hear you now if you want to tell him about your ordeal."

"Hey, Jon," Forrester said in a loud voice, "you don't want to experience the Sister's mind meddling. Trust me on that. I saw things uglier than my worst nightmares."

"And they were drawn from your own subconscious," Valery said in a mild tone. "I merely allowed you to experience them consciously."

"Yeah, well, I'd rather never see that sort of thing again for as long as I live." Forrester looked at her out of the corner of his eyes.

"And you won't unless you get into trouble again." Major Durron walked over to the door, which slid open, revealing two large, muscular, heavily armed Commission noncoms. "You may take Centurion Forrester to the detention suite."

Then, trailed by Sister Valery, he left the room, walked across the corridor and both entered the one holding Sexton.

"Good day, Sergeant. And how are you?"

Sexton looked at him with overt suspicion but didn't reply.

"You've seen your comrade enjoy the Sister's ministrations. Will you answer my questions freely, or shall I ask Sister Valery to open your subconscious and let the monsters hidden there escape?"

When Sexton still refused to speak, Durron nodded at Valery.

"Go ahead and give him a brief taste."

As she moved to stand in front of him, Sexton's expressionless eyes followed her, and he met Valery's gaze without flinching. But then her stare felt like she was plunging into his soul, and moments later, he gasped.

"Okay, you've made your point," Sexton said once he'd regained a measure of sanity. "Ask away."

Durron repeated the questions he'd put to Forrester and received the same answers. When he was done, Durron gave Sexton a satisfied nod.

"That's it, my friend. I'll be delving into details with you and your comrade over the coming days, but essentially, your ordeal is over, and we will send you home on the next ship heading to Hatshepsut. You'll now join Centurion Forrester in the detention suite, which is really a small, secure apartment where you can take your ease."

***

"That was, um, impressive," DeCarde said in a dubious tone as they watched Durron and Sister Valery leave the interrogation room, replaced by guards who untied Sexton and escorted him out. "Monsters in the subconscious? I'm not even sure the Lyonesse version of the Order knows about those."

"They do," Norum said in a soft voice. "But ever since my forbear Marta Norum's day, they avoid speaking of it, let alone going there after she unleashed monsters so depraved it killed the subject of the experiment."

"Oh." DeCarde's eyebrows shot up. "Family lore?"

Norum nodded.

"Not everyone is this susceptible to a Sister's opening their subconscious," Torma said. "In fact, apparently only those with sociopathic or psychopathic tendencies harbor monsters strong enough to cause the sort of fear we saw in Forrester and Sexton. I, for instance, know I don't have them. You see, the Commission subjects everyone who works with a Sister to the treatment you saw, so they are fully aware of its effect. Contemplating my subconscious felt strange, yes, frightening too, but not terrifying. At least not to the extent we just witnessed."

"So, what you're saying is that Forrester and Sexton are on the sociopathy spectrum?" DeCarde asked.

"Indeed." Torma nodded.

"And what if they hadn't been — if they didn't have monsters lurking in the depths of their souls?"

"Then Valery would have created them, something very few of the Sisters can do, even among those working for the Commission. But the criminals we deal with have those tendencies. Otherwise, they wouldn't end up in our interrogation rooms."

"And I suppose good spies must be a bit psycho to survive."

"The fact they were about to carry out the kill orders on you without hesitation certainly indicates psychological abnormalities."

"Contrary to Rey and Beth, who fled the LOI because they wouldn't assassinate me." Norum cocked an amused eyebrow at DeCarde. "It's good to know our companions aren't sociopaths."

"Yep." A thoughtful expression appeared on DeCarde's face. "You know, we may not be doing Forrester and Sexton any favors by shipping them back to the Republic. President-for-life Derik Juska won't be forgiving to spies who got themselves caught and interrogated. It might be a good idea if we talked to them.

"Agreed." Norum turned to Torma. "Do you think they'd be welcome to settle here?"

The latter's eyes narrowed for a few seconds.

"Perhaps. Definitely, if they work with counterintelligence, feeding disinformation to their masters. At least for a while."

"You'd let them stay if they turn double agents." Norum tilted his head to one side. "We'd appreciate a few minutes with Forrester and Sexton. Can you arrange it?"

"Certainly." Torma nodded. He pulled out his communicator and made a brief call to Major Durron. "Follow me."

He led them into the corridor, turned left, and headed toward the stairs, which he took downward. The second basement level was just as cold and impersonal as the first, with antiseptic white walls pierced by equally white doors, all bathed in harsh illumination. Torma stopped before a door marked 101 and touched the pad embedded in its jamb.

It slid open to reveal a small compartment with an inner door and a bank of displays on the wall. Those displays showed innocuous-looking rooms furnished like a mid-level apartment — a living room with an open-concept kitchen and dining room and two bedrooms with ensuite baths. Fake windows showed outside scenes even though the place was two stories underground.

As the door closed behind them, they observed Forrester and Sexton sitting in opposite chairs in the living room, glasses containing an amber liquid in hand.

"Whiskey?" DeCarde asked, eyebrow cocked.

"Yes," Torma replied. "The detention suite is for those whom we must hold for a while but will not prosecute or subject to any more coercive interrogations. It comes with every comfort."

"Interesting."

Torma touched a control pad embedded in the inner door jamb, and it slid aside silently, opening on Forrester and Sexton, who stared at them in disbelief. Norum and DeCarde entered while Torma stayed in the antechamber, letting the door close.

"Got any more of that stuff?" Norum nodded at the glass Forrester was holding.

The latter recovered after a few heartbeats and nodded.

"Sure, Admiral." He stood, went to the kitchen area, and took a pair of glasses from a cupboard. A green, triangular bottle already sat on the counter. "It's Glen Draconis. Good stuff."

Forrester poured healthy amounts into both glasses and handed them to Norum and DeCarde, who took the remaining living room chairs.

"Slainte." Norum raised his glass before taking a sip. "Yep, it's smooth. Nice of the State Security Commission to stock their detention suites with more than mere rotgut."

"What do you want?"

Forrester eyed him with naked suspicion, as did Sexton.

"To have a little chat with you."

"Seeing as we're a captive audience, go ahead and talk." He took a mouthful of whiskey.

"Major Durron said you'd be repatriated to the Republic once he finishes your debriefing."

"Yeah. Are you going to tell me that's not the case?"

"Oh, he'll put you on the next ship bound for Hatshepsut with your luggage and money. But what happens when you report to your superiors? And those superiors report to President Juska?"

Forrester shrugged.

"We'll probably be fired. Or at least removed from intelligence duty. Which doesn't matter. I'm done anyhow. Retirement doesn't look so bad."

"So am I," Sexton said.

"The problem is, people who disappoint the president find themselves vanishing permanently these days, and make no mistake, Juska will be told of your failure. How much do you want to bet you might easily join the disappeared? After all, you're no longer of any use to the government."

Norum could tell the idea surprised Forrester, but then his eyes narrowed as he thought about it.

"You realize Ambassador DeCarde and I fled the Republic one step ahead of government assassins sent at Juska's orders because our existence supposedly threatens his regime. Do you think he'll spare a pair of low-ranking failed spies when he's after us?"

"What are you suggesting, Admiral?"

"You have the option of staying in the Hegemony."

Forrester scoffed.

"After they caught us spying on them? I doubt it."

"Not if you feed your superiors whatever the Hegemony wants. I'm sure they're willing to pay handsomely. It's low risk, low effort, high reward. Plus, you get to live out a natural lifespan."

"Is that what you're doing? Working against the Republic?"

Norum shook his head.

"No. We work for the Colonial Service's Inspector General, auditing Hegemony colonies for best practices, accounting, corruption, that sort of thing."

He drained his glass and stood, imitated by DeCarde.

"I'll let you mull it over. If you're willing to act as double agents for a bit, just let Major Durron know. He'll organize everything. Of course, you'll have to surrender your codes to the Commission."

With that, they turned on their heels and headed for the door, feeling the eyes of both men burning holes in their backs.

Once out in the corridor, Torma asked, "Do you think they'll do it?"

"That depends on how far along the psychopathy spectrum they are. Pure psychopaths are out for themselves only. They have no loyalties and no attachments. For them, betraying a star nation is no bigger deal than betraying a friend. They'd do it in a second if it helps them."

— 46 —

"Do you think Admiral Norum's story that our own government might disappear us for failure holds up, Harold?" Sexton eyed his comrade as he took another sip of Glen Draconis.

Forrester shrugged and said, in an irritable tone, "How the hell should I know?"

"Still dealing with the interrogation?"

"Yeah. What's it to you?"

"Compared to me, you got a massive dose of the Sister's mind meddling, so I'm not surprised," Sexton replied, using a soft voice. "I was utterly terrified by those few seconds I experienced the monsters and thought I'd lose my sanity."

Forrester grunted.

"I'm still not sure I didn't lose mine, and this is just a manifestation of my madness." He waved his arm, indicating the room.

"Nah. It's real, and we both cracked under interrogation, which brings me back to my question. What do you figure will happen to us when we get home?"

After taking a mouthful of whiskey, Forrester stared into the dregs at the bottom of his glass.

"Nothing good, I reckon. The admiral is probably right when he says the boss won't forgive us for getting caught and spilling everything. But from there to having us executed? I dunno."

He looked up at Sexton.

"I'll tell you one thing for sure. If we defect, we'll never set foot on a Republic world for as long as we live."

"Just like Admiral Norum, Ambassador DeCarde, the two LOI officers, and a lot of high-priced folks from Lyonesse we've spotted around New Draconis over the last twelve months, which means we'd be in good company."

"Sounds to me like you've already made up your mind." Forrester stood and headed for the kitchen, where the bottle of Glen Draconis waited. "You want some more?"

"Not right now, thanks." Sexton shook his head. "I don't know that I've chosen to stay on Wyvern just yet. But since I have nothing waiting for me at home, other than a pissed-off boss and possibly a blaster round in the back of the head, I won't lie. It's an attractive option."

"Even if it comes at the price of feeding false intelligence back to the Republic?" Forrester poured himself another dram and rejoined Sexton.

"Look, it's clear to both of us that the Republic we served for such a long time is fading away if it hasn't already perished. Derik Juska made sure of that when he got the Senate to vote for removing term limits. I'm sure he's got other items on his to-do list that'll help turn Lyonesse into a dictatorship. So, yeah. I'd have no problems sending fake information back. Consider it the price for maybe saving our lives."

***

"Not bad." Sexton looked around at the flat the State Security Commission assigned to them. It was nowhere near the Raijin Arms and in a slightly shabby part of New Draconis, but still near the main amenities. "We can live here easily."

Two bedrooms with ensuite baths, a large living room and dining room combined, a separate kitchen, and a balcony completed the fifth-story apartment. It was given that the place had surveillance sensors, but in return, the larder was full, and the bar held a broad selection of alcoholic drinks.

Forrester grunted.

"And no rent, thanks to our new employers. I suppose it could be worse."

"Time to check for any messages from home. Or what used to be home," Sexton added in an acerbic tone.

The agents used a pair of darknet nodes to send and receive communications delivered by starships on the Hatshepsut run. Incoming messages — encoded — were beamed to one node address by the ship. Outbound ships queried the other for messages that would be downloaded into the Hatshepsut subspace communications array. Their connection to both nodes was untraceable. When interviewed, both men had only revealed the existence of the second, outbound node as a form of insurance to keep some sort of communications conduit with the Republic open.

Sexton switched on the apartment's communicator and accessed the inbound one via a dozen cutouts, knowing the

Commission was looking over his virtual shoulder for the outbound node. He found a single missive. And it didn't come from any starship. It came from another Hegemony darknet node. Sexton downloaded it and the decryption algorithm onto his personal communicator, which had been returned by the Commission. He assumed it was equally compromised and didn't immediately decode the message.

"How about we go get us some new clothes?"

Forrester, who'd been examining the bedrooms, grunted. "Why?"

"Because I asked."

At hearing Sexton's tone, Forrester reappeared in the living room and gave him a questioning look.

The former simply shook his head and said, "Shall we?"

They wandered to a clothing store where they bought several full sets, changing into one of them and abandoning the clothes they'd worn. Then, Sexton led Forrester to an electronics store where they each bought new communicators, turning their old ones in to be recycled after he transferred the message and the decryption algorithm.

Once back on the street, Sexton said, "There was one message on the node — and it came from the Wyvern darknet, not a ship."

"The Commission messing with us?"

"Nope. It had tags indicating the sender is from military intelligence. Our military intelligence."

"What the heck?"

"Yeah. That's why I made sure we were sanitized before telling you. That message may be other operatives trying to contact us."

"But no one should have the darknet node address."

"Except for HQ back home."

A light went on in Forrester’s eyes.

“You mean new arrivals who received the address and were instructed to contact us.”

“Yep. Should I decode it?”

“If they're expecting a reply and we don't provide one, they'll become aware that something occurred, so yeah.”

“Okay.”

Sexton led them to a sidewalk café, where they took a small table. As they sat, he pulled out his new communicator and touched the display while Forrester ordered two cups of coffee. He wasn’t particularly fond of the stuff and preferred tea. But tea wasn’t a common drink on Wyvern, and they couldn’t afford to stand out.

After a few minutes, during which their coffee was delivered, Sexton looked up from his communicator.

“They reference our report on Norum, DeCarde, and the LOI officers by the date we sent it and say they’re here to help with them and track down other defectors. They want to meet, in a public place, our choice. The message was sent three days ago with a return darknet node address, so they’re probably getting a little impatient for a reply.”

Forrester frowned.

“That’s what we really need right now — a hit team from home. Any chance it could be the Commission testing us?”

“Doubt it. Neither of us told them we sent a report, let alone the date we sent it. Whoever they are, they’re genuine. Shall I set up a meeting?”

“No.” Forrester took a sip of his coffee and suppressed a grimace.

“Does that mean we tell our Commission handler?” Sexton asked.

"And condemn two of our former comrades to either defect or face the music back home?" Forrester let out a bark of laughter. "Come to think of it, they won't be allowed to go free, not after we betray them. Otherwise, our use as providers of disinformation will be over. I figure the Hegemony will keep them — at least until we've burned ourselves with military intelligence, which could take years. And what if we know them personally? They could be old friends."

"Possibly."

"But it gets worse." Forrester raised a finger. "Consider this. If we speak to our handler about this, they'll find out we withheld a darknet node from them as insurance. And they'll take it away from us. It leaves us with only one solution. We ignore the message and pretend it doesn't exist. That way, we keep our insurance and don't betray anyone."

"And what if they communicate back to Lyonesse that we didn't get in touch with them, yet Lyonesse still gets intelligence reports from us?"

"Then, back home might begin to wonder about those reports and us. It's a winning scenario all around."

—47—

"Turgut Ienna is dead."

Norum glanced up from his workstation.

"Who?" He asked.

"Former deputy governor of Yotai. I helped him escape to the Hegemony last year. He was fleeing bogus embezzlement charges that would have seen him jailed for at least ten years."

"I vaguely remember Ienna. Or at least I remember hearing his name. How are you sure the charges were false?"

"Simple. I've known Turgut for over a decade. He's as honest as the day is long. However, he was becoming vocal in opposing Juska's policies concerning the colonies. Quite vocal, in fact. So much so that his boss, the governor, wanted nothing more than to shut him up."

Norum nodded.

"Okay. And how do you know he died?"

"With the help of our friends in the Commission, I traced the people I got out of the Republic and keep a distant watch over them. If we were targeted for assassination, why not the others, right? And just now, I received an advisory that Turgut collapsed and died in the city's pedestrian district last night, something the police are describing as suspicious. His autopsy this morning found no underlying medical issues but uncovered a tiny perimortem puncture mark on the side of his neck. The police suspect that he might have been killed by a rapidly dissipating poison that induced cardiac arrest."

"Could it have been Forrester and Sexton? Those two bastards don't inspire any confidence whatsoever."

DeCarde gave his friend a tight smile.

"Let me check."

He called up an address on his communicator.

"Major Durron, Currag DeCarde here. How are you?"

"Feeling contented, Ambassador. What can I do for you?"

"I've just seen that a former Republic citizen, Turgut Ienna, died under suspicious circumstances in New Draconis' pedestrian district yesterday. Could it have been our two turncoats?"

"Let me check." More than a minute passed in silence, then, "No, not a chance. Both were at home from eighteen hundred onward, and your man died at twenty-one hundred."

"Which means we might have a second assassin team from the Republic on Wyvern, Major. Turgut Ienna was a notable dissident, more notable even than I am. If, of course, his death wasn't from natural causes."

"The police consider his death suspicious, which is usually a pretty good sign they believe someone murdered him but have no firm evidence yet. Do you know if he had any local enemies?"

"No idea, Major, but I doubt it. Turgut Ienna wasn't the sort who made them. On the contrary."

"Then I shall speak with my superiors concerning this matter. We'll probably go through arrivals from Hatshepsut for the last few months and see what we've got, but I wouldn't hold my breath."

"Would it be possible to notify the other exiles I have on my watch list that they might be in danger?"

"Sure, although how many of them will take a warning from the Commission seriously is anyone's guess."

"Thank you, Major. Please keep me apprised of any developments. As you might recall, I am particularly interested in the exiles' fates, seeing as how I got most out of the Republic, in some cases mere hours before the Lyonesse Office of Inquiry could arrest them for various political reasons."

"Certainly, Ambassador."

"DeCarde, out." He glanced at Norum. "Let's hope they take precautions so Turgut is the only one who dies."

But DeCarde's hopes were in vain. Three days later, shortly after he sat at his desk, the office communicator pinged — Major Durron. And he looked grim.

"I'm sorry to advise you that Hasso Imric is dead. On this occasion, there's no doubt it's murder. He had time to call the police and fight back before he succumbed. But when a patrol arrived, the culprits were gone."

"Damn." DeCarde gave Norum a bleak look.

"Hasso Imric?" The latter asked. "The former permanent undersecretary for constitutional affairs? A solid man, as I recall."

DeCarde nodded.

"Yes. And he was one of the first to publicly raise the alarm about Juska's plans. I helped him escape LOI assassins almost two years ago. Did the killer or killers leave any clues behind, Major?"

"The police are still processing the scene. I'll find out the moment they're done. You'll hear about it shortly after that."

"Thanks. Of course, you checked the whereabouts of Forrester and Sexton last night, right?"

"They were at home during the time of the attack on Mister Imric. But I'll be chatting with them about these murders later today. Would you care to observe?"

"Definitely."

"Then, say, fourteen hundred hours at Commission HQ. I'll leave word with the guard post to admit you and Admiral Norum and make sure you find your way to the ground floor interview suites."

"Excellent."

"Until then. Durron, out."

Norum looked at DeCarde.

"You figure we need to up our security again?"

"What do you think?" The latter asked with an ironic expression.

That afternoon, Norum and DeCarde presented themselves at the entrance to the Commission's Wyvern HQ, produced their Colonial Service credentials, and were duly led to an observation gallery between two interview rooms on the ground floor. There, they saw Forrester in one room and Sexton in the other. Both individuals sat at bare metal tables, alone, though they were free to move around. A few minutes later, Sister Valery joined them in the gallery as Major Durron entered Sexton's room.

"Good day, Sister." Norum inclined his head in greeting. "To what do we owe the pleasure?"

Valery smiled at him.

"I'm here to serve as a lie detector."

Norum was about to ask how, but Durron spoke.

"How are you this fine afternoon, Jon?"

Sexton shrugged.

"Okay. Why were we summoned here?"

"Did you know that someone murdered two prominent exiles from the Republic in the last few days? A Turgut Ienna and a Hasso Imric."

"And you're wondering whether we did it. The answer is no."

"Oh, I'm well aware you weren't involved. But it is clear that the Republic's government is responsible for the killings. No one else has any motive."

Sister Valery spoke in a soft tone.

"He knows something, Major."

Neither Durron nor Sexton reacted, and Norum understood that the former wore an invisible earbug so he could hear Valery.

"Tell me about the Republic's hit team, Jon."

Sexton met Durron's eyes and said, "I don't know a damn thing about any hit team."

"He's definitely lying, Major," Sister Valery said.

Durron shook his head.

"Jon, please don't bullshit me. Sister Valery is watching you and just told me you're lying. I can have her come join us and put you to the question directly if you'd like."

Sexton paled.

"Okay. Yes, there's a team of intelligence agents on Wyvern who are tasked with eliminating exiles. But that's all I know."

"He's speaking the truth," Valery murmured.

"How do you know about them?"

Sexton looked away and exhaled loudly.

"Look, we didn't tell you we use two darknet nodes, one for outgoing and one for incoming messages. We gave you the outgoing node only. Call it insurance. When we were released, we found an encrypted message on the incoming node telling us an assassination team had arrived. They wanted to meet so we could coordinate action against Admiral Norum, Ambassador DeCarde, and the rest of the dissidents. We didn't answer, let alone meet with them."

"Oh, Jon." Durron tsked. "If only you'd been completely honest with me, we might have prevented those two deaths."

Sexton glanced at him before dropping his gaze, but he remained silent.

Durron abruptly stood and left the room. Moments later, he entered the other one and dropped into the chair facing Forrester.

"Tell me about the incoming darknet node you forgot to mention and the message you found on it."

Forrester's face hardened.

"I suppose you spoke with Jon already."

"Never mind who I spoke to. Just tell me."

A sigh.

"Very well. Yes, we only gave you the outgoing node, and yes, we found a message on the incoming one after you released us. It said an assassination team from back home was in town, and we should meet to coordinate hits on Norum, DeCarde, and the other exiles. That's it. We didn't contact them, seeing as how we've switched sides."

"But you didn't tell me either, and that was a mistake, Harold, one which may have cost two men their lives. You see, Turgut Ienna and Hasso Imric, both exiles from the Republic, were murdered — Imric last night."

"What do you want me to say? Sorry?" Forrester snapped. "We were trying to stay out of it."

"And now you're fully in. Come with me."

Durron led Forrester to Sexton's interview room and had him sit beside his comrade.

"Here's what we're going to do, gents. You set up a meeting with the assassination team, and when they appear, we'll arrest them. And you'll give us the address of that second darknet node, of course."

"It's been almost two weeks since they sent their message. Don't you think they'll be a little suspicious about such a delay in our replying?"

Durron shrugged.

"Can't be helped. You're our best way of stopping them. Keep in mind that they're now your enemy as well as mine."

"All right," Forrester said in a resigned tone.

"Excellent. First, forward a copy of their message to me. Then, let me think of the best place for a meeting, and finally, I'll watch you encode a reply to the assassins and send it."

"Will we have to be at the meeting place?"

"Of course. Their briefing about you will likely have included your appearance. Thus, you'll be needed as bait so they reveal themselves."

"Yeah. Figured as much."

—48—

“The Republic has begun a systematic assassination campaign against the dissidents who sought refuge in the Hegemony,” President Mandus said as she looked around the table at Magistra Abbatissa Ardrix, Chancellor Conteh, and Grand Admiral Benes. “Two of them are dead, and an attempt was made on Admiral Norum and Ambassador DeCarde. I tend to consider that a hostile act by a foreign government. If we still had diplomatic relations, I’d call in Lyonesse’s representative and read him the riot act, but unfortunately, we don’t.”

“Did President Juska go mad?” Conteh frowned. “Why kill exiles? Surely, they don’t present a threat to his regime.”

“Who knows?” Mandus shrugged. “The question is, how do we react to this unjustified and unjustifiable activity on Hegemony soil?”

"When the Commission finds them, and it will, send the assassins' bodies back with a note that says, next time, we're coming for you," Benes suggested.

"Not a bad idea," Conteh gave him a smile that didn't quite reach his eyes. But then, none of his smiles ever did. "Assuming they die under the Commission's tender mercies."

Benes cocked an eyebrow at the chancellor. "That depends on their degree of cooperation with the Commission's interrogators, no?"

"I suppose so."

"Perhaps we could return them or their bodies with another note," Ardrix said. "One that informs the Republic of Lyonesse that the Second Empire has been proclaimed on Wyvern, which retakes its place as the imperial capital and invites them to join us."

"Nice idea, but do you really believe they might?" Benes asked.

"No. Yet, considering the rapidly fading legitimacy of President Juska's regime, it will introduce further uncertainty among the Republic's various factions and worlds. There may be some, potentially a large number, especially in the reclaimed star systems, who will look to Wyvern rather than Lyonesse as the genuine inheritor of the First Empire."

"It's certainly worth a try," Mandus said. "Because there's nothing wrong with judiciously applied psychological operations. And we'll repatriate them along with the notes, in a naval ship, not a merchant. That alone will also send a message. Let's hope the Commission can track these assassins before the Conclave meets."

***

Forrester and Sexton entered the Farrier Park at the edge of New Draconis' less salubrious quarter shortly before twenty-two hundred hours and found it deserted. The night weighed heavily on both men — low cloud cover, oppressive humidity, little artificial and no natural light — and they felt a tinge of nervousness.

When they'd finally replied to the assassin team's missive using recognition code words only military intelligence agents would know, they proposed a meeting in a lower town tavern. The response, however, was filled with suspicion, demanding why they'd taken their own sweet time. When Sexton wrote that they'd been lying low for a while because they didn't want to be tracked by the State Security Commission, he received a demand that they show up in the park that very evening and sit on the bench beside the statue of Jules Farrier.

Forrester had told Major Durron about the change of venue, leaving him to question what the assassins planned. There was no cover within forty meters of the statue, giving anyone excellent lines of sight and making the surveillance job more difficult. Plus, the park had many escape routes and would be empty at twenty-two hundred hours. It meant that instead of swooping in on the assassins, they would have to determine their direction once they left the meeting and take them as they exited the park.

Forrester and Sexton entered the clearing with the statue at its center and headed for the empty bench, wondering whether their former military intelligence colleagues were watching from the darkness. They sat uncomfortably and waited. Twenty-two hundred came and passed, and there was no sign of the agents. By twenty-two-twenty, Forrester wondered whether they'd reneged, or something had happened to them. But then, two silent black-clad figures detached themselves from the ring of trees and came toward them.

They stopped three paces from the bench and studied both men with eyes hidden by the shadows of their hoods.

"Harold Forrester and Jon Sexton. Well, well, well. Who'd have thought we'd meet the two of you hundreds of light years from home?" A low female alto voice said.

"Karei Plutan." Forrester climbed to his feet, imitated by Sexton. "How the hell are you here?"

Both figures threw back their hoods, and he also recognized the second woman.

"Jayda Kwan. I should have figured the two of you would team up. I understand business is good. Two dissidents taken care of."

"And many more to come. You don't seem to have much success in taking Norum and DeCarde, though. We hear they're still alive and kicking."

"They've been lucky. You know how it is, especially with former military people. They have a sixth sense that keeps them out of trouble." He met Plutan's gaze. "Why are we meeting in this forsaken place instead of a nice, cozy tavern?"

"That sixth sense you were mentioning just now? We have it too, and something told us we'd be better off in an empty, open space after dark than a crowded pub."

"Really? I don't see any reasons."

"And that's part of the problem, Harold. It took you over two weeks to respond. I don't buy the lying low excuse. If your node had truly been compromised, you wouldn't have answered at all. So, what's the real reason?"

"Look, our attempt on Norum and DeCarde failed. We left town and stayed off the darknet until we could be sure the Commission or the police weren't onto us."

"Why do I think you're not telling me the whole truth, Harold?"

Forrester shrugged. "I have no idea. But I'm not lying to you."

"Okay. Let's get out of here and go someplace less exposed."

"Sure. Although I thought being exposed was the whole point of meeting in the park."

"Initial contact only, Harold. Now that we know who you are, we're good for a more secluded place."

"And that is?"

"Someplace you'll see in due course. Come on."

Both women turned on their heels and headed away from the statue in a different direction than the one they'd come from. Forrester glanced at Sexton, who gave him a half-shrug that said, what else are we going to do?

Plutan glanced over her shoulder and made a come-on gesture, and they followed at a quick pace.

She led them into the treeline, along a gravel path strewn with debris from the surrounding vegetation, her footsteps making soft, regular sounds. The path widened as the trees petered out, and something caught Kwan's attention. She halted and held out her hand, stopping Plutan and the others.

"What's up?" Plutan asked in a low whisper.

"I get the feeling there are people nearby, closing in on us," she replied in the same tone, pulling a handgun from beneath her jacket.

Plutan imitated her but turned to Forrester and Sexton.

"You wouldn't know anything about that, would you?"

Forrester, who'd not been told of Major Durron's plans, shook his head although he suspected those people might be Commission or police.

"Not a clue."

"Get ahead of us." She gestured with her weapon. "And keep walking until I tell you to stop."

Both men complied, hands itching to pull out their own guns, but they understood the move might be misinterpreted by Plutan and Kwan and earn them a pair of rounds in the back.

They emerged from the trees, and suddenly, two dozen dark figures appeared, brandishing weapons.

"Surrender or die," a deep male voice said.

Plutan turned on Forrester, aiming her gun at his midriff.

"You sonofabitch. You led us into an ambush."

Forrester raised both hands, palms facing outward. "Not me."

"Aw, fuck. I knew you'd gone over to the enemy." She pulled her trigger twice, and Forrester collapsed. A heartbeat later, Kwan shot Sexton, then turned her gun toward the approaching figures.

"Don't make it worse," the same man added as the figures surrounded Plutan and Kwan.

After a moment of hesitation, both dropped their weapons and raised their hands. Moments later, they were on the ground, hands being manacled behind their backs as one of the Commission officers knelt to check on Forrester and Sexton.

"Both are dead, Major," he said, climbing to his feet.

"Four murders, two of them witnessed by us." Durron stood over the prone women. "Your future is looking grim, Madames Plutan and Kwan." When both stared up at him, he chuckled. "Oh, yes. Forrester and Sexton spent some quality time in our dungeons after their failed attempt on Admiral Norum and Ambassador DeCarde. They soon saw the error of their ways and agreed to work for us. Both were wearing listening devices. We heard your conversation loud and clear."

When neither made a sound, Durron chuckled.

"We'll soon have you talking like there's no tomorrow."

—49—

Plutan, strapped to an interrogation rack, screamed like a tormented soul trapped by the greatest evil ever known. Sister Valery had released some of the darkest monsters she'd encountered in her years working for the Commission from the assassin's subconscious and was shaken by what she'd seen. She greatly feared those demons would consume Plutan's sanity and leave her an inarticulate, delirious mess that could never recover, her spirit shattered, and her consciousness trapped in an endless cycle of madness.

The screams continued for what seemed like a long time, though they rapidly diminished in volume as Plutan's tortured vocal cords gave out. But when she finally fell silent, it wasn't because of her voice giving out, but her heart. The health markers built into the rack turned red, and Plutan died without answering a single question, driven to the grave by the devils she carried in her subconscious.

A shaken Major Durron blinked a few times before turning to Valery.

"What the hell was that?" He noticed her unsettled gaze. "Are you alright, Sister?"

"No. As a matter of fact, I'm not." Even her voice was unsteady. "That woman harbored evil like I've never seen before. She was a highly controlled psychopath of the worst kind, one whose monsters grew over the years, and my releasing them killed her. If I hadn't done so, she might have lived a normal life, albeit one without a shred of empathy, remorse, or human feeling."

"If nothing else, it saves us from having to execute her. Time to check on her comrade." Durron glanced at the video pickup that fed the other interrogation suite. Kwan would have seen everything that had happened but not heard Plutan's howls. The door opened to a pair of guards, and Durron said, "Put her body in a stasis chamber. Apparently, we're sending it back to the Republic, along with those of Forrester and Sexton."

"Yes, sir."

Once in the suite next door, Durron went to stand a pace in front of Kwan while Valery hung back.

"You saw your friend die, killed by the evil within her once Sister Valery released it. It was not a good death. I believe she suffered immensely. Now the question you must ask yourself is, will you risk dying in the same manner, should you harbor monsters in your subconscious as cruel as Karei had? Or will you answer my questions?"

Kwan didn't meet Durron's gaze, nor did she speak. She simply stared at the far wall through expressionless eyes.

"So be it. Sister?"

Durron stepped back as Valery took his place.

After a few moments of probing, the Sister glanced at Durron. "This one has rudimentary awareness and primitive mental shields. We could actually train her as a member of the Order."

"But do you think she'll go crazy like Plutan? I'd rather she didn't lose her sanity, let alone die because I've received orders to leave one alive so she can tell the Republic's government what happened to her and her comrades."

"She'll be fine. I can't sense the same sort of immense pressure from within her subconscious as I could from Plutan's."

"Then please proceed."

Valery closed her eyes and within moments, Kwan's widened in fear. She gasped and began to pant as wildness overtook her gaze. Just as abruptly as it had started, the reaction to Valery's intrusion ceased as the Sister's eyes opened again.

"You got a tiny taste of the madness that engulfed Karei Plutan. Will you answer my questions now and spare yourself any more terrors? Afterward, I'll ensure you're made comfortable until we transfer you back to the Republic."

"Yes." Kwan's reply came out as a hushed croak.

"Is Jayda Kwan your real name?"

"Yes."

"And you're a member of the Lyonesse Defense Force, I presume. What is your rank and service?"

"Lieutenant, Lyonesse Navy."

"What was Karei Plutan?"

"Centurion, Lyonesse Marine Corps."

"Did you murder Turgut Ienna and Hasso Imric?"

"Yes."

"Who was next on your list?"

"Ravenna Winter. We were going to do her tomorrow."

"Are you the only assassin team on Wyvern, or are there others?"

"I don't know. We came here by ourselves aboard a merchant vessel."

"Did you kill dissidents other than Ienna and Imric?"

"Several, back home in the Republic."

"I thought the Lyonesse Office of Inquiry took care of domestic dissidents."

"They do it, we do it. It depends on who's available."

Durron was sure Kwan would have shrugged if the rack hadn't restrained her. He turned to Sister Valery.

"How's she doing?"

"Telling the truth."

"Good. Now, which ship did you take to come here?"

***

"We've captured and interrogated the assassination team, Madame President," Nero Cabreras, the head of the State Security Commission, said when Mandus accepted his call. "One of them died before she could reveal anything, but the other one told us everything. Based on our search of recent arrivals, we're pretty sure they were the only team operating on Wyvern."

Mandus felt relief at his words. The Conclave was meeting in three days, and she'd already ordered a ship to stand by, ready for the long trip to Hatshepsut with the news of her proclamation.

"That's excellent, Nero. Give the people involved my thanks for a job well done."

"Certainly, Madame."

They briefly discussed a few other items of interest, and then Cabreras rang off. Mandus returned to what she'd been doing, putting the final touches on the written proposal to the Conclave now that all its members were in New Draconis. Three days should be enough for them to absorb everything and make up their minds. Not that the issue was in doubt. The people in the capital who were aware of what she planned on broaching were uniformly enthusiastic.

And as one of the last acts of her presidency, proclaiming the Second Empire would ensure her place in history.

—50—

"You've read the proposal. It is time to break with our recent history and embrace the future by returning to our distant past."

President Vigdis Mandus let her eyes roam over the Conclave members, a hundred in all — admirals, generals, senior bureaucrats, planetary consuls, a smattering of businesspeople — and paused to let her words sink in. Ardrix and Chancellor Conteh, the other two members of the Hegemony's Executive Council, sat directly in front of her alongside Grand Admiral Benes. The three also belonged to the Conclave.

"But changing the name of the Wyvern Hegemony to the Second Empire, so it better reflects our ambitions of reuniting humanity, is only the initial step. We must also adopt the old imperial constitution first promulgated twelve hundred years ago, suitably modified to prevent the emergence of another

Stichus Ruggero. After all, it allowed for the longest-lived stable and peaceful polity in human history."

Mandus paused again and saw many nods of approval. That the Conclave would accept the proposal with the necessary two-thirds majority was never in doubt, but the Hegemony's Founding Law required her to go through the motions.

"You've read the text of the proposed imperial constitution, suitably annotated to mark where it differs from the original of twelve centuries ago." More nods greeted her words. "When you vote it into being, you're also dissolving the Conclave in favor of an Imperial Senate with representatives from every star system."

Since the Conclave had no genuine power except that of appointing the president — its primary role was to advise the Hegemony's leader — the dissolution wouldn't matter much for most members when weighed against reinstating the Empire.

"This includes Lindisfarne, which will join the Second Empire as a full-fledged member now that the Void Reborn has returned to the Order."

Ardrix had formally subordinated the Void Reborn to the Summus Abbatissa of the Order the previous week. She now wore the old star-filled orb instead of the one with the phoenix around her neck, though she was still Magistra Abbatissa. Sister Mariko had indicated she would appoint more Magistras as the Order re-propagated to oversee multiple abbeys and priories in several star systems. The Summus Abbatissa's span of control during the final years of the old Empire had simply been too great.

"That, in a nutshell, is the proposal. We elect to transform the Wyvern Hegemony into what the old Empire was in its early days when the golden age was still dawning. Or we remain as we are and fail to launch a second era of greatness for humanity." Mandus paused one last time. "Does anyone have questions?"

Five seconds passed in silence, then ten, and it became plain that everyone had made up their minds beforehand. They were ready.

"I now call upon you to vote. A yes will transform the Hegemony into the Second Empire. A no means keeping the status quo. Please go ahead."

The members of the Conclave used their communicators, tuned to a unique, secure frequency, to transmit their choice, and the results showed up on the display behind Mandus within moments.

One hundred yes votes. Mandus didn't even have to cast her own ballot.

"I hereby proclaim the Wyvern Hegemony replaced by the Second Empire. Please rise."

A hidden band struck up the ancient Imperial Anthem as the original imperial flag, a stylized galaxy on a dark blue background, appeared on the room's display.

Once the music died away, Sandor Benes said in a soft but mock plaintive voice, "And now we'll have to change our identifiers from Wyvern Hegemony Starship to Imperial Starship and add the imperial crown to every single badge in existence."

The Chief of Naval Operations, who stood behind him, chuckled.

"And we'll still be finding hulls and badges with the old identifiers five years from now."

"No doubt."

President of the Empire Vigdis Mandus cocked an amused eyebrow at Benes but said, "That was it. I believe a celebratory spread is laid out for us next door. Shall we?"

***

Word that the Conclave had proclaimed the Second Empire spread like wildfire through New Draconis and across Wyvern. Within minutes of the meeting breaking up, the newsnets were making gleeful announcements and showing freshly released video of President Mandus' address. The result had been expected by a population well aware of the vote and its impact, but spontaneous celebrations broke out everywhere.

Farrin Norum and Currag DeCarde were glued to the large display in Crevan Torma's office, watching the replay of President Mandus' speech, the ensuing vote, and the playing of the Imperial Anthem.

"You know," Norum said, smiling crookedly, "I'd love to be a fly on the wall of Derik Juska's office when news of this reaches him. He'll be livid."

"And he'll ratchet up the rhetoric to heights not seen in over a thousand years," DeCarde answered.

Torma frowned. "Do you think he'd actually order military action against us?"

DeCarde shrugged.

"Anything is possible. I think Juska is the sort who begins to believe his own bullshit and acts accordingly. Folks like that can get dangerous real quick for anyone who opposes them, as we've already seen on a personal level. From there, it's a short trip to the state of affairs where they deal with entire polities that same way — they become vengeful and violent."

"Let's hope it doesn't come to that."

***

As prearranged, the Imperial Starship *Zealous*, one of the new frigates, hastily changed her designators from WHS to IS and broke out of Wyvern orbit. She carried a copy of the video highlighting President Mandus' speech and another short video address by Mandus directed at the citizens of the Republic, expressing her hope their worlds would accede to the Second Empire. A subdued Jayda Kwan had been brought aboard in fetters earlier along with the three bodies — Forrester, Sexton, and Plutan — in stasis chambers, along with the Commission's report on their interrogations and fate.

Most figured the videos wouldn't be seen by more than a small number of people once the commander of the Lyonesse Defense Force garrison in the Hatshepsut system looked at them. But they hoped someone, somewhere along the way to President Juska's office, would leak one or the other, preferably both.

—51—

Hatshepsut
Republic of Lyonesse

"Sir, a frigate identifying itself as the Imperial Starship *Zealous* emerged from the wormhole and is requesting permission to approach Hatshepsut. She claims she carries a Lyonesse military intelligence officer and the bodies of three deceased Republic agents, which she wishes to repatriate."

"*Imperial* starship?" Commodore Al Jecks asked in an incredulous tone as he speared the senior operations duty officer with his intense gaze. She'd come in person to his office, which was just across the corridor from the operations center aboard Starbase Hatshepsut. "Don't tell me the Hegemony developed delusions of grandeur."

"Sorry, sir. That's all they said."

"Get me the frigate's captain."

"Yes, sir. Wait one, please." The duty officer vanished, and a few moments later, her voice came over Jeck's office communicator. "I have Captain Damasa Jorrier of the Imperial Starship *Zealous* for you, sir."

"Put her on."

A narrow face framed by short, graying red hair appeared on the office display, and green eyes on either side of a patrician nose met his.

"Commodore Jecks, I'm Damasa Jorrier. Your duty officer said you wished to speak with me."

"Thank you for coming online, Captain. I'm curious. Did the Hegemony transform itself into an Empire in the last few weeks?"

"Yes, sir. President Mandus proclaimed the Second Empire just before we left Wyvern. I have a copy of her speech with me, as well as a video addressed to the citizens of the Republic. Shall I transmit both now?"

"If you would."

"Certainly. Please stand by. In the meantime, may I bring *Zealous* into Hatshepsut orbit so I can transfer Lieutenant Kwan and the bodies of Centurion Plutan, Centurion Forrester, and Master Sergeant Sexton to you as the senior Defense Force authority?"

"How did the three die?"

"I also have a report from Imperial State Security concerning the events that led to Lieutenant Kwan's detention and the deaths of the others, which I shall transmit with the speech and note."

"You seem well prepared, Captain."

"I only carry out my duty, sir."

"Once you've transmitted the three reports, please go FTL for Hatshepsut. You're cleared to enter orbit."

"Thank you, Commodore."

Her face faded from his display as three messages appeared in his queue, all of them originating from IS *Zealous*.

Jecks opened the first one, the video recording of President Mandus' speech to the Conclave. He watched it with morbid fascination, knowing the duty officer and her crew were watching as well. When he got to the second message, the note from Mandus to the citizens of the Republic, Jecks suspected he should probably embargo everything and send it directly to Defense Force HQ on Lyonesse under a classified heading. This was inflammatory stuff, inviting the Republic's worlds to rejoin the Empire.

He called the duty officer and slapped a top secret designation on the three messages before reading the third. When he was done, Jecks sat back and stared at the bulkhead for a long time, wondering where the Republic had gone off the rails. Assassinating President Juska's political foes on foreign worlds? The Almighty wept.

Jecks packaged the messages under a terse note of his own, which explained how they got into his hands and sent it off. Then, he told the duty officer and her crew that any mention of the messages' contents was now covered by the Official Secrets Act and was not to be discussed unless HQ released them for public consumption.

Then, Jecks retreated to his quarters and poured himself a large glass of whiskey. Fortunately, command of the Hatshepsut system was his last assignment before he retired in six months. And once he did, he'd stay as far away from the Republic's government as possible.

***

Lannion
Republic of Lyonesse

Admiral Gerhard Glass, Chief of the Lyonesse Defense Staff, didn't know how the president would react to the messages from Wyvern he'd received via Commodore Jecks, but he was sure it wouldn't be pleasant for the messenger. At least Jecks had shown presence of mind when he classified them top secret need-to-know. A shame he wasn't more politically reliable. He could have become Chief of Naval Operations one day instead of facing early retirement.

But the president demanded all flag officer appointments be given to Lyonesse First adherents. Jecks wasn't enthusiastic about the ideology and didn't care to hide his disdain.

He couldn't decide which of the three files was worse, but the interrogation report from the Imperial State Security Commission had left him shaking his head. If it ever got out that the Republic's government was assassinating political dissidents, there could be hell to pay.

And he strongly suspected it would eventually become common knowledge, along with President Mandus' speech and appeal to the citizens of the Republic. There were enough opponents to Juska's regime still embedded in the bureaucracy, both military and civilian, who might glimpse the news from the Empire and quietly release it.

His first step, of course, would be informing the Secretary of Defense. The days when the CDS had direct access to the president were long gone. But the SecDef would make sure Glass delivered the news in case Juska reacted badly. Glass opened a link with the SecDef's office.

"What can I do for you, Admiral?" The executive assistant asked.

"I need to speak with Mister Beelen urgently. Something's come up that he needs to know about right away."

"And that would be?" The EA asked in a supercilious tone.

Glass forcibly restrained his irritation with the man who believed his place in the pecking order was determined by his control of access to the SecDef. He thus had a much higher opinion of himself than was warranted.

"Top secret, for the SecDef's ears only."

"I am cleared top secret, as you're well aware, Admiral."

"This is need-to-know, and you don't need-to-know. Now, is Mister Beelen available or not?"

"He is."

"I'll be in his office in five minutes."

Before the EA could respond, Glass cut the link and sighed. The man's innate arrogance seemed a feature of those close to the cabinet secretaries under the current government, and it was getting wearisome.

Five minutes later, the EA ushered him into the SecDef's office, and he plopped into a chair facing his desk without waiting for an invitation.

"We have problems, sir. The sort that'll give us major headaches." He fished a data wafer from his shirt pocket. "The messages on here come from what was formerly known as the Wyvern Hegemony, delivered to Hatshepsut by one of their Navy starships along with one live and three dead military intelligence agents. The live one is Jayda Kwan, who was sent to Wyvern along with her partner as an assassination team a few weeks ago, and she broke under interrogation by the State Security Commission."

Glass put the wafer on Beelen's desk.

"I think you should look at the videos starting with the one marked President's Speech."

Beelen picked up the wafer and placed it on his desk's built-in reader and a virtual display appeared hovering over the desktop, showing President Mandus.

Glass watched the expression on Beelen's face as he listened to her speech proclaiming the founding of the Second Empire, with alarm erasing his initial incredulity as the import of what she said sunk in.

"This is incredible, Admiral. It cannot be countenanced."

"Please watch the second one, marked Address to the Republic."

Beelen called it up and let it play.

"Citizens of the Republic of Lyonesse, I am Vigdis Mandus, President of the Second Human Empire, which I proclaimed based on the First Empire's old constitution, with Wyvern restored to its place as imperial capital. My goal, and that of my successors, is reuniting humanity under a single flag, a single Senate, and a single ruler. While your leaders move away from the ideals that gave birth to your Republic, turning it into a dictatorship governed by immoral men and women, we are restoring the ancient ideals that gave our species the longest period of peace and prosperity in recorded history. And we invite you to join us in creating a unified Empire, one that will bring forth a second golden age. We welcome any star system that wishes to accompany us on this journey with open arms. They will have the freedom to govern themselves according to their own lights and send representatives to the Imperial Senate. In return, they will receive the protection of the Imperial Armed Forces, be able to engage in free trade with other imperial worlds, and their citizens will be able to move freely between them as they seek to improve their lives. Join us. It's as simple as that."

Mandus was replaced by the old imperial flag, which faded away a few seconds later. Beelen, speechless, stared at the blank display.

"That's inflammatory," he said once he recovered his composure. "And I use the word advisedly. Calling on the Republic's worlds to secede from Lyonesse can almost be considered an act of war."

"I wouldn't go quite so far, sir. Besides, the last thing the Republic can afford is an interstellar war. We're at naval parity with the Hegemony — pardon me, the Second Empire — and our star systems are much more dispersed than theirs. Besides, the wormhole termini in their core star systems have forts guarding them. In a hit-and-run conflict, which is the best we can do, we'll lose a lot of ships and crews while they'll be able to strike us with near impunity."

"A cheerful assessment."

"A realistic one. The third file is the Imperial State Security report on the four intelligence operatives they repatriated."

"Three of whom they murdered."

"No. The assassination team shot and killed the two intelligence-gathering agents, while the assassin who died did so of cardiac arrest during interrogation. But read and watch for yourself, sir. It's all explained."

"A fake, no doubt."

"Perhaps, but our people on Hatshepsut will interview the survivor and either confirm the report or not. The fact that they sent it along with Lieutenant Kwan leads me to believe it's genuine. They mean for us to know they've ended the threat against the dissidents. Now, sir, we need to brief President Juska, and the sooner, the better. I cannot tell how much of this leaked, but it would be best if he were aware before the public gets a hint."

"You'll brief him, Admiral." Beelen touched his desktop, and the office door opened, admitting his EA. "Please see when the president can receive the Admiral and me on a matter of great urgency."

—52—

"This is outrageous." The President of the Republic of Lyonesse, Derik Juska, turned furious eyes on Admiral Glass. "How can she proclaim the thrice-damned Hegemony the true heir of the old Empire? We are the heirs. Us. Lyonesse."

Glass simply gazed back at Juska with an expression devoid of all emotion.

"Because she can, sir?"

Juska held Glass' gaze for a few long seconds.

"Don't get smart with me, Admiral. You are eminently replaceable."

"Yes, sir. It gets worse, I'm afraid. President Mandus recorded a message for the citizens of the Republic. If I may?"

Juska gave Glass a curt nod, and he called up the second video.

Observing the president's face while he watched Mandus was an education in itself. Juska's eyes blazed with a naked hatred, and

Glass wondered whether he was entirely sane. At the end of the message, Juska immediately turned his attention on Glass.

"What the hell was that?" He demanded in a low tone filled with menace.

"A call to arms against the Republic, sir," Ty Beelen said in a soft voice.

"If she wants war, she will have it."

"As I already explained to the Secretary of Defense, we are not in a position to wage war against the Second Empire, sir." Glass went through the same arguments he'd given Beelen. To his immense relief, Juska didn't gainsay him.

"I trust you ensured both messages are classified, Admiral."

"Yes, sir, top secret need-to-know."

"And they will stay that way. Anyone who leaks even a second of them will find themselves looking at the wrong end of an LOI blaster."

"Understood, sir. But thanks to traders, word of the Hegemony taking on the mantle of the Second Empire will eventually percolate through the Republic. It might already have reached Hatshepsut via open sources if a merchant ship was close behind the imperial frigate."

Juska rolled his eyes.

"Yes, I understand. I just don't want Mandus' pretensions that her fake Empire is humanity's true heir to surface."

"I'll do what I can, Mister President."

"Was that everything?"

Glass and Beelen exchanged glances, and the latter gave a slight nod. They would not be aggravating President Juska with word that his assassins had been unceremoniously discovered and sent home.

"Yes, sir."

They stood, bowed their heads, and turned on their heels, leaving Juska to stare at the far wall as he mulled over Mandus' pronouncements. A fresh resolve wormed its way through his anger, and he smiled.

Derik Juska would do what he did best — speak to the citizens of the Republic and denounce the Hegemony claiming the mantle of Empire in no uncertain terms. He would exhort his people to redouble their efforts in expanding Lyonesse's sphere and its military might and demand the Senate grant him special powers to make it happen. He would turn the problem of Mandus proclaiming the Second Empire into greater possibilities for his regime and consolidate supreme authority over the Republic in his hands.

Juska summoned the presidential speechwriter, a true wizard with words, and gave him his marching orders. That evening, he made a thunderous address from his office, condemning Mandus and her fake Empire and asking that full powers be vested in his office. The next day, massive demonstrations of support spontaneously materialized in Lannion and Lyonesse's main cities and quickly spread to Arietis, Yotai, Mykonos, and the other core worlds. In truth, there was nothing spontaneous about them — Juska had simply sent word to loyal activists via his political staff. But such were his powers as an orator, the sentiments motivating the public displays of support were genuine.

Nothing could stop him now.

— 53 —

New Draconis
Second Empire

Admiral Norum and Ambassador DeCarde, both wearing formal black evening suits with miniature medals and qualification insignia, entered the lobby of the Raijin Arms to find Major General Torma waiting for them. He wore the State Security Commission's silver-trimmed, high-collared black mess uniform with the stars of his rank on top of twisted silver bullion thread epaulets. Miniature medals adorned his left breast, while the insignia of the Colonial Service — a stylized lotus flower symbolizing rebirth surrounded by a wreath of stars — hung on his right side.

"Looking spiffy, Crevan," Norum said, smiling. "I like your mess kit. Very clean lines. A shame you didn't bring it with you to Lyonesse. You'd have been the center of attraction during the mess dinner you attended."

"And it is a shame you lost yours somewhere along the way. It would have afforded us some unusual variety." Movement outside the door attracted Torma's attention. "And there's our car, right on time."

They left the apartment building and climbed aboard.

"It's kind of President Mandus to invite us to her celebratory gala," Norum said, settling on the back-facing seat. "Though I fear we might be somewhat out of place."

"No more than I was back on Lyonesse," Torma replied. "You're honored guests of the Empire, high-ranking individuals in your own right."

"Kind of you to say so, but we left our ranks back in the Republic."

"Not from the president's point of view, and hers is the only one that counts tonight. You are symbols of her hopes to reunite humanity under the imperial banner one day and put together once more that which Dendera rent asunder. May she rot in hell."

DeCarde chuckled.

"How poetic of you."

"For a police officer, you mean?" Torma cocked an amused eyebrow at him. "But I'm correct in assuming your symbolic value to the president. It's how she thinks. And now, let's not speak of it anymore and enjoy ourselves. This will be the most momentous gala in living memory, which is why it's being held in the Joint Base New Draconis' largest hangar, suitably transformed for the occasion."

As if to underline the size of the event, they joined a long line of ground cars wending their way through the base, each disgorging several passengers at the entrance to the hangar in question, where Ground Forces and Navy troopers in full dress uniform stood at attention on either side.

They climbed out of their car as it stopped and joined the throng of officers and senior bureaucrats wearing their finery, waiting to enter. Once inside, Norum let out a low whistle.

"Impressive."

Hundreds of pennants hung from the rafters above, while round, eight-person tables covered the floor. A raised stage at one end held a lectern backed by a stand of flags, while a gigantic imperial banner covered one wall. A hundred-person Ground Forces band, sitting in one corner, played light airs as guests snagged full champagne glasses from passing waiters with large trays.

Torma pulled out his invitation card and checked the seating arrangements. He gestured at a table close to that of President Mandus, who hadn't arrived yet.

"I believe we're sitting over there."

"A privileged spot if we're within sight of the head table."

"Indeed. It speaks to your importance in the president's eyes."

Admiral Godfrey, the commander-in-chief of the Colonial Service, wearing a Navy mess uniform dripping with gold braid, appeared and smiled at them.

"And how are you this fine evening, one which will be for the books, I don't doubt?"

"Ready for anything, Johannes," Norum said.

"Excellent."

Just then, the band stopped, and heraldic trumpet players rose from their seats. They rang out something not heard in over two hundred years — the Imperial Ruffles and Flourishes, which had once greeted the emperor or empress and now signaled the president's arrival. The crowd fell silent, and those in uniform stood to attention as President Mandus, in formal civilian evening wear with miniature medals, strode onto the stage and stood behind the lectern. When the last peal of the trumpets faded away, she beamed at the assembly.

"Stand easy, everyone, and welcome to the first Presidential Gala of the Second Empire."

Someone stopped beside Norum, and he glanced to his right.

"Hello, Magistra Abbatissa," he whispered. "You look well."

"I am well," Ardrix replied with her usual mysterious smile. "But let us listen to the president."

"The past few weeks have been momentous," Mandus said. "We have renewed our purpose and are finally looking to a bright future, a new golden age, as we reunite humanity under the hallowed flag of the Empire. What a time to be alive!" Cheers and applause greeted her words, and she raised a hand until they quieted. "Now, please take your seats and enjoy."

Mandus climbed off the stage as the band picked up again, and people found their tables. Soon, animated conversations, underscored by music, filled the immense space, and waiters brought out the first course.

Ardrix and Admiral Godfrey had joined Norum, DeCarde, and Torma at their table, along with three other Colonial Service senior officers.

"Why aren't you sitting with the president, Ardrix?" Norum asked in a low voice, leaning toward her.

"Because I'm no longer the Head of the Order of the Void Reborn since it ceased to exist. I'm now under the Summus Abbatissa on Lindisfarne, and if she were here, she would sit with President Mandus."

"I see. Well, I'm glad you're with us."

"As am I," Torma said from Ardrix's other side. "After everything we've been through together."

The evening progressed, as did the conversation and the plates, and soon, the only items that remained on the tables were the port bottles and glasses. And as every human who'd ever served in a military capacity knew, it was time for the toasts and the marches.

A gavel was heard silencing the room, and President Mandus climbed to her feet, glass in hand.

"Officers, officials, and guests, please rise." Once they'd done so, Mandus said, "I give you the Empire." She raised her glass, imitated by every last guest.

"The Empire," hundreds of voices roared out, and the band played the Imperial Anthem.

Then, the marches followed — that of the Imperial Navy, the Imperial Ground Forces, and the Imperial Commission for State Security. Surprising Norum, the bandmaster then announced the march of the Republic of Lyonesse Navy, and he found himself the only one to stand. Naturally, the Republic's Marine Corps was named next, causing DeCarde to rise.

"More of President Mandus' symbols of hope for reunification?" Norum asked Torma with an amused air.

"Indeed."

A fist began to pound on a table distant from the center of the hanger turned impromptu officer's mess. It was joined by many more, and a voice rang out.

There once was a ship that put to space
And the name of that ship was the Golden Ace
Radiation blew hard, her bow dipped down
Blow, me bully boys blow

As soon as the last word came out of the singer's mouth, the entire assemblage called out 'huh' and accompanied him in the refrain, as did the band.

Soon may the Wellerman come
To bring us sugar and tea and rum
One day, when the tonguin' is done
We'll take our leave and go.

Torma grinned at Norum and said, "I told you we never forgot it."

Then he and the rest of their table, Ardrix included, joined in and Norum found out that Torma's voice wasn't so bad after all.

About the Author

Eric Thomson is the pen name of a retired Canadian soldier who spent more time in uniform than he expected, both in the Regular Army and the Army Reserve. He spent his Regular Army career in the Infantry and his Reserve service in the Armoured Corps. He worked as an information technology specialist for several years before retiring to become a full-time author.

Eric has been a voracious reader of science fiction, military fiction, and history all his life. Several years ago, he put fingers to keyboard and started writing his own military sci-fi, with a definite space opera slant, using many of his own experiences as a soldier for inspiration.

When he is not writing fiction, Eric indulges in his other passions: photography, hiking, and scuba diving, all of which he shares with his wife.

Join Eric Thomson at http://www.thomsonfiction.ca/

Scan to visit the site.

Where you will find news about upcoming books and more information about the universe in which his heroes fight for humanity's survival.

And read his blog at https://blog.thomsonfiction.ca

If you enjoyed this book, please consider leaving a review on Goodreads or with your favorite online retailer to help others discover it.

Also by Eric Thomson

Siobhan Dunmoore

No Honor in Death (Siobhan Dunmoore Book 1)
The Path of Duty (Siobhan Dunmoore Book 2)
Like Stars in Heaven (Siobhan Dunmoore Book 3)
Victory's Bright Dawn (Siobhan Dunmoore Book 4)
Without Mercy (Siobhan Dunmoore Book 5)
When the Guns Roar (Siobhan Dunmoore Book 6)
A Dark and Dirty Wary (Siobhan Dunmoore Book 7)
On Stormy Seas (Siobhan Dunmoore Book 8)
The Final Shore (Siobhan Dunmoore Book 9)

Decker's War

Death Comes But Once (Decker's War Book 1)
Cold Comfort (Decker's War Book 2)
Fatal Blade (Decker's War Book 3)
Howling Stars (Decker's War Book 4)
Black Sword (Decker's War Book 5)
No Remorse (Decker's War Book 6)
Hard Strike (Decker's War Book 7)

Constabulary Casefiles

The Warrior's Knife
A Colonial Murder
The Dirty and the Dead
A Peril so Dire

Ghost Squadron

We Dare (Ghost Squadron No. 1)
Deadly Intent (Ghost Squadron No. 2)
Die Like the Rest (Ghost Squadron No. 3)
Fear No Darkness (Ghost Squadron No. 4)

Ashes of Empire

Imperial Sunset (Ashes of Empire #1)
Imperial Twilight (Ashes of Empire #2)
Imperial Night (Ashes of Empire #3)
Imperial Echoes (Ashes of Empire #4)
Imperial Ghosts (Ashes of Empire #5)
Imperial Dawn (Ashes of Empire #6)

Printed in Great Britain
by Amazon

45883305R00228